ALSO BY STEVE AMICK

The Lake, the River & the Other Lake

NOTHING BUT A SMILE

NOTHING BUT A SMILE

Steve Amick

PANTHEON BOOKS

NEW YORK

Ami

Copyright © 2009 by Steve Amick

All rights reserved. Published in the United States by Pantheon Books, a division of Random House, Inc., New York, and in Canada by Random House of Canada Limited, Toronto.

Pantheon Books and colophon are registered trademarks of Random House, Inc.

Library of Congress Cataloging-in-Publication Data
Amick, Steve.
Nothing but a smile : a novel / Steve Amick.
p.   cm.
ISBN 978-0-307-37736-4
1. World War, 1939–1945—Veterans—Fiction. 2. Chicago (Ill.)—
Fiction. 3. Michigan—Fiction. I. Title.
PS3601.M53N68 2009
813'.6—dc22   2008024390

www.pantheonbooks.com

Printed in the United States of America
First Edition
2 4 6 8 9 7 5 3 1

For Sharyl, gorgeous and smart

And in memory of
Don Burau (1935–2007),
commercial illustrator, Chicago ad man,
amateur boxer, artist, father-in-law

NOTHING BUT A SMILE

Prologue

She knew what they were doing in the house. She wasn't that far gone. She even knew who they were, more or less. The strapping one with the Kirk Douglas chin and a T-shirt that said his name was Earl, though she was fairly certain it was not, was her grandson, Billy's kid. The one sorting through her silverware and boxing up the kitchen was the grandson's wife, what's-her-name. They were there to help her pack up the house, to move her to a facility of some kind.

And she wouldn't have fought them on this, even if she could get the names right. The fact was, she'd been unable to negotiate the stairs since the gladiolas, and here the leaves were turning on the sugar maple out back. So it was fine—why hang on to a place where she could only use one floor?

It had been even longer since she'd ventured beyond the upstairs, to the attic and its pull-down set of steps. But she knew that's where they'd found themselves now by the muffled distance of the voices of the grandson and his helpers and friends—the people Billy had enlisted long distance to help pack it all away. She could tell by the creaking hinge of the stairs, though she hadn't heard it in years, and she could tell, mostly, by the rise in their voices, the near yelp of surprise and discovery.

Now she'd have to explain about the trunk.

He didn't come right out and describe what he'd found—the equipment and back issues, the grease-penciled contact sheets and crumbly negatives in their tidy tin sarcophagi—but it was clear from the way he kicked at the foyer rug they had yet to roll up, and the way he tried to dismiss it as "some old junk in the attic, probably Grampa's," that they were planning to pitch it. Or maybe sell it on the computer. But either way, dispose of it, and that wouldn't do.

"It's not your grampa's," she told him, making sure to hold her chin level, keep his restless gaze fixed. "Or anyway, it's mine as well, just as much."

1

On a warm June day in 1944, Wink Dutton, known most recently to the U.S. Army as Staff Sergeant Winton S. Dutton, special correspondent and burgeoning cartoonist and illustrator, stepped out onto the streets of Chicago in his civvies. In his pocket, he had seventeen dollars, the address of his buddy's camera shop, a short list of publishers and advertising agencies, and the Purple Heart awarded to him for misunderstanding an ensign's instructions regarding a flywheel aboard a sub he was supposed to be working up a piece on for the pages of *Yank* magazine.

The ensign had probably told him more than clearly to *"Keep your finger out of this here,"* but given the effects of a bottle of peach brandy the night before—a gift from a grateful quartermaster colonel for the boldly rugged rendering he'd done of him to accompany an article about fruitcake distribution and Christmas morale—the submarine tour seemed more like a cacophony of alarms, whistles, bells, and bellowing. He couldn't think of a worse post-brandy story than, possibly, covering a riveter's competition at a shipyard. Between the banging in his head and the banging in the tin can that was the USS _____ (*name censored for military secrecy*), the only message he was able to receive was *"Be sure to touch this flywheel I'm pointing to."*

He didn't actually lose the hand, just proper use of the middle finger down to the pinky, plus the tip of the middle finger, right where he rested his pencils, pens, and paintbrushes.

"It's the fuck finger and then some," the navy doctor informed him. "You can still pinch, of course."

"Great," he'd told him. "I'll put in for a transfer to the Pinching Brigade. I'll get right on that."

Before Wink shipped out of Townsville, Queensland, Sergeant Bill Chesterton, known to his fellow correspondents and poker players as Chesty, stopped by to say good-bye and good luck—and since Wink was planning on heading to Chicago, could he check in on his wife, Sal, and tell her he loved her still and was still being true?

"Absolutely," he told him, and resisted horsing around with any cheap jokes—offering to do more than that for him or doubt the man's statement of fidelity. It was the sort of thing guys did, the way they kidded, but personally, he thought it was a little too mean and a little too easy. And a little too close to the sort of demoralizing crap guys could hear plenty just by dialing in Tokyo Rose on the radio.

Besides, he counted himself lucky for having no such serious attachments—either back in the States or in the Pacific theater—and it was only this luck, he knew, that kept him from being such a vulnerable, miserable, hang-faced slob.

He made four stabs at the job search that first day in Chicago. All three interviewers were respectful and very complimentary of his portfolio. The two that seemed at least on the ball enough to assess his new situation—that he wouldn't be able to illustrate or cartoon anymore and that the third thing he did, marginally well, writing copy, was also limited as he had yet to relearn how to write with the other hand, and it left his typing appallingly more hunt-and-peck—nevertheless agreed that he would still make a great art director. Unfortunately, neither one currently had any art director positions available. At one of the four stops, an ad agency that was doing a lot of promotional poster work for the bond drive, he was told they might be needing a new stock boy in the art department soon, but that wouldn't happen for another month and only if the husband of the girl currently holding the job got shipped stateside, in which case they imagined she would most likely want to quit work and return to taking care of her home. It hardly sounded like a long shot.

And say it worked out—what was the jackpot? Counting gum erasers and reordering Berol pads in a windowless supply room? Filling out endless ration forms just to order the stuff? Bearing the abuse and demands of actual illustrators and art directors, whose job he should have? Fun.

No, at this rate, he was likely going to have to head home to Michigan, maybe help out at his uncle's farm in St. Johns till he could retrain himself as a lefty.

So it was with a sense of defeat and lean prospects that he sought out a room at a walk-up hotel he'd gotten off a list from the VA. Jobs aside, he didn't even feel that upbeat about the chance of scrounging a good meal. It was almost five. Chow time wasn't that far off, and checking in had already put him down another buck fifty.

After hanging his one extra shirt on the hook on his door, he lay back on the clangy little bed—no worse than Government Issue, but he'd grown used to the nonreg hammocks and hooch pads of the South Pacific. He tried to lie cadaver straight, not wanting to wrinkle his suit for the job hunt ahead, and stared out the window at a billboard across the street. Of course, it was imploring him to buy U.S. bonds.

"Sure thing, Unc," he said to himself. "First nickel I earn."

He wished he at least had a book to read. Maybe, with a book, he could distract himself enough to stay in the room all night and skip going out and wasting what little coin he had in his pocket tying one on. Maybe if it were a really engaging read, he could manage to distract himself enough to skip dinner, too.

Already he was thinking what places there were to eat around the hotel and how much it would put him out.

He realized then that he was on Adams. Chesty's camera shop was on Adams, the number not far off from his hotel address. He figured he might as well go look up the guy's wife and check that errand off the list.

2

She'd been keeping it from Chesty, but the camera shop just wasn't making it. It hadn't done well before Pearl, during the Depression, but with the war on now, folks' loose money had other practical purposes than camera equipment or even getting film developed. Occasionally, someone brought in their old Brownie to be repaired, and there were ardent hobbyists who simply had to splurge, but for the most part, the shop was a leaky boat, losing money every month her husband had been away.

Sal tried to make up the difference as best she could moonlighting at the *Trib* as a darkroom tech. She'd spoken to an editor about picking up an assignment as a photographer. He was an admirer of Chesty's and so wasn't overtly rude about it, but did say, "We're not quite there yet, Sal."

He offered to put in a word for her in the secretarial pool, but she told him she couldn't type. It wasn't true—she'd earned A's in typing class two straight years in high school—but it hadn't come down to being a secretary yet. Doing that would mean full-time, daytime hours, hence closing the shop. *We're not quite there yet,* she thought.

One of the other possibilities she hadn't fully explored was something she found in the back of the photography magazines they sold at the shop—small ads, phrased with discretion, asking for girlie photos. Typically, they said things like:

WE BUY ART PHOTOS
$$$ paid for QUALITY pics
With Male Appeal
Life Study • Naturist • Sun Worship
For publishing/mass market
Very Reasonable Offers

She'd gone as far as writing a few of them—queries only, with only two or three photos enclosed—asking for a little more guidance in terms of subject matter.

She thought she had a pretty good idea what they were driving at.

The photos she enclosed she shot herself, as samples. To make sure they didn't just steal them and reproduce them—though it would be hard to do, grainy and raw looking, shooting from the print, not the negative—she'd further stymied them in any potential attempt to steal the shots by running a big *X* across the face in each with a grease pencil.

The face, of course, was her face. She'd decided to pose for these practice shots herself, using a timer gizmo of her husband's own devising. No sense going to the trouble of hunting up subjects and shelling out a modeling fee for something she wasn't sure could even turn a profit.

In the first, she was standing behind a wingback chair, her breasts resting on the back of it, peeking over the top. She didn't enjoy the look of her large nipples in that one. They seemed to be staring back at the camera like the wide eyes of an owl.

The second was her sitting in the chair, legs tucked up under her chin, her arms wrapped around the whole business, hiding her goodies as best she could. Expressionwise, she'd been trying for coy and coquettish, but she looked, she thought, more like she had some sort of intestinal issues, maybe an ulcer or just really bad heartburn.

The third, she just lay on her tummy on a towel on the floor, at a right angle to the camera, her chin propped up on her hands, her head tipped slightly in the direction of the tripod. To her, her grin seemed pasted on, but it was x-ed out, anyway, and besides, these were just test shots.

After practicing a manlier hand, she signed the queries *S. Dean Chesterton*. It was her name, after all—Dean was her maiden name—but she wasn't surprised when one of the replies began with *Dear Dean*.

Two things did surprise her: they offered up no criticism of her composition and lighting. She knew she didn't have Chesty's eye, but they'd failed to mention these flaws. And the second surprise was she'd shown too much skin:

```
Today's wartime pinups are running a tad
more conservative, Dean. Ease up on the
flesh.
   We want to show the boys in uniform what
they're fighting for, but the USO does not
like dispensing anything that might get
them thinking the girls back home are too
sexed up & easy & begging for it.
```

```
More girl-next-door brunette is big
right now--less blonde bombshell. Long leg
shots. Think mild distraction, Dean. (Just
enough to get the boys hot, not enough to
get them worried and going AWOL!)
     And speaking of uniforms, may we suggest
that's a great way to dress up your model.
Half a sailor's tunic, maybe an aviator's
cap, cocked at a flirty angle. Get the
girls saluting, waving flags, straddling
cannons--that sort of thing.
```

Another, hand scribbled, just said:

Think "home fires burning," Mac—not "my pussy's on fire."
Maybe next time.

This last had Sal a little taken aback—no one had ever used that word in addressing her before. Even if it was only written and not spoken out loud, it was a little jarring. Besides, she hadn't shown her *pussy*, for Pete's sake. Merely her bottom and her legs and her bosom, especially in that one that came off as an owl impression.

All the responses said the grease pencil Xs were unnecessary, that they were legitimate brokers and not in the business of using any photographer's work without legal authority and complete monetary compensation.

Legitimate, she thought. *Right.*

She'd have to give it a little more consideration before proceeding.

3

At first he thought he'd arrived after closing and everyone had gone home for the day, but when he stopped to scribble a note and was about to slide it into the mail slot, he caught a glimpse of something stirring in the back. There was someone in there, after all, a short blonde moving along behind the counter. Her eye caught his through the glass, and she seemed to be frowning slightly, perhaps wondering what the hell he was doing stooped over in the doorway of her shop, and so he tried the door finally, and sure enough, it shuddered open with a jangle of the shop bell.

In little subtle ways, he was finding his mind wasn't quite his own anymore, this first week back stateside. They'd warned him at the VA this would be the case, and so far, it had been true— nothing huge or fantastic, but readjusting could play tricks on a guy suddenly thrown back in with the civilians. And so it was that for one foggy moment, despite knowing Chesty, despite having held the man's forehead once when he needed to puke his guts out into some jungle plant behind a Quonset PX, despite knowing full well that the man's nickname was a shortening of his last, in the moment Wink spotted this woman behind the counter, in the no-nonsense Kate Hepburn–style trouser suit that nonetheless failed to disguise her physical assets—she was, in fact, somewhat busty, "chesty"—so it was that for that second of confusion, he had it in his mind that *this* was the Chesty referred to, in the dusty chalkboard sign in the front window that touted CHESTY'S AMAZING SPECIALS.

And then the confusion passed, and he flushed with embarrassment, thinking of the real Chesty, stuck back in the Pacific somewhere—the stand-up guy so concerned about his wife. Wink busied himself removing his hat—*Steady on, soldier*—and composed himself quickly.

She had eyes, in fact, like his very own mother's—green and wise and sharply alive, shrewd eyes—and he focused on them instead and told himself, *Her name is Sal . . . Or Mrs. Chesterton . . . Or ma'am . . .* and told her who he was and why he was there.

4

She recognized his name, she thought, from some of her husband's letters, but definitely from *Yank* and *Stars and Stripes*. She liked his sarcastic cartoons, in particular. And the straight stuff was impressive and sometimes moving—the man could draw.

But it took a moment to put it all together, since he was out of uniform. She thought that a little odd, if he'd just been discharged. Also, he shook hands with his left, which for a second she took as some genteel deferment to her being a gal, but quickly caught on that his right was game. It wasn't wrapped or in a sling, but it did appear a little twisted.

He told her Chesty hadn't had time to compose a letter for him to bring along, but her husband wanted him to personally convey that he was just fine, still in one piece, and that he missed her—according to this man—"something awful."

Sal surmised the phrase was his own. It didn't feel quite like her husband. The sentiment, sure. That was Chesty, all right.

Most days, she got along fine—chin high, no tears, eyes on the task at hand—but standing there talking about him now kind of tugged at her heart. And the fact that his friend here, Sergeant Dutton, stood roughly the same height—the same lanky, easy frame—made it tug even harder. She got the same way, a little, whenever she came across a picture of Jimmy Stewart in a photo magazine.

Her visitor seemed concerned that she really understand that her husband had zero time to pen a letter, that Chesty had run out in a jeep just to see him off—some sort of gangplank farewell, she imagined—and there was no reason to doubt this. But the man went on to tell her about some coconut he'd lost.

"We've got about thirty seconds till I have to board, so Chesty, he runs over to this palm tree, shinnies up the thing, and picks a little round coconut. Cute, little, grapefruit-sized coconut, takes out his penknife and cuts an S in the bark—you know?"

"Sure," she said. "For *Sal*."

"Right, so I get on board and I had the thing till Honolulu and I don't know what happened, but it's all my fault. It must've gotten away from me there, I figure, but all I know is I didn't have it by California, and I just feel sick about the whole thing, ma'am."

She told him not to be silly, not to concern himself over such a thing.

"Yeah, but I wanted you to know, on account of it's practically like I lost a personal love letter. I mean, it's sort of the same as him sending you that kind of a letter."

Sal just smiled and nodded, liking the story, even though (a) Chesty never carried a penknife since once pricking his privates through his trouser pocket as a young boy and (b) Chesty disliked the taste of coconut, even in her famous ranger cookie recipe, and (c) he was no climber. He almost got dizzy going up one flight to their apartment, and he'd failed the climbing part of every obstacle course in boot camp and would have been classified 4-F if they hadn't wanted his photography skills.

She didn't doubt the visitor had once had a small coconut

with an S on it. If he were making the entire thing up, he'd just make up an imaginary lost letter and be done with it. So, logically, he probably was, for a time, in possession of an actual coconut. He'd probably even carved the S on it. But it had to have been an afterthought, after he'd said good-bye to Chesty. He'd no doubt picked it up along the way, maybe while laid over in Hawaii.

Endearing, she thought, some stranger going to such trouble to make her husband look good—even if he ultimately muffed it.

As he stood there telling it, his stomach suddenly growled. It was louder than any shop bell they'd ever hung on the door—if he'd walked in with that stomach rumbling, and she were back in the darkroom, she would have heard it just fine.

"My goodness!" she said, laughing, and his face turned red. "Sounds like the call of a soldier used to three regular chow times."

He laughed a little, but he did look embarrassed. And he was starting to put on his hat.

The Italian mother side of her kicked in and she insisted he stay for a home-cooked dinner.

5

She and Chesty lived right upstairs, it turned out. Most of the top floor was an apartment, with a kitchen and living area and everything—small but cozy: street-salvaged furniture and battered family heirlooms gathered around a dingy coil rug. He imagined the two newlyweds loving this place. Even with her father living in a smaller apartment right in back, as she explained he'd been doing up until his passing two years before.

They were squeezing quite the operation into a small amount of real estate. She'd briefly showed him the darkroom lab in the rear downstairs, as they'd passed through on the way up, and there was a little studio area curtained off for shooting passport photos and the occasional baby. The stockroom, she explained, was down in the cellar.

He pointed out that if you left the doors open between the apartments, the little one might make a nice kid's room for Chesty Jr.

"Eventually," she said with a smile. "That's the plan."

Dinner was some Italian concoction he didn't quite catch the title of, though delicious as all hell, but messy and rambunctious on the plate, with all kinds of little twisty noodles that skittered away from him and a sloppy red sauce that seemed be an out-and-out convention of items, not just tomatoes.

She gave him an extra napkin and said it was fine to tuck it up into his collar—that her father always had when her mother made this sauce.

He was glad to hear it, since he had no contingency plans for ruining half his wardrobe his first night in town.

When she called him Sergeant Dutton for the umpteenth time, he told her straight and clear, he'd feel better her calling him Wink; that even when he'd been in uniform, folks tended to call him Wink.

Which raised the issue of his uniform. "Seems to me," she said, "looking for work as a vet in uniform—a decorated vet, I imagine—would be a far sight easier than just a suit and tie, nice as yours is."

So he explained the facts about his winning the Purple Heart; how he'd hurt himself through no fault of anyone but himself, and if that was his ticket home, it hardly felt right trading on the war-hero bit while meanwhile other good guys like her husband Chesty were still stuck there, only because they'd failed to get hungover and cause a stupid accident.

She shrugged lazily, sipping her coffee, and gave him a smile that seemed like an absolution of his sin. "You don't need to be apologizing to anyone. You need to 'get on with doing whatever you need to do to get on doing'—to paraphrase Ben Franklin or my parents or somebody . . ." As if to illustrate he had a right to his share, she ripped the crusty bread in the basket before them in half and handed him his portion.

It was odd, the pasta, the bread, the cannoli she said they could split for dessert—this claim she was part Italian. He wasn't quite sure he could see it. Her hair looked almost golden, backlit by the streetlight outside.

It made him think of something else he wanted to say.

"You should know, ma'am, Chesty was one of the best photographers I ever—"

She stopped him with a gesture. "*Is.* Present tense. Please."

"Oh, absolutely! I was going to say he was one of the best I ever met *while I was there.* Sorry. Not to make him sound . . . you know." *Great,* he thought. *Start talking about the guy like he's bought the farm, why don't you?*

He was telling her this because he thought she'd want to hear it—a compliment he meant sincerely. They hadn't worked on the same assignments very often, because they were both essentially picture guys, but he'd worked beside him at the typewriter a few times. And he'd worked beside him more than a few times closing various bars, but she didn't need to hear about that.

"I guess I'm trying to say he's more than just a drinking pal," he said. "The guy's got quite a reputation. Professionally."

He realized he probably thought to tell her all this, how respected his skills were, because it had struck him since laying eyes on the guy's wife how odd it was that he'd never seen a picture of her. It got him to thinking how ironic that was, considering Chesty was, in fact, a damned fine lensman. Most of the guys serving—even those not as in love as Chesty or as talented in the tricks of photography or with as much to brag on as Chesty clearly had, he could see now—at some point pulled out a picture or two from their wallets or inside their caps and passed them around. Chesty had never done that.

Of course, it didn't mean the guy hadn't carried the photos on him. Wink certainly would have, if this were *his* gal back home.

6

She loved that he brought news of Chesty—not only news, but actual stories, with details and conflict and tension and a running commentary of extra insights and asides provided by this charming, slightly goofy gentleman whom she could picture her husband immediately taking a shine to; hell, she'd already taken a shine to him herself in just a few short hours. Wink Dutton seemed to be able to take her right there, as if she were alongside the two of them lost in a jeep in some rutted road in the Solomon Islands, or sitting through a horrendous hymn recital from native schoolchildren in an unventilated brick building in which the only thing topping the acoustics and the tone deafness was the actual stink of the music director, standing between them and the kids, flapping her arms to conduct and wafting them with BO each time. It felt like she was there, whether changing flashbulbs for Chesty in a captured Jap hooch or helping barter with a village for a Thanksgiving meal, trading an admiral's personal rocking chair for a roasted goat and then trying to determine, before they got back to the base, if it was really a goat or if they'd been had.

Hearing of him, picturing him, made her eyes get a little

blurry. She wasn't going to blubber and "gal it up," as her pop used to say—not until her visitor left and she maybe ran a bath. But as much as the joy of the evening was in hearing about her husband, it was also about something else—talking to someone, having a guest, playing hostess like a regular human being, for once. Like a regular female human being.

And she found herself not exactly flirting with this man— that would be wrong, and he was clearly too much a stand-up guy not to bristle if she *had* been flirting—but she found herself feeling overly aware of her own movements, her physical actions, position, and poise, in a way she hadn't since long before she'd been married. And she knew it wasn't to attract this Wink, as much of a catch as he might be. It was something else. It was the notes she'd gotten on her girlie-shot attempts. On some level, while still taking in these marvelous tales of her beloved, she was thinking of those letters, too—the advice that the models should be more wholesome, posed in the behavior of an all-American girl. And so as she talked and listened and carried on this won-derful discussion, she also let the gears turn, imagining new, homier shots she might try—if she did try again: girl at the stove, bent over, checking the bread warming within; girl setting the table, silhouetted by the streetlight outside, girl curled up on her chair after dinner, one leg tucked up underneath her, listening with rapt attention to the young man seated across from her . . .

7

He could see from the way she talked about the camera shop and pointed out several of the furnishings that had remained in the apartment since back when she'd been a little girl that she was keeping it all going as much for her father—the original owner—as she was for Chesty. It seemed like something she cared a lot about and was struggling to hold on to.

They were sipping coffee now, and picking at the cannoli crumbs off an old spiderwebbed saucer. He was pretty sure the coffee was actually chicory.

"I'm sorry I can't offer you work here," she said, completely unprovoked. "But things are just—"

He stopped her before the details, telling her it was no problem, that it wasn't really the sort of work he had in mind, anyway. "Hey, I know next to nothing about cameras and such. I wouldn't mind learning a little something about it someday—might be handy to have in my bag of tricks now that I'm—" He waggled his bum right hand, thinking, *Now that I can't draw a simple bowl of fruit.* "You know . . . But no. Really. That's fine. I swear I wasn't fishing around for—"

"Oh, I know," she said. "But I wish we were in a position to."

He told her he had a whole list of places he hadn't exhausted yet, and then they talked a little of new movies he hadn't even heard of and actresses they both liked until the coffee was gone.

She acted very impressed when he got to the sink before her and started in on the dishes. She didn't stop him but joined him, and they worked on them together. He let her take over the washing and worked the dish towel instead, not explaining why, but, frankly, she didn't appear to have a surplus of unchipped china, and he didn't trust his right hand in the slippery suds as much as he did drying.

She went over and turned on the radio, and he didn't realize he was whistling along to "Paper Doll" until she joined in as well. It stopped him up short, and she laughed at him.

"Pardon me," he said. He'd sort of forgotten where he was, for a moment.

"No pardons necessary for a man who does dishes. If you're staying put for a while, Wink, I'm sure I have a friend or two you could ask out on a date."

He told her that staying depended on the job prospects. "Otherwise, it's me for Michigan."

When she asked where he was looking, he showed her the list in his pocket, the contacts he had left. It looked sort of pathetic, he thought, with the four so far crossed off.

She pointed to one still left—LD&M. Lampe, Deininger & Monroe. "One of these single friends I'm thinking of, actually, she works there now."

He asked what she did there.

"I'm not sure. But look out for her. Her name's Reenie."

He said he would, but it was just an interview and it was a big company with a lot of employees, so . . .

"You can't miss her," she said. "She looks like a pinup."

Downstairs, saying his thank-yous, standing by as she unlocked the shop door to let him out, he felt, if he were to be honest about it, he hadn't quite completed the assignment. He hadn't said exactly what Chesty had told him to say, and who was he to decide if the wording mattered or didn't? Maybe it mattered. Say Chesty never made it back to say everything he wanted to say— if that happened, Wink knew he'd likely kick himself a little for not being more of a stickler about the thing. More *verbatim*.

Besides, the idea of relaying the mush now felt just a hair more comfortable than it did a few hours back, when he was facing this woman for the first time. It felt like he knew her a hell of a lot better now. He could do this.

Despite that, preparing himself to say it, standing in the open front door, he chuckled a little. Even being just the messenger, he felt sheepish and tongue-tied. He turned to look down the street, in the direction of his hotel. He'd forgotten how desolate the Loop got at night, and it seemed even more so now, with all the rationing and belt tightening. "It feels a little personal to be slinging this around, but anyway, Chesty wanted me to tell you that he really . . . uh, *loves* you . . . Present tense!" It made him chuckle again. "There you go! And I'm to make it real clear he's being . . . true—you know—uh, faithful . . ." He caught her eye now, looking up at him seriously in the dim shadows of the streetlights. She wasn't chuckling. "But anyway, I'm sure you know all that, ma'am. Goes without saying." He could picture his friend's face, the last time he saw him, and it didn't take any flashing of wallet photos to see how much the guy missed her, and it was hard not to think of that, of what his friend would give to be standing there in his place in this dim doorway, in the glow of his home and his wife, without getting a little choked up himself. "And I knew it, too," he said. "Obvious to anyone who knew him—*knows* him, I mean, present tense—for even five minutes, him always keeping it in his . . . Anyway, it's true."

Finally, she said, "Truer than the coconut story?"

He felt his ears heating up, but he knew she knew he was giving her the straight dope. "Absolutely."

8

All the next morning, she never heard the bell jangle once. Which wasn't all bad—she had plenty to distract her without the public wandering in to buy very little or just look. And at least this one morning she had things on her mind to fill these restless, panicky hours in which the store was officially open but usually vacant. She had those new ideas she'd dreamed up for homier, girl-at-home girlie shots, and she hoped to get them down on paper somehow by the end of the day. Maybe this time she wouldn't bother shooting them just yet, but she'd thought she was on to something with this angle last night—the young lady in the kitchen—and it would be smart to jot them down in some manner.

Before she could get to that, though, she had the past evening's wonderful visit to recount, as best as she could piece it together, most of which was going directly into a long letter to Chesty that she'd started right after her chicory and toast. Maybe it was silly, retelling every little thing his friend had told her, since most of it Chesty probably had already heard before, and much of it he'd actually participated in himself, but she wanted him to know just how much it had meant that he'd sent this man to check in on her and, in a sort of indirect, intermediary way, call on her and share a little slice of his life there. It was romantic of Chesty, in a way, reaching out to her by proxy from across the globe.

She got so caught up in getting it all down, she started to thank him for the coconut before she had to scratch it out, forgetting for a moment that there wasn't actually a coconut, and even if there had been, it hadn't originated with her husband, but with his friend.

Plus, she had an idea to propose:

An idea has come to me, dear, that I think you may think a good one. I do not know the outcome of Mr. Dutton's job search today, but if he does in fact find a means to stay in Chic., I suggest we consider offering to rent him Pop's apartment—at a very nominal rate, of course. In exchange, maybe he could help out with some of the occasional heavy lifting. This is all only if you approve and think it wise, of course.

She decided it would be best not to upset him with two additional points: her last restocking order for some of the darkroom chemicals had been refused for a past-due back payment. Which was fine—a minor setback. And anyway, they were all set on developer, just running a little low on fix. Not that they were developing enough film these days to make the shortage an imminent crisis, exactly—that was the crux of the problem, after all: lack of customers—but if she had to dilute it much more, the quality would begin to suffer, and besides, it just felt unprofessional, running low on something so basic. Not to mention the fact that it made the shop look bad to the chemical company, an outfit that had been supplying her pop for two decades and with whom, until now, they had yet to welsh on a tab.

The second factor driving her to consider renting to Wink was the break-ins. As unpatriotic as it struck her, it being wartime and all, there'd lately been a rash of petty robberies in the neighborhood. It was probably juveniles—too young for the draft, too unsupervised with all the men away. She'd even felt nervous a few times walking home alone from the movies. Most of the other shops were dark at night, and there were sometimes groups of young boys sniffing around in the shadows, probably mostly trying to act tough to one another, having their jokes, but you never knew. It felt threatening, and the emptiness of her pocketbook was no safeguard. It was enough to keep her moving, glancing over her shoulder, and some nights, even with the doors locked and the windows grated, it got pretty spooky up above the shop. Every little sound, all the way down Adams—a distant trash can rolling or the tinkle of glass—could sometimes jangle her nerves, make her go for the radio and crank it up, let them know there were folks, *plural,* living there.

She didn't write Chesty about this second concern, either. There was no sense giving him the Tokyo Rose treatment, getting him worked up. But it *was* further reason to consider this idea of renting to Wink.

The biggest argument against it, of course, would be how it might look. As desolate as it seemed some nights, she still knew a few other people on the block—not only fellow shopkeepers but also several dear old busybodies living a few doors down, in particular, Mrs. Brablec and Mrs. Mulopulos, and she expected they'd get a lot of mileage out of a tall handsome mystery man coming and going as if he lived there, using his very own key at the door of the shop, pocketing it, and whistling on his way to work, bold as can be. They'd sprain their tongues.

One solution, of course, was to put out a sign in the window that said ROOM FOR RENT, let them get the idea ahead of time that she didn't have a boyfriend or anything like that. No, better still: APARTMENT FOR RENT. Sure. Make it clear it was a whole separate living area.

She'd do that for a week or so—hang it out there and sort of let the concept sink in. Also, she could give him a key to the back, so it would appear even more separate. Even folks working and living right on the block probably didn't know the upstairs apartments were only divided by a hallway. They might assume it was completely separate and walled off, with its own rear stairway and everything. *That* would certainly be upstanding and proper enough, if it were true.

The only other flaw in the idea would be Wink himself. He might not want to rent the apartment, even if it was at a cut-rate price. Maybe he hadn't really enjoyed talking to her that much. Maybe his visit had been entirely out of obligation—a chore to check off the list, done only out of respect for his pal Chesty—and he would rather find a place more exciting, where the action was. Maybe a place with a lot of other veterans as tenants, where you could get a poker game going at all hours or toss around a medicine ball in your undershirt. A place where unmarried, available women might be living next door, not some boring married lady.

And, of course, she needed to get her husband's okay.

9

The sun was setting on the war-bonds billboard—setting, too, on another day of dismal luck. An orangey glow washed across the sign and the oily-looking rooftop supporting it and the El track just beyond where a train was whisking all of those employed Chicagoans away from the Loop, home to their dinners and loved ones after a job well done.

The coy squint and chipper, toothy grin on the beaming, painted majorette, dressed up like Uncle Sam, seemed precisely calculated to make her just slightly naughty, implying she just might be a "victory girl," one of those notorious stateside gals who felt it was her patriotic duty to sleep with any red-blooded serviceman, whether just returned home or about to ship out.

Sure, her legs were bare, but for a legitimate reason: she was no doubt leading a war-bonds parade. And the striped stovepipe hat was tipped over one eye only because it was too large, not to be sexy, and the hand cocked on her hip was standard to twirlers and marchers, not a streetwalker stance, a come-on. But that wide, wet smile—brother, better look twice! *That* made his pecker jump, despite his glum state. Which meant the artwork was doing its job—hats off to the illustrator and art director!

Lucky employed bastards . . .

His list of prospective contacts had dwindled even faster than his meager savings (nine dollars and seventy cents). He'd crossed the last off his list today, with nothing more promising than a lot of hearty thumps on the back and words of admiration for the work in his portfolio he could no longer duplicate and the standard *welcome home, soldier!* guff. One creative director he met with, Rollo Deininger, did say that there was a *chance* he could start him off managing the in-house production studio at LD&M, and then see if he could eventually work his way up into an art director position—if Wink weren't able to eventually return to his real calling, illustration work. Production studio manager wouldn't be a great job—not much better than the near possibility of the day before at that other agency, stock boy for the art supplies. It would be a hell of a step down, in terms of pay and prestige. He'd essentially be gluing campaign comps onto presentation board and constructing one-off in-store stand-up displays and that sort of thing, along with overseeing a crew of the ad world's truly underpaid—art students and interns—as they put together all the layouts and did all the grunt work to make the creative teams look good when they pitched a client. What was worse, Deininger wasn't even actually offering him the job yet, just informing him that it *might* be a possibility.

Great to know, he thought. *So might the end of the war and my marriage to Betty Grable and the return of full function to my drawing hand—all possibilities . . .*

On that score, Deininger had come right out and asked. He seemed like a blunt man, but Wink understood the need to know.

He assured him the lame hand would present no problem in the event of either job becoming available—art director or production studio manager. The truth was, he could work an X-Acto knife and bottle of mucilage and boss around the production kids even if he had a hook for a hand. Art director, he was less sure of—it would be hard to entirely avoid drawing with that one.

But he could tell that even the crummy production room possibility was just a lot of bunk. The guy was just being upbeat
about it because he was a veteran; thought he was doing him a
favor by blowing sunshine up his ass.

And now he was looking out at the end of a day that felt only
marginally different from the end of everything, and he couldn't
for the life of him get a bead on how to make it better. Sure, he
could go get sauced. Crawl in a bottle somewhere. Except the
amount of lubrication he would need to feel better about his
prospects would mean digging pretty deep in the kitty.

There was a place back in the PTO where they'd had no real
PX, so some of the boys had thrown together a hooch speak—
part Quonset hut, part grass mat, under the brass's radar and
down jungle roads, that they'd dubbed the Corncob in honor of
their fearless leader, MacArthur. He suddenly missed that place.
He could get drunk dirt cheap there, and it felt like no one—
brass, Japs, or civilization—would ever find him.

But now, here, dollars left meant days left. So the smart thing,
the penny-pinching thing, the long-range-plans thing to do,
would be to sit there in that dingy room and take it. Besides, he
needed to buckle down and start working on the rehab. Either
figure out a way to adapt the half-dead hand or train the left.

Training his left usually seemed like the least depressing
exercise—more like a parlor trick or a party game than something to be overseen by some stern nurse at the VA back in
Hawaii.

He had no proper drawing paper, but no matter—it would be
wasted anyway, like handing a nice Borden & Riley linen sketch
pad to a toddler to hack at with crayons. Instead he had a stack
of shirt cardboard he'd salvaged from the trash cans in the show-
ers down the hall. A lot of his fellow losers in this hotel were out

going on job interviews, it seemed, based on the amount of new shirts being opened.

He tried not to look at his hand or at the so-called drawing but to just stay focused on his subject, the window and curtains, the girl on the billboard beyond. The pencil felt completely at odds with his hand, and he knew the results would be no more than a series of spasmodic swirls and herky-jerky lines, nothing resembling his subject in the least. And he was right. When he finally looked down, it was almost laughable.

He'd seen a man in the square in Canberra who owned a pet monkey that "drew" pictures for a nickel. They'd been better than this.

After only three attempts, crumpling them and tossing them into the wastebasket, his left hand already felt cramped.

Maybe alcohol would actually limber it up . . .

He really could use a belt, some kind of relief. He thought of crying and started to laugh. They'd told him at the hospital in Honolulu that a time would come when he'd need to cry over the loss and that it was natural to do that. And he had, once, unexpectedly, out on the beach, when no one was around. That was enough.

Of course, there were other fast forms of relief, some even cheaper than liquor. Sighing, giving in to it, he slid his hand down his pants. It was one of the few things he could do pretty much the same as ever with his right.

But he couldn't think of anything good. And he didn't have anything to look at. He'd had a pretty well-pawed hotbook, but someone had lifted it off him in Hawaii. The girlie card of Rita Hayworth in his wallet was so worn from sitting on it, the only part not worn away was the top of her hair and a little bit of her imprinted signature.

Brother, he thought, getting up off the bed and moving over to the window.

If he stood off to the side of the curtains, he had a better view of the girl on the sign without, hopefully, putting himself in sight of anyone down on the street or across the way.

Be just my luck, he thought, *getting hauled in now on a morals charge.*

He tried to think if she looked in any general terms like any old girlfriends, any he'd met in the service. Sometimes that helped.

Not dropping the business at hand, he slid the wastebasket over closer with his foot. Hopefully that would catch it.

He decided to go with the idea that she *was* a victory gal, easy as a breeze and "full of a generosity of spirit," as an Australian "leftenant" he knew once put it. In real life, Wink would usually try to steer clear of such wild girls—they usually came with a load of headaches, like boyfriends or brothers or remorse or disease—but what the hell, this one was only imaginary.

He was at that point where it could go either way—the quick arrival of relief, or a prolonged teeth-gnasher in which he would finally have to close up shop before he chafed himself raw. There was something about her blonde hair he found troubling . . .

He froze at the sound of someone at the door, knocking, and a muffled male voice. "Hey! Soldier. If your name's Dutton, there's a phone call for you."

"Yeah?" For some reason, the first person he imagined was Chesty's wife.

"Yeah! Some Kraut named Dining-Room-something."

Cramming it all back in his trousers, he bolted out into the hall, sliding on the floorboards in his stocking feet, and took the stairs two at a shot. Boners were for another time.

10

Once she got the idea in her head, she decided to just do it fast and not think about it too much or she'd chicken out. So she closed the shop temporarily, spinning the cardboard arrows around on the little clock-shaped sign that indicated when she'd be returning, gave herself an hour, and locked the front door. She told herself she wasn't being derelict: the film slot was still an option for any customers dropping off a roll to be developed, as unlikely as that was.

Her mom's second cousin Mia ran a beauty shop over on Racine—in fact, the place was one of those two-sided operations, spanning two storefronts, barber and beauty shop, the whole thing lately run by Mia's nephew Carlo (whatever that made him to *her*, Sal wasn't quite sure, having no interest or patience for the math). Currently, Carlo was fighting in Italy (for the U.S.A., of course), and in the meantime, his aunt Mia was doing her best to oversee the whole thing.

She could see right off, just by the dusty windows, that Mia had her hands full keeping it going. A few of the wigs displayed on the higher shelves along the top of the window showed traces of actual cobwebs.

Mia looked overstressed, but glad to see her. After the hugs and kisses, the cheek patting and hip pinching—things Sal frankly never got used to, physical affection being less of a spectacle on her side of the family—she coaxed the tiny old lady to the back of the beauty shop where they could talk. She had two customers, and both were camped out under loud hair dryers, but Sal wanted to make it appear that she was up to something shady.

She told her she thought she might have a way to collect extra ration stamps every month, but she was going to need a little help. In exchange, she'd of course pass some of the stamps along Mia's way.

To pull this off, Sal knew she was going to have to cut back on sugar and butter and a few other things, but in the end, it might pay off.

And if it *really* paid off, she could probably just buy the extra ration stamps on the black market and give them to Mia that way, rather than taking from her own supply, as she was going to have to do now.

"To pull it off," she said, "I'm going to need a wig."

The old lady didn't appear shocked at all, but turned real conspiratorial, clamping a hand on Sal's, her eyes suddenly alive. "Ah, you make the phony identifications! With the photo making and everything, yes?"

Sal tried for shifty, glancing around the beauty shop, and told her it was probably best for Mia if she didn't make her too much of an accomplice by giving her too many details. "I'm thinking maybe something much darker than my actual hair," she said, "and something you can spare for a while."

Let her think she was scamming them down at the ration center, "double dipping"—registering for a second set of ration books under an alias. Let her think whatever. Anything was probably better than telling her the real reason for borrowing the wig.

Mia began patting her hand furiously, pulling her over to the shelves of wigs. "I think maybe I got just the thing, hon. It fit you nice like it was born right on top of your head! It fool everybody, this wig I'm thinking of for you."

11

His second day at the ad agency, he spotted Sal's friend.

She came in looking for help mounting some comps, stooped over a little, her eyes on the rough sketches in her hands, shuffling through the tissues, all business, but she was tall—a long-legged whirlwind with inky hair, arched eyebrows, and a tiny pout of a mouth. Exactly like a pinup.

"You're Reenie," he announced. She had to be.

It stopped the flurry, for a second, as he introduced himself and explained who he was—who he was in relation to Sal and Chesty Chesterton, that is, not in terms of LD&M, which was evident, he felt, from his rubber smock and proximity to the layout table. She shook his hand a little too earnestly, pumping it like she was trying to get a bucket of water out of him or impress him that she could rub elbows with the boys. The way she grabbed at it, he didn't have time to offer his left instead. He wasn't sure she noticed anything about his right. If she did, she was too polite or too flustered to mention it.

Normally, he figured, it would be all right to ask her to have lunch with him, or at least take a coffee break later in the day, since Chesty's wife had been planning to maybe fix them up anyhow. And he had to hand it to Sal—she had a good eye.

But he didn't feel right bringing it up this very moment. Maybe it was the distracted way this gal let out a heavy sigh and held her shoulders so stooped, like the world was weighing her down. She was having a bad day, clearly.

Sal hadn't mentioned in what capacity she was working there, but this seemed to be her own work she needed to have boarded. "So you're an art director, I take it?"

"*Junior* art director—they're just trying me out." Then she muttered, "I'm in over my head—obviously."

That, he decided, was begging for elaboration. But he could see it would have to wait.

After meeting Sal's friend, he found himself thinking of the pleasant evening he'd had the other night. On his walk home to the hotel after work that second day, he decided he ought to stop by the camera shop again and give her the latest—that he was back among the employed, no matter the lowly position. It was a career setback, but that setback had occurred beneath the Coral Sea, inside a submarine, not in the offices of Lampe, Deininger & Monroe, and any sort of movement forward now was news worth sharing, he figured.

Besides, it wasn't just to tell Sal alone. She would write Chesty and tell him he was getting settled in, starting to make his way as a civilian, and thus spare Wink the physical chore, struggling with his left or fumbling around on a typewriter he'd have to rent—that is, after filing an Application for a Certificate to Rent a Class-B Typewriter at the ration center, then waiting for the Typewriter Rental Certificate—not to mention sparing himself the guilt of not yet writing the pals he'd left behind.

Plus, he owed the lady dinner.

12

The new roll, she kept her bosom out of it. Not even a fanny shot—well, not her *bare* fanny. She showed a lot of leg, very high up, which was trickier to orchestrate than she imagined, since she'd decided the poses should tell a story, not just be shots of her dumbly holding up her skirt like some sort of raunchy game of show-and-tell. After much struggling to make the skirt look like it was naturally positioned, she finally hit on two things. The first of these was a length of thread, sewn to her hem, that she could use to lift the skirt by tying it to some prop in the scene—for one shot, the back of the dinette chair as she bent to check the bread. The second trick was a wire clothes hanger, unlooped and straightened, that she basted into the hem—not unlike a southern belle's hoopskirt, but one that could be bent and shaped to give the appearance of being caught by the wind—like in one she did of a pie cooling in the breeze of a little electric desk fan.

The editors had just said "leg shots," with zero clarification regarding nylons, so she shot half the roll bare legged, then painted on her leg makeup and drew on the seams with her eyebrow pencil. (This last touch she never bothered with in real life—she had to take the closet mirror down and prop it against the wall to try to get the lines straight up the length of her legs—and her husband seemed to like her legs just fine without her having to glam it up so.) Once she had the fake stockings painted on, she went through all the poses a second time, thinking, *The biggest fantasy part of this fantasy is that the gal owns actual nylons. . . .* Already she was starting to think of the gal posing as someone else, not Mrs. William Chesterton, and it helped her follow through with it. Of course, the wig helped a lot, too. It was the last thing she adjusted after getting the tripod and the lamps just so. In the wig, it just seemed a good deal easier to vamp it up—dip a shoulder, pout the mouth. Overall, it felt like she was coming on pretty hotsy totsy, but it was hard to tell, as she was no longer clear on what part of herself she was supposed to show more of and what part less.

And now, in the darkroom, she still wasn't sure. Maybe these shots *weren't* an improvement on the first batch, the ones she'd mailed off like a fool. It was discouraging—how was she ever going to know what worked? These *seemed* cute, but was that cute enough to get a homesick GI smiling the right amount but not get him lava hot, AWOL hot? Who knew?

The only thing she felt certain of was the wig. To her, the dark hair looked all natural, no question, so she doubted any *man* would spot it as a phony. Maybe if the man were a hairdresser, but then what would *he* be doing shelling out good money or army scrip to look at these pictures?

But then again, as she was already rapidly learning, it was all such difficult business trying to calculate the silliness of men.

She'd just hung up the contact sheet to dry and was about to start in on the tough work of selecting shots, making cropping decisions, trying to get a few usable prints out of this, when she heard the tinkle of the shop bell out front and a friendly call of "Hello? Anyone home? Anyone hungry?"

13

Walking her back from the Berghoff where he'd gotten off cheap—she'd been merciful and simply split a corned beef with him—he stopped at the front window of the camera shop as she unlocked the front door. He hadn't noticed it earlier, but she had a sign up that read APARTMENT FOR RENT.

"You're not moving out?" he asked.

"No, no. The little one in back. My pop's. Things are really—"

He was going to touch his hat brim and say good night as soon as she had the door unlocked and got safely inside, but as she stepped in and pressed the light switch, she took only a step or two before stopping suddenly. He half expected to see someone there, staring back at them—her husband, Chesty; a burglar; an overanxious potential renter—or maybe a rat scurrying across the floor. Or maybe she'd just remembered she'd left something back in the chaos of the Berghoff.

She started to head back into the rear of the shop, turning on more lights as she went. There was apprehension in her posture. He decided he was watching woman's intuition at work: she was *sensing* there was something wrong.

"Mr. Dutton . . . ," she called, and since she'd already gotten the hang of *Wink,* he knew she was addressing him this way for some reason, some effect. He followed her in, all the way to the rear entrance, by the little staircase that led up to the second-floor living quarters.

Someone had been there. Or tried to be there. The glass was smashed in one of the little panes in the door. Fortunately, there was a steel grid bolted over the glass panes and the intruder had failed to reach the handle inside.

His first thought was kids. Hoodlum youths, up to no good, doing stuff just to be doing stuff. A practical-minded, professional burglar would know, even from the outside, reaching the lock that way was a long shot. Pointless mischief, but all the same, it had to be scary for a good-looking woman living alone.

Unlocking it now and opening it, trying the bolt and the handle on the outside, he determined they hadn't done any damage to anything but that one little pane. "The lock's fine," he said. "It'll still lock up tight, no problem."

He asked for some heavy cardboard, just to fix it temporarily, keep the wind out. She stepped back toward the darkroom and slipped past the dark purple curtain, returning with a scrap of heavy mat board and a mat cutter.

He almost chuckled: in the last two days of this new job, he'd been more involved with various mat boards and craft knives than ever before and now *this,* even after hours . . . But he could see she wasn't taking it lightly, and so he told her she was going to be fine, that the worst of it was over, that no one was going to hurt her.

"They already *have,*" she said. "Things are already so tight, and now I have to get *that* repaired!" She looked tough about it, mad and scowling, and he almost feared for the confused drunk or dimwitted teens who did this, imagining what they might face if she caught them. But the sound of her voice told something different. It was anguish, the sound of a frail, exhausted woman, one step from tears. "We can't afford any of this anymore and now—"

Dropping the mat board, he took her by the shoulders and squeezed, not feeling a hug was exactly appropriate. She remained a few inches from him, but he could feel her breath against his shirt, coming in hard little huffs. He waited for it to calm and he told her he'd put this mat board in, then he'd come back tomorrow and fix the window himself. It was mostly grunt work, no great art to it. He'd done it before for whole sash windows, and this was just a tiny little pane—easy! All he had to do was pry off the molding, pick out the broken shards, set it in, caulk it if he wanted to get fancy about it, and tack the molding back in place. The piece of glass, maybe five inches square, would cost maybe two bits—that would be his treat. The expense was in the glaziers' labor—and his labor would be free. "So stop worrying about that little pane."

She smiled up at him now, weakly, and he released his grip on her and asked her to get a broom and take care of the broken shards while he cut the cardboard to size. Before patching it, he first measured the small frame and scribbled the dimensions on a scrap of mat board he tucked into his wallet. She was done sweeping and sat down on the bottom of the stairs that led up to the apartments, her chin on her hands, still looking a little weary and worrisome, like a kid with a busted skate. But he wasn't done yet, so he ignored this for now. "Need some tape," he announced, and before she could direct him, he ducked into the darkroom and, sure enough, spotted a roll of black gallery tape.

"You shouldn't go in there," she said as he tore off some good lengths. "There might—"

"I know," he said, finishing up the patch. "I know *that* much about darkrooms. But *you* just went in there, so I figured I wouldn't be exposing anything." He got a good look at her now, trying to assess how she was doing there on the stairs. Not well. She was hugging herself, rubbing the length of her arms, either nervous or cold.

"Now," he told her, clapping his hands together, playing the know-it-all handyman, "we need just one other thing . . ."

14

The "good stiff belt apiece" that Wink had prescribed—and she had provided, shuffling up to Pop's old room and removing the bottle of bathtub gin, circa Capone, she'd found in a dusty hatbox under his bed after he'd died—had led to two more, and the two more had led to the darkroom. She kept only the safelight on, and she'd only finished the contact sheet, with its tiny frames, but she figured he could sort of make out the pictures. Well enough at least. Well enough to form an opinion.

"Come on," she said. "Tell me what you think."

She hadn't told him what they were for or where they'd come from—or that she'd taken them or that it was her in that black wig. She'd just said she had something she wanted to show him.

"Well," he said, squinting at the sheet in the dim red light, "it's a little confusing. *Contradictory,* I guess is a better word . . . See, the crisp focus, nice contrast, all that—that's all very professional. But still . . . the composition says another thing. A lot of these, if it were me, I'd 'kindergarten' the stove and the table— move the view to the side more, so the secondary objects are turned more dead-on. That way, the lines of the stove become simplified so they no longer draw focus away from your subject. See how the angle of perspective is giving the stove all these acute angles which make that part of the composition busier? They don't want all this busyness. For what this is, this kind of subject matter, there's just too much going on. Ideally, if I were *painting* this, say, for a calendar, I might just rough in the stove— barely sketch it, just give an *idea* she's in a kitchen—so we concentrate instead on the girl . . . Or in a photo, not a painting—a lot of these girlie photos, the furniture and stuff, they're all just props. Painted cardboard boxes or canvas flats. Backdrops—like an old vaudeville skit or a stage play. Same deal."

It was frustrating. These were not the kind of answers she was looking for exactly. But she wasn't sure she should give him more information than she had. "So is it professional or—"

"Amateur maybe . . . ?" He still didn't sound too sure. "If you're asking should you go to the cops or write the postmaster general, no, it's not raunchy enough to qualify for the smut laws. She's not even naked, really. But could someone make some money with these, if they wanted? Sure. Like I say, they're not *smoldering hot,* and they're not the most artful compositions, but sure, they probably could. But if it bothers you at all, I say just

don't make them any prints. You have a right to turn away customers, certainly. And if this kind of thing bothers you—"

"Ha!" She tore the contact sheet away. "You think I'm in any
position to turn anything away at this point? I'm just trying to
make ends meet." She wished now she hadn't had seconds of
the questionable Prohibition-era rotgut. It was hard not showing
she'd flared. She didn't mean to be short with him. He was just
trying to help. Heck, he *was* helping. Some of what he said were
actual artistic tips. But for the most part, he seemed to be very
focused on whether they were professional girlie shots, for the
public, or just some private people, horsing around. She knew it
was just the booze, but for a second, he struck her as being sort
of above it all, and it was hard not to come right out and admit
what she was up to and show him the new tax letter she'd received from the city and the other back-payment-due notices
and dare him to condemn her for trying this.

But, she reminded herself, she didn't need his approval, so he
didn't really need to know.

She pulled the chain on the safelight and threw open the curtain, leading him out. Somewhere between the first belt and the
second, they'd settled on the plan that he would stay in Pop's
apartment tonight, just in case whoever broke the window in
back returned, and now she still had to make up his room and
scrounge up a few toiletries Chesty had left behind.

She needed his help reaching Pop's blanket and the twin-
sized sheets, tucked away up on the top shelf of the hall linen
closet, and as he took the other end and helped with the military-
style bed making, she told him he might as well check out of the
hotel tomorrow, if he was comfortable enough tonight. He could
stay until she found a renter—if he wanted. "I know *I'd* feel safer
and you'd save your money." She was thinking privately, as she
had been earlier at dinner, offering to split the corned beef on

rye, that he probably hadn't even been paid yet at his new job and, employed or not, was probably cutting it pretty close.

She told him she was sure Chesty would appreciate his being there.

"Well . . . ," he said.

"But just to make sure, I've already written him to suggest such an arrangement." It was true, but of course she'd told her husband she'd wait for his answer before speaking to Wink. Instead, she told Wink she was sure Chesty would agree that they should offer to rent to him but only at a very nominal rate, and that Chesty would probably also say she should take care not to cramp his style, et cetera—that a young bachelor like Wink probably wouldn't want to be cooped up with a boring married lady.

"I'm sure he wouldn't call you boring," Wink said.

"No, but then *he's* not allowed to. I'm sure he will suggest that if we do offer to rent it to you, you'll feel obligated to do so, and he'll warn me not to make a nuisance of myself, that we should leave you alone to find something more suitable to your lifestyle."

"Which, believe me, is a thrill a minute," he said with a smirk.

She told him she didn't doubt that, considering the fact that in this one evening with him, she'd experienced "fine dining" at one of the city's hot spots, a crime scene, near drunkenness, lurid photographs, and two people sleeping under the same roof without benefit of marriage. "That's all since you came along, Wink Dutton. And I'm afraid life above the camera shop does not normally offer nearly that much excitement."

It was great just having someone around to laugh with, even if it was only a chuckle and it wasn't anyone with whom she could actually share the biggest laugh of all—the truth of what she'd done, flouncing around the kitchen in nearly nothing but a wig and leg paint.

. . .

All through the night, she stirred awake. First it was recalling
the jagged little broken window in back and all the scary things
that might be trying to sneak in, and then she'd remember that
Wink Dutton was there, on guard duty, in Pop's apartment. Anyone breaking in would have to pass his door to get to her, and
knowing that, she'd feel better and doze off. Then she'd remember that he had an injured hand and wonder if he could defend
her if he needed to. But then she'd remember he was a tall one—
as tall as Chesty—and other than the hand, seemed fit and ath-
letic as any boy in the service. She imagined him going through
all the training—hand-to-hand combat, jabbing mattresses with
bayonets, high stepping through a field of tires, right along with
the soldiers who *hadn't* been handed typewriters and cameras
and pen and ink. No, in a pinch, he'd be fine.

She'd doze off again, and then she'd think about the bills and
the taxes and the lack of customers and how she was there facing it alone, but then she'd remember Wink there, just through
the back wall, and think maybe he'd become a regular renter and
help out around the store even, and everything would be back in
the black.

And then, just about to doze off, she'd think of what the
neighbors might say and the few customers she still had might
say and the deliveryman and the mailman. And her relatives. And
even what Chesty himself might say. But if Chesty didn't want
Wink here, she wouldn't have him.

Except she could tell already that Wink was the kind of friend
her husband wouldn't mind having there, in fact would prefer
to be there, boarding up broken windows and looking out for her.
And it made her miss Chesty like crazy—the way he smelled of

darkroom chemicals; the way he never eased into bed, just flopped down like dead weight, perching on the edge of the bed first to wind his alarm clock. Even if she'd already started to nod off, he'd flop down with a groan, just as lanky and clueless as a high schooler, and he'd always whisper "Sorry" like it was a surprise every single goddamn night.

God, she missed him.

At one point, she had to clamp her pillow over her face to muffle her sobs. Having a guest there, right down the hall, made it tricky when she started to cry her eyes out. But still, she was glad he was there. It was good not to feel quite so overwhelmingly alone.

15

At the Zim Zam Coffee Shop, right around the corner from the agency, Sal's friend admitted two things: she had very little art direction experience and her last name was Rooney.

Reenie Rooney.

Her real first name was Maureen, which made marginal sense, he thought—as the youngest in a large "black Irish" brood, her siblings had called her Reenie for short. The part that struck him as screwy was the part where her siblings, whose last names, conceivably, were all *also* Rooney, didn't seem to fathom what hers was, in total. Maybe by the time she got to school and her name took on its full ridiculous bloom, *Reenie* had stuck. Still, he thought, she's trying to impress major clients with a name that sounds like a jump-rope chant?

And though she claimed to be underqualified, he was suitably impressed with her former place of employment—the Stevens-

Gross Studio, home to several top-notch commercial illustrators. Impressed, that is, until she told him she'd only really answered phones and processed invoices, ordered supplies, and performed other such clerical duties. No actual design, illustration, or art direction experience.

He told her not to worry. Though he privately suspected her new position at LD&M had a lot to do with wartime job vacancies, he assured her they must have all seen something special in her portfolio—in her spec work, that is, even if she'd done nothing that had actually been produced.

Those perfectly arched eyebrows made a dive-bombing maneuver again and she practically gnawed loose a fingernail. "I never really . . . put one together? *Yet,* I mean. A portfolio. Even with just spec work. And it wasn't any 'all' that hired me—just Mr. Deininger. And now, lately, he's been real . . . well, *insistent.*"

As much as he loved the looks of this long, lovely gal, right about here, Wink was hoping she would say the boss was cracking down, expecting her to produce, to show something for herself, though as near as he could figure, she'd just barely started. Wink wouldn't want to see her fired, of course, but it seemed more likely that his own movement up to something more suitable, given his experience, might come all the sooner if this creative director Deininger was getting "insistent" about winning results.

But that wasn't what she meant. "He's convinced I'm easy just because I used to—well, he figured it out that I used to also sometimes pose for Mr. Elvgren. You know who I mean? At Stevens-Gross?"

Of course he knew who Gil Elvgren was. Besides having rapidly become America's most beloved and classiest painter of calendar pinups, he'd taught a couple night courses right down the street at the American Academy of Art, back in 1940, and Wink had been lucky enough to get in. He'd been in awe of Elvgren, even more so after studying with him, and he wondered if the guy ever heard that he, one of his many students, of course, had made a little splash for himself in the army publications. Or if the man would even remember his name if he did happen across it.

"I wasn't nude or anything. I wasn't even wearing the dresses and undies he put me in. Later, I mean. He did all the clothes or no clothes later. What I mean is, I was in my *office outfits,* for Pete's sake. Dressed for work. And I was just trying to help out, you know? In between all my other work. Step on an apple crate here, lean against this stepladder there . . . They had professional models most of the time, but a lot of us girls on the office side, we'd help out, you know? Pitch in? Just so's he could get a snap-shot, something to work from. So now Mr. D. keeps coming around, thinking . . . Well, is what I did really so awful? I mean, is that supposed to make me a tramp?"

Even if she were a tramp, he thought, the girl had a right to say no when she wanted and not be pestered all day.

"No," he said. "It doesn't make you a tramp. It makes Deininger a jerk."

She seemed to be hesitating, unsure she wanted to hear his response to something.

"He said something else," she said finally.

"Which was what?"

"He said you're ready to take over my job if I'm going to be . . . 'uncooperative.' He says you're overqualified for it, except I got one qualification you don't."

"He said that?"

"Ain't it awful? Like he's talking about my privates or something!"

The bad coffee suddenly tasted even worse, and he wondered now if he'd been hired just to make the girl fear for her job.

Brought in as a Human Wedge so some paunchy 4-F hot-to-trot goldbrick could put the make on sweet little Reenie Rooney.

Nice place, this home front . . .

After work and after picking up the new glass, when he stopped by the hotel to get his things and check out, he stopped at the newsstand downstairs and scanned some of the girlie mags and considered splurging. Payday would arrive soon, and some things were sort of necessities, in a way . . . He got as far as picking up a copy of *At Ease* and scanning the cover—the photo of Ann Sheridan in a red, white, and blue bathing suit, the description of articles about "the Oomph Girl" and "Manhood Misery: Tojo's Secret Shame!" and one that made him wonder how much he'd missed while away, something on how the bosom was "back in style." Flipping through, he saw there was a photo essay on a new synthetic rubber the government was developing—they didn't seem to mean rubber as in *rubbers*—but the pictures showed them supposedly testing it with cheerleaders bouncing on a piece of it stretched like a trampoline. *Hmm,* he thought. *Very informative.*

But then he remembered he'd be taking it into his little room just down the short hall from a respectable woman—his war buddy's very good wife—and he also flashed on that lovely Reenie, with her pinup looks and her leggy ways and the sob story she'd laid out for him about that creep Deininger making it tough for her, and before he knew it, he'd soured on the idea of the magazine. Some other time, maybe.

That evening, after replacing the glass, he tried to stay out of Sal's hair, slipping out to get something vaguely meat-ish on a

bun and stroll up to Wacker before she felt compelled to make
him dinner again. When he returned, she came out into the hall
to give him fresh towels and a set of keys and to say how glad she
was he'd decided to stay a little longer.

Her apartment door was half open, and it struck him that the
basic background in those shots of the brunette she had shown
him the night before—the kitchen and table—reminded him a
lot of Sal and Chesty's kitchen. Of course, a lot of kitchens
looked like that all over Chicago.

Kidding around, but also half serious, he asked to see the
girlies again.

She looked puzzled. "The what?"

"That roll of film you processed that you were showing me.
The girlie shots. Whatever they were."

She scowled, but was smirking, too, giving him a little shove
with his stack of fresh towels. "No! You lecher! Jeez, those are
personal property. I mean, *someone's* personal property."

"So they haven't picked them up yet? Oh boy!" He rubbed
his palms together evilly and made a broad, comical Groucho
lunge toward the stairs, like he was rushing down to the darkroom, and she poked him again.

But now he was completely kidding. Because the second the
idea about her kitchen had crossed his mind, he'd pretty much
dismissed it. No way were they shot in her apartment. And anyway, how would he really get more details out of the tiny contact
sheet? It wasn't like he could tiptoe down to the darkroom and
give himself a crash course in working an enlarger and developing prints . . . Forget it.

And he wasn't looking to get his jollies, which was clearly
what she thought he was up to. But he left it at that and said
good night.

16

The next day, she got two notices from camera supply whole-salers, saying they were forwarding unpaid invoices to a collection agency; a phone call from Mia, wondering how she was coming with her ration stamp "situation"; and a brilliant idea. The brilliant idea, unlike the rest of these things, came from her gran-pop, her father's dad. Gran-pop Dean's photo hung high over the register, way up among the boxes of flash powder that hadn't been used practically since the time of tintypes. Gran-pop was dour looking, with a dour-looking mustache and dour-looking eyes, all of which drooped, but his frame was inspired. It was a cameo frame, Victorian and ornately scrolled and very, very oval.

It was how she'd fix the roll of girl-in-the-kitchen shots—salvage it, that is, rather than going back and reshooting, fussing with all those issues of perspective and building cartoonish prop stoves out of cardboard and all the rest. She had to be practical. And really, when exactly was she supposed to do all that now? With *him* there in the evenings, right down the hall, she could hardly restage the elaborate setup in her apartment. And during the day, even with tumbleweeds practically blowing through the shop, she still had to be available for the possibility of a lone customer wandering in inexplicably—she couldn't very well flounce downstairs with her flyaway skirt, black wig, and painted-on nylons anytime she heard the shop bell tinkle.

Back in the darkroom, she tried a print using a cardboard cameo frame to mask it as an oval, cutting away most of the extraneous "busyness," as he'd called it. At the same time, she did a soft "dodging" trick she'd learned from her pop—a wad of cheesecloth on a pair of forceps, wiggled, during the exposure, over the center, casting the edges she wished to obscure in further shadow.

It looked pretty good. The oval made a nice frame.

The editors had said nothing about a particular format; the shots needing to be rectangular. Maybe it was a risky choice.

But she had to admit, they did look better. Wink had been right about all the extra stuff in the background—the spice rack above the stove, the line of the dinette table jutting across one corner. In the oval of the cameo frame, the girl was the star.

She was the star.

Then she had another idea. Something about the thought of her new houseguest being right down the hall and her not being able to carry on in her apartment at night made her think of a keyhole.

It was even better.

Wink seemed impressed.

She just gave him a quick flash of the shots, not much more than a quick shuffle through the five by eights, before closing them back up in a manila envelope, but she could tell that his grin was more at her cleverness than at the naughty flash of leg.

The keyhole mask she'd cut from mat board actually blocked out even more than the extraneous elements in the kitchen, it even blocked out parts of the girl. But somehow, that seemed to make it more exciting, like the viewpoint of a Peeping Tom, getting a look at something off-limits.

"Brother!" he said. "I'd say the skills of the darkroom tech surpass the skills of the photographer!"

She shrugged. "It's hard to work all that stuff and work the camera and take the pose."

He looked at her curiously in the dim safelight. "What are you saying?"

"I'm just saying . . . I would imagine. I assume, like you say, it's an amateur, and so . . ."

"You're going to give them the regular shots, too, right? Without any cropping? These here today are better by far, artistically, professionally—no question. But I mean, in case it's just a guy who wants some record of his wife. Or a gal who wants her guy not to forget her while he's off fighting . . . Hey, that's probably what it is, actually, now that I think of it."

At this point, she remembered a plausible explanation she'd dreamed up for him the other day, and she tried it on him now: she told him the negatives had appeared in the drop slot with only a last name, so she wasn't sure yet what they were for. And, of course, the customer would only be returning to pick them up during store hours, when Wink was away.

He seemed to buy it.

"Brother . . . ," he said again. "Clearly I miss all the good stuff around here. Nothing nearly as exciting happens at *my* place of work."

17

He hadn't seen Sal's friend Reenie for two days. He'd begun to think she'd either given up and quit, or surprised herself with hidden talent and come up with a winning campaign. Or she'd given up in a more depressing way, relenting to that wolf at the helm.

And he wasn't sure at first if the latter weren't true when he finally spotted her while strolling by the supply room. He'd taken to swinging by LD&M's well-stocked supply room every chance he got—not only to pilfer sketch pads to sneak back to the little apartment over the camera shop to work on his left-hand drawing, but mostly because the sight of the stockroom reminded him, even in his most harried moments of frustration working in the production studio, that at least he hadn't had to take that other job, as a stock boy. Being King of the Craft Knife was at least better than that.

It was the raven hair that tipped him off. She was in there, standing behind a metal rack of sketch pads. He started in, grinning, thinking he'd see if she could sneak away for another coffee, when he heard another voice, male, whispering low, and her eyes flashed Wink's way with a look of distress.

So he went on ahead in, scuffling his feet, whistling "Paper Doll." Deininger was in there all right, standing awfully close, leaning in. In fact, she was pressed up against the wall, and he seemed to be blocking her exit, speaking privately to her somewhere around the neck, roughly her clavicle.

Across from them in the tight space, there was a high shelf of glue pots. Wink made a move for them, stretching and lurching, groaning dramatically with the effort, and pulled back and elbowed the guy sharply in the back of the head.

"Oh, gee!" Wink said. "I'm sorry, boss! I didn't see you there, sir. Gee, I guess I didn't expect to see you here in the supply room having a private meeting with a junior art director, sir. Guess you better go get some ice on that or have someone look at it, maybe?"

There was a *harrumph* or something from the creative director. Wink stole a glance at Reenie, who looked alarmed, but also a little like she wanted to laugh.

Carrying the glue pot, which he didn't need, Wink started to shuffle out ahead of them, lingering in the hall, waiting for the guy to beat it. But Deininger did not appear. Wink turned to go back in, when the door closed quietly.

The guy made a mistake not locking it.

Standing back, slipping the rubber apron to one side and adjusting his trouser leg for a little more slack, Wink raised one leg and kicked, hard. The door flew open, banging against a metal rack of paper clips, staples, and metal fasteners.

"Okay, clearly this is my fault," he announced, placing the glue pot on the nearest shelf and heading for him. "Obviously, I was too subtle for you." This time he used both hands and wrenched him away from Sal's friend, then shoved him hard, full on the chest. Deininger's legs slipped out from under him, his shiny brogans skittering, and he fell back into the corner against an empty, rattling filing cabinet. It boomed like a small-caliber cannon. It was the loudest thing Wink had heard since returning to civilian life—it was barroom loud, dangerous sounding, thrilling.

Deininger scrambled back to his feet like he was on fire. Wink braced himself for a punch, but the guy just squeezed past him, escaping into the hall.

Wink followed him out, with Reenie trailing close behind. Deininger was barking at his secretary coming the other way. "Mrs. Walters! Call the police! Now!"

As Wink approached, the guy whipped around like he needed to keep his eyes on him and started to back down the hall.

"Really?" Wink said, halting his pursuit, which meant he had to raise his voice the farther Deininger scrambled away. "The cops? That sound like good public relations to you, pal? Clapping cuffs on the cripple?" He was yelling now. "Want it to get around how a decorated war veteran got the better of you, despite being burdened with a lame hand?" He waggled his right, high in the air, and now people were coming out, gathering in the hall. "War injury, you know, sacrificed for my country and all."

Now that he had a crowd at his side, Deininger apparently felt safe enough to stop retreating.

"Seriously?" Wink said. "This is your plan?"

He took it as a sign of a lack of intelligence that there wasn't even a flicker of doubt in this guy's eyes. He didn't appear to even be reconsidering his position, reappraising his situation, strategizing the best diplomatic maneuver. He wasn't budging.

So Wink didn't budge either, just stood in the hall facing him, the two of them like gunfighters—one amused and crippled, the other jangled and red faced—and waited for the police. Which was fine, just fine. He didn't want to work there anyway. If the guy was that bullheaded and unable to reassess the situation and adjust, Wink knew he'd be a horrible creative director. Just lousy.

He untied his rubber apron and hung it on the nearest door-knob while they waited.

18

All the way up to the Gold Coast to visit her in-laws that morning, she tried to focus on what she should do next, exactly, and to block out the looks from the old men and young vets on the platform and on the train and walking down the street. She knew what they were looking at. It was much too warm today for a jacket, and so they were checking her out.

Though she never would admit it to anyone, not even her best girlfriends, Sal knew she had a nice figure—specifically, she was well endowed, as her aunt Patty, who shared the trait, liked to describe it. Her legs were a little stumpy for her own liking, her bottom a little flat and broad, but she knew she had a good thing going on up top. It was hard not to know it—she'd long ago grown used to the drift of men's eyes, the sudden glaze of distraction that would come over them in her presence, and the stolen glances she'd catch in the reflection of display cases and windows when they thought she couldn't see.

Which is how she knew Chesty loved her for her—he'd known her before they'd even appeared.

Chesty—known back then as Billy Chesterton—arrived in her life long before the bosom. It must have been somewhere in the beginning of junior high when he started riding his bike down to the shop from his upscale neighborhood north of the river and helped her pop sweep up and stock supplies, and generally made a nuisance of himself. It was that annoying age when boys just reeked of body odor and an earnest awkwardness, and so she tried to avoid him as much as possible. But he wasn't there for her. He was there because he'd caught the photography bug. He'd been reading magazine articles and had a brand-new camera his uncle had given him and wanted to learn everything he could. So the third or fourth time Pop saw him loitering around the store, he got the kid talking, decided there was only one way to find out how passionate he really was about tackling something that would amount to extracurricular schooling, and took him on as unpaid help, only on Saturdays. That schedule expanded, though, and by high school, he was not only getting a little pay but working three weekday afternoons as well. He even tried to talk Pop into opening the store on Sundays, but Pop told him his late wife had been raised Catholic—Sal's mom had passed by then—and though Pop didn't believe and didn't take Sal to services, they still weren't going to open up on Sundays. He told him to do his homework on Sundays—that he had to make something of himself, not just take pictures and hang out in the camera shop.

And he *was* making something of himself—somehow, between all the shuttling down to the Loop and working in the shop, he managed to become the photo editor on both his high school newspaper and yearbook.

And by then, she wasn't so annoyed that he was always there. Surprisingly, despite not having time to go out for sports teams, despite standing stooped over chemicals in the darkroom hours at a time, his growth had not been stunted and he had a beautiful head of hair. Her pop always claimed the chemicals had taken his own hair, but Chesty never had that problem.

In a way, his love was more pure than hers. Because though she'd come around when he began to bloom into a handsome young man, he'd acted moony about her from the start, back before her skin cleared and she filled out. Long before her best features, as she saw it now—when she was all "bruised knees and bee stings," as he later put it. It was clear he would have been hanging around a camera shop even if she hadn't been living above one, but it might have been a different camera shop.

Her pop always kidded her that she was, from the beginning, "the only other thing that boy likes almost as much as photography."

And maybe she was shallow for not seeing the same in him when he was all elbows and bicycle handlebars, barging in, always there—heck, she'd been aware of his presence the afternoon she got her first menses. She wasn't so clear what was going on in the toilet, but she knew Billy, as he was still known then, was working that day. He was somewhere in the shop, his constant-seeming presence something she never had a say in.

It was only in high school, when he had friends on the paper and yearbook, that other boys started calling him Chesty, and the nickname spread and seeped into other parts of his life, and soon they were calling him that at the shop as well. It was around that time that she began to blossom herself, and it came on like gangbusters, and because they were starting to gravitate toward each other, addressing each other with more care, more manners, doing little favors for each other—sharing a bottle of pop, an umbrella, eventually taking in movies, holding hands, kissing, sparking, petting, going steady—she would hear his new name Chesty and think, self-consciously, *I am too . . . We belong together.* There was no question.

And she knew that even if she hadn't grown to love him and they hadn't married, there was a good chance her pop might have willed Chesty part ownership in the shop anyway.

19

The two arresting officers who eventually arrived were pretty polite about the whole thing, like this was normal behavior among businessmen working in the Loop.

When they got down to the lobby, he realized his portfolio was still upstairs—still with Deininger, who'd asked him to bring it back in his first day, to show to the other CDs and principals in the company—and he had better get it now, when he could, because he certainly wasn't coming back.

He described it to them, and one of the cops went back up in the elevator to retrieve it while he stood in handcuffs with the other. It was just after lunchtime and the lobby was being crisscrossed with people he knew—other illustrators and art directors—with their eyebrows raised, probably inventing all manner of fantastic stories about what he'd done.

When the cop appeared in the elevator with his portfolio, his partner began moving him toward the street. "We walk to the precinct," he explained. "Do our part for the effort."

It was a beautiful June day in downtown Chicago, and other than the fact that he was handcuffed and flanked by two uniformed patrolmen, heading for jail, it felt great to be out of that windowless studio, walking around in the sun and the breeze.

The cop holding his portfolio had it unzipped and was glancing through it as they walked, maybe making sure it didn't contain any weapons.

He assured them it was just drawings and cartoons he'd done in the service.

"Really? Say! You Bill Mauldin?" The cop seemed genuinely interested in the work now, not just cracking wise, as he tried to peer closer into the little portfolio case and maintain his stride. He turned to his partner. "Joe, I think this guy's maybe Bill Mauldin!"

The one called Joe seemed to have no idea who Bill Mauldin was, so he wasn't as disappointed as the first guy to find out that Wink wasn't, in fact, the celebrated infantry cartoonist of the Forty-fifth Division and *Stars and Stripes*.

He'd never met Mauldin, having been in the Pacific theater himself, but he knew from photos that the heroic and talented bastard was sort of a runty little guy, more the rugged foot soldier type, built for trudging and ducking. Mauldin deserved all the accolades he'd been getting, and not just on account of his being an enlisted grunt, usually covered in mud, right in the flak, but because he was just straight-out talented.

"Sorry, fellas," he said. "Nearest I ever came to being Bill Mauldin is taking a mud treatment at this spa place in Tahiti."

They squinted at him like maybe they had the wrong idea about him.

"I wouldn't have done it myself, of course, but they ordered me. Working on a story on the local hot spots, opportunities for R & R and all . . ." The few he could actually get into in print, that is—not the grab-ass dime-a-dance huts and the "Special Times Movee House," which was a mobile stag show, set up in a U.S. Cavalry tent dating from probably the Spanish-American War. And, of course, the awful little cribs for the "party-time girls" who were really no more than actual girls. Compared with all that, the spa had seemed as regal as a cathedral. And if *legitimate* meant no one came right out and directly offered to work his bone, then perfectly legitimate.

The cop who'd taken down the complaint was the same one who'd gone up to Deininger's office for his portfolio, and he was flipping through his notepad as they walked. Wink noticed he'd corrected the spelling of his boss's name—probably saw it on the door when he went back up—and he was showing it to his partner. "That's a Kraut name, am I right?" He turned back to Wink and asked him, "Guy you shoved, gave me the cartoon book there—he some kind of Kraut?"

Wink just shrugged.

The one called Joe looked like he was going to spit. "Our boys are out there dying, this Kraut's busy on the make, getting all handsy with the fräuleins, probably wanted to ask her out to the next secret Bund meeting . . ."

Wink kept his mouth shut. He had some German on his mother's side. His uncle Len, the farmer over in Michigan—he was German. Not a Bund member, he was sure, but still, German enough.

At the precinct, they ushered him in through a door marked BOOKING, uncuffed him, and helped him empty his pockets, handing it all over to the sergeant, an older, rounder guy with a pure white handlebar mustache. They moved on to his jacket, with everything going into a manila envelope, until one of them pulled out his Purple Heart.

He'd honestly thought he'd misplaced the stupid thing.

The sergeant glowered at him for a second, breathing through his nose, sounding not unlike livestock, then went back behind the swinging gate, back into the noise and bustle of ringing phones and clacking typewriters, farther in. Meanwhile, the arresting officers eased up on their grip. The one called Joe asked if he was okay, they hadn't hurt anything on him or anything? Like he had prosthetic limbs, maybe, or a metal plate. Wink assured them he was fine. The other one asked where he'd gotten it, and he told them in the Pacific, and then the sergeant reappeared and handed him back the medal and waggled a meaty finger in some kind of fidgety gesture between the other two that seemed to suggest they were dropping the charges, letting him go.

The sergeant waddled closer and placed a hand on his shoulder. "Just don't go back there, okay, soldier? I think we can take it you're fired." As he gently guided him toward the door, he leaned in and said quietly, "My wife and I have three Blue Stars in our front parlor window, so I'm telling you like I'd tell any one of my own boys. You did your fight. Now get a job that isn't run by punks and pantywaists. You don't need that crap."

It was true. He really didn't.

20

Whitcomb and Sarah Chesterton weren't actually her in-laws in the truest sense. But as Chesty's elderly, childless aunt and uncle, the ones who'd raised him and sheltered him from age ten on, they were the closest thing she knew to in-laws. His real mother was still alive, she understood, back in Nebraska, but Sal had yet to meet her—or any other Chestertons. She'd seen photos of both his real parents, and thought he favored his father the most—William Sr., Chesty's dad, the less successful of the two bank president brothers, died on a railroad track outside of Breakey, Nebraska, in 1930, a few days after his small bank there failed.

Once a month, at the elderly uncle's request, she traveled up to the Gold Coast area and let him look at the books. Though she felt it was really none of his business and Chesty would no doubt object on her behalf if she told him he was doing this, she went along with it, but, of course, brought him an entirely different set of books, pure fiction, doctored to make it appear the camera shop was still operating firmly in the black. She would never misrepresent her finances in another situation—certainly not to the government or anything—but he wasn't the government. He was just the man who'd raised her husband and someone who knew something about finances. And frankly, someone who was nosy. He didn't own any of the store or anything. So let him have the fairy-tale version, she always told herself every month. In her place, Chesty would at least give him the fairy-tale version, if not a stern telling off. And frankly, technically, it mattered less what Chesty would do, because technically, it was more her store than his.

These days, though he was retired as president of the bank, Whitcomb Chesterton maintained office hours for half a day every week—Wednesday morning. It was more out of respect for the man than for any real purpose, as far as she could see. It gave him a routine and a place to open his business correspondence and read the various financial newspapers. She noticed, on the once-monthly Wednesdays she visited, the occasional young bank employee might stick his head in and ask Mr. Chesterton's advice or opinion on this or that, though she suspected they did this either out of genuine kindness, to make him feel useful, or as part of some sort of sycophantic clambering up the corporate ladder, she wasn't sure—a waggling of their eager, bushy tails. She was pretty sure they didn't actually need his advice. She knew *she* didn't.

But she was polite, just like they were. She would show him the books and he would frown over them and make various small grunting noises and work his substantial eyebrows and ask her one or two questions about inventory and the like that she would try to answer as vaguely as possible, and then, usually, his wife, Sarah, would appear in the office and she and Mrs. Chesterton would go have tea over at the Drake, and she would share clippings of Chesty's latest contributions to *Yank* or *Stars and Stripes* with the elderly woman, and they would compare letters, assuring each other that he sounded just fine and perfectly far removed from the so-called action. For some reason, Sal was the only one who seemed to get original prints from him, and she'd show these to his aunt as well, always quietly irritated that the old lady never seemed to get the hang of holding them by the edges and not getting her fingerprints all over them, and then Sal would peck her on the cheek and tell her she had to catch her train and she would see them both next month.

Except, sometimes, something else happened first.

Of the two of these dear old relatives of her husband, Sal felt that, on the whole, the more interesting one was Chesty's aunt Sarah, mostly because Sal never knew exactly what to expect with her. She strongly suspected the old gal's faculties were prone to a wide fluctuation, because though half the visits went pretty much as she expected, nearly half the time, right near the end, Sarah Chesterton would announce that he'd sent her some cash by mistake. Whenever she did this, she presented it with almost the exact same speech, like something she'd scripted and memorized: *Oh, by the way, I think young William made an error. He seems to have sent me some money he intended to send you, dear. I could tell from the note he included it was for you, to deposit in your account, but I'm sad to say I must have misplaced the accompanying note. So sorry* . . . And then she'd slip Sal anywhere from twenty to fifty dollars in a banker's security envelope, never once dropping the charade, never winking or smiling.

And then, on other visits, there was just no envelope and no mention of money. The visit would be as pleasant as these more lucrative occasions, except there was no cash gift dressed up as a misaddressed letter from Chesty. Sal couldn't pick up on any pattern of disapproval. It was possible Mrs. Chesterton was slightly fuzzier on these days, and that was what made Sal think it had to do more with her failing faculties than with her frugality. When she was on the ball, she knew they needed some help. When she was having an off day, it was probably all she could do to keep it straight who "young William" was and where in the world he was.

Sal had tried, the first few times, to refuse the money, but on the days there was money, the old girl was so sharp, she played her part to the hilt, laying it on thick about this missing letter from her nephew in which he made it absolutely clear this was for his wife, to be deposited in their account. So when there was a security envelope, Sal played along.

Unfortunately, today, when she really needed it more than ever, there was no envelope.

Sal smiled and kissed her husband's guardian on the cheek and squeezed her birdlike hand and took her exit, knowing she would have to hurry now. She was going to have to make another stop. Because there was no envelope today, she was going to have to go through with the contingency plan—the one involving another envelope she'd been carrying in her purse.

All in all, her morning up here had been a bust.

The bell captain who held the door open for her made no attempt to hide that he was staring her smack in the blouse.

Speaking of busts, she thought.

And all the way back, as if she had actually been speaking out loud of busts, men passing in the street and fellow passengers on the El resumed their perusal of her physical attributes. Some smiled—affably enough, without cruelty, as if they were doing her a favor. She couldn't help think they were getting something for free. *All these men . . .* She wished, too late, that she'd taken a silent tally since starting out this morning: how many had grabbed a look? It got her to thinking.

Not only had she never been with another man, she'd never let another man see even a little of her body naked, except for maybe the women's doctor her pop had insisted she visit once, before she got married, and even he seemed to be looking away through most of it. Also, she was dressed in a hospital gown and he only opened the ties as necessary. It wasn't exactly the same.

But that had changed, she realized, since she'd sent in those first test shots. Some unknown, unseen strangers—strange *men,* no doubt—had now seen her. Maybe not in the flesh, but still.

It was strange to think that if she sold something—something maybe not as coy as the keyhole shots where she showed no nipples or even the full cheeks of her bottom, but something beyond, something more risqué, like the first batch, it would skyrocket her entire solar systems past any other gal she knew in terms of number-of-men-who've-seen-me-naked. Even more than her wilder friends like Reenie. Strange, she thought, how doing something simple like dropping a garment here or a towel there, mailing a letter, signing a simple release form, might so suddenly and completely alter the category of woman into which she fell.

She stopped for a second, at the post office on the corner of Clark, removed the photo-mailer envelope she'd been lugging around all morning from her purse, and slipped it through the OUT OF TOWN slot. It was done.

Arriving home, she saw someone was standing at the locked front door, facing the other way, waiting for her. A few steps closer and she saw it wasn't a customer but an unexpected, friendly face.

Something was up.

21

It already felt strange strolling up Adams when all the shops were still open, heading back to the camera shop in the middle of the workday, but his was over—and how!—and he could see now there would be no point waiting around for a phone call from any of the other places where he'd interviewed. Without illustration in his quiver, without his trusty right hand, he was done here. Time for the farm.

The best thing, he'd decided, would be if Sal were in the darkroom. Or better yet, out running an errand. He had his key and he could sneak upstairs and get his things together—strip the bed, pack his grip—leave his uncle's address for Chesty, for Christmas cards or something, and then he'd find her and tell her once he was all set to go; on his way to Union Station to catch the train to Michigan. He was afraid, if he did it the other way around, if he saw her beaming face first and got to laughing with her, he'd cling to some hope of eventually finding proper work, of things being rosy in the Windy City, and he'd linger till he was down to his last dime. He really might.

Before he reached the shop, though, he spotted wavy blonde hair on a gal seated by the window of the coffee shop—right across from a brunette with killer bedroom eyes and a pinup pout. He stopped and rapped on the glass, and as down as he felt on this awful afternoon, the sight of the wide smiles on those two gorgeous gals got him chuckling like a shell-shock case all the way in.

They had a chair pushed out for him by the time he reached their table. Flopping down in it, he set his portfolio beside him on the floor and checked his watch, frowning at Reenie. "Shouldn't you be at the office playing dodge 'em and tag with Rollo Deininger?"

The arched eyebrows arched still farther. "Oh, he fired me as soon as you were out of the building."

"What? Why?"

She shrugged. "He's the boss. He can fire anyone he wants."

He wasn't fully aware he'd banged his good hand on the table till he saw the girls flinch and the old couple seated next to them turn and frown.

"Excuse me," he said. "But that's ridiculous. *I'm* the one who shoved him."

"Yes, but I'm the one who wouldn't sleep with him."

He took a deep breath and let it out slowly, watching the pedestrians going by out on Adams. It seemed there were a lot more people on foot these days—not just him and Joe and the other cop.

"Not true," he said, placing his hand gently on her wrist. "I wouldn't sleep with him, either."

Reenie laughed, short and fast, like a concession, a small ac-knowledgment that he at least was making an effort to cheer her up. Sal laughed a little heartier, but then she hadn't been the one to lose her job.

He laid it on. "He never *tried* to sleep with me, mind you, but just so we're crystal clear on my position on that, if he *had* tried . . ."

Turning to Sal now, he decided to tell her straight out. His plan for the smooth getaway was a bust. "Listen, I'll be leaving in the morning. You're going to need to get a tenant soon, and I don't think I'm going to make it here."

"Stay anyway," she said. "Help out when you can part-time. Do some of the heavy lifting—that'll be your rent."

He told her she couldn't afford to do that. "You say yourself there's hardly any business."

"That doesn't make the boxes and equipment any lighter. And you want to learn photography. I'll teach you all about the camera and the darkroom, you teach me about composition and lighting and that sort of stuff. When business does pick up, we'll be quite a team."

"Wink and Sal," Reenie said, smirking and lighting up. "Sounds like a soft-shoe vaudeville team, more like."

Sal started snickering and it was fun to see. "And another thing," she said. "Any boardinghouse, most hotels you find, a lot of them are going to cramp your style more than I ever will. You'll never hear me squawk about visitors."

The girls were shooting each other looks he couldn't quite follow and it made him uneasy.

He told her he'd stay until the end of the month or until Chesty responded to her letter proposing the scheme. And if he did other work, he'd start paying whatever she was going to charge whomever else she would have rented it to.

It didn't seem like all that much of a plan and it even felt a little wrong somehow, but he couldn't help feeling glad that he wouldn't be packing his grip and taking the train back to Michigan. Not today, anyway.

22

Sal arrived at the *Trib* by nine that evening and reported to the editor who'd called her in. She'd had a long day, between the visit to the in-laws and meeting with her friend Reenie—and then Wink—and the two of them being fired, and frankly, she wished this wasn't an evening that the paper had work for her. Logically, she could use the money, but it had indeed been a long day.

The one who'd called her in wasn't the guy she normally dealt with, Bob, but a narrow-faced weaselly 4-F type who actually looked too young to draft, named Dickie Something. She'd never really trusted Dickie, the way he grinned at her.

Maybe it was just for this evening, but he'd commandeered Bob's office. She poked her head in just to give him a wave, to let him know she was there, she was heading for the darkroom, when he pushed up out of his desk chair with a *sproing* and said, "Oh, hey, doll. Sorry heaps, really, but as it turns out, we got no work for you tonight."

"You called me in," she pointed out.

"It was before I knew Burt was back. He needed some hours."

She couldn't help it: her hands went automatically to her hips. "So you're admitting you called me *first*."

Dickie shrugged. "He's a veteran, Sal. I'm supposed to turn away a veteran?"

Sighing, she glanced at the clock. "My escort won't be returning for me till one a.m., Dickie. What about that?"

Despite the fact that he was grinning like an acne-covered jack-o'-lantern the whole time, Dickie claimed again that he was sorry. He said he would send her back home in a cab—on the paper this time. "Or," he said, gesturing to Bob's office, Bob's couch, as if it were his own, "you can wait for your escort *here*. Sit! Read some magazines, help yourself to the bar . . . In fact, I'll have a drink with you, Sal. We can talk about you coming to work full-time on the day shift. Or maybe there's something better. Who knows?"

She didn't like the way he raised his eyebrow. It was a move much cuter on Reenie.

23

That night, he felt jumpy as an Army Air Corps Benzedrine fiend. Part of it was that he knew he couldn't fall asleep: around half past midnight, he would need to start out for the *Trib*, to fetch Sal and escort her back home. She'd gotten called in to pick up some darkroom tech work that wouldn't be over till one a.m. She'd insisted she was fine walking up there alone. There was still light in the sky when she set out. About twenty minutes after she'd left, the phone started ringing downstairs in the shop, but they hadn't yet worked out a policy on his answering it, so he let it ring. The jangling went on and on, making him even more rattled and restless.

But even if he were to try setting an alarm clock, just resting for forty winks, he knew he wouldn't be able to do it. He figured he had about five dollars left, plus a pocket watch his uncle had given him, and a few other things he might pawn. This was blockheaded, staying here—no job, no prospects—and just lying down flat as if he didn't have a care in the world didn't seem like a sensible way to do it.

They'd originally given him some pills for his hand, but those were gone. As was the pain. He considered, for a moment, where that putrid bathtub gin might be that Sal had squirreled away somewhere . . . Another time, another place, maybe if he were more settled in, he'd be thinking of *other* distractions to the restlessness as well—like trying to meet a girl. Though knowing Sal would be sleeping right next door would make that idea a little awkward.

Was she really serious about being a lax landlord? Meaning, say, some night he did invite a girl home with him—that would actually fly?

That idea made him think of Reenie. She was a stunner—something out of a magazine—but *maybe* he'd have a chance; an outside shot . . . Except he didn't want to act the drooling ape Deininger had been. Better take it easy on that front.

Seeing Reenie and Sal together that afternoon, he'd thought how lucky he was, this newly returned to Chicago and still finding his way around, and already he knew two very cute, very fun gals, even if they were just pals—one being off-limits, the other being in the caution-slow lane. It still was a hell of a kick, hanging out in the afternoon, watching the civilians bustle past while idly laughing it up with two great, spunky women. It was just nice to have new friends.

And he hated to be the kind of guy who got *ideas*, but seeing them together this afternoon made him wonder about one other thing: was it possible that the dark-haired model in those shots Sal had been processing, supposedly for some customer, was actually Reenie? Meaning what—Sal was the photographer? Or someone else entirely—some guy Reenie knew or worked with somewhere?

It made him wish he'd gotten a better look. But the first time, the contacts had been too tiny. And the second time, the prints had been too coyly obstructed by that keyhole silhouette. In both cases, she'd barely let him get a good look, just flashing them and then kicking him out.

But it wasn't like there was a lock on the darkroom. Hell, there wasn't even a door. It was just a curtain.

The darkroom was very organized, and she appeared not to be sugarcoating it about the state of business—there were only a few strips of negatives clipped up on a corkboard on the far wall and nothing hanging on the line to dry and nothing in the chemical baths.

He found a few shots of Chesty, in his uniform, next to a kangaroo. Ones he'd sent home, Wink figured.

The manila envelope that he remembered was gone.

He did locate a wide drawer under the workbench, and it contained a lot of papers, including what looked like tables with a lot of information about ratios of dilution of various chemicals, and some pieces of mat board cut out in different shapes, including the keyhole, and a manila envelope. Uncoiling the string enclosure, he found it contained photos, all right, but these were different. These were nudes, or seminudes—girl curled up in a chair, girl bare assed on a towel, girl resting her bazooms on the back of a chair—all with their faces x-ed out with a grease pencil. All clearly blonde.

With his fingernail, he scratched at the X on the one suntanning her ass. And it stared back. It was Sal.

The lady who would be sleeping right down the hall. His buddy's wife.

In his shock, he stepped back and banged his head on the

unlit overhead light. He yelped out and swore, and the chains rattled and adrenaline shot through him; fear he'd disrupt everything here and she'd see it later and realize he knew.

Except . . . she'd been the one to bring him in there initially. She'd shown the other ones to him, asked him for his opinion. On some level, she'd *wanted* him to know. She wanted him to look.

Didn't she?

He stood there, trying to catch his breath as he scratched away the other Xs and stared, frozen, not sure what to do.

He could still pack his grip and sneak out. That was still a viable plan. If he could pull it together and stop bumping into things. If he could stop staring at the photos.

Christ on a crutch, he thought. *What does she want from me? She was the one pushing for me to stay here . . . Christ on a cracker . . .*

He was only human, after all. He was only a guy. He was a good guy, sure, or tried to be, but he was only—what was that again?—human.

And he was just out of the service, for Christ's sake. Maybe it wasn't the same as being away in prison for a while, but still, a thing like that left a guy weak in certain areas.

Yeah, he had to get out of there. Pronto.

"What are you doing?" It was Sal, stepping through the curtain.

He blurted out some question about picking her up at one a.m.

"Never mind that," she said. "What're you doing?"

He reminded her that she'd brought him into the darkroom before. Twice. The part he didn't say out loud, but wanted to say was, *You wanted me to find these.*

Except when she finally did look down and her eyes adjusted and he saw that she saw what he held in his hand, he wasn't so sure anymore. Maybe she didn't want that. Maybe she was disappointed. She looked deflated, smaller than her normal petite frame, if that was possible.

"Wait." She didn't say anything more, but stepped back through the curtain. He heard her back behind the counter in front, the ding of the register, and then she returned with a stack of clippings and letters and handed them to him.

The letters were business envelopes. The clippings were ads he'd seen a hundred times before—"Art Photos Needed."

"Look at the response," she said.

He opened the letters and glanced at them just enough to see they appeared to be correspondence with the people who'd placed the ads. He wasn't sure what to say. Why was she thrusting all this stuff at him? "Chesty is my friend, Sal. I'm really not comfortable—"

"I don't play around, if that's what you're wondering." She sounded a little peeved now, and glared at him. "I love my husband and I'm *true* to him—that thing you seemed to have such difficulty relaying the first night you came by. *I* say it easily. I am true to the man I love. That's not at issue."

She told him how she'd been fooling around with these girlie shots, thinking it might be a way to bring in some extra cash fast, that they really needed it, and that she was, in a number of ways, way out of her realm, and she could use a little help from someone like him—a friend, someone who respected her husband and her and knew scads of things about pictures and men and girls. "Someone," she said, "who I don't think will judge me." She showed him where she'd hidden the contact sheet for the shots of the brunette in the kitchen and a stack of five by eights of the same, unobscured by the keyhole-shaped frame. And then she showed him a wig, pulling it from a hatbox he'd missed, under the workbench. She was the brunette.

"Just one more thing about all this," she said. "Chesty doesn't need to know."

Without meaning to, he let out a little gasp of air. There was only so much he could promise. This fell firmly in the *a little much* category, and it was hard not letting her see that.

"I'm not going to cheat on him," she said, "but that doesn't mean I'm not going to lie to him. Only not because I'm trying to hide something that's really all that shameful." He looked away, staring at the large luminous numbers on the glow-in-the-dark timer as she said, "I need to lie because if he knows I'm doing this, he'll be concerned about our *finances,* how bad off we must be. Which we are, unfortunately."

She pulled out a stack of bills, including what appeared to be a letter from the city about property taxes, and laid them out on the workbench and tapped them once, like a poker player laying down the killer hand.

"So I need you not to tell him."

She waited for his response. He sighed again, trying to think of something noncommittal. Finally, he said, "I'm terrible at letter writing." He held up his lame hand. "Even before this."

Apparently, it wasn't enough. Her eyes narrowed. She was growing impatient. "I'm serious, Wink Dutton!"

He threw his hands up, in surrender. "Okay, okay. I won't tell him. I promise." He wished she hadn't pressed him. He still had a lingering feeling that he had no idea what the hell he might be signing up for.

24

As near as she could figure it, based on what she tried to learn from Wink over the following days—and there was no telling really, how much he actually knew about such things or how much he was shielding her from, still withholding information, maybe trying to be genteel—it wasn't so cut-and-dried as there not being *any* nudity in girlie pictures. Not at all. In fact, when she showed him the publishers' responses from the first batch, his brow got a little crinkled with an expression that seemed to say something was not quite right.

"No, no," he said. "There are nudes. Sure there are. I've—I've seen them."

"You own some, you mean."

He hesitated. "*Owned* some. Past tense." He seemed a little fidgety, saying this, like he wanted to change the subject, and he launched into a complicated spiel about the range and variety of girlie photos, then seemed to be backtracking, claiming there really wasn't that much skin. He tried to explain something he said he'd been led to understand back when he was contributing to *Yank*—that both they and the civilian publications were making an effort to show more "good girls" these days, as well as fewer Aryan blondes. Girls next door who were still next door waiting for the poor sap to come home safe. But there were different tones for different kinds of magazines.

"But the girls are never actually naked?"

His face screwed up again—Wink was either wincing or thinking. "You can *find* it . . ."

It felt impossible, sitting in the camera shop, trying to understand all the distinctions he claimed there were. "This requires a field trip," she told him. "I'll go get my wig."

At the nearest indoor news shop, she let him enter first, counted to twenty Mississippi, then followed him in, disguised in her borrowed black wig and Wink's dark aviator glasses.

Immediately, the owner, a slightly scaled-down version of Sydney Greenstreet, started giving her the evil eye from his perch on a stool beside the cash register, but she went right into her investigation anyway, glancing at *McCall's* only briefly before drifting over to the more lurid covers.

The covers were what she'd call cheesecake, and at first, it was hard to tell them apart. A few times, when it seemed like the owner wasn't looking, Wink, standing down the aisle at a fair distance, would jerk his head a little or nod in the direction of a particular title, and she'd investigate.

Between the gossip confidentials and the "adult humor" cartoon-gag magazines and the nudist and burlesque promotionals, there were dozens of titles. Of course they didn't have sufficient funds to purchase all of them, so they had to study them there.

Knowing she could never remember everything she found important, she slipped her grocery pad out of her pocketbook, concealing it in her hand, and tried to discreetly jot down a few notes and titles of potential magazines. A lot of them, according to the addresses listed on the mastheads, were published by the same people, and most she recognized as the places she'd been writing.

Suddenly, the newsdealer was at her side, breathing like an inbred pug. "Hey, lady." She returned the magazine in her

hand to the rack and picked up a *Stars and Stripes*, ignoring him.
" 'Scuse me," he said. "Princess? This here is not a *scenic view*,
okay?"

It was, however, a free country, so she sniffed a little and
moved on, continuing to browse. Maybe he thought it scared off
the shy customers, seeing a woman looking at the men's magazines. Well, it wasn't something she was going to make a big
scene doing, but it certainly wasn't fair for him to object, as long
as she was discreet. He hadn't said anything at all to Wink yet,
who was down the aisle a ways, acting like they weren't together,
and *he* was browsing just the same. Possibly the man just didn't
want to tangle with Wink, the way the big lump was huffing and
puffing to catch his breath just venturing away from his stool.

But he wouldn't drop it. "Oh, I see! Either you can't hear me
or you're too *royal* to address the rabble . . ."

With a somewhat-menacing throat clearing, Wink glanced
over her way, at which point the newsdealer, to her surprise, redi-
rected his abuse, fearlessly waddling over to face Wink instead.
"Maybe *you* can tell me, Slim. Can't figure out for the life of me,
your friend here"—Sal was stunned that he'd put them together
with one mere rasp of the throat. She decided he must be more
on the ball than he appeared—"is she Miss Helen Keller herself
or is she maybe the lost Anastasia, empress of Russia? I ask on
account of she's either deaf as a door knocker or too royal for me
to be speaking to, is that it?"

"None," Wink said, "of the above. We are conducting a scien-
tific survey, sir, that has far-reaching, global ramifications for all
our young boys out there still fighting for freedom, country, and
sweet little Janie next door."

"Yeah? That so? Well, buy or leave, pal: there's your American
way right there. Ramificate *that*, friend. And if you don't like my
policies, you can buy me out and I'll be off to the Sunshine State

and you can stay here and run this place however god-awful way you want. Run it into the ground, the fuck all I care, I'm in Florida, basking in the sunshine with the beautiful babes like in these here girlie magazines, but until then, Slim—and Mrs. Slim—you gotta play by the rules!"

Ignoring this, Wink offered her his arm, escorting her out.

She thought she had a better general idea now of the range he'd been talking about—though nothing but the half-hidden ones over to the side, some of which seemed like they were from France or somewhere, bore any similarity to the first batch of shots she'd taken.

All in all, it felt helpful, getting a glimpse into the male world like this. She felt just a hair closer to understanding what they were looking for. On the walk home, she suggested that, for future research, they could find another magazine shop, to which Wink said, "You kidding me? As long as we're too broke for a lot of movies and nightclub entertainment and the Book-of-the-Month Club, I don't know about you, but I'm going back for the free floor show." He gave her a wink, adding, "These days, Mrs. Slim, we gotta grab our smiles wherever we can."

The first real lesson she gave him was the one Pop had first given her: she showed him how to build a simple pinhole camera, using cardboard shoe boxes she got from the old gent at the Florsheim's. (The old man had teased her, telling her, "Need to see some ration coupons for those, darling," as if she were buying the shoes, and she laughed for him, as if it were funny.)

Building the pinhole camera felt almost childish, the kind of assignment she would give a grade-school class, but it was where she knew to start. It was fun, too, carrying them out onto the sidewalk and exposing the photo paper, custom cut by hand in the darkroom to fit in the back of the box, to the June sunlight as it drew lines from the lamppost across the sidewalk and the awning and the bricks, slanting into the alley that ran alongside the shop. They stood close, following the sweep hand on his watch, counting the seconds out loud.

This way he could work immediately on developing prints and skip right over the fussiness of film; the process of winding and developing a roll of negatives—all that manual dexterity and chemistry—that could be so frustrating to the novice.

This way they could talk about contrast and graininess and all that good stuff, and he could feel satisfied with the results without a long struggle.

She could tell he wanted to get started for real, really jump in feet first and move ahead, but he also seemed to understand that all good things took time and patience.

Which was maybe, when Pop had first given it, also part of the lesson.

25

The end of June came with the departure of the Republicans and the arrival of summer fashions he found almost startling to his Wac-weary eyes. The Grand Ol' Party had come to town to nominate a Michigan boy from about twenty miles down the road from Wink's uncle Len's farm—Thomas E. Dewey, originally of Owosso—and it felt almost like all the gals of Chicago had been waiting for the stodgy old conventioneers to leave town before pulling out these breezier outfits. Sal told him no, these looks were all the rage now all over the States. Women were showing bare midriffs these days, and the skirts were so slim and figure hugging—except for the enormous flat hats that also appeared on the scene like a fleet of aircraft carriers and would argue against this trend—that he generally had to wonder if this season's fashions were a result of rationing; you could do your part for the war effort by skimping on material.

Not that he didn't like it. And it reminded him about something that he'd strangely pushed to the mental back burner since he'd moved into Sal and Chesty's spare apartment—the idea that a major element of being back among civilians was being back among civilian *women*. It seemed his thoughts had roamed almost exclusively in that direction at the time of his discharge— or even before, lollygagging in the navy hospital, watching the nurses and wondering what they'd look like in something other than white. And yet, since he'd moved into the back apartment, the only lady friend he was spending any solid time with was the lady of the house.

Sure, her friend Reenie stopped in, too, and he was relieved to hear she was employed again, back at the Stevens-Gross Studio, doing pretty much her old job there. He felt a little sorry for her, that it hadn't worked out in a creative position at LD&M, but try as he might, he couldn't quite bring himself to regret his part in getting her out of there. What else could he have done— sat back and let that masher go about his business? Maybe she was right back where she'd started, performing menial clerical duties for the pinup illustrators. Maybe it was unfulfilling. But at least she wasn't getting herself pawed in the supply room.

It was ironic, he thought, that an illustration studio where the artists were known for producing some of the nation's most popular pinup paintings was kinder and more civil in its treatment of a vulnerable young girl than a prominent and supposedly upstanding ad agency that produced work for America's most wholesome packaged goods.

"That's not entirely true," Reenie pointed out. "I heard LD&M gets calendar contracts and stuff, too. They just don't flash it around. Bad for the image. Their big clients think it's kind of lowbrow."

He told her "lowbrow" was carrying on the way that wolf had and then canning her for it. She told him he was sweet, and that felt like the end of it.

In the time since the two of them had been fired, she began to drop by in the late afternoons and evenings, ostensibly to see Sal. He couldn't help feeling a little flattered by the frequency of her visits, until Sal picked up on it and told him, "Don't get a swelled head. She used to hang out here all the time before she started at that ad agency and was always working late and trying to brainstorm some winning idea and just trying to keep up and one step away from the creeps. So this isn't new for her—this is back to normal, Mr. Swellhead."

Wink told her he didn't have a swelled head, he'd just wondered how her friend was doing, is all. He told her he wasn't planning on bothering her or anything.

"Oh, go ahead and bother her," Sal said, smiling now. "I did want you two to go out, remember? I'm just saying she's not *currently* coming by to see you. Doesn't mean she won't be, eventually, if you get off your rear end and talk to her like you're halfway interested."

He was interested, sure, but Sal had been keeping him more than busy, showing him the ropes. He wasn't exactly twiddling his thumbs, looking for ways to kill time by trying to decipher the intent of a complicated big city girl like Reenie. He had skills to learn.

He was getting it.

He'd always done well in science, back in school. Especially chemistry. So the darkroom part of Sal's photography lessons, breaking down the development of the negatives and the prints, felt to Wink like it was falling into place pretty logically. Every once in a while, he required just the slightest adjustment—a subtle eyebrow or intake of breath from Sal, teaching him in the womblike reddish haze behind the heavy curtain. But he hadn't yet made one move so completely wrong she had to raise her voice. He didn't want to get too cocky too soon, but it seemed like he was really getting it.

He liked the narrow margin of error in this part of "Sal's Crash Camera Course," as they'd been jokingly calling it. For once, at least some part of producing a picture was measurable. All his life, he'd worked in the terrifying abyss of relatively few restrictions that was the other two-dimensional arts. He had taken one ceramics studio class, before the war, and with that, too, like this, he'd been comforted by the limitations of the medium and the part that seemed almost like a recipe out of a cookbook, as tried-and-true as something from the *Farmer's Almanac*—"Corn should be picked when acorns are the size of squirrels' ears . . ." With a drawing or a painting, you started down a path, and you either kept going in that direction or altered what you'd done and tried something else, but there weren't the same absolutes, no *Crosshatching must always be done at a diagonal angle to the object being textured, except in the case of a herringbone suit . . . The human nose must be drawn for no more than ten and no less than five minutes . . .* He'd never felt the comfort of the rigid parameters Sal laid out for him here in terms of stop bath, developer, fix. There was security in the control of a measuring cup.

In a way, it was a little like being in the service. When he'd been in, he'd grumbled as much as the next guy about the whole lousy deal, plotting the demise of everyone from that day's mess cook on up to FDR himself, but the truth was, the structure and lack of freedom did make it easier to concentrate on the fun part—what he would do on his next leave or what he could possibly trade for in exchange for painting another cheesecake bomber girl. And in the darkroom, not being able to wing it—not just throwing various chemicals into a tub like a Creole gumbo and hoping for the best—made it easier to concentrate on the parts of it over which he *could* make choices, the whole *art* part of it.

The choices available through selection of shutter speed, as she'd been showing him, plus the range of diaphragm openings—the list of oddly sporadic and specific fractions called f-stops—he found as exciting as a full palette of fine oils. He'd never really thought about it, even watching a pro like Chesty at work back in the PTO, but there were more options found in these gizmos than properly utilized by the average weekend slob peering down into his Brownie in the park, waiting for his kid to stop drilling for boogers, so many choices that could affect lighting, color, and that area Sal particularly wanted him to help *her* with, composition.

Besides, being in the darkroom for any length of time soon felt peaceful; removed. If the store was closed and they didn't have to listen for customers out front, he would commandeer Sal's radio, and between the low music and the low lights, it was almost like he was back in the better parts of the Pacific theater, like that illegal speakeasy hooch, and there weren't any car horns honking or El trains rumbling or newsboys crying out about destruction, just the night and the close proximity of a nice-looking girl.

Except, of course, if they were both there now, in the PTO, back on the bottom of the world, Sal would be too busy to be giving him photography lessons. She'd be off with her husband on a three-day pass, enjoying herself a hell of a lot more than she had to be now, and Wink would have to find himself another date to stand beside, talking low, lost in the dark of the Corncob and the tropical night.

Part of his side of the bargain was to teach her a little art theory, such as the elements of composition, and he wasn't sure at first how serious she was about this, nor how he would teach her. He wasn't an instructor—had no lectures worked up, nor the patience to ever design such things. If he had a good textbook, with full-color examples from the masters, he could much easier lay out the whole deal about the Golden Ratio and the rule of thirds and balance and framing . . . But the only textbook he'd ever owned like that—this would have been back when he was taking classes at the Academy in 1940—had been swapped, if he remembered right, for a half-drunk pint of mint schnapps and a pair of winter gloves.

It wasn't long, though, before he realized he was staying right in the neighborhood of what amounted to perhaps one of the world's largest art textbooks—guarded only by two stone lions. Being right on Adams, it was only a matter of blocks to the Art Institute. And on Mondays, admission was free.

26

At first, she wasn't quite clear what he wanted her to see in this room and began to glance around, hoping not to appear nearly as dumb and inartistic as she felt. The one dead ahead, barely taken in, registered only as something as mundane as a claim check for the cleaners, found at the bottom of her purse.

But he was pointing at it, redirecting her. *Okay* . . . Yes, it still struck her as commonplace, in the way of a magazine ad or a billboard or a snapshot taken out the front window of the camera shop, just to get the roll spooling. Maybe a candid at the Berghoff. And as modern as this summer's ladies' fashions—it could have been painted earlier that day. Maybe the day before, to allow the paint to dry.

And yet, despite that first reaction, there was actually something captivating about it. It drew her in, physically, pulling her into the room, right up close.

NIGHTHAWKS, the plate on the wall said. EDWARD HOPPER.

"This one's new since I was here last, back before the war," he said. "Brand spankin'! Two years old. Kind of different, may not be your cup of tea, but I think you'll see a lot of what we've been talking about at work here. The way the fellow's got it worked up, compositionwise . . ."

It was just three people and a soda jerk or maybe a short-order cook, late night at a lunch counter. These people weren't special, they weren't doing anything fancy, they weren't even shown in enough detail to qualify as a portrait, to determine the degree of their beauty or grotesqueness or what the heck they even looked like. They were just sitting there like lumps. Lonesome lumps.

But the triangle of yellow—the bright light of the seedy little eatery—did cut through the darkness, the brackish gray-green of the dead intersection, to frame them so sharply.

And the way they were isolated off to one side, counterbalancing the empty, darker, practically unused portion of the composition—it did really focus her eye on them in a way that began to feel not only intentional but powerful, even masterful.

Moving right up to it now, she started calling out things she saw in it; things he'd been teaching her. They'd been talking about framing and lines of perspective and balance and something he called the rule of thirds.

With all she'd known of photography, learned from her pop and then Chesty, they'd never bothered getting into any of this with her. All she'd managed were the practical fundamentals of recording a pretty image: how to determine if something was worth the cost of film and photo paper, how to determine which part should be in focus, how to get it in focus, and how to line it up inside the frame.

"Also, there's the juxtaposed complementaries . . ."

It sounded like Reenie. She turned to see her sitting on the bench at the back of the room, reading from a brochure. She wasn't sure how long she'd been there.

"Or are you two not covering color theory today?"

With a smile, Sal greeted her, noticing that Wink was looking away now, drawn to something across the room that looked like a storm at sea. He didn't appear particularly surprised that Reenie had joined them.

Rather than make a scene, Sal did what any dignified person would do—she announced she was going back downstairs to the ladies' room, knowing Reenie would feel duty-bound to tag along.

It worked, but her friend didn't volunteer any explanation once they were down there, just grabbed a smoke by the sinks and waited.

After faking it in a stall, then pretending to wash up, Sal told her, at the mirror, "Say, Reen? Why don't you just meet us after, hon? You're not missing out on anything . . . *social*. He's just giving me a little art tutorial, you understand?" She pulled the steno pad she'd been scribbling on from her pocketbook and flashed it at her friend. "I'm actually trying to learn something, so—"

"So *I'm* not? I'm just the dumb bunny?" Reenie slipped into

a comical breathy voice, somewhere between Mae West and
Baby Snooks. " 'Looka all the pretty *pischers*! *Ooh . . . !*' " She
stubbed out her cigarette against the marble. "Who's the blonde
here, sister?"

Sal took a deep breath and waited, hoping to calm the impulse to smack her. When she thought she could say it nicely,
she told Reenie she'd never called her names like that and did
not think she was dumb, but that she was serious about this,
that she was trying to improve her understanding for the sake of
her *business,* not just—

"Listen." Reenie was shaking her head now. "That business
back at the ad agency? That's not over. I intend to be an art director again one day, maybe even an artist—a *great* artist. And
I'm not going to let a bunch of wolves like that Rollo Deininger
get in my way, either."

"That's great, Reenie." She checked her lipstick. "I want that
for you, too, and I'm sorry. But if you're really serious about it—
like it sure sounds you are—maybe you should actually apply to
an art school."

Reenie smirked. "And pay the tuition with what—my good
looks? No, I'll have to do this myself. Big picture, down the road,
I see myself marrying a guy rich enough he doesn't need me playing housewife, he can just put me through art school."

Sal told her it was a hell of plan. "Do it all yourself . . ."

"Darn tootin'," Reenie said. "In the meantime, though, I
wouldn't mind soaking up anything 'the Handsome Hothead' has
to say on the subject."

"I take it that's your nickname for Wink now."

"I figure it will do," she said, "until such time as he graduates
to 'the Shover Lover.' "

The first part, Sal figured, was a reference to him shoving

Reenie's former boss in the supply closet. The latter part meant she'd set her sights on him—as more than an art teacher. Maybe already had her hooks in him.

Which was fine, really. It was what Sal wanted all along, the two of them to hit it off.

27

Wink ignored the jingle of the shop bell. Sal was out front and would handle it. Besides, it sounded like it was just the mailman.

This was his first solo turn at developing a customer's roll of film, and he needed to concentrate. He couldn't afford to botch this.

He would have assumed Sal was even more concerned than he was about staying on good footing with the customers these days. So he was surprised when she bothered him, speaking to him through the curtain, telling him to be sure to come out and see her as soon as he could.

He gave her a muttery *Yeah, fine,* considering for a moment that she might just be trying to test him further—heap on the distractions to make him concentrate harder on his work. Like the kind of crap they pulled back in basic training—the DI putting his foot on your back and barking obscenities and unintelligible Arkansas slang while you did your push-ups, just to make you really sweat. Hell, maybe this roll wasn't even from a customer—maybe it was all just a test.

"How's it coming, by the way?"

He told her it was fine, no problem.

He found this initial stage, developing the negatives, to be the least fun part of the whole process—fumbling around in the pitch dark, trying to distinguish small details of the wire spool and load it by touch. There was too much pressure and chance to screw the pooch. Too Houdini; too much like his earliest, heart-pumping battles with a brassiere, on the dark rural roads back in Michigan.

When he was pretty sure he was done with the last step, he ran through the checklist again, in his head. And then once more, just to make sure he hadn't missed anything. With so few customers these days, Sal couldn't afford to get one of them riled up and screaming at her and never returning. And as for him, he'd become even more convinced, handling the cameras and working in the darkroom, that he was seriously going to have to make this his new medium. He hadn't entirely abandoned his growly, teeth-gnashing practice sessions, trying to draw with the old hand and retrain the new, but the results hadn't yet shown much improvement. The other night, while trying to sketch his bedroom dresser—a simple rectangle, at its heart—he ended the evening by punching a nice hole in the plaster wall. He was pretty sure Sal had heard him, though she hadn't mentioned it.

Finally, taking a deep breath, he decided to turn on the safe-light.

As near as he could tell as he hung up the strips to dry, it appeared to be shots of a toddler at his first birthday party—judging from the size of the blob that was the baby and the size of the darker blob that was the little birthday cake.

Then he took another breath, pulled back the curtain, and walked up to the front counter, a little wobbly as his eyes re-adjusted to the daylight.

She stood behind the counter, beaming, her hands flat on the display case. There on the glass was what looked like a check.

He stepped closer, saw the amount: seventy-five dollars. The payer was some publishing company. The payee was S. *Dean Chesterton.*

"The girl-in-the-kitchen photos," she said. "They *bought* them."

He was surprised she hadn't rushed to the bank to deposit it yet, and he told her so.

"I wanted you to see it first. And admire it."

"Nice one," he said admiringly.

"That's it?" She sounded disappointed.

"It's gorgeous," he said, laughing at her. Picking it up for a closer inspection, he noticed the memo line read *Titter 7/44.* Jabbing a finger at it, he explained that that had to be the magazine issue.

She looked like he'd notified her that she was pregnant. "You mean—it's—it's *out?* It's on newsstands and—? Lord love a duck!"

"My sentiments exactly," he said. They grabbed their hats and headed out to find it. Somewhere out there—not just somewhere, but *all over* out there—Sal was sashaying around in a flipped-up skirt, showing off her legs, and making some lucky, unseen GI a wonderful home-cooked meal.

The grouchy newsdealer eyed him suspiciously, but maybe he wasn't sure he had a browser this time or saw that Wink was quicker about it now, finding the one he wanted, because this time he didn't make with the wisecracks. Perhaps he thought Sal was a whole different gal or they weren't even together. She waited off to one side while he made the purchase, not having brought her disguise, the black wig.

Wink suspected she might not listen to him—wouldn't wait till they got back to the shop to search through it for her pictures, and so he bought a copy of *Life* as well, and tucked it in there.

He was right: she only made it a few doors down before she had the copy of *Titter* flipped open, hidden behind the *Life* cover of Admiral Nimitz, and was yanking at his arm like a kid, like he'd taken her to Riverside for a ride on the merry-go-round.

He noticed now she was wearing his Ray-Bans again, and when she spoke, she was peeking over them, like a spy, quietly declaring: "We, my friend, are in business."

28

The first thing she paid off was the past-due invoice for darkroom chemicals. She called the suppliers and told them it was in the mail and to please ship the last order; that they were almost out of fix and potassium ferricyanide for reducer. Playing it safe, she sent in half what was owed for the city tax—enough to keep them happy.

Fifteen dollars, she decided, would go to Wink.

He frowned when she handed him the five spots, but she told him it was pay for helping around the store. "Walking around money," she said. "Take Reenie to see *Double Indemnity*."

The frown remained. "I feel funny taking a cut. I mean, I'm not sure how I feel about capitalizing on your . . . well, I don't want to take *advantage* . . ."

She knew what he was driving at, and she didn't like it. The word he was stumbling over trying to avoid was *pimp*. If he really felt that way then he was as much as saying she was a whore.

"Work it out," she told him, "because if you're calling yourself a certain thing, you're calling *me* something, too. And I don't think that's very nice."

He lost the frown. "Sorry."

"And if that's your attitude, it's going to get in the way be-cause we'd be fools not to keep going with this."

He sighed, but he wasn't really shaking his head anymore. "It just doesn't sound like a *we* situation, Sal . . ."

She handed him another five spot and told him he was to go out and find some black-market ration stamps he could purchase—maybe sugar or butter—to give Mia in exchange for the use of the wig. And to make her continue to think she was just doing something as harmless as bilking the government.

"That's your part," she said. "So the fifteen bucks is well earned." She shoved the money back his way, and this time, after a moment of consideration he picked it up.

29

She had a lot of questions, it seemed to Wink, about what was enticing and what was more enticing—this or this—and though it started out seeming like *she* was the confused one, the more she probed for some kind of exact formula for what made an image hot stuff, the more it seemed like maybe *he* was.

But then he remembered something strange and amusing that he'd experienced four years back, when he was first in Chicago, taking classes just south of where they were now, at the Academy. It seemed, now, like it might serve as some kind of a response—if not an exact enough answer, at least a place-holder. So he told her about the first anatomy class he took there and how the "life model"—which in this case was just a fancy code name for "stunning leggy blonde"—came out from behind a little Japanese screen, dressed in a plain silk dressing gown, and moved, all business, to the wooden crates the instructor had laid out in the center of the circled wagon train that was their easels. Then she dropped the robe, like it was nothing.

Of course, he managed perfectly well to keep his face in order, his jaw from dropping into his tackle box, and so did his fellow classmates, mostly all male. They were all adults, at least, if not quite yet professionals. Nobody giggled, drooled, or gawked.

But then an odd thing happened. The next class, while they were getting settled at their easels and the instructor was convoluting another structure for her to pose on, Wink noticed movement behind the little Japanese screen in the corner. And he noticed the other male students were starting to notice, too. The model was just changing out of her street clothes, a perfectly normal thing for her to do, but she'd somehow jostled the screen slightly, inadvertently allowing a nice peekaboo slit of several inches through which they could see her getting ready, resting one foot at a time on a rung of her changing stool, unbuckling the strap of each pump, removing the shoe, unrolling the stocking—"Yes, this was 1940, remember actual stockings, Sal?"— and then straightening to unhook the clasp of her skirt and let it drop. In that narrow window, they glimpsed the vaguest *idea* of her white, pedestrian underwear, the unfrilly, utilitarian garter belt; gathered, in a moment, some idea of how her blouse came undone, and her serious-minded, overkill bra—and though it was only a matter of thirty seconds, tops, it was wildly exciting. Not just to him, judging by the mouth-breather gapes from his fellow artistes. The simple, partially obstructed view of her untucking the shirttails of her blouse from her waistband, the underhand flick of hand to hair as she freed it from the collar of her blouse, was stunning—far more so, even, than the two or three hours of almost boring nudity she'd subjected them to in the last class.

"That first time," he explained to Sal, "it wasn't nakedness so much as *barrenness*."

But on this following day, the model appeared, in that little glimpse of a private moment, to be nothing like the seemingly freewheeling, free spirit who'd posed before. Hell, her underpants were all wrong.

"It was amazing," he said. "And when she finally realized we were all watching her taking it off—just *beginning* to take it off— she shrieked and snatched up her clothes and bolted. From the room. From the school."

He laughed, remembering now how steamed the instructor got, how he called them all silly children for behaving in that way. And since the model never returned, the teacher took her place until he eventually found a new girl. But Wink had always felt it was more punishment than practicality, making them all stare at his wizened old pecker and saddlebag of a scrotum, his gray pubes and sagging chest and ass cheeks.

Sal seemed stymied by the story. "Really? This wasn't just some weird reaction on your part alone? *All* the guys were more worked up over her slipping out of her skirt than being able to study her in the buff? You're putting me on, aren't you?"

He shrugged, not sure how else to explain it. "Guys . . . are guys."

She looked like she was having an epiphany, and when she spoke, it was like she was sounding it out, trying it on for size. "It's the closest thing they can have to being romantic."

When he heard her say it, he knew it was true.

30

Talking about it and finally doing it, she found, were two entirely different animals.

She'd assumed, with all the planning and rationalizing they'd done—talking it to death, both agreeing that this was the responsible thing to do—that they could be shrewd businessmen about it, adults about it. But now that she was standing there in a bathrobe, it was hard enough to keep her breathing even and steady, let alone keep a firm grasp on the rationalities and logic, and she gripped the flannel lapels tight, not so much out of modesty, but simply to hang on.

It was so silly and illogical, but she couldn't help wanting to hold off to the last minute to shed it—waiting till they both agreed they had everything in place; waiting for the chill to stop shooting up her spine, giving her goose bumps, making her cheeks tingle, her fingers shake.

Summertime, she told herself. *It's summertime. You're* not *cold.*

For his part, Wink didn't seem exactly kid-glove smooth himself, fidgeting with the lights, checking and double-checking the shutter speed, no time to stop and look her in the eye.

For this first session, his role would have to merely be that of art director, wardrobe assistant, corner man, maybe cheerleader. Since he didn't trust himself adjusting the focus yet, she would still have to supervise the actual operation of the camera, then hop back around in front of it.

The bathrobe was Chesty's, so it dragged on the floor, and underneath, she had on leg makeup and Wink's khaki dress tunic from his army uniform—all of which exposed far less than he'd already seen in pictures from the other two shoots. Heck, the first one, she'd been topless, even. So being jumpy about this didn't make any sense—*rationally.*

Of course, those two earlier times, he hadn't been standing right there, right in the room with her. Suddenly, this whole thing felt pretty cockamamy.

"You need a belt?" he asked, and she thought he must be as

flummoxed by this as she was, because he should have understood that she wasn't going to wear the bathrobe once they
started. So no, she wouldn't need a belt.

"I don't think so . . ." She scooted over to the mirror one more
time and opened the robe to take a peek. They were set up in the
little studio area in back that they normally used for passport
photos and children's portraits. The mirror was a little low—just
about bow-tie height for the grade-schoolers.

The plan was to mince around in various configurations of
his old uniform, like she was trying it on, clowning around for her
soldier boy. It wasn't much of a theme, but she thought they'd
better keep it simple: it was going to be hard enough concentrating on posing and being sexy with Wink there for the first
time.

Adjusting her wig, she turned back to take her place and saw
he had slipped away. She could hear him on the stairs, clumping back down, in a hurry.

He appeared with her pop's antique bathtub gin, taking a
pull. She'd misunderstood about the belt.

With a gasp and a wipe of his mouth, he held it out for her,
giving her another chance to refuse. This time, she took it.

And then she took her place on the X they'd marked on the
floor with black tape, put on a smile, slipped off the robe, and
tossed it clear of the shot.

31

He was trying his hand at making prints, practicing on their first
roll of girlies together, when he heard a rap on the door frame
that held the blackout curtain that was the darkroom door.

Sal was running the shop, so either it was even deader out front than it normally was or he'd lost track of the time and she'd already locked up for the day and wanted to see about dinner.

He grunted that it was safe to come in, not looking up, concentrating on the print in the developer tray, watching each click in the sweep of the luminescent clock. He figured she was watching pretty intently—the teacher and her apprentice—and it only made him concentrate harder as he gripped the photo with the rubber tongs, lifted it from the developer, and dropped it into the stop bath. Swishing it around gently, he turned it over, curious to see how he'd done.

There seemed to be a nice range of black and white. This business of contrast was a tricky one. The line of Sal's cleavage needed to be deep and dark but not so overexposed that she looked like she had a stripe of chest hair.

"Hmm," she murmured, noncommittal.

With the tongs tugging one corner, he held it up to the safe-light for a closer look.

He felt her sliding up behind him, peering over his shoulder. Her hair brushed his neck and he got a whiff of her. Even over the stink of the chemical baths, there was a difference: her perfume was more hibiscus and lavender; Sal's, he'd noticed, was more lilac. This was Reenie. It had to be—it wasn't just her hair brushing his neck now, but her lips.

"Oh," he said, and she found his mouth.

"Oh yourself," she said.

He pulled away, realizing she was peering down at the photo in the fix. Flipping it back over, thinking he'd better cover up the work he had hanging up to dry, he said, "Listen, that's not who you think it is."

"Please," she said. "Don't hand me that. I'd recognize that cleavage anywhere." She had that evil arch to her eyebrow she did so well. "Looks like you and Sal're teaching each other all *kinds* of things."

Reenie's reaction was not quite what he expected. Instead of acting jealous or disgusted or accusing the two of them of carrying on together, she simply said, "I want in."

"In?" he said.

Her black pageboy bobbed as she nodded enthusiastically. "On the fun. And the cash, of course. I'm assuming there's cash to be made."

It was Sal who said, before he could even think of it, "We'd pay a straight modeling fee, sure."

In other words, Reenie would not be getting a third. Sal was shrewd like that, full of business savvy, and it was amazing to Wink that she and Chesty were having financial problems, with that kind of tough talk.

Reenie didn't seem to be thrown by this. She seemed more concerned with cooking up creative possibilities they could explore, immediately spewing half a dozen ideas for cheap and easy themes for pinup pictures, just off the top of her head, which would involve only a few readily attainable props and costumes. "You're using leg makeup, right? Well, you should shoot her *putting on* the leg makeup as a separate shoot first—one about a gal making do without real nylons—then change the wig and do whatever you were going to shoot. That way you've got two photo stories for the price and trouble of one."

Sal shot him a look that told him she was damn impressed and would file that idea away.

Reenie asked what Sal got paid for the first batch, and she told her. Reenie then suggested they might consider, at some point down the line, making some bigger bucks with some of the so-called after-hours clients she'd heard about back at LD&M. "There are people like this character Mr. Price or Pace or something—they come in and hire the art department for special jobs, unofficial. Deininger especially. Girlie calendars, card decks, that angle. Some of it's kind of, you know . . . *French.* I'm just thinking, if you ever want to cut out the middleman, skip over these magazine publishers. I understand it can be very heavy on the do-re-mi, and that's always a good thing."

"We're fine for now," Sal said, a little stiffly, he thought. "But thank you for your suggestion."

"I'm just saying," Reenie said, "if you're doing it, do it all out, is all . . ."

He knew that she wanted to go back to school to study properly to be an art director. Maybe she was thinking that between the pay from her day job at Stevens-Gross and some extra cash on the side from posing, it would be enough to get her that degree.

Or maybe she was just a little nuts. That was also a strong possibility.

He'd suspected as much the night he'd given his little art lecture for the two gals down the street at the Art Institute, when, after they both said good night to Sal, Reenie quietly tiptoed back up the stairs and slipped into his apartment.

As soon as she had the door closed, she leaned back against it, looked him earnestly in the eye while gliding her hand down his pants, and whispered, "You know I'm not one of those victory girls, right?"

He said he knew.

"I don't just throw myself at every boy who serves, okay? I'm *fun,* sure. Or I can be. But I don't just push right over for every man in uniform. Get me, buster?"

He was having trouble swallowing. "Gotten," he said, and it came out funny.

"Like you, for inst—you're not in uniform. And I'm planning on climbing all over *you* like ivy on a trellis. So what kind of a golldarn victory girl is that, huh, dreamboat? There goes that theory right out the ever-lovin' window."

He didn't tell her he'd given up having *any* theories about *anything* having to do with *any* woman *at all* ever since arriving back in Chicago. He didn't tell her anything because she had her tongue in his mouth, and she was pushing him back toward the narrow bed.

32

She enjoyed it best of all when the letters from Chesty were typewritten, like this one was. Not because his handwriting was so awful, but she had to think that it meant he was safely back out of the fray, working closer to civilization (if they had such a thing down there on the other side of the world) and not pinned down in some jungle skirmish, assigned to cover the wrong story at the wrong time. A typewriter meant he had a chair and probably a desk—both good signs, in terms of danger.

There were six pages to the thing, and this last she handed to Wink to read:

```
6
can imagine we laughed our a---s off over
that one!
   Oh, also--rc'ved your letter re: Wink
Dutton staying in your Pop's apt. and that
is aces w/me. I will worry considerably
less than I do now knowing he is there.
```

```
Just don't let him become TOO handy w/a
camera than yours truly--I would not
welcome the competition!
     Seriously, though, that boy has the eye,
I tell you. He is one talented ason-of-a-
gun and if you have ever wanted to learn
more in re: art theory etc., as I know you
do, I suggest you take advantage of his
presence, his generosity and his thick-
headed tendency to drive a point into the
£ground.
     I'm just razzing the lucky so-and-so, of
course, dear. Dutton is a good egg and I'm
glad to know he'll be around--not that you
ever needed any looking after, kiddo.
     My love to you and a sock on that bony
jaw to Dutton--


                              Chesty.
```

She showed it to him just so he would know she wasn't mis-interpreting or misrepresenting her husband's desires in any way.

"Well, okay," Wink said. "I guess that settles that. Should I run out and get a little throw rug or a potted geranium, maybe a pretty frame for that picture of my girlfriend, really settle in for good?"

She wasn't sure why he was being so sarcastic about it—it wasn't like they were holding a gun to his head and making him stay there.

"You have a girlfriend?" she asked, thinking maybe Reenie had already succeeded in working her charms on him.

He snapped his fingers like she'd suggested a crackerjack

idea. "Oh right!" he said. "I should probably pick up one of those, as well. I mean, as long as I'm getting the comfy rug and the geranium and the picture frame."

The conversation just sort of ended. When he shuffled off to his end of the hall, and closed his door, she had a good idea he was having a belt of something.

The man took a nip more frequently than she remembered her husband doing, but maybe she was just idealizing Chesty, since he was gone. And maybe her husband would be drinking more now, too; perhaps as much as Wink. War changed men. One more drink or two here and there could hardly be the worst result, given the other choices, like shell shock or paraplegism or trench foot. Or, well, *death.*

She thought that if she didn't know better, she'd think Wink was peeved about something, even acting a little hostile.

She'd never felt like she was head of her class in guessing what went on in the thick domes of men, and she was sure as hell out of practice lately.

Tuning in one of the least dreary soaps on the radio, she sat down at her kitchen to write Chesty a nice long response and cram it full of love and understanding and other sweet nothings.

33

The next check arrived with an advance copy and a friendly note saying, *Send us more of "Winkin' Sally." Love her!*

He stared at it like it was Japanese.

With no idea what they were talking about, he flipped

through the pulpy pages of the magazine till he recognized Sal's smile.

Two pages of familiar photos, with this headline:

WINKIN' SALLY,
YOUR BARRACKS GAL-PALLY!
This stunning soldier-ette's making a surprise inspection!

Under the photos of Sal in his tunic and overseas cap were the following inane captions: "<u>DRESS</u> *inspection? Gee, I'm not sure* <u>where I left it</u> *last!"* . . . *"To be fair, I'm only* <u>half</u> *out of uniform"* . . . *"GI must stand for 'Getting Ideas'!"* . . . *"At* <u>EASE</u>*? Who you calling* <u>EASY</u>, *soldier?!"* . . . *"Let's try bouncing a quarter off your bed— or* <u>something</u>*! . . ."* . . . *"So does my uniform pass muster, buster?"*

He stared at it for the longest time before he could even begin to piece together what in Jesus' name happened.

He'd been plastered. Always a fair guess, but he was pretty sure, thinking back, he'd been feeling mopey and blue up in his room, burned up about his hand, unable to draw, feeling lonesome and still thinking about those shots he'd taken of Sal the night before, half in his uniform, as the corny copy said, and how they were right downstairs, all printed out and the negatives safe in their waxpaper sleeves, all set to go off to the magazine publisher. He remembered that they hadn't sealed the manila envelope, but agreed to leave it there, unsealed, for twenty-four hours, just in case they changed their minds. Also in the envelope was a release form the publisher had sent along when they bought Sal's first series, the shots she'd done on her own in the kitchen.

The late hour and the low spirits and the descending hash mark on his bottle got the better of him, and he snuck downstairs with the bold determination to spread the photos out on the darkroom workbench and whack his pecker. Wax the dolphin, as someone used to say back in the PTO. Except he couldn't go through with it. Instead, he looked at each of them, in the red glow of the safelight, and took another pull on his bottle each time, toasting her: "To Mrs. Chesty Chesterton . . ."

And the form was there on the workbench, having spilled out of the envelope with the rest of the contents. She had almost completed it, but it had gotten kind of late, so she'd agreed to finish it when the waiting period was over and they mailed it in.

He was pretty sure now, thinking back to that hazy night, he must have snatched up a grease pencil and, with his shaky left hand, scribbled *Wink-n-Sal* encircled by a heart, right on the form, then shoved it in the envelope and licked it closed. He seemed to remember thinking he was filling out the space for *Contributing artist(s):* but possibly it hit a little closer to the line that read *Working title, if applc.*

When he told the girls, he showed them both the editor's note and the magazine, but kept this theory of its origin to himself, along with any admission of having scrawled an illegible valentine on the official submission form. Not only wasn't he sure he could explain to either one of them what would possess him to do such a thing, alcohol notwithstanding; he wasn't sure, given even the far future stretches of his own living days, he could ever explain such a thing even to himself.

He would tell them it was a mystery; that her name and his must have appeared somewhere in the correspondence and the magazine folks took it upon themselves to combine them, maybe as a joke, trying to be cute; maybe out of confusion.

Besides, it didn't matter how it had happened, he figured, so much as what the hell they were going to do about it.

"You've got yourself a *brand name!*" Reenie said when he showed the photo spread to the two of them. "Just because you weren't looking for it, doesn't mean it's not a good thing. A lot of great things in life are accidents. This penicillin they've got now? Some scientist got sloppy with his sandwich, his bread got all moldy . . . bingo! He's cured the clap."

"Yeah, but . . ." Sal looked a little stricken, as he thought she might. "I mean, it's got *my name* in the name!"

Reenie gave her a playful shove. "Bilge! You go by Sal, they know Sally. Whole different gal."

It was hard to convince himself that Sal seemed very persuaded by her friend's logic, and he felt a little guilty about the whole snafu. He wished, in a way, he'd just gone ahead and waxed the dolphin to her photos and been done with it; skipped the graffiti and kept her name out of the whole thing.

Sal studied the two-page spread again while he and Reenie stood by, as if waiting for her final, official verdict. "Maybe I wouldn't feel so iffy about it if the stuff they wrote wasn't so . . ."

Reenie was tapping the magazine with a pencil, studying it closer. "The copy's corny as hell, granted. We could do better than they did—maybe send in our own copy next time."

"And it does worry me a little," Sal said. "Some guy might connect the name with the face, here in the shop, maybe cause trouble. It feels a little . . . exposed."

He told her if that was how she felt, then absolutely, they could call it quits right there, no problem. But he could see from her face that she wasn't ready to toss in the towel over a silly nickname. And the way her pal was fired up, there was no way Reenie would allow her to.

"The only thing you two should be worrying about is how much longer you can keep this up without getting some proper stockings. Have you seen many of these girlie magazines? Lots of legs, my friend. And rationing or no rationing, a pinup girl with

her very own name like that has to at least own one decent pair
of stockings. End of discussion."

Except it wasn't—the discussion did not end, but simply sidetracked to the issue of how best to procure nylons without getting tangled up with black-market thugs and then sidetracked
again to stocking varieties and classifications he'd never heard
of (Sal appeared a little in the dark, as well) or ever guessed ex-
isted, such as something Reenie called Cuban heels, shifting
next to a primer on the anatomy of the female calf and how it
could be rendered more aesthetically pleasing by positioning and
flexing and which pumps created the best effects.

Frankly, Wink felt they'd stepped far out of his wheelhouse.
The more they talked about great legs and disreputable contacts,
the more it became clear to him that Reenie would now be their
resident expert on both.

34

The first one they did together, they went once more with a military theme. It seemed to Sal, between what Wink told her and
the comments she'd received from the publishers, plus hearing
Reenie's own two cents, backed up with evidence *she* lugged
in—stacks of recent girlies she'd pilfered from her brothers—
the military angle, these days, was a surefire bet.

It was beyond Sal why this would be—did these GIs, far
away, really fantasize that their sweethearts back home might
sneak in one night, get past the sentries and land mines, possibly get a bullet through their brain pan at every step, possibly
fall into enemy hands and be ravished beyond all mercy, all to
then parade around in a strictly confined area that included le-

gions of equally sex-starved men, who, no matter if they shared his uniform, might also ravish her beyond all mercy? When she really thought about it, it was pretty fruity.

But they cobbled together the bare semblance of two quasi-military uniforms and, borrowing an old Scout pup tent from Reenie's brother Patrick, went through a series of comic poses, each of which exposed their legs and cleavage and showed off the muscles on Reenie's calves and the bulge of Sal's own bosom as she tugged with exaggeration on the line, as if trying to stake it into the hard studio floor.

They both had their long suits, she figured, and even if she wore her wig, as she was, rendering them both raven-haired cuties, they each had their special feature that would distinguish them: she was the busty one, Reenie had the gams. But were they both going to be Winkin' Sally, she wondered, or would the editors come up with something completely new? There was a part of her that felt petty worrying about such things, but she wondered if men might like Reenie better. Maybe they were equally pretty, each in her own way, but her friend was certainly the bolder of the two. And she was also the one with the great, expressive eyebrows, the big sexy wink. It was right in the name—maybe *she* was Winkin' Sally, not Sal herself.

Well, she thought, that wasn't their end of it. That was beyond their domain. Their job here was to toss their bodies around in front of the camera and not worry about anything other than exposing parts of themselves in ridiculous predicaments.

It wasn't hard to fumble and fall on the floor—the tent was a shambles and neither of them had a clue how to raise the moldy old thing—and when they'd fall, they'd hold the pose, Reenie's legs up over her head, Sal's buttons popping. It was ridiculous and so much fun. Much more so now that she had a girlfriend to do it with her, and the hardest part to all this, she was starting to realize, was not cracking up so hard they broke the pose and fell all over each other laughing.

It felt wonderful paying off the creditors, starting to set things right. With the second sale of photos, she felt confident enough about this turn of fortune to write Chesty and tell him . . . *something.* Of course, she wasn't ready to tell him that she'd been producing girlie pictures, not to mention posing for them. She liked to think he was understanding enough that later on, when he was no longer far off and in harm's way, he might be able to hear the whole truth and not fly off the handle. Wink seemed to think he would be able to—he claimed he never would have gotten involved in all this himself if he really thought Chesty wouldn't understand, over time, given some perspective.

"But don't tell him now, no," he agreed. "You should see what a mess worry and distance makes of the married guys back there. You're right keeping him in the dark till he's Stateside. Or maybe till you two have had your third child or so."

And the other thing that made it tricky writing Chesty and telling him things were turning around was he wasn't actually aware things *hadn't* been hunky-dory—she'd been sugarcoating the shop's finances for him almost as much as she had been for his uncle in their monthly visits at his bank, so how could she tell her husband, *Hey, we're no longer in danger of losing the shop to creditors!?*

She knew it was pride that made her want to spill the beans. Some sort of bravado about rolling up her sleeves, taking care of her man. She felt, in her way, a little like Rosie the Riveter, doing what had to be done when times turned hard. Except, in her case, the rivet gun was a camera, and the assembly line of bombers she produced was an assembly line of boners and grins for all the young men out there.

She was all set to wad up her airmail letter when Wink came to her rescue. He'd been watching her struggle through the better part of two cups of coffee, the two of them having developed the habit of breakfast together at her end of the hall. Decorum hadn't gotten *so* lax—they still both dressed before he appeared in her kitchen—but still, it had grown considerably familiar and casual between them. For instance, he made no pretense about glancing over at what she was writing in this private letter to her husband.

"Tell him *Business has improved nicely. I'm doing very well.* You can get into the particulars later."

She was growing rather fond of this trait of his—he seemed to be able to sum up a situation and the best course of action all in the same moment. It made her wonder, sometimes—if he hadn't once been such a good illustrator and cartoonist—whether he would have been given men to command in battle.

She told him his suggestion made sense, it was just that she kind of wanted Chesty to be proud of her and . . . well . . .

He'd been doing his "left-hand doodling," as he called it, too discouraged to refer to it as actual drawing. She would never admit it to him, but she could see why he was discouraged. The retraining process didn't seem to be working—which made it all the more admirable that he kept slugging away at it. His usual procedure, during their breakfast coffee and toast, was to do what he was doing now—sketch, with his left, on a stack of scrap paper while alternating sips of coffee and bites of dry toast with his crippled right.

But now he stopped all motion, setting down his pencil and his toast, and intertwined his unsatisfying hands, looking at her directly in a way that made her squirm. "Let me ask you something, Sal. Are *you* proud of yourself?"

She hesitated, though she knew the answer. "Yes, I am."

"Then you're all set. Case closed."

He smiled that sad smile she'd grown so accustomed to mornings of late and went back to his scribbling.

35

He felt pretty nervous stopping by the Stevens-Gross Studio, home of such talented commercial artists as Haddon Sundblom and Gil Elvgren, but it made sense to pick Reenie up from work. He was taking her to a retrospective show of war-bonds poster art, then to grab a bite, then maybe take in a picture, then swing by a porch party some of her ad friends were throwing to celebrate the liberation of Paris, and the first stop of the evening, the poster art show, was just down the block from Stevens-Gross.

She gave him a halfhearted tour. Every artist there had their own individual studio. Two were still hard at work, artists Wink failed to recognize—he might have had better luck if he could see their canvases. Reenie just waved as they passed, not introducing him; probably not wanting to interrupt. They seemed young, and Wink wondered if they were maybe staying late to make a good impression. One of them looked younger than him, and it was hard not to imagine himself getting that slot in another version of the world, in a life in which he wasn't stupidly hungover and not paying attention on a submarine tour.

He asked about Elvgren. The prospect of running into his hero and former painting instructor was both exciting and scary. Wink wasn't sure what he would say to explain what he was up to these days.

"Home with the wife and kids by now," she said. "He's a nine-to-fiver. You wouldn't know it for all the naughtiness the guy likes to paint, but he's a real family man. All business. Very professional."

Sundblom's studio was filled with work for Coke—warm, rosy-cheeked girls tipping back the hourglass bottle. On the easel there was one of his famous Coke Santas, the red suit and the window of what had to be his workshop still only roughed in.

"Man alive," Wink said, and told Reenie that this was like walking through the commercial artist's equivalent of the Art Institute of Chicago.

Reenie shrugged. "You get used to it."

For the Paris party, all the guests were supposed to bring cheese if they could get their hands on it, but at least wear berets.

"What kind of world is this now," he'd said earlier, "where it's become easier to find berets than cheese?"

Reenie thought there might be some in the costume and prop bins the illustrators kept in the back, and she left him alone in Elvgren's studio to go dig around for berets.

"Man alive . . . ," he said again, to himself this time, unable to keep it in.

The girl on the canvas, though barely completed, was beautiful—that face so rosy and smiling, eyeing him coyly. There was a portion of the painting roughed out for the boilerplate print—he had no idea yet what the box would double as. Maybe a crate, a radio, something like that. This was how they did it: leaving a section of the illustration ready and blank where they could slug in the advertiser's copy later.

There were props and stools and various risers shoved over in the corner. He'd understood from Reenie that Elvgren didn't work from live models but from reference photos he posed and shot himself, and these were all over one side of the studio. Wink moved closer, inspecting the rows of black-and-white shots of a blonde model with a pageboy straddling an overturned chair like it was a horse, cowboy hat in hand; then supine on the floor with her legs propped up on a Kodak box, holding a yardstick like it was a fishing rod. There were even a few of Reenie. She appeared to be in her everyday work clothes, no doubt just pitching in and helping out. In one, Wink could see the string holding her skirt back as she peered over her shoulder at a point marked on the wall with an X of adhesive tape. This was the bare bones of . . . what? A fence, a bush, something that would snag the girl's dress.

Even the photos were great. Hell, they were as good if not better than the best stuff *they'd* been shooting. And this, for these guys, these real artists, was just the beginning of the process. *Imagine that . . .*

Returning to the easel, he leaned close, loving the texture of the brushstrokes, still damp, and the garage smell of the oil paint. He picked up the man's palette, disappointed that he was apparently one of those diligently organized artists who cleaned his palette at the end of each workday. He would have liked to see how he was mixing the colors.

Wink missed mixing the colors, layering it on, building it up.

"Listen," Reenie said, suddenly behind him, "if this place makes you so gaga, we could wait till everyone leaves and . . ."

He hadn't realized he was caressing the glass palette. He turned to face her, trying to puzzle out if it was a sincere offer or not. The short time they'd been fooling around, he'd learned enough of Reenie's ways to suspect it was possible she was on the level. She might want him to take her right there, maybe on the drop cloth.

She rolled her eyes up to the beret on her head, gave him a smirk. "Kidding, chum. I'm not doing it in here! You nuts? Someday, I *am* leaving again—mark my words—moving up to bigger and better, brother, and I'll need to ask these folks for references, believe you me. So ix-nay on the ooky-nay."

As they left the studio, he secretly wished they didn't have a full evening ahead of them. Something about visiting this place really had him blue.

36

The picture was called *To Have and Have Not,* and they sat right up front, so close she could make out the rips and patches in the screen. When the Warner Bros. shield came up like a badge, followed by a map of the Caribbean, they still had the whole front row to themselves.

It was difficult to watch, this close up, but this was where they were supposed to sit, so she didn't complain, other than a few sighs and slouching down in her seat, trying to make it easier to crane her neck to see.

"Bogie's lips do look huge," Reenie whispered.

Sal told her to hush, not wanting her to ruin it.

Anyway, his lips had always seemed large to her, even before today, but now, it was hard not to focus on them and wonder if these sluglike lips ran in the Bogart family.

They sat through a bunch of marlin fishing and talk of bees, then the leading lady appeared in an upstairs hallway with *Anybody got a match?* and Reenie's elbow jabbed Sal, pulling her from the story as two men with long coats joined them, taking a seat on either side of them. Neither bookend man said hello or acknowledged them in any way.

She didn't want to be too obvious about it, but she snuck a peek out of her periphery. The man next to her looked like a tough customer. On the biggish side, dark curly hair, possible broken nose, but good-looking. He'd assumed possession of the armrest and he had thick piano-mover hands. The one two seats down, on the far side of Reenie, had a thin, childlike face, a delicate nose, and long lashes. This one was the one who finally spoke, saying, "Bogie's lips look *huge*."

That was the password. These were the black marketeers with the nylons.

Sal turned and glanced at Reenie one last time, as if to make sure—as if there were any way to possibly *be* sure about such a thing—and slid the envelope from her pocketbook, slipping it into the paw dangling at the end of her armrest. Like small prey swallowed by a snake, the envelope retracted up into his coat sleeve. Meanwhile, to her left, the thin fellow allowed a paper bundle to drop from his coat. He was very elegant about it as he bent and rested the package against Reenie's leg.

A minute or two passed, and then there was some lively hustle and bustle on the screen—Hoagy Carmichael singing "Am I Blue?" and the gal joining in and the nightclub breaking out in applause. The two men took this moment to remove themselves, the small one executing the slightest nod of a bow, and they retreated to seats in the back.

Her heart was pumping, even after they'd gone.

She'd suggested, several times, they ask Wink to come along, just to be safe.

"No, no," Reenie had insisted. "Patrick says if we show up with a fella, they may think he's a cop or a G-man or something. So just you and me, toots."

This hadn't sounded like such a red-hot plan. Sal asked her if she really thought that would be safe, the two of them meeting strange men unescorted.

"They know my brothers," Reenie said. "Or know *of* them.

Believe me, that's like having an entire armored division gunning their engines behind us. We could show up naked, they wouldn't touch us. We'll be *fine!*"

And they were fine. There was no monkey business, not even so much as a leer. She even wondered, though it was hard to tell in the brief glimpses she got of him, if one of the men wasn't a sissy. He seemed overly gentle handling the stockings. And not once did his glance detour even briefly toward her bosom.

All the way home, she'd expected J. Edgar Hoover or Eliot Ness to step out from an alley, flash a badge, demand to see what was in the Marshall Field's bag. She imagined the unflattering photographic skills of the police department, ugly mug shots, printed on the crime page of the *Trib,* spinning forward as if in a newsreel or cheap movie, and the headline: CHEESECAKE DUO NABBED IN NYLON RING. The drop head would read "Illicit Photographs Seized as Evidence."

But no such cinematic-style calamity befell them, and as she locked the shop door behind them, she busted out grinning, not believing their good luck. "Sister," she announced, "we are rolling in clover."

It was a surprise—since they hadn't needed his help anyway, they'd kept it from Wink. She stashed the little package in the hatbox in the darkroom until later that night. They'd get him to set up for a shoot, and then they'd pull out the nylons.

They used the darkroom to change, and Reenie went in ahead of her while Sal double-checked the way Wink had the camera set up.

"Hey, Sal?" she said, calling out to her from behind the curtain. "You said something earlier about us rolling in clover? I think maybe we're rolling in something else."

She didn't like the sound of this. Leaving Wink to it, she marched over and pulled back the curtain. Reenie was down to her panties and bra, the lacy black set that went well with her hair, but she wasn't wearing the nylons. Instead, she held one stretched out between her hands as if playing cat's cradle.

Sal could see for herself. "They're a little big?"

"A little? Seabiscuit might be able to pull it off. *Maybe.*"

Wink joined them and they gathered around the big surprise. According to the labels, only one pair was XL. The other three were XXL.

"Nice surprise," Wink said. "You shouldn't have."

Reenie reached around her and slapped him on the head. "Any ideas, mister, or are you just going to stand there looking dashing?"

Sal came up with the idea of pulling them back tight with clothespins, but the other two outvoted her on this, claiming it would be too hard to shoot every shot so that the stockings never wrinkled and the clothespins never showed.

Wink asked, just for the sake of argument, what if they just let them be big and wrinkly—how would that look?

"Like a safari," Reenie said matter-of-factly. "Like we're elephants. Or rhinos."

But ultimately, Reenie was the one who came up with the solution. They wouldn't wear the stockings. They'd use them as a prop, as the main theme. Holding them up, dangling them, inspecting them, they didn't look outrageously huge. They would shoot a storyline of girls *buying* a pair of nylon stockings—the last one on a sales table—and then they would fight over it.

So Sal and Wink carried the dinette down from upstairs while Reenie made some hand-lettered sales signs out of cardboard. Reenie borrowed a couple of Sal's hats from the closet and the two they'd both worn that day and arranged them on the far wall on pushpins. It looked a *little* like a ladies' department.

The best shots, she could tell, even as they were doing it, were the ones Wink got once they got going, once the poses moved beyond the wide-eyed surprise and the two "customers" discover the one pair of stockings for sale, once the struggle had begun and their clothes "accidentally" began to fall away. The giant nylon worked wonderfully for tug-of-war, stretching outrageously. They grimaced and sneered, putting on their most ferocious faces, and it was hard to hold their expressions long enough for the shot without busting out laughing. In one shot Reenie dreamed up, they both stood on either side of the sales display and braced themselves, each with one leg up, a foot jammed against the table.

At one point, they were both up *on* the table, with Sal on top, pinning her down, but Reenie holding fast to the prized nylons. Another shot, Sal was on all fours on the floor, the nylons between her teeth, with Reenie straddling her, working the ends like reins.

"Next time," Reenie said when they'd shot the roll and Sal had begun gathering up the oversize, seemingly useless hosiery, "we'll string them up and make hammocks, do a whole desert island fantasy . . ."

The girl was just chock-full of ideas.

37

It was Chesty's birthday, and Sal was hitting the sauce. The three of them had had dinner earlier, and one drink there, toasting him in his absence, and then she'd opted out of the movie after and had the two of them drop her back at the shop. She said she just wanted to sit and think happy birthday wishes that he was safe.

He and Reenie took in a picture featuring Joan Fontaine as some poor gal just trying to get married but pestered by her fiancé and three old flames, all trying to dig up dirt on her and tell tales on her. It appeared to be a comedy.

After, they necked in the park by the Buckingham Fountain for a little bit, watching the twinkling lights on Lake Michigan, and though she worked him over a little through his trousers, with her hand, Reenie insisted he not try to sneak into her place with her tonight but that he better go back alone and check on her friend. "Even though she was acting all perky and all," Reenie said. "It was maybe just an act, you know? And we don't want to rub the couple-y thing in her face too much today."

So he went back and found the light was on under her door, and she had "I Don't Want to Set the World on Fire" on the phonograph, which stopped with a jolt when he rapped lightly.

When she appeared in the hallway, it was clear she'd been crying and even clearer the drinking hadn't stopped with the one birthday toast at dinner.

She wasn't crying now, just smeary eyed and red cheeked, and when he gave her a little smile, meant to say he understood, her face twisted in silent pain. He opened his arms and she walked right in, her hands at her sides. He felt her wet face pressed up against his shirt, throbbing with silent sobs. He patted her back, said, "There, there," said something about it being the last birthday Chesty would spend away from her, he was sure.

He couldn't tell if she was breathing heavily now or sniffling or what it was, but she pulled aside his jacket lapels and kept her face buried in his chest. And something else—was she unbuttoning his shirt?

She was, but not in the normal way, from the top down. She seemed to be working somewhere in the middle, just opening it enough to press her nose in against his undershirt. Then the sniffing became more audible. She was *smelling* him, taking big whiffs and laughing and whimpering.

"I never get to smell that man smell anymore," she mumbled.

She was so sloppy and pathetic, he couldn't take it as a come-on. He let her sniff a few more solid ones, patting her head a little, and chuckling at how silly it felt, standing there in his friend's hallway, letting his wife inhale his chest.

Then he pulled her away and helped her back into her apartment and got her started getting ready for bed, leaving her to the more private stuff, and then he beat it out of there, back to his apartment down the hall.

The next day, Sal seemed pretty embarrassed, avoiding him at every turn. Reenie came by, and Sal seemed glad to have an excuse to leave. The two went over to the coffee shop and were gone for almost two hours.

That night, Reenie stayed over. He'd been able to get hold of some rubbers, and they did it standing up, her grabbing hold of the top of the dresser, watching him wryly in the mirror. The bed, they'd found, was squeaky as hell.

It wasn't till they'd turned off the light and turned in that she said, "Oh, Sal told me how she came a little unglued last night— Chesty's birthday and all."

"She did?"

Reenie started giggling. "I told her she's welcome to smell you all she wants."

He didn't say anything. Across the alley, Ella Fitzgerald was singing with the Ink Spots, "I'm Making Believe."

"She wanted my—you know—blessing," Reenie said. "I told her it wasn't mine to give."

He could hear her breathing and enjoying her smoke. He wondered if he should say something, but she beat him to it: "That was right, wasn't it?"

"That she could smell me again?" Wink said.

"That it wasn't mine to give. That we don't have that kind of—"

"Is it possible I really smell that much like Chesty?"

There was a long pause and she said, "I don't really recall what Chesty smelled like, distinctly. Not that I could put into words."

He suggested then that maybe it was just that all men smelled alike.

She seemed to be thinking that over. "I'm Making Believe" was a record, he decided, not the radio. They were starting it up again.

When she spoke next, Reenie's voice was so low, it felt like they were behind enemy lines: "I just want to make sure it was okay—everything I said to Sal."

Reaching across the dimness, he patted her hip. "Sure. Everything's jake."

He knew it wasn't the kind of answer she wanted. She wanted some kind of definition about their relationship.

He adjusted his breathing, making it steady, as if he'd already started to fall asleep.

38

The name Winkin' Sally now regularly appeared in print with almost all their photos, as well as a second name, Weekend Sally. The two names were either rotated interchangeably or paired inseparably, like a comic book duo. It was still fuzzy to Sal which one *she* was supposed to be and which one was Reenie. It seemed, too, in correspondence, that the editors didn't make any distinction themselves and possibly *couldn't* make any distinction. It was possible they weren't aware at the magazines that they were actually two separate real-life girls rather than a double exposure or a dozen different girls, someone new each time.

She and Reenie were drinking coffee at the Zim Zam and checking out their latest work. Four magazines were spread out before them, one with Sal identified by the editors as Winkin' Sally, another with Reenie identified as the same, another with Sal as Weekend Sally, and the last with both of them, jointly billed as Winkin' Sally and Weekend Sally, but nothing more itemized than that.

They'd moved beyond feeling cowed by the grouch at the news shop and had marched in there, without wigs or Wink this time, bold as royalty or streetwalkers, and bought exactly what they were looking for. Bringing them out in public, sitting at a small table by the window, with other patrons giving them frowns and raised eyebrows, felt like nothing compared with facing the newsdealer earlier, staring him down. So, as Reenie had put it, "to hell with it—if they don't have bigger things to think about, then let 'em frown themselves silly . . ."

She was right—they certainly had more important things to think about. The American army had just crossed the Rhine; victory in Europe was close at hand; MacArthur had even returned to Manila—all things more important than two gals looking at girlie magazines at the coffee shop.

The one Sal was looking at was a copy of *At Ease* and a photo story someone had cobbled together out of shots of her attempting to bathe in an army helmet Wink had taken with him at discharge: "Weekend Sally on a Saturday Nite!" She'd kept her towel on the whole time and had unseen panties on underneath—along with even some pasties Reenie had lent her—and of course never managed to get down in the helmet, but just stuck her toe in the thing and pretended to pour water from an empty teakettle into it and generally acted like a moron, doing the pouty face Reenie had taught her. She remembered Wink asking her, in a moment alone after the shoot, where Reenie had gotten pasties, and Sal had told her she had no idea.

"Not so crazy about *weekend*," Sal said now, privately thinking that had to be *her* now, by default. Since Reenie always made a point in each shoot of winking every other second in a way that almost appeared painful, a physical exertion, like she might throw out her back, Reenie had probably commandeered the first name, the one they'd originally given Sal. "*Weekend* sounds awfully close to *party girl*. A pushover you call in a pinch, when you've got nothing better lined up. A girl just for the weekends, or one who'll go away with a man."

"I think it's maybe a pun," Reenie said. "Like she's *weakened* by something. You know—worn down, dropping her defenses, giving in."

"Eww!" Sal hadn't even thought of that. "Now I'm even less crazy about it."

"Relax," Reenie said. "If anyone thinks one of us is the easy one, it's me. Men smell it on me or something. Trust me. *I'm* the part-timer they don't take seriously."

She sounded irked about something. Sal wondered if she was upset in some sort of delayed way about what she'd told her about Chesty's birthday, about getting drunk and sniffing Wink the other night, but Reenie had seemed understanding about that—even laughed with her about it. Sal studied her friend for a moment, but Reenie didn't look up from the page, flipping through, biting the corner of her lip, and Sal didn't pursue it. She loved the girl, but there was that black Irish streak that was just plain *scary*.

.   .   .

The next day, Sal opened a letter she thought she should share with Reenie. Normally, she would have taken it to Wink and the two of them would have decided on it, but given the content, she thought she should leave the vote up to herself and Reenie. It said:

Dean—
    Great stuff this last time, as usual!
Keep 'em comin', old boy!
    Thought you should know that we on the
"Editorial Board," such as it is, have
been thinking that the time is ripe, for
"loosening up" a little around here. You
might have noticed in the last few issues
of our various titles, we've allowed
pictorial content to get a bit "zestier."
Now that we as a society almost have this
great hardship behind us, we feel our
boys, at home in peacetime America, will
be ooking to "let their hair down," just a
tad- and we for one feel they deserve it.
Without some of the ~~stickru~~ strictures
placed on us by military censors and the
PX concessions, etc--who felt our boys
wouldn't handle certain "distractions," we
foresee being no longer under quite as
tight strictures.
    Basically, we're looking for "nipple-
peepers" and a little of the tushy.

```
    See what you can do with your beautiful
babes, friend.
    *Fees will be increased accordingly, of
course--say, double your current rate to
start? How does that grab you?
```

It seemed to grab them differently. Sal immediately went back to the first impulse she felt when she'd opened it—working the numbers, considering what they could potentially make—while it appeared that Reenie was thinking more like the art director she wanted to be, imagining the new storylines and gimmicks they could concoct.

But when they presented the possibility to Wink, inviting him in to sit at her kitchen table, Reenie surprised her by suddenly starting in with the coy stuff, saying, "I don't know, Sal . . . Show my *business*? Really show it?"

It seemed peculiar she'd be playing fainthearted and delicate now. Especially after talking a big game about the quick bucks they could make with the various after-hours clients she thought she could get them, the ones whose products purported to run a little more to the blue, the French.

"Not your *business*, Reen," Sal said, trying to be patient with the little faker. "Your bazooms, that's all. Just a little. It's not that big a deal, actually. I mean, it's *all* a little nerve-racking, isn't it, whatever you're showing? Even if it's just thighs you don't feel so great about or—"

"Sal," Wink said. "Show her those first ones. Whattaya think?"

It was a good idea, so she took Reenie down to the darkroom, alone, and showed her the first things she shot, before Wink had even arrived last year—without a wig, even, and without a stitch on top.

"Jeezo Pete, Sal!" Reenie's shock seemed legitimate. And they'd left Wink upstairs, so she didn't have any reason to be putting her on, playing it up, acting demure. "And you were showing all this to Wink?"

"What—you think my husband's going to be all that much *more* upset, if he were to find out?" It was a legitimate question, actually, the answer to which she wasn't really sure. Was Wink alone seeing her nudes worse than the clothed cheesecake appearing in print, available to anyone? "I sort of figure 'In for a penny . . .' "

"Not what I mean—Chesty's reaction." Reenie sneered, giving her a shot with her elbow. "I mean thanks a heap for letting *me* know you're showing him this! . . . *Pal!*"

Sal explained that she took them all on her own, that Wink wasn't in the room. Still, she was curious about her reaction. "Does it bother you, really, him seeing . . . more of me like this?"

"Not really." Reenie shrugged, poker faced now, with the slightest little pout maybe just slipping out. "He can do what he wants."

"He didn't *do* anything, Reen. Not with me, at least." She would hope her dear old pal would know her better than that, that she wasn't that kind of wife to Chesty, no matter how far away he was or how long he was gone. Sal wasn't positive Wink wasn't seeing *other* women, but she didn't mention that.

Reenie said, "Well, he can look at what he wants, is what I mean, then. They're his eyes, not mine. And we don't have that kind of a setup, he and I. We just don't."

The first concept they tried under these new relaxed guidelines was one dreamed up by Reenie. The theme was an artist and her life model. "Cheap as heck," Reenie said. "We won't need to buy a thing."

Except she did need to "borrow" an easel from her day job. And an old white dress shirt from Wink—he'd ruined it in the darkroom, so it would serve as a perfect artist's smock.

When she'd heard the pitch, Sal had assumed her friend would play the artist's model herself. After all, she'd posed for the calendar artists over at her work, and she knew the real "model poses"—the corny, vampy stuff—far better than Sal.

"No, no," Reenie said. "I'm the artist. You're the nude."

Reenie had it all worked out for her: if Sal stood with one leg cocked slightly, holding her bosom, and her leg turned just so, all you really saw was the side of her bare bottom and the tops of her bosom and a long, bare leg, but none of her private business. The long expanse of bare leg felt the most scandalous, personally, though really didn't count as nudity, in Sal's mind. What did make her feel most exposed was just getting in that position. She felt her face burning up, her heartbeat pumping in her neck, her fingers getting tingly against her goose-pimpled bosom, because what the magazine reader got to see and what Wink had to see, waiting for her to get safely in position, were two different things.

To his credit, he seemed unduly preoccupied with the lights and reflectors and fussing with the cords in the time between throwing her robe clear of the shot and Reenie aligning her and declaring her in position, ready to go.

It seemed to her that Reenie ought to be the one so very exposed, at least in this first series, since she was already used to stripping down for Wink, in private. For her part, Reenie did have her bottom peeking out from beneath the shirttails of her paint smock as she extended her paintbrush to squint one-eyed and measure the proportions of her model. And when the thing escalated into a paint fight, as they'd scripted it to, there was more of Reenie's bare fanny and even a nipple or two popping out of her torn smock, but for Sal, being actually stark naked, every shot had to be carefully and slowly choreographed, to make sure she was still strategically covered—by a splotch of paint or the palette or a corner of the easel—and each shot, waiting for the two of them to confer, Reenie saying, "No, wait, I think we can still see her puss," was excruciating.

This time, she got good and loaded, starting before the session was over and continuing on, alone in her bathtub upstairs while the two of them ran the negs. She could hear them laughing and having a good time down there. It came right up through the floorboards and the pipes.

Mostly, she worried that if she wasn't completely plastered, she'd sneak down there and destroy the film. So she drank up.

39

He was starting to feel self-conscious about his efforts to retrain his right hand. Thinking that Sal could hear him banging around and cussing and carrying on whenever he tried, he'd started to remove himself from not only his apartment but the whole camera shop, taking a tablet over to Grant Park or Navy Pier, if the weather was bearable, or sometimes—if he wasn't feeling too down about it—to the Art Institute, though usually that was a bad idea. Sometimes folks in the museum sidled up close alongside him, thinking they were about to catch a glimpse of a budding talent at work and, boy, were they in for a shock. He could feel them stiffen next to him, holding their breath for an instant as they zeroed in on the swirly, shaky lines and distorted proportion. They probably thought he was delusional.

And, of course, since taking it outside, his diligence in retraining his hands was waning. After all, he wasn't simple. He knew what was what. He'd been working on it for a well over a year, and still no luck. Here it was, August 1945 already. Hell, just last week, when the fight with the Japs was finally over, they announced that scientists had managed to retrain atomic particles, for Christ's sake. They'd found a way to make atoms go from basically lying there unnoticed and useless to blowing two whole cities to dust. And yet he couldn't coax a few lousy fingers on one hand to behave normally.

The left, uninjured hand wasn't getting much better. As they'd explained it to him way back at the VA hospital in Hawaii, that hand was like a radio that was all wired up right, only no one had taken the time to tune it properly. While meanwhile the right was shorting out on some of the wires, but the wires that were still connected were already well tuned.

The young doctor was just trying to be helpful, using these comparisons, but really they were unrelatable as hell and still weren't any less so, all this time later. Radio was about sound. Art was about sight. Some things didn't take a medical degree to know.

"Doctors do that," Sal told him once. "They try to find a way to illustrate what's going on—"

"Sure," he told her, "but dragging radios into it doesn't help! Christ, I could illustrate better with the bum hand itself . . ."

The problem was, he still didn't know which hand had a better shot of drawing properly, if either was even possible.

With his right hand, he found the best thing he still had going, if anything, was tonal control. He could still shade and vary the degree of shading, as long as he could keep the charcoal or the flat of the pencil gripped between his okay thumb and his iffy middle finger, because that hand still had a memory of finesse; it still had a looseness in gesture. He just couldn't make all the fingers work right.

The left hand, he found, was slightly better—though still not great—at blind contour drawing, the classic first-year exercise of following the outline of a thing without looking at the paper. It was supposed to strengthen hand-eye coordination. The results with his left were shaky and jerky, but that was often the case with this exercise.

He did a lot of these—simple still lifes he found around him, staring out at the view from a bench, letting his hand do its worst without interference. For one thing, at least he didn't have to stare at his monstrosities as he produced them. He could glance at them once, at the end, and just toss them into a trash basket.

When V-J Day, as the newsreels were calling it now, had happened last week, he felt a little unpatriotic that he wasn't feeling more worked up about it. Of course it was great that the war was over, but for some reason, he didn't feel all that compelled to go looking for a parade. And there were plenty. In a town like Chicago that loves its parades, they were popping up spontaneously every six feet. There was dancing and kissing and carrying on right out in public. Reenie confessed she lost count of the guys who kissed her on August 15.

He'd thought about grabbing someone and kissing them like that—acting crazy. Maybe kiss Sal, just to play it safe, not grab some stranger's girl on the street, maybe get his block knocked off. But it just wasn't in him to do any of that.

For one thing, he didn't have a clue what he was going to do with his life. For as long as he could remember, the answer to that question lay on the white drawing tablet in his lap. And though that had been closed to him for more than a year now, somehow, he hadn't really felt a need to think about it as seriously because he could always tell himself *There's a war on.* Now, with peace suddenly dropped on them like a ton of bricks, it felt like nothing more than pressure to make serious plans.

Sal had even seemed a little thrown by this sudden peace. Chesty would eventually be coming home, and Wink got the idea that she'd grown fond of their unofficial side business.

The night of V-J Day, in fact, she'd confessed that she'd secretly felt she was doing something to help. "I always imagined," she said, "or I guess hoped, that one day some vet would come up and tell me that the photos, you know, *helped* just a little."

She seemed almost glum, and he'd decided to tease her out of it. "So we haven't been doing this for the money?" She laughed and he told her, "Hey, just because no one's ever come up and told you that yet, about the girlies helping, doesn't mean it's not true."

When he got home from trying to draw in the park, she must have seen him coming because she was standing out on the sidewalk, waiting for him, hugging herself though it wasn't quite yet Labor Day, the sun golden in her hair, on her yellow dress. She started in when he was still half a block away, calling out to him as he approached. "Hey. You know how we've talked about how someday we're going to have to explain to Chesty what we've been doing here? The photos and all?"

He saw she was grinning, which maybe meant she'd come up with a good explanation. Which was good, because he wasn't sure himself that he'd be able to explain it to the guy when the time came.

"Yeah . . ." He stepped into the shop, and she followed him in.

"Well, better start working on that explanation," she said, and he noticed now she was clutching a postcard with a palm tree. "He's coming home."

40

Sergeant William "Chesty" Chesterton stood looking out at the San Francisco Bay, his ears filled with the clamor of seagulls. Pretty, but not five hours' worth of pretty.

There would be a bus arriving, eventually, that would get him from the naval yard to the train station, but that wasn't for five hours, and he didn't even have a magazine. He'd been cleaned out, the whole collection pilfered during the crossing from Hawaii. A fellow couldn't even go topside for ten minutes without risking having his gear tossed and pawed through. It was like traveling with monkeys, really. He especially wished he hadn't lost the girlies he'd been thinking about showing Sal; the couple issues with the girl that looked so much like her—that is, if you squinted a little and ignored the fact the hair was all wrong. Anyway, he still hadn't fully decided if he would show them to her, let alone tell her about them. Probably he would. Sal was pretty all right. She might actually get a charge out of it, knowing some sexy girl in a magazine looked—to him at least—just like her.

He was shooting with the Argus—boring long perspectives of the docks, close-ups of the moorings, panoramas of the disappointingly unfoggy Bay, all a bit unpeopled for his taste—when he heard someone calling him.

"Hey, shutterbug—84 Charlie!"

They'd been calling him that all the way from Hawaii. He squinted into the sun at a shadowy figure on the gangplank of a navy freighter. He was pretty sure it was an ensign he recognized from the trip over.

"Over here! You wanna get an eyeful of something really wild, check this out."

The cargo class was docked right next to the cattleboat they'd just come over on. He imagined this guy wasn't going home, like him, but probably shipping out on another troopship. Chesty felt sorry for the poor bastard.

Grinning like he was camp happy, gesturing to follow, the ensign called over his shoulder, by way of explanation, "You gotta see this. It's relief for the Japs, right, but you tell me what the jumping Jesus the skibbies plan on doing with all *this*."

Stepping down into the hold, the metal clang of the stairs got quiet about halfway down, the reverberation muffled. He strained to see why in the dark, his eyes slowly adjusting to take in mountains of white powder only partially contained by a scattering of wooden crates. It was everywhere, floating in the air like misty breath on a winter's morning.

"Wow . . ."

"Right?" the ensign said. "Crazy, huh?"

Through the blizzard of white, he strained to make out words stamped on a nearby crate: SWANS DOWN, it read—a strange phrase that nonetheless stirred a gray memory he couldn't quite place, an earlier time, a younger time, safe back home, maybe in the kitchen.

"Cake flour," the ensign said, and then it all made sense.

Except for the part where it was filling the hold of this ship, and he pointed that out to him. "*This* is a basic necessity?"

"Yeah, right? Thing hits me just the same. Only who knows? Maybe someone up top feels *so solly* for the little fuckers. Wants 'em to have a nice treat, maybe a nice red velvet cake. Who knows. Maybe someone's idea of a joke or it's something someone had in surplus or it was going rotten anyway, maybe boll weevils, a tax write-off—who knows how the brass thinks, am I right?"

Farther back, narrow sunlight shafted in like it would in the nave of a cathedral. Beautiful, but maybe not enough light. He lifted the Argus and adjusted the f-stop, hoping that would compensate for the lack, and fired away. The one-striper beside him stopped talking, as if watching him work or afraid sound would disrupt the shots. Chesty had a half a roll still and no real conviction he'd captured anything but blackness. Digging out the flash rig from his pack, he really started to imagine he was standing in a snowstorm. The ensign started giggling.

Framing the shot again, including the guy in this one, off to one side, turned three-quarters, Chesty saw himself back home, standing in the first heavy snowfall of the season—my God, that would be soon! two months at the most, knowing Chicago—and he thought how it had been so long since he'd seen snow, he'd missed entire winters with his wife, and he thought of her warm little kitchen and Sal in the front window, looking out at the snow blowing around outside, and pressed the trigger for the biggest flash he had ever seen, white, white, white.

41

They traveled, with bereavement vouchers procured through his contacts at the New York offices of *Yank*, on the Southern Pacific's Overland Route. Separate accommodations. Boarding in Chicago, he slipped the porter a couple bucks to make sure they were properly situated—not in adjoining sleepers, which might elicit disapproval from fellow passengers, but kitty-corner from each other, across the aisle and down three doors. Distant enough, he hoped, for her to feel some privacy in her grieving, but close enough that she didn't feel completely abandoned.

The body—or, as near as he'd been able to determine, an assortment of parts they'd been able to recover and box up in a coffin—was waiting on ice at the Port of San Francisco. Once they took possession, they would reboard the train and escort Sergeant William Chesterton to his final resting place—the family plot in Breakey, Nebraska.

Initially, he'd offered to travel to California in her place and bring Chesty back for burial, but Sal said no, that didn't make sense, since they wouldn't be burying him in Chicago.

This had been news to Wink. It didn't seem like the right time to pester her with a lot of questions, but he'd had no idea his friend was from Nebraska.

Somewhere beyond Laramie, he got to talking to an auburn-haired gal named Carol in the lounge car. She looked a little like Rita Hayworth, except one eye was visibly smaller than the other. Though it was somewhere between ten and midnight (he couldn't keep track of these time zones they were passing through), the lady was drinking a lot of coffee, and when he declined to join her in a cup, saying the stuff would keep him from sleeping, she seemed like she was about to say something, then thought better of it and smiled to herself instead. They talked about the steamy novel she was reading, *Forever Amber,* and when he asked if it was as scandalous as he'd heard, her mouth curled in a way he liked a great deal and she said, "It'll do." Asking to see it, he riffled through the pages, expecting something nasty to pop out at him and grab his attention, which it didn't.

While he was still glancing at it, she stretched a little in her seat, long and lovely, and he strained a little to keep his eyes on the page. "You have to read it terribly closely to find the juicy stuff," she explained, and that settled it for him. He handed it back and she ordered another little pot of coffee from a passing porter—a woman, as were several of the mechanics he'd seen so far. He expected they'd all be out of work soon, sent back home now that the men were returning.

Wink wondered, a little, how she was affording all this coffee, and how she rated a travel voucher, but he didn't try to pry it out of her. She seemed either well off or accustomed to being well off, if she didn't happen to be at this particular time.

Instead of delving back into her book, she turned and gazed out the window. It was still very flat out there and dark and starry.

"Do you know your stars?" she asked.

"Sure," he lied. "You've got your various Dippers, Big and Little, your Cassiopeia . . ."

"Which is where?"

He stared out at the night as she pulled the chain in their little table-side lamp. It helped with the illumination outside by cutting down on the reflection, but sacrificed the image of her profile he'd been checking out in the window.

"No idea," he said. "These are Wyoming stars."

When the coffee replacement came, along with an extra cup, presumably for him, he declined again and asked her how the hell she planned on sleeping tonight.

"That isn't my plan," she said. "I never can on trains, anyway, so I might as well have some fun—just stay up and be wicked."

He thought she winked. He might have imagined it—the lamp was still off and there was that oddity with her smaller eye—and then she eased a slender silver flask from her handbag and added to her half-full cup. This he didn't decline, accepting a belt minus the coffee, and it was a relief, a warm balm that allowed him to rest his eyes for just a moment, and imagine, for that moment, that the train's motion was a mothering rocking, a gentle lulling, not the friction of pistons, and for just that moment, he imagined he didn't have Chesty's widow a few cars down that he must watch over like an orphaned ward, and so he would follow this overly stimulated stranger's lead wherever it went, which quite probably would be down to her roomette or compartment or possibly high-class drawing room, and down to her undergarments, and he would follow her hints and insinuations to her wordless gestures and finally to her husky, grunted urgings . . . But it was only for a moment, and then there was a return to the knowledge that his friend needed him at this crucial time to watch over his wife and make it as bearable as it could be and his other friend needed him as well, or possibly might, and even if it were only an outside chance that she would need him in the next hour or so—even for something as small as a clean handkerchief or an aspirin powder or something as big as a hug, he should be there. And so, in a moment, he said good night to lovely, possible Carol in the lounge car and returned, alone, to his roomette.

The flat farmland streaming past made him occasionally think of his uncle in Michigan. He would always have a place there, he knew, if this ever became too much for him. A place, of course, wasn't *necessarily* a life. He wondered about that. If it ever came down to that, if he turned to Uncle Len, would there be room for growth there? Could he expand the acreage, down the line— find his own farmhouse, his own wife? The pickings around St. Johns, he imagined, quite probably paled compared with what he'd seen in Chicago. Hell, what he'd seen on board this train, even. Of course, a guy could hunt a little farther afield than a five or ten mile radius around his uncle's farm.

Theoretically, he could bring someone in, like a hothouse flower. Go down to Ann Arbor or Lansing, some highbrow hot spot like that, meet a gal with a little more of a sense of the great big world, maybe even a coed with some education . . . But what would stop that gal from pining for that great big world? For that matter, what would stop him from doing the same?

In Cheyenne, the porter barked past, announcing they had a half-hour stop to refuel and restock the dining car, so folks should get out and stretch if they wanted.

Wink wanted. The station was still hopping—it was not quite nine p.m. He got a milk shake at a soda fountain across the street, then returned to the station and drank it in the shoeshine chair, getting a shine. Since the newsstand was still open, he bought a copy of *Stars and Stripes,* the Denver *Post*—the old man said they didn't carry the Chicago *Tribune*—two paperback books of crossword puzzles, a handful of Hollywood gossip magazines for Sal, the latest *Esquire* for him, and a stack of girlies off the half-hidden side shelf for both of them to peruse. *At Ease* and *Wink* were among the bunch he grabbed, and he was pretty sure they had some work in both of these. Finally, he spotted that steamy novel, *Forever Amber,* and threw that on the pile, too. He wasn't sure which one of them that was for, but he figured it would, at the least, hand them a laugh. Maybe he'd read it to her out loud like a kiddie story.

"These two are the same," the old man pointed out, holding up the two copies of the crossword puzzle book he'd selected.

Wink was aware of that. Not bothering to explain that one was for him and one was for his traveling companion, he said, "The same is fine."

As the old guy groused over his pad, working a nubby pencil stub, adding it up, Wink was flipping through *At Ease* when he caught a glimpse of Reenie's unmistakable half-open pout and remembered what time of month it was. He was missing the

once-monthly treat she gave him with her mouth, and since
she'd recently confided that she and Sal had managed to magi-
cally synchronize their monthlies since spending so much time
together in the past year, he told the old guy to toss some Midol
on the pile as well.

"Hmm," the guy grumbled, as if sympathizing with him, taking
it down from the small pharmaceutical section. "The wife, huh?"

Wink just nodded, not bothering to correct him.

"Guess we all know how that is, brother."

"Yes," Wink said, "we do," though he had no earthly idea how
it was.

While the man retabulated, Wink slid the *Wink* from the
stack and flipped through it. There was Weekend Sally, as they
were calling her in this one, topless and squeezing them together
like ripe fruit, the fingers of her black opera gloves just hiding the
nipples, but beaming like everything was jake and A-okay, not a
care in the world, not a husband in a box, not a dream out the
window, not at all like she was trapped in a cramped compartment in a lonely train in a strange countryside, with nowhere to
go, with the stuffing knocked out of her and all the tears drained
out of her, too.

42

Her jawbone and her cheekbones ached from the constant crying; her mouth set in a nearly fixed expression of anguish.

Her whole body ached, in fact. She never thought it would
hurt like this, so physically. She'd almost forgotten the feel of
deep, steady breathing, getting so used to her breath only coming in small, halting gasps.

She saw it, too—didn't just feel it—catching a glimpse of her ghastly face in the dark window of nighttime farmland rolling endlessly past, or in the horrible mirror on the back of her sliver of a closet. The word *grief-stricken* suddenly made sense in a way it never had before—she looked *seized* by something, in the grip of something that twisted and distorted her features to the point where even she almost failed to recognize herself.

She heard them sometimes, walking past, chatting in the corridor. Already there were soldiers returning, heading home upright and lucky. She knew she'd have to steel herself to it: on the return trip, heading back from the West Coast, there'd no doubt be waves of them, rushing back into the heart of the country in a massive, boyish, awkward gallop.

Even muffled through the door, they sounded giddy and nervous, hurtling with the speed of the train into the uncharted lands of *peacetime* and *Stateside*. Mostly it was girls and jobs and "getting back to goddamn *normal*." And there was still talk of the bomb they'd dropped on the Japs: *This here's where they're testing them, isn't it? Out here in the flat-and-nothin'? That's how I heard it, anyway* . . .

It reached her, talk like this, drifting in like cigarette smoke, and she'd stare out her private window, as if expecting to see the unexpected—a flash brighter than the sun; a shudder deeper than any chill.

43

In the naval yard in San Francisco, Wink stood by as an MP went over Chesty's personal effects—the contents of his duffel and a footlocker crammed with exposed film, clippings of his work, files of prints, boxes of lenses, a light meter, and a portrait-sized bellows camera. Separate from this collection was the camera he'd been using at the moment of the explosion. Sal held it up to her eye, as if calmly assessing the damage, but he could see her gloved hand was shaking.

Maybe she'd thought, in a stunned moment that got away from her, she'd see Chesty in there, or at least some explanation as to what in the name of heaven . . .

Despite the smudges and scrapes, Wink could still make out the ARGUS next to her trembling fingers. It appeared to be more or less intact.

"Maybe got thrown clear of the blast," the MP said, a little too softly.

"I'm afraid . . . ," she said, and Wink reached out and steadied her, his hand on her elbow before she could finish. "I'm afraid I don't understand what . . ."

"I'm sorry, ma'am—folks. Again, that's classified." The MP made a twisted little face like he had heartburn.

So she signed for the whole caboodle and thanked him, and Wink steered her gently to the door. Outside, squinting in the California sun, he started looking around for the Quonset-hut number for their next stop, the remains. He was thinking of letting her in on the fact that when he was still serving, they called any soldier stuck in an office like that guy back there a Gertrude—try to hand her a laugh—when another door at the opposite end of the office they'd just visited opened, and it was the same MP, beckoning them closer.

Wink motioned for Sal to stay put and went to see what the guy had to say for himself.

"I don't know much," the MP said, glancing around with a mixture of what appeared to be equal parts nervousness and annoyance, "strictly scuttlebutt, but you know there was a survivor, right?"

. . .

Once he made sure he had the right bed, checking the clipboard chart and the dog tags on the bandaged patient—the guy probably faking sleep anyway, trying to stretch out his hospital time— Wink yanked the privacy curtain around, and the metal rake of the curtain rings made a clatter that even someone faking sleep couldn't ignore.

Once the ensign's eyes came open in a groggy squint, Wink launched into it. "Love to hear what happened to you and Chesty—Sergeant Chesterton, that is. Something exploded?"

"You're a civilian," he said. "Who wants to know?"

"His widow, actually. But you can tell me."

The guy's face softened a little at this. He looked disappointed that he couldn't very well keep being a hard-on, and he sat up a little in the bed, a very loose approximation of standing at attention, as if a slightly higher altitude would convey more respect.

"Swans Down. Going as relief to Japan."

After checking to be sure he was talking about the brand of cake flour, Wink pointed out that that hardly seemed like much of a necessity.

The ensign shrugged. "No kidding, right? Something like fourteen tons of unboxed Swans Down cake flour. Loose. Looked harmless, too. Like Christmas Eve. Only the shit went up like no snowflakes, believe me. More like it was gunpowder . . . Hey, on the widow? You can tell her it was my fault, really. I'm the one who took Chesty in there, thought he should get a picture . . ."

For a second, Wink wanted to hop on that guilt train, thinking how if *he'd* been there, he could have told him how combustible finely milled flours can be. It wasn't Chesty's fault he wasn't raised on a farm.

The ensign seemed to be warming up now. "You know what's worse than dying young, brother? Dying *silly*, in some lacy way. Seriously, I'm terrified of going some way frivolous like that now. It's all I can think about. Hey, but on the widow—don't tell her that, okay, friend? About it being silly and frivolous? Tell her it was real pretty. 'Cause it really was. I mean—you know, the most he probably knew of it. Like fairy dust. A man should go out that way, looking at something beautiful. I guess no way it can be a silly death if that's the case."

It wasn't enough, his description of it. She said she needed to hear it straight from the eyewitness.

But when he returned to the hospital with her, the ensign had dummied up. Someone had gotten to him. When he spoke today, his speech was louder than Wink remembered, and he rattled it off like something on a bad radio drama.

"Like I was telling the gentleman here yesterday, it must've been some type of unavoidable naturally occurring chemical breakdown that ignited that heating fuel, down in that hold. That's all I know."

"Heating fuel?" Wink wasn't sure he was hearing right.

"Or maybe, possibly, some manner of sabotage orchestrated by outside agitators or subversives of a political nature."

Wink asked him about the cake flour.

The guy's lip twitched a little, and then he said, "I guess I'm not clear what you're talking about, friend."

It felt like they were being watched. Wink glanced up and spotted a gray-haired, gray-skinned lieutenant commander with a hefty row of tossed salad on his chest, down at the end of the room, talking to a nurse and a man in a plain brown suit who looked like one of Hoover's men. Wink caught the officer's eye and gave him a disgusted frown.

Turning back, he saw that the ensign was letting his eyes droop, and the nurse who'd been conferring with the two muckety-mucks swooped in and said he needed rest and his bandages changed and they would need to go. Right now.

It was pathetic. He glanced down at Sal, and she just seemed disappointed. Standing, hat in hand, he helped her up, and as they were filing out, he thought he heard the ensign say, very faintly, "Sorry . . ."

Outside, it was overcast and he heard seagulls crying. Sal's hair whipped around in the wind, uncontainable in her black hat and veil. "None of that matters," she said. "Let's just get him home."

44

Heading back east, the train couldn't go fast enough for Sal. She would never say it out loud, but already there was something else piggybacked onto the grief, and that was *monotony*.

It brought on waves of guilt like something actually jabbing her gut, but already, sometimes, she wanted desperately to be done crying, to bust out of her compartment, to come out and play and join Wink and even strangers in the lounge car. Maybe play a hand of bridge and just talk about normal things like normal people. And then the guilt she felt for feeling this way would bring on the gushing sobs even stronger, making such a public appearance beyond the little door of her compartment an impossibility.

During the day, she sometimes unsnapped Chesty's Argus

and fiddled with it. There was no telling yet if the casing was intact, if light was seeping in through hairline cracks, but the film advanced without the whisper of any mechanical problems. She took pictures, not just boring straight-on shots that she knew would contain trace elements of reflections somewhere in the shot, the glass catching the light and ruining it with wispy ghosts and sunspots—what had her pop called them? "Circles of confusion" . . . ? Maybe that was something else. Everything seemed unfocused these days, out of kilter. Instead, she sat to one side and included the window frame in the composition, almost as an admission as to what this was, a nod to the realism of the setting, the sloppy intrusion of the train, not just the pure elegance of the scenery. She thought of the framing Wink had first shown her in the Hopper up the street at the Art Institute well over a year ago. She'd returned many times since and had grown to love it, though she knew she could never fully understand it or approach it the way Wink could. Already, with what little technical tricks she could pass along to him, he had moved far beyond anything *she* could do with a camera, and in a way, it was one of the things that made her saddest about losing Chesty right at this point in their lives—as trivial as it seemed, it made her heart ache to think what a kick her husband would have gotten out of seeing his friend's progress with the camera, the way he was steadily learning to transfer everything he'd trained his hands to do, finding other ways to utilize that eye of his that Chesty had so admired.

She wondered sometimes if she should have filled him in earlier. It hadn't seemed like the kind of thing to lay out in a letter, especially one going through someone else's hands, with the military censors, but now he would never know about their little adventure together. Their success, their enterprise . . .

Sitting off to one side like that, she would set the focus on a spot in the middle distance, checking it against the next thing that lined up with her crosshairs—a barn, say, but shot at an angle, so it wasn't simply rolling past in a blur.

If the camera turned out to be undamaged, she hoped to discover she'd created startling, rushing panoramas with a single item locked in focus, crisp as a maple leaf.

It was here she first thought of teaching Wink about depth of field. Somehow, they hadn't gotten to that yet—the technique of manipulating the range and portion of a photograph that appears in focus. Looking out at the long vista stretched out through the range finder of the Argus, she knew, even in that bleakness, someone with Wink's eye could make a lot of interesting stuff happen. The technique would never be needed for their girlie shoots, which was most likely why it had yet to come up, but in his own artistic studies, the "assignments" she still occasionally gave him to prod him and encourage him, depth of field might just be a fruitful one for him to explore.

When she felt she could sit with a visitor without blubbering instantly, she invited Wink in to talk. The porter brought tea, and once they were settled, she asked Wink if he had any questions about the logistics of stopping in Breakey, and he said, "Yeah, actually, I wasn't real clear *what* we're doing out here, really . . ."

It turned out he not only meant the funeral but was pretty much in the dark about Chesty's entire family history. It was surprising and made her wonder what exactly war buddies talked about all that time they spent together.

So she explained how Chesty came to move to Chicago at the age of ten; how his uncle Whitcomb was the more successful of two brothers in banking. Growing up, Whitcomb Chesterton had been the better student and gone to a better college—Dartmouth, out east, rather than staying in Nebraska

at a state school, like Chesty's dad. In fact, Chesty's uncle managed to keep his bank from failing, even in the worst years that
followed the Crash.

"So," Wink said, looking puzzled, "Chesty came to live in
Chicago just because his uncle was doing better?"

She wasn't very good at telling it, she thought, not having
talked about it much. "Chesty's dad, William Sr.—*his* bank
failed. The bank in Breakey, Nebraska, where they lived. Well,
he felt horrible about it and drove out of town a ways and parked
his car in front of a freight train."

Wink frowned. "That happens sometimes, a car stuck on the
tracks. It *could* have been an accident."

She explained that it was a slow-moving freight train—one
that had barely picked up speed coming out of Breakey—and
they sat quietly with that for a good long while, watching the
land roll by.

She was gaunt and haggard, looking more like one of those FSA
portraits of Okies by Dorthea Lange than the widow of a bank
president. And she looked older than her years—at least as old
as Chesty's aunt and uncle back in Chicago. But she also looked
more like Chesty than they ever did. Sal had never met anyone
who shared his narrow nose and distinctive brow. It made her
wonder if her husband's mother was also artistic. She'd never
thought to ask him.

The family plot Chesty's mother took them to wasn't actually
in the Breakey cemetery but in a tiny rural cemetery twenty minutes down the road. Sal got the feeling there was a good reason
they'd removed themselves to this exile. Back in town, there
were no doubt many citizens of Breakey still smarting from the
collapse of the savings and loan fifteen years before.

The grave had been dug in one of the few remaining spaces, near other Chesterton headstones, including that of Chesty's dad and another awaiting his weary-looking mother, the final date still unchiseled. "It's nothing much," she said. "Hardly anything left to it, nowadays, the rate they seem to be dropping like flies, the Chestertons . . . But still, we managed to hang on to a little space yet. This, for William, and a spot for me, which'll be soon enough, I imagine. And of course I been saving a spot for you, too, child. I knew William would be coming back one day, and now he has and he brought me my never-before-seen daughter-in-law along in the bargain, and I couldn't be happier to finally lay eyes on you, I just couldn't, and the Lord did finally deliver my boy back to me."

Sal wasn't sure what to say about the plot the nice lady had saved for her—if she should thank her, if she should say she wasn't sure yet what she'd be doing when the time came. She was only twenty-five. Her own folks were buried north of Chicago, and she had no idea if they had room for her. And did this mean she would never fall in love again, the next fifty or sixty years? Right now, the idea felt as improbable as her becoming a jungle explorer or learning to fly, but she wasn't unrealistic. The heart could mend. And even now, in her grief, the idea that it wouldn't, that she could actually face the remainder—heck, the majority—of her life alone, *decades* of solitude, made something catch in her lungs or her sternum. So she said nothing, pulling the slender woman toward her, hugging her. Chesty's mom had a hard boniness to her that made her almost painful to hug, and Sal thought, *I wouldn't have it any other way.*

The honor guard was a pimply corporal with bottle-bottom glasses who'd come by bus from the nearest Army Reserve unit.

He didn't appear to have ever traveled beyond the borders of Nebraska, let alone seen action. As he folded the flag, his hands shook—a sign she interpreted as more likely meaning he was a novice than any indicator he was particularly moved. Once he'd performed this little bit of patriotic origami, he presented it to Sal, along with a rigid salute.

As much as she kind of wanted it, after considering a moment, stroking her gloved hand across the crisp fabric, she turned and placed it in her mother-in-law's lap. From the way Mrs. Chesterton's shoulders shuddered and her veil swayed with her sobs, Sal could tell she'd done the right thing. She'd cherish that flag. And while Sal had a hard time reconciling the notion that Chesty had never touched this particular American flag, had never had anything to do with this *specific* flag, had probably never even strode the same continent as this flag—unless this happened to be an old one they found in some warehouse where it had been collecting dust since before his induction and shipping out—his mom might have less of a sense of that mattering since she'd had no real connection with him anyway, his personal inventory, as it were, since he was ten. Sal could hand the poor lady a purple hand-painted necktie with a hula girl on it and say it was his all-time favorite, and she'd cherish it, certainly. What else did she have?

45

"Wink," she said. "What did you think would happen to you?"

They were about an hour out of Breakey. She'd invited him into her compartment, and they were standing by her window, staring out at the flat scenery and the sunset just beginning to start its slow maneuver.

He started to tell her *Nothing,* he just thought she'd need an escort, that the train might be packed with rowdy soldiers.

"In life," she said. "Is all this pretty much how you thought, or . . . ?"

He *had* been thinking about that a little since the late-breaking news of Chesty's childhood. The whole business had made him wonder why the two of them had hit it off so easily, back in the PTO. Though neither one had been aware of it, they had something big in common: they had both been shipped off to an uncle. True, Wink's dad hadn't parked his car in front of the Southern Pacific, and his uncle only owned a small bean, beet, and wheat farm, not a bank. His surroundings had been nothing like Chicago's Gold Coast. In fact, the school district he'd been moved into at Uncle Len's was the same one where, back in '27, some madman dynamited the new school building—a very different background, Wink figured.

But before that, before they shipped him to the country where, according to his dad, even the dirt was healthy, Wink had spent most of the previous year sick in bed with scarlet fever.

It hadn't gone over so well with his mother. Two years before he was born, there was another boy, Carl, who would have been his older brother. Carl was four when he caught the Spanish flu.

Wink remembered a gaggle of aunts and near aunts attending when Wink was ill—cute fun ones who played checkers and *I spy with my little eye* . . . Also old bluehairs from the church who tried to catch him up on his schoolwork.

That year in bed, he read a lot and drew a lot and followed the funnies like a religious zealot, especially Rube Goldberg. The man's hilarious, overengineered machines, designed to complete

the most mundane tasks, captivated him, and soon he was drawing his own third-grade versions. He loved the idea of being able
to do all kinds of things, all on his own, with no help from anyone else. All he would need would be one of those wonderful
machines. Then he'd get by just fine and never feel lonesome.

As near as he could puzzle it out in hindsight, his mother just
couldn't stomach seeing another kid so sick, so hit the sauce and
eventually ran off while he was still bedridden. "Which was why
all the ladies coming by," he explained now to Sal, "bringing covered dishes. I didn't know it till I recovered—just thought she
didn't want to catch it. Figured she was just keeping out of my
bedroom, that she was still right down the hall."

"Christ on a crutch," Sal said, and he felt her hand lightly on
the small of his back before she withdrew it.

Meaning to rope it back to the subject at hand, he told her he
remembered wanting to be Rube Goldberg for a while, or at least
a syndicated cartoonist or illustrator of some sort, and then after
being shipped up to the farm in St. Johns, he thought he wanted
to be his uncle Len, or at least live there for a time, two un-
bathed bachelors without a care in the world.

He wasn't sure any of this was really addressing her question,
but beyond the career dreams, maybe it *was* all sort of the way
he'd pictured. For one thing, he never thought he'd settle down
and marry. Even as a boy, it had seemed as much a long shot as
it seemed now. One thing he'd always noticed was babies and
kids gave him the most difficulty drawing. Early on, he got quite
good at women's faces and even the female form, maybe because
of the many doting women who visited him and took care of him
that year in bed, and the close proximity of their faces and breasts
as they loomed over him. But his children, even after years of art
instruction, looked more like fairies or leprechauns and his babies
looked corrupt, like fat captains of industry or surly beat cops.

"Oh, brother," Sal said, when he laid it all out for her. "And what did Reenie say when you told her this story—you not wanting to settle down?"

"Or bathe."

"Or bathe."

"Actually, I never thought to tell her any of this."

She turned to face him. "Never *thought* to, or . . . ?"

"I didn't see how it was relevant to her."

She gave him an arched look that was an awful lot like something Reenie would work up, the eyebrow taking wing like that. *Winkin' Sally . . .* It was the closest Sal had come to *amused* since they'd started out from Chicago. She turned back to face the window.

"Still not sure," he said.

About any of it, he thought.

She gave him the Argus. It was the C-3, for 35mm—the popular model folks called the Brick, on account of it was no bigger than one, really. "And Chesty's favorite, too," she said. "Fits in your hand pretty nicely, huh?"

"Wonderful," he said, hefting it.

She pointed out, in case he didn't know, that it was made in Michigan, and he gave her a grin, saying, "As if I needed anything more to recommend it, it being Chesty's personal favorite and all . . ."

She reminded him they wouldn't know if it was damaged until they got home and developed the film. "But either way," she said, "even if it's a paperweight, I want you to have it. He'd be so glad you're doing what you're doing now—moving forward, I mean, trying new things . . ." She seemed to choke a little, saying it. "I'm feeling like some hokey sob sister here, Wink, like

I'm going to burst out with the waterworks again, but at any rate, he would be proud."

He fiddled with the Brick a little, hoping she might pull it together.

"When we get home," she said, "I'd *like* you to stick around. I suspect you've been planning to jump ship on me now. And maybe it seems like even less fun than it did before, babysitting a married lady, now that you'd be babysitting a boring old widow lady. You know I'm only teasing about 'jumping ship'—I'd understand perfectly if you decide to move on. You've done more than enough, coming out here. So if you'd rather go, that's fine, but—"

He told her he hadn't entertained any such thoughts, though of course he had. He wasn't sure why, but in his mind, he'd pictured getting home, gathering his satchel together, and cleaning out his room above the shop. Somehow, his friend never coming back seemed to change things in terms of Wink's living arrangement. Maybe, before, it had seemed temporary in a way it couldn't now, as if he might just be living down the little hall from her until the day he died.

46

The first thing she did when they got back to Chicago was develop Chesty's last roll of film.

The good news was, the Argus seemed to in fact be undamaged. The shots at the end of the roll, taken on the train by her and a few by Wink, were just as crisp and unblemished by light leaks as the shots at the front of the roll, taken on a stopover in Hawaii, was Wink's guess—of beach and jeeps and a couple pretty Wacs pretending to hold up a leaning palm tree.

The bad news was, the ones in the middle, taken in the hold of the cargo ship, were mostly underexposed. Two were beautiful, though confusing—abstract mounds of white cut by shafts of light ranged toward the rear of the hold, and the last of these, the one that had probably caused the explosion, showed the powder, misty, airborne; the drifts beyond; the about-to-be-injured ensign grinning back at the camera. The problem was, it wasn't damning evidence of anything one way or the other. But it was, she felt, worth taking up to the Tower to show Bob, her editor friend on the *Trib*.

Reenie and Wink both told her she needed to give herself time before going out, that her job right now was to just let herself grieve.

"I'll do that as soon as I do this," she said, and set up an appointment to show Bob the shots the next day.

Bob looked pained. "So they were sending cake flour to Nagasaki—not sure where the scandal is in that . . . Incompetence? Misuse of government funds? Maybe . . . And the photos don't show all that much the reader can even recognize."

She tried to explain that it wasn't so much what Chesty was able to capture on film in those last seconds, but the way the military showed no interest in really investigating, even failing to bother examining his film. "It was as if they already had their own story, and anything else only stood to complicate things for them."

Bob shrugged, sighing. "Unfortunately, hon, that's usually how it works."

She could see him almost physically trying to control his glance shifting to the clock on the wall. Compared with his normal gruff demeanor, this seemed an almost heartbreakingly tender attitude.

When she began to gather up the shots, slipping them back in their envelope to go, he heaved up out of his leather chair and sort of lurched at her, draping one arm across her shoulders in a half hug. It was like being embraced by a halfhearted, geriatric bear.

"You're young, kid. You really are." He said it so quietly, she had to think about it to understand what he was saying, and then he pulled away and turned his back to her, looking down at Lake Michigan, an act she wasn't so offended by because she thought she'd caught the slightest little hitch in his voice, and besides, this kind of a scene wasn't his usual area of expertise.

That evening, the three of them sat at her kitchen table, Chesty's photos splayed out before them.

Reenie sounded ready for a fight. "Maybe we could take it to the Swans Down people, see what they have to say for themselves. Or try to start some sort of boycott, get folks to stop using the stuff till someone—"

"Forget it," Sal said. "I just wanted to see if anyone needed to see this."

They sat there for at least another minute, staring at the blurry blizzard in the pictures—the last image Chesty had ever seen.

She wasn't looking for a fight herself, just an explanation. Or an apology or . . . something.

Finally, clearing her throat, she announced, "I tell you one thing, though, I'm never baking or eating another goddamn cake in my life."

They both laughed with her, then got up and came around and put their arms around her, hugging her between them.

"Fair enough," Wink said. "Long as that still leaves cookies and pie."

47

A few days after they got back from California, he was minding the store and Sal was out visiting Chesty's aunt and uncle when two men wearing dark suits and sour pusses stepped in. One pulled the shade and flicked the door locked before Wink could come around the counter with a sash weight he'd been using to strengthen his gimp hand.

A second before he had the sash weight up and ready, he saw the flash of leather and metal—badges. They were government men.

"A little privacy, is all, Mr. Dutton." The bigger one went on to introduce himself and his partner—nondescript Pilgrim names that slipped away a moment after he heard them.

They asked to look around, but started in on that before he could answer. One had a camera, he noticed, but they didn't seem to be there to have their camera looked at.

"This photo," the bigger one said, "the one you people just tried to fob off on the editors of—"

"Fob off?"

"What exactly were you trying to accomplish with something like that, friend? You looking to give someone a black eye? The military? State Department? Foreign relations? The good people who make Swans Down?"

Wink noticed the guy had phrased it as if he'd been the one taking Chesty's film to the newspaper himself. He didn't bother correcting him because he'd felt just as invested as Sal.

He told him no to the black-eye question, they were just try-

ing to make some information available to the public; see if it
was deemed worthy of attention. He said, pointedly, "Since my
buddy apparently *died* taking that photo, seems to me maybe the
least we could do was take a peek at *why* . . ."

They both looked at him wryly, as if it were a silly, silly answer.

"Would you call yourself subversive, Mr. Dutton?"

Subversive? Where were they getting this stuff? He sure
wasn't up on all his crossword puzzle words, but if by "subversive" they meant some kind of boat-rocker, out to buck the brass,
they clearly didn't realize they were talking to a guy who'd once
consented, in exchange for a crate of canned apricots and an
introduction to a certain nurse, to paint an oil for a company
commander that placed him square in the middle of his own air-
field during a Jap attack, hands on his hips and shouting orders,
even though he'd allegedly been in the laundry at the time,
closely inspecting the bottom of a mountain of sacks of dirty
clothes. And hadn't they seen his rah-rah drawings in *Yank,* for
chrissake?

"You fellows looking to find out what happened with the cake
flour," Wink asked, "or just find out who's asking about the
cake flour?"

"Smart guy," the short one told the other one, pointing at
Wink as if he'd identified a breed of rare bird.

"No kidding," Wink said. "You act like we—like *I'm* the subject of your investigation."

The short one gave him a sick smile, like he was trying to sell
him a used car, swampland, or a Bible. "Just trying to get a sense
of where things stand now." He gestured dismissively in roughly
the direction of the West Coast. "Back then is back then. Ship's
bills of lading, cake flour . . . not my deal. I don't question the
wherebys and *therefores* of whoever back *there,* what happened
then, I question *you,* what's happening in *here, now.*"

They poked around in the darkroom and the basement and even upstairs in both apartments.

He wasn't crazy about the look they gave each other in his room, lifting the narrow mattress, exchanging a smirk.

One took photos in every room. The other took notes in a reporter's pad he clutched close to his chest like an old lady playing cards.

After nosing around through what little reading material he kept stashed under his bed plus all the books Sal kept down the hall on her side, including those on her bedside bookshelf, the guy jotting down titles as they went, they returned to the darkroom and took pictures of pictures. It was just odd.

The way they pawed through the stacks of girlie prints, the extras and rejects, taking shots with their own camera of any prints that had nudity, he was starting to think his lack of attention in school was showing: might "subversive" mean something else? (Or was he thinking of something like "perversive"? "Perverted . . ."?) It had seemed, at first, like these two were on the hunt for troublemakers, but maybe they were looking into deviants.

He kind of wanted to ask them what in the wide world they were doing there, poking through their personal things, and what exactly they were driving at with this "subversive" jazz; maybe ask them to please draw a clearer picture for him, define their terms. But he wasn't about to stir things up further by asking a lot of ignorant questions. *I may be a dope,* he thought, *but I know when to keep my neck tucked in tight.*

They didn't ask where Sal was. Maybe they didn't care.

"If you really have to do this," Wink said, hoping to make them feel bad, "I'm glad you came this afternoon, on account of Mrs. Chesterton—the widow—is out visiting her grieving in-laws. She'd probably find this a little upsetting."

"Relax, Mr. Considerate. We knew you were alone." The G-man patted him on the shoulder in a condescending way that made him want to knock the guy's block off.

But he didn't, of course.

48

Now that she was back home, she kept going, kept on with all her normal routines, brushing aside suggestions from Wink and Reenie and other well-meaning friends that she might need a period of adjustment. She might want to close the camera shop for a while or cut back on hours, maybe go away for a little rest.

The Chestertons suggested she consider selling the store, or at least taking on a partner or manager and moving out of there—discontinue her part in keeping it going and see it more as a source of income, an investment. It was as if they'd forgotten that her own father had started the store and raised her above it, long before their nephew even came to Chicago. They told her she could come stay in one of their extra bedrooms, an offer she declined politely.

Reenie offered a hunting cabin up in the Wisconsin Dells that her oldest brother, Ryan, owned with a policeman friend. She could stay there as long as she wanted—well, until deer season opened, but it would make a quiet getaway if she just wanted to go somewhere and think.

Wink, who had no place to offer her, instead offered her privacy—suggesting again that he could move out, if she wanted. And now she honestly gave it a little more consideration than she had out west on the train. She knew Reenie would take him in, at least until he found his own apartment. But given what

Sal had been hearing about the housing crunch with all these boys coming home now, she didn't imagine he would find it all that easy to find a place. And then maybe he'd stay longer with Reenie than he'd planned. And those two would fall into some sort of new phase, based only on convenience and an increased sense of familiarity, and they'd maybe get married without truly meaning to and regret it later and start drinking . . . Too many young people these days were getting paired up for far more terrible reasons than that—shipping out, coming home, needing housing, needing citizenship . . . Besides, Sal didn't particularly want him to leave. Enough had changed in her life, with no way to fix it, ever, so why add to the list? Better to keep Wink there, and keep running the shop and, yes, keep at the girlie photos.

Except, when it came down to it, she didn't feel like posing just yet. She couldn't quite put it into words, but right now, it didn't feel the same.

49

"You don't get it," Reenie said. "She didn't *think* you'd get it."

It was true. He didn't get it, but maybe that was because it didn't make a whole heap of sense. The fact that it was taking more than one woman to explain it and deliver it and interpret it left him even less sure it was something that could *ever* be gotten by a guy. According to Reenie, Sal was ready to get back to business, done with her mourning enough to roll up her sleeves and produce some more girlie material, except she didn't want to pose for the shots.

"So she's still too upset or . . . ?" He wasn't sure he bought that, though she had stopped the louder crying jags at least a week ago. She no longer seemed as down in the dumps. If not peppy, she at least seemed to be getting on with her routine, making it, more or less, through her day.

"Of course she still misses him," Reenie said. "But no. She just thinks it's not quite right, now that she doesn't have a husband."

Wink would be the last one to push a gal into peeling for the camera if she had any beef with it. Hell, Sal *originally* practically had to talk him into the whole deal. But he could not for the life of him get his head around *this* screwy reasoning: having a husband had made it *more* proper to pose naked for the public?

Reenie moved closer, right up against him, so her explanation was an intimate whisper. She was doing it, mostly, he knew, so Sal wouldn't hear her relaying their private conversation word for word, but he also figured she was being cozy, settling him down by touching his chest and breathing on his neck as she spoke—a thing he didn't mind one bit. She smelled of Wrigley's spearmint gum and hairspray. "The way *she* sees it, *before,* she could always tell herself, while she was doing it, she was really posing for *him,* playing it up for him, batting her eyes, sticking out her can, whatever. All for Chesty. Not flaunting it for some other guy, stepping out on him, but fantasizing it was just the two of them there. More of a 'pure' thing, was the way she put it."

Even as she said it, Wink could see it—there had always been a wholesome, good-girl quality to Sal's photos. No matter what she was actually doing in them, no matter what she was showing, she came off as decent and true. So maybe she was right. Maybe the pictures wouldn't work as well if she felt loose and available or something. It was odd thinking, women's logic, but he couldn't help but get it, a little.

"Plus," Reenie said, "as long as Chesty was alive out there somewhere, she could kid herself that she *was* posing for him. She liked to think he'd actually see one of her pictures somewhere and be fooled by the wig and all—which, by the way, I personally think is nuts. I mean men are thick, sure, and husbands apparently more so, but don't those married types know every square inch of each other after a while? Anyway, Sal thought he'd never recognize her but hoped a photo would catch his eye all the same. He'd get a kick out of it, put it in his wallet or his helmet, look at it on lonely nights . . . Basically, she was hoping to give her husband a thrill long distance. Boners from home, sort of a naughty Red Cross package . . . Now, she just figures she'd be getting naked for strangers."

Wink bit his lip, waiting for the urge to subside that made him want to bark, *But she* has *been posing for strangers!*

Reenie volunteered to help—in fact, insisted—in searching for some new girls to model. "You need me," she said, patting his cheek so it stung a little and giving him that wry arched eyebrow of hers. "Even creeps and killers can be matinee idol handsome, dollface. You might be some white slaver with a panel truck and a hypo full of opium—how would a gal know?"

So she went with him, to the burlesque shows and the dime-a-dance halls. Trying to help, he offered up the suggestion that they contact his alma mater, the American Academy of Art, see if they'd share their list of life models, but Reenie made a sour face. "The kind of gal who shows her beav to a room full of longhairs and brooding artistes? Gotta be a little short in the face department, am I right? Maybe a little flabby, too?"

She was right. Except for that time he'd told Sal about, when the model hadn't known they were watching her disrobe, the models hadn't been much in the way of va-va-va-voom. And the instructors, except for maybe Elvgren, had chosen them for having "interesting definition," which translated to meat on their bones, and not usually in the preferred locations.

Of the two, they had the most luck at the burly shows. The dime-a-dance girls were mostly either offended or *too* agreeable in a lackluster, dead-eyed way that made him sad and made it clear they were also part-time prostitutes. He passed on these.

And a few girls came from Reenie's workplace, the Stevens-Gross Studio—fellow girl Fridays like herself who sometimes modeled for the painters there, and the idea that he might get to shoot a model who'd inspired the great Gil Elvgren made him feel, in theory, one step closer to being what he'd meant to be, an actual artist. The thought both pleased and depressed him.

Mostly, the process of looking for more girls was an awkward one. He felt like a traveling salesman, seeking out company, and even letting Reenie do most of the talking wasn't much better. That just made him feel like a pimp, like she was in his stable and they were trying to break in someone new.

He thought about sitting on the porch of his uncle's farmhouse in St. Johns, sketching a deer that had wandered into the yard during the thaw, trying to get the wide wet eyes and beautiful, trembling legs just right, and it struck him that he'd literally been around the world since then.

"Thirty bucks," Reenie told them. "Easy as pie."

The first shoot with a new girl, Sal didn't even come down to watch. Actually, he heard her on the stairs, the creak of the old wood as she stood and listened, then sat for a while, smoking, which was not her usual habit. And though the shoot was just dandy—a goofy lion-tamer bit, with a whip Reenie had rounded up somewhere, no doubt from one of her scary brothers, and the girl, a slightly bucktoothed redhead named Rox, in a pith helmet and a belted safari shirt, holding a wooden chair for protection, ran through a series of silly poses with a ratty, floppy-necked lion rag doll, which was minus one of its button eyes. Reenie, ever the disgruntled art director, had added the touch of a sketched-in big top on the canvas scrim behind, nicely free-handed in charcoal swoops. And they had no problem getting Rox to sign the release form Sal had come up with, relinquishing all rights for a flat thirty-dollar modeling fee.

Still, it didn't feel the same without Sal down there with them. It felt like he was doing something wrong, and it was enough to make him speak up and say something. When they were done, he told Reenie he'd rather wait to develop the film till the next day and that he was bushed, begging off from having her linger and spend the night. Instead, he went upstairs, checked to see that light was still seeping out from under Sal's door, and rapped lightly. When she answered, he told her he thought maybe they should pack it in on the girlies.

She gave him a put-on pout, frowning like a little girl. "That's no fun," she said. "Only one of us can be no fun at a time, and it's still my turn. So go about your business, Wink. Really. I'll be all right. Honor bright."

She told him again how he needed the practice; told him how good he was getting behind the camera. And with a gentle little push, she sent him back out into the hall with instructions to go downstairs to the darkroom and develop the night's work and "keep plugging away."

"Really," she said. "Just ignore me and I'll let you know when I'm ready to come out and play."

50

All this attention, well meaning as it was, actually made her nervous. She didn't consider herself much like Reenie, who probably wouldn't mind folks fussing over her, paying attention nonstop. But it felt as though Wink was watching her all the time—not in any creepy, vulture way, but like a parent, as if she were a small child again, toddling, unsteady on her feet, capable of cracking her head on a coffee table at every shaky step. She appreciated him being there, in theory, but somehow, in the moment, he made her more uncomfortably self-conscious than she might have been if she were trying to get through her days all on her own.

She decided he needed another photography lesson—not just to distract him from his hovering, attending to her like some unnatural crossbreeding of a personal valet and a guard dog, but also because she genuinely felt she'd fallen short on her end of their bargain. His artistic eye had taken him far in terms of competent, pleasing picture taking, but there were still several technical areas to explore. In the past year or more, they'd been keeping themselves so busy in the confines of the studio, she'd grown lax in challenging him.

Once she was fairly certain she'd harangued him enough about the concept of depth of field—what it was and how to manipulate it—she sent him out on the same assignment Pop had given her at eleven, and Chesty a couple years later: *One roll, two hours. Go out where there's some distance—walk west to Michigan Avenue or Grant Park or down south to the Shedd or wherever you want. Go up in a skyscraper and shoot down, if you want. Let's see some interesting shots that utilize depth of field.*

Even as she laid it out for him, she couldn't help wondering if Pop had given these field assignments to her and then Chesty for exactly the same reason she was giving it now—to get them out of the shop, to stop the hovering and grab a little peace.

But he wasn't gone long, returning in a little over an hour. She reminded him it wasn't a race, but he only shrugged, heading for the darkroom. "Ran out of film!" He was smiling in a distant, distracted way—that and his pace in getting to the darkroom tipped her off that he might have something interesting.

Because there were two boxes of film stock, just delivered, to open and count, double-checking it all against the bill, she didn't follow him in even when she knew he was safely past the fix, and the negatives were hanging to dry.

By the time she had a moment to check on her "student," she found him pulling his contact sheet from the stop bath.

She could see right away he had some nice stuff. It was hard to see yet, on that small scale, how integral the manipulation of depth of field was in any of the shots, but even to someone like her who admittedly only knew the technical side, and lacked that artistic eye that he and Chesty had, she could see that several of them had great contrast—bold black-and-white lines at pleasing angles. But when he pointed to the one he wanted to work up as a print, she honestly felt disappointed in him. And concerned. *He* was supposed to be the expert on composition and lighting and all those good artsy things, but this one he was hopping around about—stepping lively as he rearranged the chemicals and retrieved the single strip of 35mm negative, getting it ready for the enlarger—seemed, at that scale, at least, like it should be titled *Ho Hum*. Or possibly *Ho Hum Man on the Corner*. She didn't see it at all. And where was the tricky use of depth of field? The fact that everything looked pretty sharp, from a close-up section of commercial signage in the foreground to a plate-glass window on the far side of a cluttered intersection? Whoop-de-do.

"Well," she grumbled, leaving him to it, "don't forget we're not made of photo paper . . ."

She tried to remember what she had come up with for her own depth-of-field assignment when she was eleven. Obviously nothing so great it had remained memorable. Neither could she recall what Chesty had come up with, though she knew Pop had been pleased enough with both of their efforts.

At five by eight, she could see it. It was something. At first glance, it had the candid appearance of something accidental, maybe even a mistake or throwaway shot, loading the film. It seemed chaotic and real, but there was solid composition to it, a wounded GI framed by two distinct vertical lines, a perfect division for the rule of thirds, and it put her in mind of Hopper's painting and the way that image had seeped into her the longer she looked, the first glance brushed off, registering, as this one did, as just some urban crossroad somewhere, bleak and unimportant.

The left third of the picture was taken up by what seemed to be the rear end of a panel truck—mostly just part of the advertising painted there, two stark words in white: COLD CUTS. The right third of the picture was defined by a utility pole with a metal sign bolted to it: NO LOITERING—NO STANDING ANYTIME. This second part, she knew, referred to cars and cabs, but still, the combination was clever, because in the middle distance, framed by these two bold verticals, but just a tad off center, to keep it interesting, was a beefy but rumpled-looking marine in a peacoat, not only standing, but reading a newspaper.

His left hand was a prosthetic, the metal pinchers crimping the pages. It was startlingly sharp, surgically shiny. "Oh my," she said, despite herself, hoping she didn't sound insensitive. It was just there was something so unsettling about it, something that went beyond a young man losing his hand.

The focus was clean enough to read his glum expression and the detail of a five o'clock shadow along his jawline. On the open page, the clear, short blocks of type told her it was the classified section—want ads, she imagined, looking for work.

At his side, slumped like a dead body, just visible at the bottom of the shot, was a duffel bag. She could make out part of the stenciled lettering: CPL. A. KE-something. She wondered if it constituted all his worldly possessions—lugging them around everywhere he wandered, like a turtle.

Beyond him still, counterbalancing the middle third, were three words, WELCOME HOME, SERVICEMEN, on a banner draped along a line of perspective that drew her eye farther in, toward what must be the building across the street, brick with a plate-glass window. An American flag filled most of the curtained window, except for a card at the bottom that read SORRY NO VACANCY.

"I'm standing two blocks back," Wink said. "Guy thinks I'm shooting this blossoming crab apple in someone's yard, way down the street, maybe the delicatessen truck, at the most."

The picture was incredibly moving. It made her sad, of course, but also a little angry. And, also, almost want to laugh.

"I got to thinking," Wink said. "You told me all about depth of field—what it is, how to adjust it—but you never told me why you'd want to use it."

He was right. She'd never asked Pop either, and she didn't think Chesty ever had. It was just a tool, to use or not use.

This is an artist, she thought. *That's the difference.*

For the first time in a long time, she wished her pop could be there, just to put his two cents in.

Wink had his hands shoved down in his trouser pockets now. She hadn't seen him look this anxious since the time he tried to convey Chesty's message, that first night in June of '44, nearly two years back. "You know," he said, "maybe this doesn't make any sense and this is probably crap here, just something I'm goofing around with, but . . . it's the first time I've done anything since . . ." He held up his right hand, the uncooperative one. "You know—that feels like when I used to do my cartoons. Like I'm almost *saying* something, you know? Leastways, working with juxtaposition, irony, all that good stuff. Not just making an interesting picture or a cute picture or—"

"It's exactly like that," she told him. "And it belongs in print."

She told him she'd talk to Bob at the *Trib* and see if he'd take a look at it and gave him a little cuff on the shoulder on the way out of the darkroom, the way she imagined Chesty would have.

51

There was a male face at the front door of the shop. Wink had been expecting Reenie for more than two hours, but that hardly looked like her. Not so much around the mustache; the much rounder, Germanic-looking head.

But she was there, too, about to let herself in. He heard her husky laugh and another woman's, too, and the rattle of her keys.

They'd been planning to do a shoot of Reenie doing calisthenics with a set of chest expanders and fake barbells she'd made the night before with balloons and a carpet tube, all painted black. She'd been clear she'd come straight over after clocking out at the Stevens-Gross Studio. Now here it was almost nine, and she'd brought guests?

He'd been heading down the back hallway, making strides into the darkened front part of the shop, intending to throw the bolt on the door just to save Reenie the trouble of unlocking it and to impress upon her, with his quick steps and glowering, that she'd been wasting his evening and there was lost time to make up, when he stopped up short, only halfway down the hall, recognizing the face in the glass.

It was a face that took him back five years now, before the war, to art classes here in town—classes where he could properly hold a brush or a piece of charcoal, pinched precisely between his marvelously engineered fingers.

It was Gil Elvgren. His hero.

Why in the *wide* world had she brought him here?

Sidestepping into the cellar doorway, he peered back just as Reenie's spare key finally came through for her and they burst in, the shop bell jangling. He heard the click of the front lights and the other woman say, "Looks like maybe we kept you a bit late, dear . . ."

There was a reason Wink had never gone over to see her during her day job. He didn't want to run into Elvgren. He thought she understood that. So the maniac tells him he should swing by?

Elvgren would look down on all this, he bet. When he'd taken a class with him, Wink remembered how his uncle back in Michigan frowned at Elvgren's calendar work, which was vibrant and lustrous, with glowing skin and masterful composition. His uncle was of the mind that that was smut, because the girls were overly pretty and underly clothed. But it was all relative: *Elvgren* would frown in turn, he was sure, at what *they* were doing now—

comparatively, the basest sort of puerile provocation, having so little to do with art.

If she brought them all the way in, they'd see everything. There was no time to hide the props and break down the lights they had set up in back, and he had no idea what this lunatic he sometimes considered his girlfriend had told the great artist.

"Whoopsadaisy . . . ," the other woman said, and he took it to mean she'd realized they were no longer alone. Wink had heard it, too—the shush of slippers on the backstairs; Sal clicking on the light on that end and heading down the hall toward them. He was caught in between, flanked at both exits.

From the top cellar step, pressed against the open door, he watched as she approached, wrapped in her housecoat. She paused for a second and looked directly at him, then kept going, not giving him away. He withdrew down into the cellar, creeping step by step so they wouldn't hear, hoping Reenie's introduction of her guests would cover the sound of his retreat.

He was surprised to see Sal coming down to investigate. Earlier, when Reenie had failed to show at the appointed hour, he'd gone upstairs to wait with her for a while, in the back of his mind wondering if this might be the night that Sal decided it was time to pose again. But she'd told him she was going to heat up a hot-water bottle, of all things, and curl up with her old cookbooks and plan some hearty meals she'd been without for a few years, on account of the rationing. He'd thought to himself, *What are you now, lady—sixty-five years old?* but he'd just told her, instead, that it sounded like a great idea.

Below the floorboards, the conversation was muted, with sudden snatches breaking through intact. Sal was no more than a low, silky sound, the genteel murmur of a lady playing the well-mannered hostess. The mysterious other woman, Wink decided, was Elvgren's wife.

"We wanted to make certain our Reenie got to her destination," Mrs. Elvgren said, her voice rising, emphatic with apology or alcohol or both. "We're so sorry it's so late, but Gil and I *had* to drag Reenie out to dinner with us. Look at her! The girl requires fattening."

"Pure rot," Elvgren said, and Wink could picture him up there, looking even more than he remembered like a sort of Ernest Hemingway. "Don't listen to the missus. It's claptrap. We understand you've got one of my former students here, so we thought we'd tag along and—"

"Intrude," Mrs. Elvgren said.

There was polite laughter and some muffled pleasantries Wink couldn't quite make out regarding restaurants and which places were back to snuff, menuwise, and which ones still needed to get back on their legs. He couldn't tell what Sal was saying about where he was. He assumed she offered some excuse, or was at least playing dumb. Except for Sal, they all sounded tipsy, which seemed like a swell idea.

Wink fished out the flask he'd been carrying to loosen Reenie up for the shoot—not that she ever needed anything to loosen her up, but it made the thing more fun for both of them, especially since they'd lost Sal. He wasn't sure how he could go back up there now.

There was an old wooden display counter down there, smack in the center of the cellar, that was missing all its glass sides and now served as storage for stocking cardboard boxes, keeping them off the damp floor. Rearranging the row on top so the boxes were all relatively level, he took off his jacket and spread it out for a makeshift navy bunk. For a pillow, he propped up the busted bellows from a portrait camera he estimated as old enough to be Mathew Brady's, climbed up, and stretched out.

Lying there in the dark, staring up at the low beams, he tried to imagine what his hero would have said to him, if he'd faced him.

Maybe he'd be polite. It was possible. Maybe he'd say, *Say there, fella, I saw a few illustrations of yours that ran in* Yank *and* Stars and Stripes *and I recognized the name and I was proud to recall that you'd studied with me . . .*

Maybe he'd call him son or kiddo or my good man— something more encouraging than smutmonger. Maybe he wouldn't tell him he was a disgrace.

Sure, Wink thought, pulling back on the flask. *Dream on, pal.*

Gnawing, Wink thought, opening his eyes in the dark. He supposed he'd nodded off. He didn't think he heard anyone moving around up there. Feeling around, he couldn't put his hands on the flask and couldn't remember if there was much left but backwash.

There'd been laughter, hadn't there? Hearty *good nights* and shuffling and footfalls and the jangle of the shop bell on the door?

He couldn't be certain and so wasn't going anywhere yet, just to be safe.

Easing himself down to stretch, he found his way carefully to a nearby filing cabinet where he'd hidden a stash of black market Glenlivet that one of Reenie's brothers had acquired for him.

It was in behind the unclaimed wedding photos, which had their own drawer. The file went back a few decades, but it still seemed surprisingly large, and he'd wondered, when he'd discovered them, how many were unclaimed out of an inability to pay or pure forgetfulness and how many because things had all gone to smash.

Quietly slipping the bottle out and unpeeling the seal, he climbed back onto his nest. Lying there waiting, with nothing to do but imagine, put him in mind of the year he got scarlet fever, and how he thought his mom was still out there in the other room. At least then, he was able to draw his Rube Goldbergs to pass the time. Plus, he could turn a light on.

Pathetic, he thought. *And if that man caught you here, he'd tell you so to your face.*

The scotch burned beautifully, and he made it a double.

No, he wouldn't, he corrected himself. *He wouldn't say that. This is* my *make-believe, damn it. I'll cook it up any way I see fit, thank you very much.*

The gnawing was some critter off in a corner. He wanted to fling something over there, get it to back off, but he remembered he was hiding and so lay still.

Listen, Elvgren would tell him, slurring just a little, because, in his mind, Wink had joined him for dinner and drinks. Good ol' Gil had treated. *I know about your hand,* he'd say. *I know about these naughty pictures you're doing, and no, it is not what you had in mind, I'm sure . . . And it's not necessarily what I'd have in mind for any of my students—ideally. And if you could still paint and draw, I'd say get to it! What's keeping you? But . . .*

It was a significant *but,* looming there like the low beams overhead. He'd take this moment to pull out his pipe, tamping down the cherry tobacco, and Wink decided he would smoke one, too. They'd draw on their twin pipes like respectable bankers knocking back a few at the country club . . . no! Better yet—chaired professors emeritus hobnobbing in the oaken faculty lounge. Some ivy-covered ivory tower where they could look out through stained glass and watch coeds crossing campus in tight sweaters. *But you ready for the speech?* Elvgren would say. *Here it is, friend. There can be a little art in anything you do. Even stuff you do because you have to do it, there's no other ready option . . . The thing is, that little bit of art isn't just in there, au-*

tomatically, rising and bubbling like yeast in a loaf of bread. You have to go to the trouble of putting it in there.

He could see the crackling fireplace, the wingback club chairs, their wool blazers with suede patches on the elbows. *Hear, hear!* Chesty would chime in, and how swell it was that he was there, too, to hear this pep talk, hardly looking even the least bit blown up. *The putting-it-in-there step! Indeed! Quite crucial!*

They'd nod together, gesturing with their meerschaums as the great man elaborated: *If you get up and do something every day— even if it's working a camera, even if it's shooting snapshots of Reenie's very pretty legs and immaculate keister, you're still doing more than some blowhard who's decided he's Rembrandt but is holding out for a patron of the arts to come calling—some sponsor nobler than a razor blade company or bottler of soda pop or the makers of in-home laundry machines . . .*

Now he'd clamp his solid hand on Wink's shoulder. (And in so doing, not really look all that different from his uncle's neighbors back in St. Johns, the simple farmers of German, Dutch, and Swedish stock. Pry them out of the barn coat or overalls, catch them in town on Sunday—sure: hardworking, God-fearing men, all. Elvgren included.) His former teacher would pause a moment, either for effect or because he was slightly wobbly on his feet, a little in his cups, and, finally, give the command, *Now say "Amen" and get to work.*

"Amen," Wink said now, barely a whisper, though he knew no one was still upstairs to hear him. The little coffee klatch had no doubt broken up very soon after he'd started drinking. Even the girls, he imagined, had given up on him for the night.

He was going to have to hang out down there and sleep it off. And unless he cared to go up and face them, he realized that if he needed to water his horse or get sick, it was all probably going to have to happen in the laundry tub.

52

"It's like going to a candy store, nowadays," Reenie said, "coming in here."

This comment, said to her, not the butcher, nonetheless seemed to get his attention. Through the display case, Sal saw his gaze move from the veal he was scooping onto a little paper boat to the long loveliness of her pal, who was digging through her pocketbook, waiting her turn along with Sal for the fat German-looking lady to get her makings for her Wiener schnitzel.

Sal knew what she meant—it was a treat just shopping for meat, no longer having to hassle with ration stamps. The restrictions for buying meat and butter had finally been lifted around Thanksgiving.

The butcher gave them a wry smile when it was their turn, pointing a big thick finger at Reenie. "Candy store, huh? That's a hot one." Then he cocked his head to one side like the RCA Victor dog. "Hey, I think I know you . . ."

Sal spoke up, pointing out that she came in here all her life. "Well, more before the war, of course."

"No, no," he said, leaning on the glass case, revealing the marine insignia, a bluey splotch, tattooed on a hairy forearm. "*You* I recognize, sure. How you doing, ma'am? Nice to have your trade once again. But your friend here—*her* I think I know maybe . . ."

Reenie gave a little saucy shake of her head, and for a second, Sal thought she might actually strike one of her sexy poses. "You *think* you know me," she said with a broad wink, "or you think you *wanna* know me?"

The butcher laughed hard, big stevedore-style *har-hars,* jabbing that thick finger in Reenie's direction again. "Don't you start
with that, doll! Believe you me, the missus can handle a cleaver
better than yours truly, so we gotta scuttle any of *that* talk!"

Sal bought sirloin, and Reenie said she wanted the same.
When he was ringing it up, Sal tried to indicate *What the hell was
that?* with her eyes, nodding toward the butcher with his back
turned to them, but Reenie was acting oblivious. So she said
something to her instead about how Wink was really going to get
his fill of beef, only Reenie explained that the steaks were in fact
for another gentleman—her old partner at LD&M, a copywriter
named Cal. She was going to make him dinner that night.

Sal wondered to herself if Wink knew about this, but then
again, it had been clear for a while that their relationship ran
pretty catch-as-catch-can, so who was she to judge?

Reenie went on to say she was going to see if she couldn't get
the skinny from this Cal on some so-called after-hours clients
they could possibly steal away. "Maybe take one of their big calendar deals," she said. "Fix that old goat Deininger's wagon."

"Sounds like a plan," Sal said, unsure if it was. She was
watching the butcher over her friend's shoulder, and he was definitely checking out her figure like she was different from all the
other respectable lady customers whose trade he depended on.
He just *had* to know who she was. Reenie, that is—he wouldn't
have known Sal from a veal. In fact, when they left, he gave Reenie a big wink right back at her.

Out on the sidewalk, Sal had to let her have it. "That man
completely recognized you. From the . . . you know!"

"No, he didn't! He was just handing me a line, flirting with
me a little."

"Maybe." Though she wasn't buying it, she decided to drop it
for now. And she didn't raise, as pretty damning evidence that he

had recognized her, the fact that he had clearly given Reenie the better cut of meat. Which, besides being a little alarming—men on their block possibly drawing the connection to the girlies—it just wasn't fair. So she hadn't posed for a while—she had done it *first,* after all. It wasn't as if Reenie had become a Hollywood starlet. Lord love a duck, didn't she have just as much right to the good steaks?

It was around this time, the spring of '46, that a wave of mail descended on the camera shop. Most of it had been delayed some time. Both *Stars and Stripes* and the civilian places they'd appeared—*Wink* and *Titter* and *Giggles* and *At Ease*—were still playing catch-up with much of the correspondence received from soldiers back when the war was still on. The military censors had loosened their restrictions, and so, like an unclogged drain, the mailbags now arrived with stacks of forwarded fan mail. "My, my!" the mailman said. "*Someone's* popular!"

But it was unclear who. Half of them loved Weekend Sally. The other adored Winkin' Sally. It still wasn't clear to Sal who was whom in the minds of either the editors or the readers or if they even knew there were sometimes two of them. The editors had been playing so fast and loose with the titles and "copy," as Reenie called it, who *knew* what the fan mail meant—other than they'd done something right.

Looking at it all, piled up like bags of loot, she started to feel as if she owned something—something beyond the camera shop. There was something here that belonged uniquely to her. And to Wink and Reenie, of course, but no one else. Not even, really, the publishers of these magazines.

She wasn't certain she had the right word when it first hit her, but trying it on, mulling it over, then walking up to the library on Michigan Avenue and looking it up in the big dictionary in the reference section, she was pretty sure this was what she was talking about: *franchise.*

53

The Kilroy shoot was Reenie's brainstorm. Kilroy had been popping up everywhere in the past year, mostly since the boys started coming back—that enigmatic announcement KILROY WAS HERE! sometimes with a snout-nosed creature peeking over a straight-edge, implying a fence or rim of some kind.

He'd first started noticing the graffiti on the trip to fetch Chesty home—it was all over the naval yard, on crates and even buildings—and then coming back, he saw it on the train, left by troops heading home, inland, scratched on the walls when he visited the head.

He wasn't a big fan of it, as unbelievably popular and widespread as it was, never being particularly fond of unsigned art. He'd always admired that about Gil Elvgren—signing all his pinup illustrations with a big swooping *Elvgren,* right up in the meat of the canvas, not the slightest bit timid or cautious about it.

It was true that he himself had used pseudonyms for the girlie photos—when they'd bothered to ask for credits. But that was different: he could tell by scanning the masthead of all those girlie mags that none of those contributors' names were real— Ima Wolf, Lenny Lens, Mr. Snapp, O. G. Whillikers, Barry Medeep, I. C. Lovelies, Scopes Magillicuddy . . . Besides, he was saving his actual name—both Winton S. Dutton and Wink Dutton—for his real work, for the legitimate photography and, if he ever got his hand working properly again, illustration work. So he used things like W. S. Dee or Win Studdon or Winston St. Johns or just Mr. Winston or Mr. Wink for photo credits. Often the editors just made something up on their own (once it was Dusty Sink), but at least he provided a name when asked. It wasn't like cave drawings, like this Kilroy crapola.

But beyond the anonymity angle, this Kilroy business, at its core, maybe also didn't grab him the way it seemed to grab so many others because, if he were to be completely honest about it, he really just didn't get it. It felt, a little, like an inside gag or like he'd stepped away too soon from a group of jokers yucking it up at a cocktail party and missed the big punch line. It re-minded him, frankly, that he'd been discharged early. Maybe if he hadn't injured his hand, this would be yet another thing he would have been included in, and though he suspected most of the vandals and scribblers out there were just as in the dark about what the galloping Jesus it meant, unreasonably, when he saw it growing around him like a spreading mold—on the alley wall beside the camera shop, on a drainpipe at the corner, scratched into the side of the cigarette machine at the Zim Zam—he couldn't help but feel as if he'd been left out; that he hadn't served the way the other guys had.

But in terms of a girlie shoot, Kilroy seemed as good a gim-mick as any—topical, even, without being political. And now that they didn't have the more blatantly military themes to fall back on, this felt connected to that—*of* the service if not *in* the service—and maybe that was why the vets were doing it in the first place. Maybe they were trying to scratch out something that connected them to what they'd known for the past four years as they now jumped feetfirst into the world of the civvies.

Reenie's premise was simple: she would be the vandal, trying to paint the Kilroy message wherever she could. They didn't have a lot of set dressing, of course, so "everywhere" in this case would mean the canvas drop cloth on the floor and a cartoon picket fence he'd made to her specifications from a piece of piano crate she'd found in an alley a few blocks east, behind Orchestra Hall. It made a fine picket fence. The only other prop was an apple crate, which she stood on to get a better angle—not to draw her Kilroy graffiti so much as to cock her calf muscle and tip her pelvis, presenting the stretched expanse of "accidentally" exposed underpants to the camera. There were various poses she had planned, culminating in a few capper shots that would be a cop arriving just as she exposed herself, popping the buttons on her blouse and flashing a graffiti-painted bare torso, at which point the cop would lean back in shock, followed by shots of him cuffing her, wrestling her to haul her off to jail. In the last shot, with the kicking and screaming "Winkin' Sally" flung over the cop's shoulder, the reader would see that she'd managed to Kilroy him across the back of his dark cop uniform, the message written in white chalk.

Before they got to these shots, Reenie raised the idea that they shoot a couple where she scratched out KILROY and scrawled in WINKIN' SALLY instead.

"Yeah. Or WEEKEND SALLY?" he suggested, still confused about these names. "Which one, you think?"

Reenie shrugged. "Make any difference, really? I mean, especially *now*. . . ."

She was right. The names would be more interchangeable than ever now that there was only one girl playing the part. He was hoping Sal would pipe up and vote on this idea, but it was left hanging there, unsettled, as they shifted attention to the role of the cop.

The plan was that he himself would play the cop, a role he

wasn't so keen on, though she assured him if they shot it just right, his face would never be seen.

Sal was helping out, of course, minding the props and over-seeing his camera settings and lighting, and she was still sitting over on the bottom step of the stairs in back, when he heard her getting to her feet and caught, out of the corner of his eye, the gymnastics of a woman reaching back and trying to unhook her own dress.

"I'll be the cop," she said. "It'll be funnier."

He liked it. And not just because it got him off the hook. The whole thing was so clearly a fantasy, adding the goofiness of a lady cop to the mess couldn't hurt.

Glancing at Reenie, hoping to decipher what she thought about this, she appeared to be okay with the plan, shrugging, giving him a small smile. But she looked a little puzzled as well, like she was probably as unclear as he was as to what exactly Sal was offering here.

And he wasn't sure till she had the uniform on—or the parts of it she'd opted to use: no pants; the blue tunic tied up around her belly button, Bahamian style; the hat tipped at a rakish angle—but she'd decided, apparently, that she was back in the game. She would be showing skin, he realized, when she laid out her adjustment to Reenie's storyline.

It would go like this now: in the end, after wrestling to cuff the vandal, the lady cop would look down her own shirt, show ex-aggerated heights of horror and surprise, then open it to reveal the KILROY WAS HERE painted across her own bare bosom.

It made no sense, but it didn't have to. The main thing was she was back.

"I love it," Reenie announced. "Really, really love it!" and she gave Sal a little hug before they got started.

It wasn't clear to Wink if she really loved it or she just loved that Sal was in again.

He wondered if it had something to do with the sack of fan mail that had arrived the other day. Sal had seemed different since then. He wasn't sure why or how this would have motivated her to share the shoot with Reenie, but whatever the reason, he was very glad.

Reenie would have pulled it off alone just fine, he had no doubt, but this way, there was actual laughter, female laughter ringing through the camera shop, carrying out into the dark street, along with the music he found on the radio—delicious, brassy, pre-army Harry James—and he wouldn't have been anywhere else on a bet.

54

There was a lawyer who'd been frequenting the shop for years now, named Doerbom. She'd seen the name on the claim slips for his prints (mostly of statues in Grant and Lincoln parks and the occasional policeman) and had only recently learned his first name was Mort and that he was a lawyer. At some point in the time since they'd returned from burying Chesty, he'd begun signing with *Esquire* at the tail end—which she at first took as a clue that he worked at the men's magazine of that name. When it did finally hit her that he was announcing his field of work, not his specific place of employment, she experienced just the smallest moment of wonder—had he possibly added it on to impress her? She *was* widowed now and had only just begun to slip away, slightly, from the darker dresses, but maybe he was looking ahead, laying the groundwork for down the line.

It was a silly notion, and it left her, for a short breath or two, remembering the sweet unattached adventure of high school.

But that was too silly. And anyway, she wasn't interested in him in that way. He was decent enough looking, though not exactly filled to the gills with what she would call pizzazz.

Still, if he was an attorney, she might want to talk to him about the business of registering both *Winkin' Sally* and *Weekend Sally* as some kind of trademarks. After all, he was a camera buff of the first order. He might take it out in trade.

55

It was Reenie who called the meeting. She'd managed to get them in on a pitch for a so-called after-hours client her friend Cal, over at Lampe, Deininger & Monroe, had tipped her to.

They were gathered around the kitchen table in Sal's apartment. Sal had made ranger cookies, now that she was able to finally get some decent coconut. Reenie laid off, saying she needed to watch her weight, but Wink couldn't see how either was possible—Reenie needing to watch her weight or anybody being able to lay off Sal's ranger cookies.

"Cal's moved up from junior copywriter since I was there," she said, laying her fingers on Wink's knee, "and since *you* were there, too—same day, right? Anyway, Cal's moved up and up, from junior copywriter to senior copywriter to assistant creative director—even though, according to Cal, I was the one who should've gotten the credit for all our best work together. But hey, did you know I'm a *girl* apparently, and he's not?"

"We knew," Sal said dryly.

"On account of your underwear's usually pink," he said.

"Smart mouth!" Reenie said. "Anyway, Cal says, this man Mr. Price does all kinds of big business 'after hours,' with a few in the know at LD&M—stuff that competes with the stuff coming out of France, with most of the dough going directly into the pocket of Mr. Rollo Deininger."

"Our old friend," Wink said.

"Yes, the man with the hands."

Wink didn't think this was a crack at him and his own limited ability to get quite as "handsy," having restricted use of the right to the point where he actually couldn't caress a nipple the way he once had. She'd never complained, but then, he'd always managed to keep her going in some other way.

Though, of course, lately such run-ins had grown pretty inconsistent.

"Anyway," she said, "word is Mr. Price puts out a girlie card deck every year or so, and this year he's looking for a doozy."

"Going more nude?"

She nodded like he'd answered the winning round on *Quiz Kids*. "He's going more nude. The boys are home now, they can handle knowing their gals occasionally need it, their sweethearts have actual blood running through their veins. . . ."

She had packets for her presentation, and she handed them out now. Her cozy chum Cal had slipped her not only the budget requirements and all the facts and figures that Sal would be most interested in but also a couple packs of playing cards Mr. Price had produced in the past, so they could see what they were trying to top.

She said she even had a plan. "First, we need fifteen models."

Wink snorted. "How do you figure?"

"I *figure* we want to do it better and bigger than they normally do it, that's how I figure. And the client, this Mr. Price, he's also looking to have his socks blown off. *So* . . . we don't just put a girl on the back. We put one girl on the back, yes, but also one girl on the other side, for each of the face cards—four jacks, four queens, four kings—"

He finished the math for her. "Two jokers."

"Right. Fifteen girls. Thirteen, plus us." Reenie gestured to herself and Sal.

"Whew!" was all Sal said.

"They're paying a *lot*," Reenie reminded them.

Still, a *lot* minus thirteen more model fees wouldn't divvy up very impressively.

"We don't need any fifteen girls," Sal said, speaking up finally. "Please! We just need some more wigs. And costumes and props."

She was right. She usually was.

56

The photo ran in a Sunday edition in late May, over a comprehensive, multiauthor piece called "Where We Are Now"—the kind of extra-effort story, she thought, that meant someone up in the Tower was bucking for a Pulitzer. Which made it even more of a triumph—to have his photo attached to a big, serious article like that.

She'd actually gotten wind of it before him, her editor friend Bob calling the shop the night before.

"Congrats!" he'd said. "Your guy's up there with the big boys now!"

She thought for a second he might possibly be implying that Wink was *her* guy, but she decided not to correct him. Even a rough slob like Bob wouldn't be hinting she had a boyfriend so soon after her husband's death. Doubtless, he'd meant it the way she decided to take it: that they should all be proud of Wink, which, of course, she was.

The next morning, the three of them—she and Reenie and Wink—camped out in front of the news shop to watch the grumpy old man open up the roll gate and cut the band on the newspapers. Bundled like that, she thought of Christmas presents waiting to be opened, full of wonder and promise.

57

The two men strode into the shop, checking left, then right, as if they were crossing Adams, not simply crossing from the door to the counter where he stood. They flipped their badges too quickly to properly inspect, and Wink wasn't about to ask for seconds. The names they gave, Agent Something and Something-else-ski, were equally rushed.

"Right," Wink said. "You're back for more. Okay: no, I'm still not a subversive."

This stopped them up short, and they exchanged a frown that he took as one of confusion with just a hint of annoyance.

They were pretty convincing in their claim that they had never been by before, that that must have been some other agency back in the fall.

"You people need to have regular weekly meetings, so you can get it straight. I already told him, no, I am not a subversive. Don't you have some sort of easy form—if I suddenly *become* a subversive, I can check the little box and mail it in?"

"Oh, don't worry," the slim one said. "We've got eyes out there much faster than anything you could send through the U.S. mail—believe it. Now, is there a reason you've made *this* your headquarters—"

"Headquarters?"

"Being rather close to the site of the Haymarket Riot, isn't it?"

Wink was confused. History had never been his long suit, but he was pretty sure that happened back in the days of handlebar mustaches—maybe 1880-something. Did ladies take their clothes off in olden times? Probably they were calling him a political subversive, not that other kind of subversive. A socialist, maybe? But if they were implying he was cooking up bombs in the back, printing out Commie leaflets or the like, then this had to be a different bunch from the last visitors. Those two had poked their noses in the darkroom, upstairs, even the basement. It had to be on file somewhere that he was harmless, not up to any nonsense. But this one seemed stupid on top of just nosy.

"Are you asking if I'm a . . . a labor organizer or something?"

"I'm asking are you a Red, are you a Wobbly—what the Jesus are you, friend?"

The stouter of the two had a pad out, and he seemed less concerned with intimidation and more with the gathering of facts. "This picture you created for the *Tribune,* ran the other day—there some sort of hidden message in that? Were you trying to do something with that?"

He was tempted to tell them he'd intended to snap only the pretty flag in the window, but he still hadn't mastered framing the shot properly, and all that "extra" stuff just got in the way. But he remembered seeing men, ever since the government men had visited him about Chesty's cake-flour shots, dressed in this same overly insignificant way, walking a few blocks behind him or across the street, glancing at him funny, and though he could have been imagining it—and so never mentioned it to the girls— it felt a little like he was being followed. So he answered as forthrightly as he could manage and then steered the conversation over to the Argus and the other examples they'd recently stocked of the latest in miniature handhelds, and they seemed interested in this, professionally, and eventually put the notepads away.

"Okay," the slim one said, after they played with several cameras and listened to his spiel on each one, "I wanna think you're a good egg and maybe you are—you seem to be an upstanding businessman here, trying to make an honest sale, but just so we're clear, because believe you me, we had trouble plenty with these Red types back twenty years ago, not to mention going back even further—though there's folks alive still recall it like it was Wednesday—the Haymarket Riot with your Bolshevik types, like I said, which was right around here, just a bomb's throw away . . . Coincidence? Anyway, we do not want to go through all that again, now do we?"

Wink shook his head like it was too ridiculous to even answer and mentioned instead that they gave a twenty percent discount on merchandise sold to government employees, and that seemed like enough.

58

She might not have known at all about the editorial that followed if it hadn't been for the old grouch at the news shop. He'd grown curious a few days before when they'd been waiting for him early that morning the photo ran—even more so when they bought six copies (she'd put one clipping in the store window; one on the glass case at the register, where customers were certain to see it if they'd rushed past it on the way in; one went in her scrapbook; one Wink sent to his uncle who lived on a farm in Michigan; and Reenie snatched up the last two), and he asked them what was so damned special they needed to run down his supply for the day.

When they'd shown him, he studied the photograph for the longest time, not showing any signs of approving or being impressed, but more like he was trying to make certain they weren't trying to pull one over on him. Finally, he just tipped his head in almost reluctant recognition. "Eghh. Mr. Big Shot! So *not* just a fella likes to look at the girlie pictures. *Dimension,* this guy has. *Multifaceted,* this guy. I guess one never truly knows what goes on, does one?" She thought for a second he might grace them with an impression of the radio announcer from *The Shadow,* but he laid off and returned his mouth to its interrupted activity regarding a cigar.

But today, a few days later, he seemed expectant, anxious to show them there'd been a follow-up to the photo. The editors had placed what amounted to a retraction or an apology:

Regarding our recent publication on May 15 of a photograph on p. A8 by Mr. Winton S. Dutton accompanying an article about the reintroduction of service veterans to civilian home-life, we the Editors find the image, upon further consideration, potentially inflammatory and insensitive to a number of parties. The inclusion of this photograph within these pages in no way was meant to make specific allegations regarding, nor insult to, the Veterans Administration, city officials, landlords or the housing industry as a whole, the handicapped or anyone else.

We submit that the happenstance location of certain

words and phrases, appearing naturally on signage in the street, and juxtaposed within the image, may, in fact, inadvertently create a certain reading of intent. Any such "message" this may create lies within the culpability of the photographer, Mr. Dutton, and not the *Chicago Tribune.*

Though there was no intention by the publisher or our editorial staff to imply a state of animosity, negligence, nor apathy on the part of any known parties—not the least of which being the actual anonymous disabled veteran at its center—we hereby apologize for any offense it may have given.

The Editors

"It's that head guy they got up there," the news dealer said, breathing on her with the stink of chewed seegar. "What's-his-name—isolationist conservative guy. Never wanted us in the fight. Any opportunity, he loves to stick it to the Dems. This way, he sticks it to 'em, then turns around, eats his cake, too."

The mention of cake only made her think of Chesty, lost in that blizzard of white, and it only made her sadder. Wink had done something wonderful—a great, thought-provoking picture, beautifully composed—and they were using it to poke, not provoke, then leave him holding the bag.

Sons of bitches . . . It was a good thing they'd stopped calling her for tech work since the men came back. If they were letting her in the building late at night these days, who knew what she'd do?

Despite this cold-footed second-guessing by the editors, readers, it turned out, appeared to feel differently. The letters to the editor regarding this—at least the ones they printed—ran in favor two to one, with the supportive readers writing that Wink's photo "perfectly illustrated the present plight of the GI lucky enough to make it home," as opposed to the single dissenter who wrote, "Mr. Dutton's sick trick photography gives voice unnecessarily to the grousers and radicals who wouldn't know a bootstrap or how to pull themselves up by said strap, if their life depended on it."

Sal contacted a gal she knew who'd somehow hung on to her proofreader job at the paper even after V-J Day, despite being a gal, and her friend told her, "Fact is, we've apparently received *sacks* of letters and almost all of them *loved* your beau's cock-eyed photo."

Sal explained that he was not her beau.

But she *was* proud of him and concerned that the public not misinterpret his great picture or get the wrong idea about him, and all of this was to a degree that she couldn't imagine topping even for a guy who *was* her beau.

59

They shot the whole card deck in one weekend, starting with the shop closing at five on Saturday and working all Sunday.

They did the queens first, with crowns they cut out of shirt cardboard. Four years of rationing now made the idea of using tinfoil for this feel wasteful and unpatriotic, so they settled for merely bejeweled by gluing on the contents of a box of Jujubes Reenie hadn't finished the last time they went to the pictures. Sal constructed a scepter out of an old curtain rod, and they were in business. The queens were Sal in her natural blonde hair, Sal in her black wig, Reenie in her natural black hair, and Reenie in her redhead wig. One was outfitted in Sal's late mother's faux-mink stole, another in her bathrobe, another in Reenie's high school prom dress, and another in something she had to wear as a bridesmaid at her brother's wedding. The queens struck hilariously regal poses, thrusting to the heavens with the scepter and allowing the costume to fall open slightly, revealing Her Majesty's surprisingly fine legs or deep cleavage. In one, which he was pretty sure they would *have* to use, Reenie appeared to be screaming in a way that had to have been inspired by the Queen of Hearts in *Alice in Wonderland*.

For the jacks, they put their hair in ponytails and pigtails and posed on the floor, in short skirts, as if they were playing jacks. Wink had to admit, he never would have thought of this. The girls dreamed up this one on their own. In one shot, they might have their legs angled out before them, the toy jacks scattered on the floor in between. Another, they might be on all fours, hovering over the jacks and dropping the ball. He was pretty sure all other parties bidding for this job wouldn't have come up with anything quite like that, as simple as it seemed.

As for the kings, he didn't have any good ideas himself, other than maybe something political, dressing them up like Stalin and Churchill and Truman and . . . who would be the fourth? The late FDR? Except, strictly speaking, dressing them up as unattractive men, let alone dragging tense postwar politics into it, hardly qualified as a good idea. He was afraid, too, that they might want to try something similar to the queen shots—maybe don the robe and crown and just add a beard . . . ? Not very sexy, either.

But they didn't. They came up with something even better.

"I'll set up the shots in these," Sal said, motioning him away from behind the camera. "You just sit."

They had a chair for him and a velvet footstool they sometimes used for family photos, for the youngest one who always knelt in front. Reenie tugged at him, giggling. "You're the king."

"Oh, no!" This wasn't right. He wasn't having any of this. He could just see it, if he allowed himself to be a model for these things, the double takes of old war buddies—dressing up in a cardboard crown like some burlesque comedian; like those clownish oafs in the worst girlies, with their greasepaint mustaches and overblown leers—not to mention he might be a serious artist one day, somehow, or at least a news photographer, and he couldn't afford to risk his potentially professional reputation.

Besides, the chair she was leading him to could hardly pass for a throne—nothing but a wooden straight-backed chair, the one from his room that he sat on every morning to tie his shoes and test the endurance of his ancient laces. "Nice throne," he said. "No, we've got to do better than this! I mean, the *king*—now that's an important card."

But they promised they weren't going to show him in the shot—Sal had it framed so his upper torso was cropped away. All that would appear would be his legs, stretched out on the footstool, maybe an arm, and the girls, in various wigs. He was king by inference, only. It was brilliant.

"Mr. Elvgren always says," Reenie explained, "that the second most important subject in his pinups isn't *in* the painting. It's the guy looking at it."

It was true. Elvgren's stuff often drew you in because the girl looked back at the viewer, like she was in on the gag. It always felt participatory and entirely possible.

In the king shots, Reenie straddled his legs, helping him on with his slippers, her skirt hiked up as she braced herself, and Wink remained unseen behind the newspaper he was reading. In another, a blonde Reenie, in a French maid's outfit, bent at the waist, lifted his feet off the ottoman, feather duster attending to his shoes. In another, Sal was lighting his pipe, but starting it herself, both elbows out in a tomboyish pose. And in the last, Sal, looking more like Sal than he'd ever seen in any of these photo sessions, decked out in a frilly hostess dress with a respectable expanse of cleavage and pearls, offered him a martini.

Later, looking at these king shots in particular, he was amazed at how titillating they felt. Of the batch, they showed the least amount of skin, but the *idea* of them felt much more powerful than all the rest combined. These king shots felt a lot like a column in *Esquire* magazine come to life.

Sal came up with the idea for the main shot, the one that would appear on the back of the entire deck. It was nicely simple—Weekend Sally, playing cards. They'd rustled up some poker chips and a bowl of pretzels, an ashtray with cigars, and, best of all, a green eyeshade. Reenie thought it was great, too, and insisted Sal be the model.

He shot it straight on, so the hand she held, fanned out, could cover her nipples. Reenie lit her cigar and got it going while she primped Sal, and he got the lights just right. They put a lacy bra on the pot in the center of the table, as if the game had devolved to strip poker. Reenie found a loose tress and pulled it down over Sal's cheek, just so, giving her that vampy tousled look, then stood behind her and squeezed her shoulders together a little, coaxing her into a more vulnerable attitude. Reenie was still puffing away on the cigar, coaching her. "You're in a tight spot, you've bet your last buck, but you *know* you've got the winning hand . . ." Sal adjusted her facial expression accordingly, and damn if she didn't get it. One eye narrowed, her lip curled with undisguised moxie. Reenie tipped the ashes on her stogie—it was considerably shorter now, the perfect, iconic seegar—and jammed it into the corner of Sal's curled lips.

He had it framed tight so you saw the smoke and disorder of the game, but only needed to imagine her opponents seated at the table. You were right there, in the midst and heat of it.

When he squeezed the bulb for the first shot, he knew they had a winner. He could see it finished, packaged, and practically selling itself once any normal guy got a gander. It was even easy to see what would ultimately be printed on these: *Playin' Around with Weekend Sally. . . .* Or *Weekend Sally's Game.* Yes, even better—making a pun with the apostrophe *s*.

They thought they were all set until Sal went through the list and saw the two jokers hadn't been checked off. In what Wink read as a gesture of grace and diplomacy, Sal insisted her friend do the two jokers, since she'd done the back of the cards herself. Unfortunately, Reenie had forgotten to bring the Harlequin mask—the masquerade-style kind, with feathers and sequins and a stick handle to hold it up to her face. Her brother Jamie got it at Mardi Gras when he went through basic outside New Orleans, and she'd been claiming it made her look like a court jester. "Except," Sal told her, "for all the rest of you which would *not* be in checkerboard but would be naked and female and offering *nothing* worthy of ridicule, believe me. The man who laughs at you in the altogether is a little too lacy to be buying these cards."

So when they learned that Reenie didn't have the mask with her, Sal came up with a solution on the spot. Wink suspected it had been brewing for a while, that Reenie's art director talents were beginning to rub off on her friend.

Sal had Reenie—topless but turned and cropped, arms and such obstructing, so you still only partly saw her bazooms— grinning and winking that exaggerated trademark wink of hers (throwing her whole jaw into it, as if trying to dislodge a seed stuck in a back molar), and pulling a different practical joke in both of them: in one, she was lighting a match, about to hold it to a fan of Blue Tips jammed under the heel of a stiletto pump, worn by an otherwise unseen Sal, the imminent recipient of a hotfoot. In the other one, she was placing a tack on a wooden chair—again, crouched low to include her nude upper torso and wink and grin in the frame, and Sal posed as if about to sit, her can, in nothing but a lacy slip, roundly hovering over the thumbtack. "By rights," Sal said, "you should be doing these leg shots, too," but Reenie couldn't be in two places in one shot, unless they wanted to get into tricky darkroom work—double exposures and the like—and he did not feel up to that. This was hard enough, considering they might not even win the pitch. Mr. Price might not even be interested.

Wink felt proud of them both, though, for their creativity and hard work, and their generosity toward each other. These jokers, he knew, would be thought of almost certainly as Winkin' Sally, as much as the backs would further establish Sal as Weekend Sally.

Now if only they could get this Mr. Price to love it as much as he loved it.

60

"I love it," Mr. Price said. "I love it a lot. Except it's . . . no good."

Mr. Jericho Price, Sal thought, looked an awful lot like Chesty's uncle Whitcomb. Maybe twenty years younger, less involved in banking, more involved in girlie pictures and the brown-paper-wrapper stuff sold behind the counter. But otherwise, very similar. Elegant and genteel.

"The production cost," he said, "doing all these separate face cards . . . I was expecting *one* girl, on the back. You've got—what? One, two, three—"

"It's wigs," Wink said. "Two girls with wigs."

Mr. Price looked a little more impressed. "Still, production costs—it's not like a boilerplate—boom, boom, boom, every card the same."

"Mr. Price," Sal said, "how fast is this world changing? How many new things have popped up just since the war?"

"Since *Tuesday*," Reenie said. "Since *breakfast* . . ."

"Do you want to buy a deck of girlie cards next month and find someone else beat you to this idea? Because you weren't sure it would make enough money? That's really your style, being cautious?"

She felt his gaze lingering on her, studying her, and thought for a moment that the look was one of someone about to slap her. As cold as Uncle Whitcomb was, she'd never felt that possibility for an instant. But Mr. Price opted for smiling, not slapping. "We'll make it a larger run," he announced. "Volume. More units, lower cost per unit, more potential sales. Gotta take a risk to make the big bucks. That's my philosophy, anyway."

He shook hands all around with them, stopping at Reenie because she didn't seem to want to let go till he agreed to "be sure to tell that rat Rollo Deininger who beat him when you tell him he lost the pitch."

"With pleasure, my dear, with pleasure." He patted her cheek, mentioning again that soon "you two lovely ladies will be in the hands of men all over the globe." Sal thought she saw Wink wince a little at this, but he held his tongue.

On his way out, she noticed his coat was more of a cape than an overcoat, and he looked slightly Continental, swooping a silk scarf around his neck like a vanilla swirl. Clutching each of their hands a second time, he declared, "It's a pleasure doing business, and it's a business doing pleasure."

A little creepy, Sal thought, the way a phrase like that rolls off the guy's tongue. He might have just left it at *thanks* and a hand-shake.

61

The money from the card deck was just the nest egg they'd been needing to put Sal's plan into action. She wanted to start their own publishing company. Nothing big. They would operate pretty much the same as usual, even continue to sell photos to the existing girlies, but they would also put out their own. Specials, they were called—one-time titles under their own masthead. This meant contracting for print jobs and distribution, but the profit share would be higher.

He would have been fine, himself, just putzing along as they always had, but for Sal, it seemed more like an emotional need, less a business decision. "I want to be in charge," she said. "At least of some of it, some of the time. It's *my* fanny, after all."

He had an impulse to say, *Well, it's not very often your fanny, actually.* Fanny shots were more Reenie's domain. Sal's was nothing to cry about, but her top feature was definitely her top drawer.

He didn't say this, obviously, not looking to have his teeth handed to him, not looking to be out wandering the streets with those ex-GIs who couldn't find a place to live.

"First," she told him, "we need a company name."

Wink thought S&W Publishing would pretty much cover it, but Sal thought it was "too bland; too forgettable." Plus, she wasn't sure, but she felt as if there was *already* a publisher with, if not exactly that name, something close enough to be confusing. "And then there's the issue of Reenie, her feeling left out."

Reenie wouldn't be involved financially in this, just the modeling and art directing she already did, for her regular cut of the fee. But he saw her point. Reenie might still take it wrong. There was no accounting for Reenie.

"Hey!" Sal said, "how about Left-Hand Publishing? On account of all your—well, *both* of our, really—personal setbacks we had to overcome and make do, not just your hand, but . . ."

Personally, he wasn't so keen on a name that made it sound like you maybe held the magazine with your left hand to free up your right.

In the end, they settled on S&W. Reenie would just have to get over herself if she felt left out.

They managed to put out two specials in the first month operating as S&W Publishing. In the interest of keeping things friendly, one was called *Winkin' with Weekend Sally,* starring Sal, and the other, *A Weekend with Winkin' Sally,* featured Reenie. The latter was shot up at Reenie's brother's rustic cabin in Wisconsin; the former shot around the Loop—right in the alley next door and Grant Park for the harmless stuff, Sal walking around in the wind, turning actual, real-life nonmodel heads when her skirts got away from her. (The topless stuff was all done in the studio, on a park bench one of Reenie's brothers "borrowed" from the city a few years back that had been sitting in her mother's rose garden all this time. Reenie found a guy to help Wink borrow it once again.)

She also brought in a couple friends for cheap temporary help on the pasteup, including her former partner from her brief stint in advertising, Cal from LD&M, whom she obviously was seeing now, at least on some level. Wink tried not to react when he caught a glimpse of her, late one night, goosing the guy as he bent over the layout table. The rest included a hatchet-faced young guy named Hef who had a day job as an intern over at *Es-quire* and all variety of overeager notions about what they should do that went on and on and on.

Sal confided in him the second night Hef was around that the kid made her anxious. "All that energy! He's like a Pepsi-drinking, pipe-smoking machine you can't shut off! We don't need to reinvent anything," she said. "Let's just keep it simple and put this out at a profit."

"Okay," Wink said. He'd come to find that, all in all, Sal's plans were generally always okay.

It was also Sal's idea, in the interest of boosting goodwill with the man they now called Sunshine State, the grumpy proprietor of the neighborhood news shop, to give him a special rate on their S&W titles—for him, they would work directly, cutting out, for his store only, the distributor they'd acquired. In exchange, she felt certain he would give them special placement on the shelves, maybe push the titles with his regulars. "Think of it as a foothold," she said. "If it works, we expand the offer to a few other places around the area, maybe even regionally. It's a little more work, but it's a way to get some notice, have it build. . . ."

Wink saw himself in a truck, delivering the things store by store, but she told him that would never happen. "Limited offer," she said. "Just enough to get things rolling. And if nothing else comes of it, at least good ol' Sunshine might be a touch more polite next time we're supposedly 'loitering.'"

When she presented the idea to the man himself, disguised in a dark wig, she took along an autographed photo and signed it for him from Weekend Sally with big Xs and Os and suggested he put it on display over his stool.

The man's grumbles and gripes seemed to drop down a full

register. "So that's you, then, lady? With your butt-knocks hanging out and all?"

Sal gave him a wormy smile. "In the flesh!"

Wink noticed, as they were leaving, that the publicity photo was actually one of Reenie, with a sun hat barely covering her bare ass, pouting over her shoulder. He recognized her back. But he didn't say anything. He was sure Sal was more than aware and knew what she was doing.

A week or so after the first special came out, he was up on a stepladder behind the counter, rearranging boxes of flashbulbs, and Sal was at the other end, balancing the cash drawer, when Mr. Price walked in with two bouquets of cream-colored roses.

He said, "One is for you, Mrs. Chesterton, and—"

"The other's *all* mine!" Wink called down from the ladder.

Mr. Price glanced up, acknowledging him with a weak smile, then returned his attention to Sal. He told her the other bouquet was of course for her friend, Miss Rooney—"Or is she going by 'Winkin' Sally' these days?"

This guy made him even edgier now that Reenie had managed to learn more about their onetime client, apparently from her brother Dennis. Jericho Price, it was said, traded in more than girlie pictures or even dirty pictures, his most legitimate enterprise being prizefighters—he was said to back a few title contenders, in fact—but Wink assumed being a promoter was just a sliver of his involvement in the fight world.

Of course they were learning this a little late in the game— a fact he found rather annoying. It sounded like maybe Reenie could have dug up a tad more background on the guy before they conducted business with him on the card deck. For one thing, he might be one of those guys who, if you *conduct* business with them, presto chango!—you're *in* business with him. That wasn't what he and Sal had in mind.

Now Mr. Price was saying he'd heard a few things around, rumors only, about them starting their own publishing venture and trademarking the two girls, and he said it in such a disbelieving way that Sal was quick to say—almost bragging, Wink felt—that it was absolutely true; they'd done all those things since the last time they saw him.

Mr. Price's look of concern seemed almost fatherly. "Oh, I wish you hadn't done that, my dear. Risky, going out on your own like that, the little guy, all alone. It sounds like fun at first, but there are a variety of obstacles and headaches that may befall you that you will *not* see coming, I promise you."

He took a moment to tsk-tsk and shake his head, casting his eyes down to the glass display case and polishing it with his cuff in a way that looked absentminded.

But then he somehow managed to perk up, smiling again, beaming back at them. "Well! No reason to fret: if you ever feel the need for a partner in this venture—or you would like to be rid of it entirely—merely give me a jingle."

It gave Wink the creepy crawlies, the way he said *jingle*. It was like a man of his stature and influence asking if there was a *little boys' room* where he might go *tinkle*.

62

It was the anniversary of their anniversary and, admittedly, she'd had a few. *Sauced,* Wink would say she was, which was probably a load of hooey because she could still feel her legs, so what the hell did he know? *Big judgmental lug . . .*

Just to make sure, she started feeling her legs, and they felt great, leaning over in her kitchen chair and running her hands down the length of them. It was some time ago now that she and Reenie had gone out and each purchased a pair of actual nylons—their first since the war, not counting the giant-sized black-market fiasco—and *her* pair had been sitting in her top drawer, remaining untouched in their original package like prissy, nonparticipatory little prudes while Reenie's pair was no doubt ruined by now, with scandalous runs from some guy's greedy, grabby paws, probably lost in some bachelor's couch cushions somewhere in the city, maybe snaked around a bedpost, maybe even in the apartment of Mr. Judgy McJudge'em down the hall.

Practically *anywhere,* Reen's hose could be now! The girl had an old prewar Buick some new guy had just out and out given her for "no reason," and she was lately forever driving all over the city, to this party and that. . . . *Crazy* . . .

The motion of leaning over, feeling herself up, made Sal a little tipsy and light-headed, so she stopped and sat up, still admiring how great they looked.

What a gyp, she thought. *A person's anniversary, and no one to even comment on that person's great-looking legs, let alone* . . .

She remembered the last time he'd told her she was sauced— the night she got a little tipsy because it was Chesty's birthday, back when they still counted, when he was alive, and she unbuttoned his shirt and took a big whiff of him.

Wink, that is, not Chesty. Wink's chest . . .

And where *was* that long, man-smelling judgy man, anyway? What did a person have to do around here to just smell a good-looking man once in a blue moon, it being a special occasion and all?

Pushing herself up from the kitchen table, she first put away the bottle so he wouldn't judge, then went out into the hall and meant to knock on his door, and perhaps she did, but it seemed as if he simply appeared, opening up and stepping out. Maybe he'd heard her coming.

When she spoke, it didn't come out nearly as clear or forceful as she'd hoped: "Sorry I said all that . . . mean stuff . . ."

He looked puzzled. "Mean stuff?"

It dawned on her that she hadn't said anything, just drinking alone in her kitchen, so she moved on. "I got married today. We were married."

He just nodded a little and pulled her close. She was still talking, trying to tell him something, though she wasn't clear what, so her mouth was still somewhat open when it landed on him, on his neck, and she felt the salt of his skin against her lips and wondered if he would think she'd kissed him. She hadn't meant to. She could smell the starch in his shirt collar and just a hint of sweat and tobacco and maybe perfume—Reenie's, still, or someone else now? maybe just hair oil?—and she wanted to smell him again like that last time, smell his chest for just a second.

She pulled away a little, unsure herself if it was in order to step away or just to unbutton his shirt and smell his chest. He let her go, his hands lingering lightly on her arms as if meaning to steady her, and something in his eyes that she caught only out of the corner of hers, as she looked down now, at his shirt, looked about as much like pity as she thought she could bear.

She opened her mouth to tell him off or thank him or cry, she wasn't sure, but something else happened instead. It was hard to think of it as a kiss. It was more like she pressed her mouth against his to keep herself from yelping and breathed in deeply and held her breath, not moving from this perilous perch until a sob came over her that came crashing out, and she let go, turning away, unable to look him in the eye, and went back into her apartment and closed the door, knowing she'd be out flat in a matter of seconds and wouldn't remember much of this in the morning, thank God.

63

He rose before he heard her stirring down the hall and slipped out, leaving through the back door of the shop. His first stop was the hotel he'd first stayed in—when was that? Jesus, over two *years* ago . . . What the hell had he been doing sitting down the hall from her like a maiden aunt for two-plus goddamn years? It was sick, this thing they had. He couldn't very well put the make on his dead buddy's wife, but he also couldn't just sit there like a nutless pansy.

It took almost five minutes to raise a response at the front desk. The fact that the desk clerk appeared in his bathrobe, none too pleased to be answering the bell, did not bode well for their having a room. "What," the guy said, an entirely new guy since he'd last been there, "the NO VACANCY sign was too complicated for you?"

After explaining that the kid was a smartass and possibly looking to have his teeth handed to him, Wink asked about potential vacancies, anything coming up in the near future. "Long term, I'm talking about." It didn't make any difference in the answer he got, other than the addition of a *sir,* and the kid lowering his voice.

His next stop was the news shop, to get the papers and scour the apartment listings.

It was incredible. A year after the boys had started coming home, and there still wasn't enough room for them. The only listings were in Elmhurst, Park Ridge, Mount Prospect, Downers Grove, Palatine—places that seemed as far-flung as Tunisia.

On the off chance he might have heard of something, he asked the old grouch who owned the shop. "Listen, *you* see people every day, you hear stuff—I should ask you: got any idea where I might rent a room?"

"And I should ask *you*," he said, "got any idea where I could maybe rent a unicorn?"

So that was that. He stopped for a couple bear claws in a sack, breakfast for him and his "roomie," and started home, turning, somewhere en route, toward Union Station.

He was on his uncle Len's farm in St. Johns, Michigan, by late afternoon. It was the heart of soft red winter wheat season, so his uncle wasted little time on catching up and instead put him immediately to work on the combine.

He hadn't seen the old guy in years, but he didn't look significantly different. He claimed his old bedroom hadn't changed, either. "It's always here for you," he said. "Kept it just like it always was."

Which wasn't even remotely accurate, Wink saw, when he finally went up to wash for supper. His old bed remained, true, and his bookshelf and the birch-bark lamp he'd made, but a lot of the clutter was gone. Also missing was the rest of the furniture, replaced by a long metal and glass rectangle crammed into one end of the room that looked to be—and the lingering odor confirmed it—a chick incubator.

The majority of pictures he'd tacked up were gone, replaced with a couple sketches he recognized as his own that he was pretty sure he'd never hung himself, certainly not framed, as they now were. The calendar hadn't been touched. It was an Elvgren boilerplate, compliments of a Saginaw seed company for the year 1941—the one called *A Knockout,* with the smiling blonde in the corner of a boxing ring, wearing boxing gloves and leaning casually on the ropes like it was all over. One of the man's least steamy, so Wink wasn't that surprised his uncle had failed to purge it.

He recalled having stacks of books that had piled up on the floor, overflowing the bookshelf. And a dresser, topped with a collection of rocks and other treasures he'd found, plus a desk, scattered with more of the same, including jelly jars, containing various homemade experimental rocket fuels, and the science project he'd made in the eighth grade—a working model of stalactites and stalagmites using yarn and reservoirs of water and washing soda. It hadn't been pretty, and it had smelled moldy even back then, but it hadn't been easy to make, so he'd been reluctant to pitch it.

The rug was new—a gaudy rag oval that looked like his uncle had run a circus tent through his combine, though more likely something purchased at a craft bazaar at the church. The souvenir pennant from a Tigers game he'd been too young to remember attending was still there, faded a slate gray and peach and thumbtacked to the back of the door.

After supper, out on the old glider on the screened-in porch, Wink finally dropped a hint that he'd actually found his room to be a little more sparse than he recalled.

"Well, I pared it down some, sure. But the *essentials* haven't changed. I didn't toss any of the important stuff, is what I meant."

Wink asked him specifically about his missing science project.

"Did you become a scientist? You did not. So how important could it have been? You hang on to what you need. The *rest . . .*"

He flicked at the air like he was brushing away a bug. Maybe he was.

"Plus, you got rid of my old desk and my dresser . . . What is that—an incubator?"

Uncle Len grinned. "Last year I hatched two hundred baby chicks in there." He appeared to be proud of himself.

Wink stared at him. This is what happened when men were allowed to remain bachelors for so long.

"I'm not lying."

He told his uncle he didn't think he was lying; that he could still pick up faint whiffs of "something I'd call Eau de Bad Easter."

The old man snorted. "Nephew, are you unable to open a window?"

"I *did*, believe me. And it was nice to see you hadn't gotten rid of the *windows* . . ."

"You've still got that smart mouth, I see. I'm sure that served you well in the big city?"

"Yes, sir."

"And the war?"

"There, too. The United States military values nothing higher than a smart mouth."

Uncle Len chuckled, then seemed to choke it back, and he reached over, still looking out at the darkening fields, not looking Wink's way, and clamped him firmly on his shoulder. Wink took the cue to look away, too, but sit still and listen: the man had rarely touched him, even when he was little, so this meant he had something important to say.

"I'm sure you were disappointed about your hand, Nephew. Real disappointed—your drawing hand and all. And that *is* too bad. But I don't mind telling you, I was praying real hard every night that you'd just make it back."

For a second, Wink felt guilty for not coming to the farm sooner, but weighing people down with guilt wasn't really his uncle's habit, and sure enough, as if reading his mind, Uncle Len added, "Didn't have to be *here*, of course—just *back*."

When they turned in and he was back in his room, he stood studying the moonlight pouring in on the incubator and wondered if he'd be able to sleep with that thing in his room. Even empty of chicks, it did in fact retain an odor. And it made him think of babies and breeding, that impulse to see life continue—as if some cosmic commanding officer in the sky or maybe in their blood told them *As you were, soldier*—that all his fellow GIs seemed to embrace so strongly these days, and he had yet to feel.

The old farmhouse was so quiet. He tried to listen for sounds from the next room, but he couldn't make any out. He'd gotten pretty used to at least hearing footsteps and the occasional piece of furniture shifting down the hall and the city outside, rattling itself.

He stood there, looking down at the fields and the darkness stretching out for miles. If he had to long for her, he guessed he'd rather do it close up.

His uncle really didn't seem hurt or put out when he took the first train back the next morning.

Leaving Union Station, he decided to stop at the Zim Zam for a new sack of bear claws, even though these, too, were not the freshest this late in the day, and even though she wasn't expecting bear claws and he hadn't even told her where he was going, anyway.

At the camera shop, she was back behind the counter. She gave him a normal enough smile and a hello, and he offered her some of the pastry as if he hadn't disappeared for a day and a half. She probably assumed he'd been staying at Reenie's or something. She didn't ask, and he made no mention of what happened in the hallway the other night.

They were stuck with each other, no matter how cockeyed things had become between them; no matter if he *was* starting to wonder if he wasn't maybe a little in love with her.

64

A few days after she embarrassed herself with Wink—and, she suspected, nearly scared him off—Mort Doerbom, the lawyer, stopped by. He'd always appeared chipper and fresh scrubbed when he was helping them form S&W Publishing and set up the legal papers for the trademarks and all of that, but today she noticed he sported an actual carnation in his lapel.

For some reason, she found herself feeling a little glad that Wink was out visiting a printing plant. Maybe it was because, though Mort had been nothing but kind to them, taking what she considered a very minimal fee, considering what she'd heard a lawyer's help would cost, Wink had made a few disparaging remarks behind his back. It seemed uncharacteristic of Wink, who could be cutting at times, but only when someone was asking for it. She recalled how he'd described Mort after the two men first met: "I don't know," he'd said. "This character Doerbom— he strikes me as a guy who should wear glasses."

She told him Mr. Doerbom probably didn't need glasses. As a customer, he never squinted at his negatives or his prints, which he nonetheless examined carefully each time right at the counter before leaving the shop.

"I'm not saying he needs glasses but shirks them; I'm saying he just . . . should wear glasses. By rights."

She still wasn't clear on what he was getting at. Maybe it was some sort of 4-F, goldbricker crack, but when she asked him to clarify further, he couldn't—just said, "Forget it, Sal," shrugged his shoulders, and retreated into the darkroom.

If it was meant to be a crack, it wasn't one of his best, and she wondered why he couldn't do better.

When Mr. Doerbom came by now, starting off asking if she had any issues or questions about the forms he'd helped her file, he led so quickly into a question about having dinner, at first she put the two subjects together and told him if they were going to discuss business, she'd have to check with Wink; that she didn't know his schedule.

"Forgive me, Mrs. Chesterton," he said, looking a little embarrassed. "I'm afraid I haven't been clear, but I meant this not so much as a business dinner but rather, socially—a chance for the two of us to—"

"Oh. Right."

She was still thinking of Wink, actually—thinking he might walk in, back early from the printers, and it was with the further thought that perhaps if she opened herself up to such offers a little, she might not find herself at such a humiliating low point as she had the other night, lonely and drunk.

So she told him that would be fine, but reminded him that it hadn't been quite a year since her husband passed, so she would ask that he consider the socializing aspect of the dinner as being "very low key." She felt rude saying it, but he seemed pleased all the same.

As they settled their plans, she agreed to meet him at the restaurant, thinking, for now, there was no reason to advertise to Wink or Reenie or anyone else for that matter that she was possibly—maybe—going on a sort of a *date,* of all things.

65

They figured they were safe enough, given it was September and a little cold to go into the water. The chance of unwanted company, it seemed to him, was slim. He wasn't sure which one of the two girls came up with North Shore Beach—it was a bit of an expedition, all the way up past the Loyola campus—and he hadn't been able to picture which beach it was before they arrived. But when he saw it, lurking quietly at the end of North Shore Avenue, he was glad they'd taken the trouble to travel so far. Oak Street Beach, for example, facing every window on the north side of the Drake Hotel, would have been far more convenient but far less private, open in a big expansive arc to the snooty Gold Coast—the home, of course, of Chesty's rich guardians—besides affording an unobstructed view to every driver and passenger among the constant stream of traffic whizzing along Lake Shore Drive.

This section of beach, in contrast, seemed like a secret; an afterthought tacked on, off to one side, of a residential dead end, shielded from the houses by a very comforting treeline. The nearest prying eyes, it seemed, would probably have to be way on the other side, unseen, over in Michigan, fifty miles to the east.

It was overcast, the big heavy gray sky, in fact, reminding him of Michigan, the time spent on his uncle's farm. It felt just about as isolated as that. The greatest potential for interruption, he felt, lay in the gulls. They pecked and jabbered at the sand, feeding off some sort of miniature fish that silvered the beach.

Even Reenie, normally game for most anything, appeared to be a little thrown by the carpet of dead sardine-sized fish. She kicked at them with the side of the sneakers she had yet to shed. Sal seemed more interested in getting the beach towels arranged in a position that would put them at nice angles and still frame the long perspective of the shoreline, while simultaneously pestering him about f-stops and the possible need for a filter to correct the overcast sky.

There wasn't any clever story here today or any sort of special props, other than the beach towels and suntan lotion they'd brought more as practical concerns than as gimmicks for visual gags. He'd suggested a picnic basket and an inflatable beach ball or perhaps an inner tube, but the girls had nixed both of these ideas. "Naw," Reenie had said. "Gee, let's just *go to the beach.* You know?"

But now, planning to change into their suits by taking turns holding up the beach towel, ass out to Lake Michigan, Wink suggested he shoot that as well, maybe work it into more of a "narrative," as the publishers of *Wink* and *Titter* had always encouraged them to do.

So Sal went first, and Reenie clowned it up, holding the towel but posing as well, cocking her hip and glancing over her shoulder with an *uh-oh* pout, as if they were being watched.

And, in fact, they *were* being watched. He didn't catch on till several more shots. They were both in their suits now, Reenie in one of those new two-pieces, lying facedown on her towel. Thinking "narrative," he had Sal sit up on her elbows—great shot deep down the cleavage—and reach out, leering mischievously over her sunglasses, as if undoing the ties on Reenie's top. Then he shot another in which Reenie appeared to sit up—they could shoot a close-up later, maybe of Sal's hand smacking her on her back or a crab placed there or a splash of cold water—and he got off a couple of nipple peepers as she gaped, wide eyed, her mouth a perfect O, Sal grinning like a scamp, and then one more in which nothing showed, technically, but Reenie was up on both knees, clutching at her bosom, fingers splayed to reveal more flesh than hide it, looking like she had her hands full, a minor crisis.

He was about to shoot the capper—Sal standing behind her, being a pal now, tying her friend's top back up, when he heard a single evolution—one slow windup—of a police siren. It faded just as suddenly, but it was enough to make him trip over a leg of his tripod and make Reenie fumble for her top, and Sal scramble to cover herself with her towel, though they were in bathing suits, for the love of Mike, at a public beach, with no one else around—no children, clergy, old men with heart conditions. Not even a stray dog.

Just a cop.

The cop had pulled down there to "coop," as Wink had heard it called. He was sure of it: when the guy cuffed them and put them in the cruiser, Wink noticed he had a pillow up front with him and a blanket, a thermos, a copy of *Esquire,* and what looked like a corned beef sandwich wrapped in waxpaper. This was probably his secret secluded spot where he took a nap every day, and no one was the wiser. Except today the guy pulled in, saw them shooting on the beach, and decided, since it had plopped right into his lap with virtually no effort on his part, he would do some bona fide police work for a change.

On the ride in to be booked, Wink tried to appeal to him. Remembering the guys who'd let him go, way back when he had just arrived in Chicago, he asked this guy if he knew them.

"A beat cop named Joe?" the officer repeated. "Seriously? You're asking do I know a Joe? Way down in the Loop?"

"Or the other guy. He had a partner."

The cop was clearly laughing at him now. Wink was beginning to wish he still had his Purple Heart with him.

"Oh, this Keystone Kop doesn't know anybody!" Reenie sneered. "What are you talking about?" She leaned forward between him and Sal, getting up closer to the back of the cop's head, and Wink could see the flash of her dark eyes. He imagined she'd been nipping at her liquid courage right before the shoot began. "This clown's too busy sneaking off and taking naps to ever get to know any other cops, isn't that right?" Clearly, she was looking to take a different approach than he'd been hoping to try. He sort of doubted anger and ridicule would save the day, but it was too late now. Reenie was on a roll: "You're that dwarf in the cartoon picture, right—Sleepy? That's you? Listen, Melvin Purvis, aren't we keeping you from your beauty rest? Why don't you let us go and go back to your little cooping nest and curl up with your blanky? Have your little nappy-wappy?"

Sal managed to hook her friend with her elbow and pry her back in the seat. "Do us all a favor," she said quietly. "Both of you just clam up, okay?"

He had to admit, as usual, of the three of them, Sal seemed to have the best plan.

It was Sal again who knew whom to call. Mort, the lawyer she'd used to file the trademark registrations, met with all three of them in a small interview room prior to sentencing. He was very reassuring in the things he said, and it was swell of the guy to leg it up there so fast, but Wink would have preferred if the guy were a little more smooth, less nervous, especially in talking to the girls and discussing exactly what did and did not happen. He had a bottle of what appeared to be antacid tablets that he popped like Junior Mints.

Reenie had her own ideas for a legal defense, suggesting they file a Peeping Tom charge against the cop—maybe subpoena his call sheet from the switchboard, try to establish that he'd been parked there long enough to get his jollies, maybe even subpoena the blanket and see if it contained any traces of, as she put it, "horny cop sauce."

Looking at the two of them there, sitting at the table with him, it struck him that he shouldn't ever feel guilty about not making Reenie an "honest" woman. She was lovely and fun and a great pal and sexy as hell, but just seeing her idea of a normal reaction to life's curveballs like this, compared with that of an actual normal woman, say Sal, sitting next to her, made it clear in his mind that he'd done the safe and sensible thing by not making her a mother or a wife.

Her theory was entertaining, and as much as he would have liked to subscribe to it himself—the guy stroking off to the whole scene under his blanket, then buttoning up and busting them— he knew it wasn't true. The blanket was neatly folded, and the engine hood had still been warm when he leaned against it, getting cuffed. No, the cop was a pain, but he wasn't "having his cake and beating it, too," as Reenie cleverly put it at one point.

It seemed clear, the shy way he looked at Sal, this Mort had maybe a little crush on her, and Wink worried at one point, when he started asking for specifics about who was actually exposed and who had done what and for how long, that he might be trying to divvy up the responsibility, maybe hang the bulk of it on Reenie. Except the facts didn't work that way, and anyway, he soon dropped that line of pursuit, telling them it was pretty clearcut, that they'd all be okay.

Originally, the charges were obscenity and indecent exposure. The first charge was thrown out, early on, with the lawyer tossing around phrases like *artistic expression* and *free speech,* which, frankly, Wink didn't get, on account of they weren't shooting a movie and no one had said a goddamn word, but he figured why start now, since they seemed to be persuaded by this, leaving only the indecent exposure rap. Here, the fellow argued that no one was there; that her top had very briefly slipped off; that she wasn't "parading around" while thus exposed. In the end, this Mort character got it all reduced down to a fine of thirty dollars apiece for one count of disturbing the peace.

"The peace of who," Reenie mumbled, "the seagulls?" But she managed to leave well enough alone with a jab of Sal's elbow.

"Let's just go home," Wink said. "We're now, officially, a scourge on society."

Reenie exhaled a small puff of a laugh. Sal didn't seem to hear. She was hanging back, still talking to Mort.

66

Just two days after the arrest at the beach, she received a certified letter from Chesty's uncle Whitcomb, the entire contents of which were:

Shame on you.
  Am withdrawing my services forthwith.

                    Whitcomb P. Chesterton

It was even notarized by someone at his bank. And though he had been acting as a business adviser and custodian on her accounts, she'd never really thought of their relationship as a "service." When she showed it to Wink, he let out a heavy sigh and patted her arm, saying, "Well, why don't we just file this away under 'Unkind and Completely Unnecessary Overreactions'?" and, balling it up, tossed it in the trash can and wrapped his long arms around her.

She didn't let go right away, and he added, whispering into her hair, "Not a very gentlemanly thing to do, I'd say" as he stroked it away from her eyes.

It helped. It really did.

Wink agreed that he must somehow know about their recent arrest. The only other explanation—that Chesty's elderly uncle bought girlie magazines and very recently just happened to recognize her—was too coincidental and far too disturbing to imagine.

Soon it became clear that word *was* somehow getting around. Tiny cousin Mia ventured away from the beauty shop just to appear in person before Sal to disown her—though Sal still remained fuzzy on exactly what level of relation the old crone was severing. And her "Next time you want the wigs, you forget it!" didn't bother Sal. But it did kind of hurt when she said, "Manuela, she would *weep!*" because Manuela had been Sal's mom.

Mia was the same woman who had, theoretically, made no bones about bilking the government during wartime and whose nephew Carlo was widely known to be using the barbershop as a front.

She tapped her bony talons so rapidly against the display counter, the clacking on the glass sounded like a woodpecker. "I know why you get the wigs. You make the dirty! You no get extra eggs, extra butter, extra *benzina*—it all for to make the dirty! Shame on top of your head!"

At which point, she reached up with a tottering little hop and rapped Sal sharply on top of her head.

"Ow," Sal said. "What the hell?"

When she left the shop, she backed out the whole way, as if afraid to turn her back, and she was muttering *puttana*, which Sal felt pretty sure meant *whore*.

Two days after that, a brown-papered package the size of a footlocker arrived by courier. Sal tipped the delivery boy and followed him back to the door to lock it behind him. The package had no return information on it, and she didn't like the looks of it.

Cutting the jute away, peeling back the butcher paper, she found it *was* a footlocker. She lifted the lid, saw something dark and mysterious topped by tissue and a regal-looking calling card embossed with the initials SEC. It was from Sarah Chesterton. She'd written:

> For further "art projects," dear. Thought you might stay
> indoors with this. I must confess, I myself found it quite
> irresistible for such repose, in my day.
>   Not a word to Whitcomb!

It was furry under the tissue paper. And heavy. Bravely, she dug it out and lay it out on the floor. It was a full-size, luxuriant, snarling bear rug.

It felt as if a full minute passed before she could even move.

Less amusing, but equally disturbing, she received a call that same day from Mort Doerbom, explaining that the *Herald-*

American had just run a small item about the arrest. "They didn't name the shop, Sal, nor include the address, but it does say that 'those taken into custody are alleged to also operate a camera shop in the Loop reputed to be a front for degenerate smut.'"

"*Reputed?* Who's reputing *that?*"

"Well, basically, *they* are. Just them. I'm sorry, Sal. But as long as it's all sort of anonymous, they're in the clear."

She asked if it was in all the papers, and he said it wasn't in the *Trib*. Hearing that, she suspected that might have been why the stinkers at the *Herald* included that unnecessary information about the shop. They probably knew of her occasional association with the *Trib*. Or Wink's great photo for them back in May.

Rotten stinkers . . .

"Also . . . ," he said.

"Also? There's an *also?*"

Mort tended to cough a lot as he spoke, at least lately. She didn't remember any sort of tic like that when he'd been an occasional customer.

He told her he'd received a phone call from a Mr. Jericho Price, who he believed was a boxing promoter, but he presented himself as a "free speech advocate," a phrase Sal had never heard and imagined Mr. Price had cooked up for the occasion. "He asked to cover my expenses, Sal. I told him there weren't any. I hope that was, well . . ."

She could tell he was feeling a little awkward about this. It probably wasn't quite the picture he'd had of her when he first started coming into the camera shop, back when she was a married, decent woman, and how much easier that might be for him now, if she weren't the kind of woman who owned a genuine bearskin rug, on which she very well might pose naked for photographs.

67

Something was different this time. These guys had shinier suits and noses that looked broken. They didn't flop out their badges, and they didn't scour the room as they talked but kept their eyes on him the whole time, staring him down.

Also, they didn't pepper him with questions. They approached, and he expected to hear the usual *Are you a subversive?* but what they said wasn't even a question:

"It's not so good, the things you're doing."

He asked for clarification on this, and the guy said, "What *could* it mean? It means what it means, friend."

The other guy took this opportunity to jab him in the chest with a big finger. "Yeah. *That's* what it means."

At the door, as they left, the first one almost smiled. "We'll be seeing you."

Wink had a strong feeling they would, even when he didn't know they were there.

68

Shopping for proper stockings one day, ones with actual price tags in an actual store, Sal found herself blurting it out, for no real reason she could understand, telling Reenie that she'd been seeing Mort Doerbom.

"The character got us off the hook up at the beach?" Reenie

shot her the elbow and, of course, a wink. "That's the way, kiddo! Just about time you start, I'd say." Privately, Sal thought Reenie was hardly the one to be preaching about moving on, but let her friend continue her chatter. "An *attorney at law,* no less! Say, he got any friends? I can't seem to reel in any of these good-looking artsy-fartsy boys."

Sal could see that she meant to poke fun at Wink, saying that. Yet she noticed it didn't seem to keep her from giving the guy an occasional thrill.

"Maybe I'll pick out an Uncle Moneybags for myself," Reenie announced. "Some sweet, sweet sugar-daddy who'll put me through art school."

She was clowning around, but the Uncle Moneybags comment kind of stung. Sal told her it was nothing like that, that yes, Mort had taken her for a nice dinner, but mostly, she was just trying to get out there and give it a try again while keeping it very casual, taking "baby steps." She explained that he was a camera bug and belonged to several clubs that went on bimonthly photography excursions, and that was more the type of thing she'd been doing with him. "Like this evening," she said, "we're going to tour an applesauce factory."

Reenie eyed her blankly. "You're putting me on. Is that some kind of slang for something?"

"Like *banana oil?*" Sal had to laugh. "No, it's an actual factory that makes applesauce. We'll be taking pictures."

"Brother . . . ," Reenie said.

"I'd rather you didn't say anything to Wink. Or anybody, I mean. I'm not sure yet how I—"

Reenie rolled her eyes. "Don't worry, I won't! I'm not sure I could keep a straight face."

Sal left it at that and didn't tell her the rest, though Reenie's comment about keeping a straight face reminded her of it—she'd felt almost that same pressure to compose herself at the end of their last date. It was the first time since the tenth grade that she'd kissed anyone other than Chesty—excluding, of course, that strange run-in with Wink the night of her anniversary, the nature of which she still couldn't quite catalog. That had felt more like a drunken fumble, like a fuzzy dream. With Mort, it had incontrovertibly been a kiss, not so much because she felt more than she had with that blurry slipup with Wink—she didn't, actually—but because this time, she'd known it was coming and allowed it. Mort had asked, "May I kiss you, please?" and she'd nodded, which was assent enough, and she hadn't moved away—though of course she didn't exactly step into it— and it was all she could do to keep from trembling.

69

He woke to a metallic rapping downstairs, like someone knocking on the front door with a cane.

Wink was on the floor. Reenie was there, in the narrow bed. She'd spent the night, but as far as he could tell, she'd only done so in order to kick him to the floor. They hadn't fooled around— an activity that had become more and more infrequent, as of late.

"What the good Lord . . ." she said.

Pulling on his pants, he lurched out into the hall, ready to step down the stairs for a peek, but Sal was already up and standing out there, listening. She pulled him into her apartment, handing him a cup of coffee and leading him over to the front window. Kneeling on the big steamer trunk that served as a window seat, and that he'd always thought of as Sal's hope chest, he unlatched the window and got a blast of brisk autumn morning and a glimpse of a solid man, bird's-eye view, stationed at the front door.

Wink called down to him: "It's Sunday, friend. Day of rest, you know?"

The guy looked up at him, and he realized he'd studied that sad face for hours. It was the maimed vet from his photo. The metallic rapping had come from his prosthetic hand.

"Day of rest," the guy repeated. "Not a problem. I was just looking to rest my boot in your ass."

He rapped on the glass again, only this time, lining it up, Wink had a good hunch he was actually pointing to the clipping of the photo he'd had in the *Tribune* back in May—his depth-of-field "assignment." Sal had pasted it up there months ago, with a hand-lettered note that read:

OUR OWN WINK DUTTON ! !
Come In & Have This <u>PRO</u>
Help You w. <u>Your</u> Prints.

"Someone told me they saw this here. You this Dutton character? The guy took my picture without my say-so?"

Wink started to say he was very far away, meaning when he shot the photo—not sure himself how that made any difference, legally or morally—but the guy was taking it another way.

"Then come down and talk to me man to man, you can't hear so well up there . . ."

It was hard to judge if he meant that sincerely—if the guy would wait and hear him out before getting to the part where he would rest his boot in his ass. He sounded more and more reasonable, but the metal hook he had for a hand still looked awfully steely.

Wink was already feeling some relief that this was what it was apparently about—that it wasn't yet another cop or mysterious government man or lurking threat in the shadows—though he wondered if this confrontation hadn't somehow been triggered by the recent beach bust. Possibly, they'd brought more attention on themselves because of that—folks starting to know who they were and talk about them, especially around the neighborhood. He wasn't sure he liked that, the public connecting their work to the shop, to where they lived.

"We should feed him," Sal whispered, pressing on his back, trying to see around him. "It's the *least*. And maybe he'll be more reasonable, after a full meal."

He heard Reenie sneering back there behind him, "Your cupboard is bare, Mother Hubbard. Unless you just want to give him the last of that coffee and some toast. Plus, you don't want that mug up here. Looks a little nervous-in-the-service, you ask me. Very well could be a shell shock, go wild man on us."

She said she had an idea. Wink turned to see she'd just about finished pulling on her street clothes and her jacket and was heading for the stairs. He said nothing. If he'd learned anything about these two gals in the last two and some years, it was that he knew nothing. There would be little point in trying to guess what Reenie was about to do, let alone stop her. And then there was the sound of the back door downstairs, Reenie slipping out into the alley, gone.

So they watched, leaving the window cracked, peering down on the steamed marine.

Every now and then he'd squint back up at them and scowl, but it felt to Wink like the guy was losing just a little of his steam, as if each scowl felt a little more forced, each second a little more awkward.

Wink was starting to consider the idea that Reenie's plan was possibly to ditch them, just tear out the back, every man for herself, as it were. He hadn't exactly been her favorite person these days, even if she had commandeered his bed last night. He even wondered if Sal had confessed to her about the night she got drunk and weepy over her wedding anniversary and kissed him— or rather, to be more accurate, jammed her mouth against his and breathed until she sobbed. Fun stuff to be sure, and nothing he had any say in, really, but maybe Reenie would have felt territorial about it even though she seemed to have moved on from such feelings and didn't, mostly, give a hang. Still, one never knew.

"There she is," Sal said.

Wink spotted her, too, turning the corner at the end of the block. She'd come around the long way and was heading in their direction, swinging her pocketbook as if out for a Sunday stroll, not even looking straight ahead at the one-handed marine taking up sidewalk.

When she bumped into him, Wink saw the look on her face and guessed at the general direction this was going to go: she was going to do her best acting routine.

Sal cracked the window a hair more so they could hear.

"Cheese and crackers!" she said, practically gulping with the wide-eyed ingenue bit and touching his chest where she'd just plowed into him. "I'm *so* sorry. But say! Don't I know you?"

They were looking down at basically the top of his head, but they didn't need to be able to see his face any better to know the guy was thrown.

"Hold on a sec! You're *him.* You're the handsome marine from the paper." Now she was the one rapping on the glass, pointing to the clipping in the window. "Sure! Why, I've stared at that photograph so many times!"

The guy appeared to be having some trouble forming words.

"I swear I have! Almost *too* many times, really."

Wink exchanged a sideways glance with Sal. That crack had been for him, he was sure. Which wasn't fair—he'd never really bothered her with his work, anything other than the girlies.

"Say," she said again, digging through her pocketbook like a rabid squirrel. "Would you mind terribly giving me your autograph? My friends will never believe I met an honest-to-goodness cultural icon!"

The marine was speaking up now, finally forming words. "Lady, I don't know what you just called me, but—"

"That's how I heard it described, just the other day. Someone describing that photograph of you. A cultural icon, they said."

It was nice to know she was still reading the art critics, trying to improve her understanding, though he was pretty certain whoever used the term wasn't talking about his photo in the *Trib*.

"Please," she said, handing him an envelope and what looked like maybe an eyebrow pencil. "Please just sign your name. You don't need to write it out personal or anything. I'd *really* appreciate it."

Oh Christ, Wink thought. *What if he's a lefty?*

But he wasn't. He took the envelope and eyebrow pencil in his good hand and, as Reenie turned to offer her back as a writing surface, winking up at them, the marine pinned the envelope in place with his prosthetic and wrote with his right.

He must have scribbled it, though, because when he handed it back to Reenie she squinted at it disapprovingly and said, "I can't even read what this says . . . Gee, you must still be learning how to use that thing, huh?"

"You making fun or something, sister? It says my name. Keeney. Trust me. Now why don't you—"

She must have sensed, as Wink did, that the guy was about to give her the brush-off and reapply his energy to working his angry-villagers-at-the-gate bit, because she moved in on him again, beaming, all hands, patting him and hooking his arm. "Say! I was just about to collect my friends and get a late breakfast. Are you game?"

The marine shrugged. "Sure. And I can afford to pay my own way, okay? I *do* work, no matter what they're trying to make it look like in this horseshit picture—pardon my French."

Reenie said, "Great," and with that she turned and let herself in with the spare Wink gave her long ago and honestly had forgotten about, and the guy looked frozen in place down on the sidewalk, staring at her slipping into the shop, clearly surprised that the friends they'd be joining included the very guy he was yelling up at. But he didn't walk away, and he didn't rampage in after her. He stood his ground, took off his hat, wiped his forehead with his nonhook hand, and squinted up at him, giving him a smirk like, *Well, don't that just about beat all.*

They rushed back to confer in the hallway.

"He's a lot of bluster," Reenie said, when she met them at the top of the stairs. "I think he just wanted to be asked permission first. We should do this."

So they hopped to, throwing on their shoes and coats, and let her lead on.

Halfway down the stairs, Reenie stopped up short and said, "Listen, you two maybe better act like you're together, and I'll smile and make nice with the one-handed grouch. Don't you think? He seems like putty, if you know what I mean."

He and Sal exchanged an awkward sideways glance. He wasn't sure which one of them spoke up in agreement first, but, of course, it made sense.

Keeney preferred to just be called Keeney.

Sal tried calling him Mr. Keeney and Corporal Keeney a couple times, but it sounded too formal.

Pressed for a first name, the only hint he gave was, "Well, see, I'm half Irish, and I'm half German, on my mother's side, so . . ."

Wink remembered the photo and the name stenciled on his seabag. "His first initial is *A*."

They sat there for a long moment, he and the girls presumably running through the *A*'s.

Reenie was the first to put it together. "*Adolf? Really? Well, I, for one, am not calling you Adolf!*"

Keeney smiled sadly. "Exactly. So it's Keeney."

They'd secured a booth at the Zim Zam, where the breakfast left room for improvement, but it was served late into the afternoon, and the wide windows faced the sun and felt inviting on a chilly September day like this.

Despite his earlier venting outside the shop, he was surprisingly slow in voicing his complaints about the photo, and Wink took this as a good sign—that he waited to examine the menu and order before launching into any real harangue.

He did make a point again of explaining that he wasn't jobless. He said he worked a corner newsstand, which he thought wouldn't be a bad life, if it continued, but he'd like to eventually *own* his own newsstand, if that was going to be his career, not work it for the owner the way he did now in an arrangement that sounded, to Wink, a little better than a sharecropper's setup and a little worse than that of a cabbie who didn't own his hack. "Either own my own corner stand one day, or at least get inside— one of them slightly bigger, indoor deals—a news *shop*. If I have to work for someone else, I might as well be cozy. Don't feature freezing anything *else* off . . ."

Wink liked him for making this crack. The guy was brassy about his handicap without coming off too bitter. According to Keeney, it rarely got in the way with his current work. "In fact, a

couple tasks, it actually helps. I can sling a stack of bound newspapers like nothing, cut the twine if I flick it just right." The
metal on his left glinted in the bright sunlight as he demonstrated.

He said he served aboard a North Atlantic sub that was tor-
pedoed, and he was left floating on a crate in the water so long,
in and out of consciousness, that his fingers rotted and they had
to remove the hand.

"Wink here got himself a Purple Heart, too," Reenie blurted
out, being less than helpful.

"That right?" said Keeney. "Where'd you get it?"

Because the guy didn't seem particularly sarcastic or challenging, Wink decided he must be simply asking where it had occurred.

"Same," he said, withdrawing his bum hand under the table.
"I mean, I was also on a submarine when it happened. . . ."
Hopefully, he could avoid the silly details.

Compared with this guy, he felt like a fraud, and he didn't really appreciate the arched eyebrow Reenie was shooting him
across the table, like she was about to bust out laughing any
second.

He liked the guy. He was bold and funny. And talking to him
here, the four of them getting along now like old pals, it sort of
put things in perspective. So they'd screwed the pooch up at
North Shore Beach and with Sal and her in-laws, the Chestertons, and these strange visits from shadowy men in overcoats
seemed to be on the upswing. . . . Still, obviously, things could
be worse.

He remembered how Uncle Len had always said *Feeling better don't mean feeling better than* and *Life's not a misery contest*—
meaning not to go around grinning because you've lost a row of
corn to locusts but your neighbor's lost sight of the sun on ac-

count of locusts. And it wasn't that—it wasn't just feeling better about things because the guy had a hook while he himself only had some loss of use, *dysfunction,* as the doctor put it. It wasn't a misery contest.

Because things could even be worse for this guy, too. After all, Keeney did still have his dominant hand intact, which was more than Wink could say for himself. If he were truly getting into comparisons, unlike him, the guy could still draw—if he *could* draw. So it wasn't a matter of feeling better through pity.

It just felt nice. It just felt like things could be a hell of a lot worse for Wink if he didn't have great folks to sit with in a booth and just bull and laugh about whatever came up. And it was nice to have another guy be a part of that.

Of course, the fact they were getting along didn't mean the guy didn't let him have it. His objections were quite clear, as if he'd had them ready to lay out for some time now, storing them up to reel off if he ever ran into the "sumbitch who made that picture."

As he counted them off, he touched his hook to his right hand, working his way down the intact fingers. "First of all, I had a job at the time. I was working the afternoon you snapped the photo, actually. Right around the corner there's that outdoor newsstand where I work. Second, I wasn't anywhere near that NO LOITERING sign. You've got it worked out so it looks like I'm leaning up against the mother! Pardon my Swahili, ladies. . . . Any rate, I *wasn't* loitering, I was taking a five-minute smoke break on account of the owner gets all hinky I'm gonna burn his shack down. Had one too many run-ins with O'Bannion and the protection racket back in the dinosaur days. Guy gets worked up anytime some punk kid walks by with a bottle of pop—guy's convinced it could be kerosene . . . Any rate, I'm actually minding the store. Also—"

"But your duffel bag," Sal said, speaking up. "I'm not doubting your claim, but it *appears*—"

"That's my laundry, lady, if that's quite all right with you. I'm waiting for Vin at the cleaners there to reopen after his lunch— you can't see it behind that deli truck that's in the way, sticking out of an alley." He turned back to Wink. "And I know you want that to look like it's want ads I'm reading, like it's job listings, but it's the Business Opportunities section, friend. Big difference. I'm keeping my eyes peeled for someone wants to unload their newsstand, you know—buy my own. Now, the NO VACANCY sign across the street? It says that, partly, on account of me. I got one of the last apartments they had. And the cold cuts part—what is that, some kind of sick crack about my hand? Maybe you need to be a college boy to get that one. That's your idea of a sophisticated joke, yucking it up over the handicapped?"

At this, Wink decided it was time to show him his own hand "in action or, rather, lack thereof." He demonstrated with a fountain pen how he could no longer sign his name even, let alone do the work he'd been trained to do, had his heart set on doing. "I know it's maybe not the same," he said, "but I know *something* about that. A little." Then he told him he was sorry, that he'd write a public letter of apology or maybe request a different sort of retraction, if he wanted, but he should know, a lot of people who saw that photo saw a lot of different things in it. And none of them were meant to ridicule *him*.

"Yeah, I know," Keeney said, waving him off. "Skip the letter. This is just junk I've been saving up. I pretty much figured a lot of that out myself, since. I just promised myself, if I ever met the fella, I'd give him a piece of my mind. So I did. You're lucky— if I'd run into you a few months back, you'da gotten more than a piece of my mind, believe it."

It still felt like he should do something to make it up to the guy, and he had the thought, though he knew better than to promise it yet, that maybe he could talk to the grump at the news shop, that Sunshine character, about taking this guy on. It was the same work, but at least he'd be indoors.

But for now, Wink put out his good hand, which was his left, and Keeney put out his good hand, his right, and they shook, a little awkwardly, like old ladies shake, he thought. But it also felt deeply personal, like he'd known the guy for years, the two of them putting what was left of themselves out there, reaching out with no more apologies or excuses, just clutching hands.

70

If she hadn't gone back for her gloves—the white evening gloves she felt necessary for an opening like the one Mort was taking her to—she would have been in the clear. But she imagined herself among the posh patrons and art critics mingling at the new photography exhibit, a dowdy shopkeeper with fingers pickled from darkroom chemicals, and she insisted they return to the shop.

Mort stayed on the street to smoke his pipe while she looked for the gloves, unsure if they were still in her apartment somewhere or down in the overstuffed prop trunk that had blossomed in the studio area on the first floor.

She heard a man calling *Hello?* and footsteps and knew it was Wink, back from shooting some bridal party portraits. He knocked on her open bedroom door. "Sal? You okay? Why's the front door unlocked and our lawyer's standing out front? Were the cops here? Something happen?"

"No, no," she managed to say.

He tried a smile, but she could see he was confused, anxious. "Doerbom guarding the place or something? We don't have him on that kind of a retainer, I hope."

She pictured the carnation in Mort's lapel. And in an instant, it seemed as if Wink pictured it, too, or put it all together as he took her in, glancing down at her dress for the first time.

"Oh," he said. "Sorry. My mistake." Nodding, red faced, he pulled the door closed behind him, stopping when it was just ajar to say, "You look nice, by the way. Real nice."

She heard him walking slowly down the hall and entering his own apartment, and the radio coming on. She had the gloves now and put them on, then took them off, then tugged them back on, and, thinking of Reenie, took them off once more to dial the phone.

While she waited, she hurried to the window and rapped her ring against the glass to get Mort's attention. When he glanced up, she held up one finger: a minute.

When her friend picked up, she told her what had just happened and asked her to come over and keep Wink company.

"Can't," Reenie said. "Got a date myself. With the *pirate*, if you can feature that . . ."

"Who?"

"The troublemaker with the hook. Keeney. The marine?"

"But—"

"I'm doing you both a large, is the way I see it," Reenie said. "You want another favor on top of—"

"But no one asked you to—"

"Guy appears to be sweet on me, so I figure I let him buy me a nice dinner, listen to his war stories, his *hand* story, he's less likely to come pounding on your door again—maybe sometime when we're both indisposed, if you catch my meaning. I mean, what—we're doing a shoot and he just barges in again? Maybe he sues Wink? Besides, Sal, so what that Wink knows you've got a date? What's *his* beef? He's got no say-so in this. You two have some sort of . . . *thing* you're not—?"

Sal told her she was just concerned he might be a little thrown by it—by any kind of change. And maybe a little hurt that she hadn't confided in him. As a friend.

"Bilge," Reenie said. "If things change around there, I'm sure he'll find another place to live. He's a big boy. People adapt. That's life."

Sal didn't bring up the widespread housing problem these days. Reenie was certainly aware of that. Besides, she was pretty sure her friend wasn't just talking about him having a place to sleep and get his mail. She was talking about learning to look out for herself, putting herself first. But she knew, too, that as much as Reenie had been a part of everything that had happened since Wink came to town more than two years ago, she could never be as in on the little everyday things, the way they inter-acted throughout the day with certain glances and certain *hmms* and grunts and smart-mouthed inside jokes, that made it so com-fortable to think of him remaining down there at the end of the hall until they were both very old. Because even now they felt like an old couple—one that had never actually been a couple, of course, one that had never made love.

"You owe it to yourself to try," Reenie said. "Go. Get out of there."

71

Wink could tell. She had *him* in there, alone in her apartment. He lay there listening to muted conversation, lingering murmurs, for more than an hour, afraid to move for fear of rustling too loud and missing something, though he couldn't make any of it out, anyway. They were getting along—that's all he could tell.

He turned off his reading lamp at twelve-thirty, but was still wide awake at one when there was some kind of an outburst coming from Sal's end of the hall, followed by a general state of ruckus, enough to bring him out into the hallway in time to see Mort leaving, heading down the stairs. It wasn't anger on his face, but something else. And then Sal was right there and they were rushing past too fast for Wink to put it together. "Everything all right?" he asked, but she waved him off, following her new lawyer boyfriend down. She had her hand over her mouth, and at first he thought the guy had gotten rough with her— in which case, he was begging for a soaking, no matter how much she waved him off. Wink hesitated at the top of the stairs, thinking only now to dart back in and grab his bathrobe, which he did, though he imagined after more than two years it couldn't be the first time she'd caught a glimpse of his boxers.

She didn't follow Mort far. Wink heard the jangle of the shop bell as the guy exited into the street, and she started back up the stairs, looking distraught and yet smiling, kind of, shaking her head like she was trying to laugh off a bad piece of news or something.

She was gesturing in the air—a thing she only did when she was pretty worked up. She'd told him once her mother had done that—"got all Italian" with her hands.

"I thought I was ready!" she announced, and Wink shuffled in after her, into her apartment. "I really did. I mean, it's been so long and he really is a dear man, but I guess maybe it's *too* soon or maybe it's been *too long, too* much time has passed, because I . . ." She stopped for a second, as if uncertain she should continue with the details. Wink flopped down on her love seat and waited, bathrobe folded genteelly, crossing his legs like he had all night to hear this. "I *started* giggling, okay? And I just couldn't stop."

She flopped down next to him dejectedly, and he threw his arm around her, giving her a squeeze that made him feel a little like a gym coach about to launch into a pep talk. "Giggling's okay, Sal. Really. Guys like a girl who's . . . you know, having a good time and enjoying herself and . . . It's cute."

She shook her head. "The giggling didn't really start till he got out his *thing*. I tried not to—I bit my lip, actually—but it only got worse and I *don't* think it was okay with him."

Extricating himself, he got up and mixed them both an old-fashioned, assuring her it would happen when it happened. Maybe not with Mort Doerbom, but rushing it wasn't a good idea at all. And even if it had been a while, which maybe it had— Chesty had been dead a year but gone much longer than that— the giggling might be a hint to herself that she was too nervous and needed even more time.

She seemed to be deliberating before announcing, "It was smaller than I remembered. That's why I started giggling."

"Than you *remembered*?" He was confused. "But I thought you and Mort just—"

"Than I remembered . . . you know, *the only other one I've ever seen,* is what I meant." She punched him in the arm, maybe thinking he'd been trying to make a crack. The punch felt awfully like something a sister would do. He hadn't meant to make a crack; he'd just been confused about her sex life and if she already, prior to tonight, had one up and running. He'd been operating under the assumption all along that she hadn't made that step yet, which, apparently, was still true.

Sal took a big swig of her drink, then said, "But maybe my memory's playing tricks on me. Who knows?"

"Maybe . . ."

She elbowed him now, and he turned to see she was waggling her eyebrows, Groucho style, grinning, and nodded at his lap as if . . .

But no. She *had* to be kidding. He just knew she had to. So he played along, leaping from the love seat as if outraged. "Listen here, ma'am! If you're expecting me to whip it out and give you something to compare it to, you can forget it right now, sister!"

She laughed, clearly drunk. He decided she must have had more than a few before he'd mixed the old-fashioneds.

"Seriously. Mine is not to be used for some sort of Gallup Poll. It's *special.*"

She howled, shoving him. "You said *pole!*"

"Unintentional." He took a step toward the door. "Good night, Sal."

"Hey!" She shoved him back down onto the love seat, thumping him on the chest. "Just so we're clear, bub. I didn't want to see your pole, either! I'm still in mourning!"

Mort stood in the half-open doorway. They froze. Wink could feel Sal's hand still lingering on his chest as if stuck there, caught in something sticky.

Mort was studying the floor. "I . . . got to thinking: I let myself out but I can't lock it and I . . . I wanted to make sure you locked it behind me, and you *didn't,* so . . ."

When Sal spoke, it was all Wink could manage to make it out. He wondered how the hell Mort was supposed to hear it all the way across the room. "Thank you, Mort," she said. "That was very considerate of you. I'll be sure to do that."

Mort nodded, still staring down at the floor. The poor guy looked stunned.

"You're very kind, Mort," Sal said, and he nodded twice and

shrank back into the hall, pulling the door only halfway closed behind him, as if unsure of even what was expected of him in this. They listened, neither one breathing, to his footsteps clumping dejectedly down the stairs and then the distant jangle of the shop bell as he let himself out again.

They both swiveled to the window, craning to see just his hat as he hurried back down the street. It looked cold and dead out there, windy with garbage, the streetlights trembling, and then Sal burst out laughing, breathing at last. It was an uncontrollable laugh that bordered on hysterics, he thought—not entirely sure she wouldn't slip into sobbing. But no, she was laughing.

"I hope you're laughing at the situation," he said. "The awkwardness and all . . ."

She couldn't respond other than nodding.

". . . and not *mocking* the Sad Sack."

This made her shriek now, and she added a wavy gesture as if objecting to something she couldn't currently voice, what with all the shrieking and silliness.

"Brother," Wink said.

But she just kept laughing.

"Man alive," he said finally, getting up to take his leave as well now. "You're cold, lady. Very cold. You shall never, ever take the measure of my Gallup pole. That settles it." But he knew he was smiling when he said it.

Just not cackling and guffawing, as Sal continued to do, long after he was back in his own apartment, down the hall.

But going back to bed and going back to sleep were two different things. He found himself wondering if she had really been kidding or not about wanting to compare his pecker. And maybe even horsing around about it was in some way her way of leveling the playing field. After all, he'd seen her naked plenty.

Maybe the decent, gentlemanly thing would have been to just

show her what he looked like. Maybe he should have done that way back, when they were first shooting the girlies. Just to put her at ease, make it more fair.

Christ on a cracker, he thought. *It's almost three in the morning, pal, and you are not thinking straight. . . .*

He told himself he really ought to get up again and lock the door. He didn't really think she would carry the horseplay any further, sneaking into his apartment or anything ridiculous, but he might need to wax the dolphin, just to keep himself as noble and resolute as he wanted to be. He was pretty sure she wasn't ready—for any man—and no amount of kidding around or booze, no matter how outrageous and desperate she was acting, would make her honestly any more ready.

72

Manners told her she should be calling Mort Doerbom and smoothing over her behavior with him, but she found herself, late the next morning, her head still pounding from last night's cocktails, more concerned with smoothing over things with Wink. Her behavior was coming back to her in snatches, and it made her wince, thinking how she'd carried on, teasing Wink about having him whip it out.

She imagined him already packed and gone, scared off by the crazy widow, just as she felt she'd almost done the night she sort of kissed him.

There was no answer when she knocked. His door was unlocked as she pushed it ajar to call his name and heard the shower running. Thinking she'd check for a packed satchel or other signs he was leaving, she opened the door wider.

There was stuff laid out, all right, all over his mattress and chair, which was pulled closer to the bed.

Stepping in, she saw they were magazines—girlie magazines—splayed open and arranged around the bed, with only a small area left to sit back against the dented pillow and the headrest. A jar of Vaseline sat open on the bedside table.

She was about to hightail it out of there when she noticed it was her. Every page had photos of her—some in different colored wigs, one also with Reenie in some kind of a catfight pose, but mainly, it was her.

Turning to leave, she saw him standing there in his bathrobe, dripping wet, looking crushed, she thought, maybe even heartbroken.

"It's none of my business," she said, "but I'm just curious why—"

"Obviously," he said, plain as a radio weather report, "I was waxing the dolphin."

73

In a flurry of picking up and covering up, attending to the bed and the magazines, pulling the covers over the mayhem, putting away the Vaseline, eyes only on the business at hand, he explained the whole deal, how he'd stuck by his self-imposed policy for two years of *only* looking at the photos that actually ran in the magazines. That looking at any pictures of her just lying around the darkroom felt disrespectful, that this way he at least was no different from the average Joe, and—

"By *looking*, you mean . . . What did you just call it? Waxing the . . . ?"

He stopped and faced her. No amount of housekeeping was going to make this better. She'd retreated to the doorway and had her back half turned to him, her own eyes cast down to the worn runner in the hallway.

"Waxing the dolphin," he said. "I figured it was less creepy if I stuck to only what every other guy can get hold of, only—"

He stopped, wondering if he should just say, unapologetically, that every guy waxed the dolphin, tell her to knock next time, and be done with it. But she wasn't bolting; she was sticking it out. So he decided to tell her.

He told her how he'd decided, over time, that he *wasn't* the average Joe because the average Joe looking at her in the girlies didn't see what *he* got to see—a smart, gorgeous woman with an inquisitive mind and a scrappy soul who made him laugh and believe in himself and want to get up every morning. "The rack," he said, "is swell, too."

She looked him in the eye now, turning, stepping back into this room and slipping slowly into his arms. He held her there against him, her hand pinned against his chest, and they stood there for the longest time.

She sounded so small when she said, finally, "I think my not being ready, with Mort, I think that was just—I always thought you sort of pitied me, or—"

"Pitied you?" Where the Jesus did she get that?

"I never imagined you felt so—I mean, when I said I wasn't ready last night—"

"I know *I'm* not ready," he said, trying to make a joke because he really wasn't ready, in a lot of ways. "I just got through waxing the dolphin. I couldn't be ready for another half hour at least."

She socked him lightly in the breadbasket, but kept hugging him.

"Also, I refuse to whip it out for your scrutiny until you're sure you're over your giggle fits. So *that's* another roadblock."

But seriously, there was something else standing in their way, and he wasn't sure it could ever be fixed by time. He told her she could be ready to open her heart to a man anywhere from today to years from today, but to Wink, whenever it was, she would still be Chesty's widow.

"Always?" She actually sounded hurt. "Even after more than two straight years of being *my* best friend?"

He'd never thought of himself as that before. He hated the way she sounded almost offended—rejected or something—and he had to wonder now if she might have a point.

"I guess I'll have to think about this some more," he said. "A lot more."

"You do that," she said. "In the meantime, feel free to look at any pictures your heart—or your *dolphin*—desires."

She gave him a final squeeze, hands around his waist, and a kiss on the cheek, and then she let herself out, pressing the button lock first before pulling it closed behind her.

Christ on a crutch, he thought. *Like I'll be able to think about anything else . . .*

74

She woke to the realization that someone was in her bedroom.

By the sound of his breath and his smell alone, she knew it was Wink, even before the hushed repetition of her name. He was standing at the end of her bed, wiggling her foot gently, trying to quietly wake her.

It was too dark to read the clock, but it had to be at least midnight. "Let me guess . . . ," she managed to mutter, "you need to borrow more Vaseline."

"No, smart mouth." He kept up the whispering, though she thought she'd made it clear he'd already woken her. "Knock it off and listen." Even with his voice low, he sounded urgent and worked up about something, straining to get it out. "Here's why it's okay: *I never heard of Breakey, Nebraska.*"

"Excuse me?"

"Before we buried Chesty there, I mean. Before the trip out west. I never even heard of Breakey, Nebraska."

With a groan, she rolled over and worked herself up to a seated position. "Fascinating, but what does it mean?"

"It *means*," he said, almost sounding annoyed now, "maybe we'll do it with the lights off and air-raid curtains pulled tight or something, just so you don't bust a gut laughing at the equipment like you did with the last poor sap you let in here—but I am *not* in the wrong here, that's what that means. Chesty was a good guy, a great guy, a pal as far as that goes, but we weren't pals-to-the-bitter-end kind of pals, clearly. I didn't even know the guy was from Nebraska, for the love of Jesus! That whole story of being shipped off to Chicago to live with his aunt and uncle, leaving his mom back there, his dad parking on the train tracks— none of that! He never told me a bit of it! And I never told *him* about taking ill as a kid and my mom leaving and . . . I'd say that that puts me squarely in the 'friendly professional acquaintance' category, *not* the 'best buddies' category."

"And in the 'okay to pursue the widow of' category?"

"Exactly," he said, and that was the last he said for a very long while.

75

He'd never enjoyed the "aftermath" all that much. He usually felt like getting up and moving around. Maybe not fleeing, but doing something else, going out for a bite or walking the girl home. But he didn't mind this at all, this time, just lying there with Sal, her body still warm and tingly against his. In fact, he was kind of hoping he could just lie there till he fell asleep, even if it meant waking up in her bed in the morning and facing what they'd done. Already, in his heart, he knew he'd done the right thing.

She said, "I imagine we're going to probably skip a few steps, you and me. The normal rituals."

He wasn't sure he necessarily wanted to skip the rituals with her. But maybe that wasn't what she meant.

"I mean . . . the slow getting-to-know-each-other part. We've done that. And we get along . . . and it turns out you're attracted to me."

"Very," he said.

"And you don't seem to be playing the field with other women lately. You seem to have knocked off fooling around with my friend . . ."

"On account," he said, "of I'm in love with you."

She adjusted the covers and rolled over on top of him, her hair falling in his face. He'd noticed, already, even when they were doing it, that her hair made him itch. All that time he'd known her and been so close to her, relatively, and yet he'd never had an inkling her hair would make him itch. Something about it being so fine and a little wavy, maybe. He'd never known a woman to make him itch with just the touch of her hair to his skin, but he imagined he could get used to it.

She stared down into his face. There was little light coming in from the alley-side window, but he could feel her breath. "Everything you're telling me?" she said. "Same here, pal. Why do you think that's any different for me?"

"No fooling?"

"Honor bright. All of it. Well, except for looking at your picture and thinking of you and waxing my—not sure what I wax. Touching myself, then."

"Right. Of course not."

"Yeah," she said. "I don't look at your picture while I think of you and touch myself. But, hey, two out of three . . ."

For a second, he couldn't breathe. He'd never known another woman to make both his heart and his pecker leap at the dead same instant.

76

Packing her suitcase for their long weekend alone in Reenie's brother's hunting cabin up north in the Wisconsin Dells, she dug deep in her pile of old sweaters, knowing the warmer and woollier the better—patches and moth holes and unraveling be damned—and so even included the tight, slightly shrunken turtleneck she'd owned since senior year in high school. She stopped, examining the old monogram on the breast, constructed from her maiden name Dean, and realized the initials fit again; acknowledging, for the first clear moment that day, that her name was now Dutton. Sally Ann Dutton.

A few of the other girls growing up teased her about this a little—her initials spelling out *SAD*—but she'd never been particularly morose growing up, except the year her mother got sick and died, and she certainly wasn't feeling sad now. Far from it.

They'd taken care of the whole thing, in a civil service devoid of all frills, earlier that morning, down at city hall. Reenie and Keeney were the official witnesses, but Chesty's aunt Sarah had attended as well, sneaking away from her husband Whitcomb by coming downtown in a regular taxi, of all things. Sal was moved, seeing her there, touched that she would go to the bother, both logistically and emotionally, of showing. She appeared markedly older and frailer, despite the smart suit and new hat, and it was hard not to think it had a lot to do with the loss of her "young William" a little more than a year before. But she smiled sweetly through the whole proceeding. And though it seemed a little awkward, introducing her to Wink for the first time, out in the lobby, the grand old gal showed her true breeding and grace and took them all to lunch at the Palmer House.

"William would be happy for you, dear," she said. "I'm certain."

It was hard not to bust out crying, hearing this. "They liked each other a great deal," Sal told her, "my two husbands." The phrase made her laugh, despite herself, and it came out as a silly little hiccup.

Mrs. Chesterton patted Sal's white-gloved hand with her own white-gloved hand, and it felt as close as she'd felt, in a long time, to having an actual family alive and walking around on the earth.

Or perhaps the feeling had come from the glimpse she'd just caught of Wink and Reenie and Keeney, whom her friend had, thankfully, stopped calling the pirate (a sign, Sal felt, that meant something), all beaming with mischief, up to something conspiratorial with the waiter. Those nitwits were certainly her family, too.

Chesty's aunt told her then that she thought her father would have liked Wink as well, and Sal had to admit, she was probably right—Pop was no fool—and soon their surprise arrived, wheeled in on a dessert cart. They would be served cherry pie, not wedding cake, out of deference to Chesty.

"A toast to my friend," Wink said, raising his champagne to Sal, "and to my friend who has gone on—no cake, buddy—"

"Well, except maybe *cheesecake*," Reenie said, making a naughty. They all laughed—even Mrs. Chesterton, whom Sal figured didn't actually get it—and then Wink continued, turning to Reenie and Keeney.

"And to my friends now and evermore: may you find the riches I have found and the patience to find it. Dig in!"

There were *hear-hears* and gulps of champagne and then they dug in, and when she lay her fork into the flaky crust and down into the rich red goo, Wink already had a bite held out on his fork before her, offering her his in that traditional, first-bite barter, and they fed each other, and she thought of the rite of communion.

77

He watched Keeney wave off the old German bartender when he brought up the two beer bottles, insisting on opening them himself with his prosthetic hand.

"Very impressive," Wink said. "If we'd ordered wine, could you flip out a corkscrew on that thing, too?"

It had been Reenie's idea, about a week after they got back from her brother's cabin, to double-date at the Berghoff, and they'd split off, the men heading to the bar, the women waiting at the table for their salads. He watched them in the mirror behind the bar, back at the table giggling, no doubt about the honeymoon he and Sal just had.

It seemed clear halfway through the first beer that Keeney had a few declarations he wanted to make. Number one seemed to be that he had an open mind about Reenie's "moonlighting," meaning her posing, and that Wink wasn't in danger of losing "one of the Sallys" on his account, "at least not anytime soon."

He wondered if Keeney assumed Wink had already lost "one of the Sallys" by marrying her, and frankly Wink hadn't even thought about that yet.

Keeney said, "Someone else less well adjusted than myself, maybe he'd get it stuck in his craw, his girlfriend doing that kind of work, but no. I figure she doesn't knock *me* for being the way I am"—he gestured with his hook, jabbing at his own necktie—"you know, a Republican and only *half* Irish. So I gotta accept *her*."

This guy . . . Wink slapped him on the back. He was damn glad they'd found this crazy bastard.

"At least for a little while," Keeney said. "I can't really feature her peeling for the cameras once she starts having my kids."

Wink kept smiling automatically, but inside he was wondering what the hell Keeney was thinking. Didn't he know Reenie wasn't a settler? And if she did settle, the plan was to at least settle for someone who could either give her riches or a career as an art director. She wouldn't be going through art school and trying to make it at some ad agency while also making babies with this poor deluded sap.

Of course, he hadn't had a solid talk with Reenie for some time now. Maybe her plans had altered, maybe the situation had changed. But he seriously doubted it.

Keeney straightened a little in his stool. "You should know, also, we're jake, you and me. No grudge here."

"Jake on what?" He had a feeling he was talking about Reenie. "The photo in the *Trib,* you're talking about?" He knew he'd made that jake already—especially once he got him work indoors before snowfall, actually having managed to talk that grump Sunshine State into hiring him at his news shop.

"Uh-uh." Keeney jerked his thumb back toward the table behind them, which Wink took as a confirmation of his suspicion. "We're jake about the 'crossed swords,' if you'll pardon my Latin. Most situations like this, knowing another guy used to . . ." He raised his eyebrows. "You know. And then that guy moves on or whatever, the *next* guy might feel he's getting leftovers, like he turned his nose up or she got passed over, like what the Jesus this guy see wrong with *her?* But I'm saying no, I don't feel that way. I mean, just get a *load* of her . . . !"

They swiveled on their bar stools, taking in the two striking girls back at the table, the wavy-haired blonde and the dark brunette, whispering and laughing like honest-to-God starlets.

"Does she *look* like leftovers to you?"

Wink told him that she absolutely did not. He liked this guy a lot and hoped she'd somehow decide to give him a half a chance.

Keeney elbowed him, nodding back at the table again, meaning now, as Wink took it, to indicate Sal. "You just had other good things already on your plate you just weren't aware of all that time."

78

Sal took a plate of her best ranger cookies to the old coot at the news shop.

Keeney wasn't working, and she wasn't sure the owner recognized her, and so she asked.

"Sure, sure," he growled, gesturing to the pinup on the wall behind him with the stub of his cigar. She noticed the one she'd signed, actually of Reenie, had been replaced, probably by Keeney, with this one of Sal herself holding two milk jugs in front of her otherwise bare bosom. "The lady what gets her tits out." He held up his meaty paws as if not wanting to offend. "On *occasion.*" Then he affected a small, almost motionless, and completely seated bow. "Salutations."

Ignoring this, she told him she'd been curious about how some of their S&W titles were selling, and she'd come by to look around.

"You're here to window-shop?"

She reminded him again of the cookies—that bringing them for him was half the purpose of her visit—and opened the tin for him, insisting he try one.

He took one bite and didn't so much spit it out as let it fall from his mouth, leaving a wet splotch on a newspaper bundle at his feet, obliterating what she thought was probably Pogo Possum.

"Christ!" he barked. "Coconut?"

"You don't care for—"

"Coconut gives me the screaming yips! You want I should crap my pants, lady? I wouldn't feed that to a duck . . ."

This was it, she realized. She could turn tail right now and give up, or she could face this ogre.

"I *want you should*," she said, imitating his ignorant grammar, "I *want you should* consider better placement for our titles, okay, maybe even a face-out now and again, and I *want you should* consider perhaps some sort of in-store promotional appearance, meet Winkin' Sally, something like that. And I *want you should* consider we did you a huge favor finding you Keeney, a guy who probably does ninety percent of the heavy lifting around here now while you no doubt sit on your wide bottom thinking up wise remarks. And while you're at it, I *want you should* stop being so fucking *rude!*"

He stared at her for so long, so still, she thought for a second he'd had some sort of small seizure. But then he just said, "Fair enough."

"Fair enough meaning you'll give us better placement?"

"No, but I will try to work on the rude. What's that going to cost me, right? As for better placement, I'm afraid I don't want to tangle with a certain Mr. Price. Things can get hot with a gentleman like that, and when I say *hot,* I mean like *fire* hot. So you can either take him a bunch of your coconut what-have-yous here, or you can always buy me out and put me on a train to the Sunshine State, and I'll be all set. Otherwise, sorry, ma'am."

On her way out, she heard him say, so quietly perhaps it wasn't meant for her to hear, "And really—I really am gonna work on the rude."

79

In February of '47, Wink got a message from Bob, the photo editor at the *Trib,* that he wanted him to come in. He had no idea what the guy wanted.

He told Sal he was being summoned to the Tower the next day, but she claimed she knew nothing about it, either. It had been a long time since she'd moonlighted there as a darkroom tech.

All the way up there, Wink tried to confine his guesses to the mundane—maybe Bob was offering *him* some darkroom work or, at the most, a freelance assignment, though probably on spec. He tried to keep it out of his head that it could be anything more than that.

After waving him into his office, throwing out a "Congrats on the recent nuptials," and pointing to a cluttered leather hump Wink assumed was a love seat, somewhere under the papers, the exhausted-looking Bob leaned back in his massive desk chair and stretched, saying, "Real interesting, the way reactions to that photo of yours went, huh? The back and forth of it? Provocative."

Wink agreed that it was.

"Good stuff, all in all. Real good stuff." Bob sat forward now and began shuffling papers on his desk as if he'd actually made some kind of a clear statement. It felt, for a moment, as if Wink had been dismissed or at least forgotten.

But then the guy produced a slip of paper, signed it, and handed it over, explaining that he was now officially on staff.

"Yeah, but—"

Bob waved him off. "Think of it as on retainer. You don't even have to show up. You'll receive a weekly paycheck, and *this* is for back pay, we'll call it, back to May of '46. We're going to back-date the books, in terms of taxes and such."

He didn't fully understand. And he wasn't sure he'd actually said he *accepted* a job.

"Don't worry," Bob said, rising with a groan. "No meetings, no time card. You got something good in the pipes, give me a jingle. Otherwise . . ."

He had his hand out to shake, like it was over.

Wink shook it, not clear at all what had just happened, too thrown to offer his left instead. It sounded, frankly, too good to be true. The numbers on the piece of paper in his hand accounted for nearly nine months of salary.

Still, it was free money, really. He'd already been paid a flat fee for the photo. And it sounded like he was going to be better than a staff photographer, some sort of *special* photographer with a direct line to the top. This was, possibly, his big chance to finally do the sort of creative things he'd been striving to do all along.

All the way back to the shop, he felt like a respected artist.

80

Sal felt herself being jostled awake. She opened her eyes to a hand—too slender and long to be Wink's mangled right—being thrust inches from her face. "Shake, sister!" someone whispered, a woman. "Shake hands, toots, with your ol' pal Mrs. Reenie Keeney."

She forced her eyes open. It was Reenie, all right, kneeling beside the bed, grinning like someone deranged, offering her her hand. Trying to sit up a little, she started to reach out drowsily and then saw the ring and grabbed instead.

"I know, I know!" Reenie's normally husky voice now sounded like a leaky balloon. "It's very, very fast, and it's crazy, and I always said the main reason I'd ever get hitched was to shed this ridiculous name, and I think maybe I made it worse, but there you are—from Reenie Rooney to Reenie Keeney. Doesn't *that* just hand you a laugh? I know you two are going to bust a gut over that so go ahead and get it over with! Let's hear it!"

Sal turned to her husband beside her, just starting to roll over and focus. He looked about as amazed and disoriented as she felt. "What state were you—?"

"We were just a *little* tipsy, if you must know, Mr. Nosy-pants. He doesn't drink quite like you do, you know. We were perfectly in our right minds, so—"

"Indiana," Sal said, explaining it to Wink. "There's no waiting period."

"Right," Reenie said, then sourly, "So gee, where's the hug? Don't everybody throw rice at once, for Pete's sake!"

Sal hopped out of bed and threw her arms around her friend. She felt bad for hesitating. Of course she was happy for her. She stroked her back a little and whispered as much.

When she let her go, Reenie next turned to Wink, like he was supposed to come over and hug her, too. But he was staying put, with his knees up under the covers. "You're going to have to, uh"—he gestured for her to come around to his side—"I'm not really . . ." He held out his hands like he *wanted* to hug her, but he wasn't going to stand right now.

"Oh yes, of course," Reenie said, clicking around to Wink's side in her high heels. "The private stands at attention for reveille."

It felt a little strange, her pal so casually expressing her familiarity with her own husband's morning erections, but Sal supposed they were all well beyond that at this point.

Reenie bent over him, and he gave her a little shoulder hug,
their bodies not coming into contact much below the chest. He
was trying to be discreet. As she patted his back, Sal noticed she
still wore long opera-length gloves from the night before. They
probably hadn't been to sleep.

Wink asked where the lucky groom was. "Downstairs," she
said. "He felt funny enough me letting myself in with my keys.
He thought barging into your bedroom was too much."

"The guy's funny like that," Wink said. "Real old-fashioned."
Then he announced that the Duttons would be taking the
Keeneys out for a celebratory breakfast, not the same old Zim
Zam, either—"maybe someplace with fancy crepes"—but she
needed to "get the hell out" first so they could get dressed.

Reenie snorted. "Get *you*! Mr. Modest! Like I've never seen
either one of you a billion times."

Sal pointed out that her friend had never had a husband before. Especially one waiting downstairs, all alone.

81

Reenie Keeney, née Rooney, felt a glow inside that she knew was
only partially due to the champagne Keeney had smuggled in in
his peacoat to spike the orange juice for a toast.

True, it wasn't the grand shindig she'd dreamed of as a little
girl. Hell, it wasn't even the swank little luncheon that elderly
aunt of Chesty's sprang for when *they* got hitched, Sal and Wink,

back before Christmas. This little crepe place, though cute enough, was hardly the Palmer House.

But life wasn't all about following plans. Especially these days. If the world had learned anything in the years since Pearl, it was that. *Life is what actually happens,* she kept telling herself now, *not what should* ideally *happen.*

The place was crowded and clattering with dishes and chatter, and they had to lean close, even at the little table, to be heard over the din.

It was a joyful din, though, and she wanted Wink to know she really truly *was* happy. They'd made honeymoon plans for next weekend, and she told him about this now—the cabin Gil Elvgren had up in Wisconsin. "Forever he's being saying if I ever made it legal, he'd let me borrow the place."

Wink was having trouble disguising the jealousy in his eyes, but she suspected it had less to do with wanting her back so much as wanting to be pals with Gil.

"Not your brother's?"

She reminded him that he and Sal honeymooned there and gave him the crinkled nose she'd been perfecting lately, cribbed from Miss Myrna Loy. "That might feel kind of . . . strange. Don't you think?"

"You could change the sheets, I suppose," he said, dry as Utah, so she stuck out her tongue at the evil little wisenheimer. He leaned in close and whispered in her ear, "What happened to him being 'the pirate'?"

"Hush it," she said. "The big galoot's grown on me. I'm proud of him, I can count on him, he makes me laugh . . . He's a noble beast."

"You love him?"

"Just watch me."

She knew on some level she'd only mentioned Gil's cabin to Wink to try to top him—maybe that was even the reason she'd accepted the pinup painter's kind offer—and she chided herself now for giving in to that sort of pettiness. She needed to let that kind of stuff go and just worry about manipulating her own man from now on.

So she gave Wink a smile and a kiss on the cheek, then rubbed the lipstick off with her thumb and patted him there with a little slap, and he smiled back, looking just a little sad, which was—she knew—something they could both live with.

Sal was giving her the high sign to join her in the powder room, so she rose, and the two of them negotiated the crowded tables with their arms looped together as if they were back on the playground, wearing each other's ribbons. Sal was stroking her arm frenetically, clearly excited for her, or at least pretending to be.

In the powder room, through the stall, Sal said, "So— congrats and all, but I guess this throws your dream of marrying a Daddy Warbucks who'll put you through art school right out the window."

"Just a slight change of plans," she said, and laid out her new scheme: how she'd send Keeney off to art school free on the GI Bill—he could take night classes up at Navy Pier, maybe, after closing the news shop for the day, then he would come home and teach her everything he learned. His writing and drawing hand was still intact. Even if it turned out he had no real artistic talent, he could still take detailed notes.

Of course, this new plan wouldn't leave her with a sheepskin, but she thought she had enough contacts in the business that skills and gumption just might be plenty to land her a job— another chance—even if the men *were* back and the girls' time *was* supposedly over.

"Sounds like a doozy of a plan," Sal said, and they flushed in unison.

Washing up at the sinks, it felt like they were back in junior high, standing side by side in the bathroom there, and she felt she could admit now that she'd first gone out with Keeney just to rile Wink—and when she told her, Sal didn't look all that surprised—but once she'd given the guy a chance, she found he really cracked her up and he was sweet as hell. "And he reminds me of that kid in *The Best Years of Our Lives*," she said. "Not just the prosthetic hand. Well, mostly that. But anyway, I'm serious about this one. For once. Might even stop dating other guys— hell, *anything* could happen!"

She made a big show of giving her a wink, catching Sal's reflection in the mirror, trying to be bawdy about it. But she could see in Sal's face that she'd known her too long to fool her. She couldn't hide the fact that she was hooked.

Without rubbing it in or teasing her, Sal turned to her and put her arms around her, and they had a good, squealy, girly, hokey cry.

82

"So why'd you call me in," she said, "if this is about my husband?"

She was seated across from Bob, the photo editor, in his office in the Tower. She hadn't been in for almost a year and a half, since trying to show him Chesty's last photos of the cake flour, but the office looked exactly the same, even down to the half-eaten sandwich—possibly a Reuben—he appeared to be using as a paperweight.

Bob cleared his throat. "Your husband, Sal—and by the way,

all the best on that, best wishes or whatever you're supposed to say . . . Seriously, I mean it, babe. Anyway, he's *rumored* to have once beaten a certain top ad exec here in town to a bloody pulp over a trifling, so—"

"*Pushed* him only," she said. "And the bastard was *molesting* my best friend." She knew the *molesting* part was wrong, but as long as the story was getting distorted, what the hell.

"Anyway, there's no sense inviting trouble. So we're telling *you* this, and you can explain it to him. If you choose. Or don't. The arrangement we've had with him the past couple months has been a little unusual, so frankly, I don't even need to give this much explanation. He'd just stop getting checks and—"

"Wonderful! So continue this big favor of an explanation and actually *explain* it, Bob!"

"Right. Okay. So the Pulitzer Prize committee, as you may or may not know, does not *officially* announce finalists, Sal, just the actual winner of each category, *but* . . ." Here Bob took a moment to smirk, as if feeling self-satisfied with his ranking as one of the newspaper trade's inside elite; one of the boys, privy to the straight scoop. "In February of this year, we learned that Wink's shot—the one that caused that little bit of a dustup, you remember? Back the spring of last year—May of '46, this would have been. . . ."

"I *know* the shot, Bob." She'd created the assignment for Wink, for cripes' sake. And it was the only "straight" photo he'd ever had published. Of course she knew the shot. It was still pasted to the front window of their shop. It had become the thing Keeney and Reenie pointed to as the cupid's arrow that brought them together. The shot was *the* shot.

"Anyway, just a couple months ago, in February, we learned it was up for the prize. Which was great news for the paper, except, well, Wink wasn't actually on staff, so . . ."

"But that amateur just won that category, didn't he? With the lady leaping to her death in a hotel fire? The Georgia Tech student, right? Andy Hardy or—?"

"*Arnold* Hardy, his name is. Fucking lamebrain, siren-chasing luck-out artist . . . Twenty-six lousy years old! You believe that?"

She believed it, because that actually made the guy just about the same age as Wink, but she didn't offer up this information. Besides, she got Bob's meaning—age wasn't really the issue, but a perception of seriousness or professionalism.

As if to confirm this, he said, "If we'd known the committee would consider any jackass who could get his mitts on a camera, no press credentials whatsoever—something that just gets sent out over the AP wire . . . !"

She could see now what they'd been up to, thinking they had to establish Wink's official credentials, get him tied to the paper as a staffer since the time they'd published his photo.

She suspected, though she kept it to herself, that perhaps the paper's own actions rather than any flaw in Wink's photo had more to do with the judges' final decision. It easily could have been partly a matter of that pussyfooted stance they took, publishing the picture one day but running that apology a few days later, immediately disavowing themselves of any of its editorial content. Not exactly a bold move that would go down in the annals of heroic journalism.

She looked past Bob at the blue of Lake Michigan, out his magnificent window, imagining how high they were, how awful it would be to fall even at a fraction of this height. What must it have been like for that poor woman in the winning photo—no matter how unimpressive Sal had personally found the hotel fire shot.

"You think," she asked, "the judges picked it because the woman died? Is that what makes it so compelling? Because, frankly, Bob, maybe it's just me, but I didn't really—"

"She *didn't* die! That's what kills me! She's been in hospitals since December, yes, but that caption the AP ran—that's a blatant lie! And the Pulitzer committee put the same hooey in their *own* press release when they announced the award! 'Girl Leaping to Her Death' my ass!"

She hadn't heard any of that before, but she supposed Bob would know the facts, if anyone would. And it did sort of affect the way she thought about the picture now, knowing the subject in it had survived.

"Why don't you just offer him a real job?" she said. "He might take it."

"We talking about the kid in Georgia now or your new hubby?"

"Wink," she said, knowing he was kidding.

"Well, besides the fact we got staffers coming out the gills since the war's over and never mind the stars probably just aligned right for your guy, once in a lifetime, with that marine-with-a-hook-for-a-hand lucky shot which he couldn't top in a million tries, there is *also*—"

"That's talent," she said. "Not luck."

"Besides which, there is *also* the little insurmountable problem that your new husband, Sal, handsome and lucky and possibly talented though he may be, *is* reputed to be a smutmonger. This business up at North Shore Beach. The *Tribune* has an illustrious and elevated history of—"

"North Shore Beach happened *before* you put him on the payroll! What are you talking about, North Shore Beach? That was last *September.* You started giving him all that supposed back pay well after that, sometime in February, just two or three months ago! You knew about the beach thing back in February."

Bob shrugged. "True, but . . . Sal, come on. In February, the guy was a contender for the fucking *Pulitzer.*"

She turned at the sound of Dickie what's-his-name at the open door—the one who'd once called her in one evening just to try to get cozy. He was dressed more respectably than she'd ever seen him, and she suspected he'd been given a promotion since she'd last been in.

"Whereas today," Dickie said, "he's just a troublemaker who takes dirty pictures on the beach."

He took it pretty darn well, she thought. He was awfully quiet, sitting on his stool in the darkroom, swiveling a little and picking at his fingernails.

She had such an urge to kid him, though, just to get some kind of reaction out of him. "You want to say *shucks* or *drat* or something," she said, "you go right ahead, honey."

He snorted a half-passable laugh and hugged himself a little. After a long moment he said, "I've been sitting here listening to everything you're telling me, and I get it, I do, only . . . I'm trying like hell to feel bad about it or mad, and well, all that's really sticking to me is (a) I got paid almost a whole year's worth of salary for doing nothing and (b) I came close to winning a Pulitzer—a goddamn Pulitzer, Sal—for the first real photo I ever published. Only decent photo I ever made, you ask me."

She told him it wasn't the only decent photo, nor was it the last.

"That's pretty wild, though, isn't it? First time out?"

She had to admit, it was. There were staff photographers all over the country, working for years, who never won a Pulitzer, nor probably came close—though just knowing about being a finalist was pretty special, too. They weren't supposed to know that, and she reminded him of this. He might never have known he even came close. "Which is why I was a little unsure about telling you," she said. "I didn't know if it was a glass half full or—"

He pulled her in and hugged her. After a time, he told her, almost whispering now, "When I got to do cartoons, in the service, I kidded myself, but I used to daydream about one day winning one of those. For political cartooning, you know? And then Mauldin got one in '45 for *his* war stuff. . . ."

"Maybe you will," she said. "For *this* now. This is your field now, Wink—photography. It really is. You kidding me?"

He shrugged, looking about ten years old. "I guess if I can come close this early in the game, I've got a pretty good shot of pulling it off before I kick, right?"

"Right." And she truly meant it. She had this feeling, just talking about what lay ahead, that there would come a day when photojournalists talked about the saphead editor who once canned Wink Dutton, and the young kids wouldn't even believe it.

"I've got this real urge to be mad at the paper, like they were trying to trick me, because they were a little tricky about it all, but how did it hurt me any? Them not bringing me in for meetings, letting me pitch other stories? The time I wasted sending in a few spec shots here and there on my own? Maybe . . . But mostly they were just trying to trick the Pulitzer, right? But even if they *were* pulling a fast one, I guess I can't really gripe too much about that."

She reminded him how he'd mentioned several times that he and Chesty had been friendly with a marine combat photographer who'd gone on to *Stars and Stripes* and was an editor at *Life* magazine now, that he ought to try pitching him on a photo essay, and Wink agreed that maybe he would, that he might just have a shot at it.

She had to slug the big dope, right on the arm. "Of course you do!" she said. "You're a Pulitzer Prize finalist, for pity's sake— no matter if you can prove it or not."

"Now, I *do* sort of feel funny about keeping the money," he said. "But I've maybe got a plan brewing should take care of that. . . ."

She told him she didn't doubt it for a minute.

Sometimes, moments like this, she had the strangest desire to have both her men there, living and breathing at the same time, Wink *and* Chesty, working and living with her there in the camera shop, just to enjoy watching the two of them as the gears started to move.

83

Arriving at the news shop on a Saturday morning, Keeney knew he was at least a couple minutes late. The roll gate was already up. Usually he got there in time to help Sunshine unlock it and grunt it up, but he'd apparently already done it on his own, had the lights on and everything. He imagined the earful of griping he'd get from the old man on this one.

Even before he reached the shop, he had a hunch he was running late. He figured as much when Reenie had started in on him that morning. He'd eyed his alarm clock through the whole proceeding, but she'd insisted on riding him like a rodeo star, clowning it up the whole time, even throwing out a couple *yahoo!*s, which actually added even more time to the event rather than hurrying it along. *Keep it up, sweetie,* he thought, *and that landlady's going to kick us loose.* Reenie had been especially atten- tive since they eloped, and he imagined it would wind down eventually. Then again, he hadn't known the girl all that long *be-fore* they eloped, so really, he had no way to judge it. Maybe this was the way she always was.

Anyhow, he figured the old man could like it or lump it. He was a newlywed, damn it. He was entitled to a little slack in regards to rolling out of the marriage bed.

But Sunshine wasn't there. Wink Dutton was there. Inside, standing by the cash register.

"Sunshine State is coming in late," Wink informed him. "If he comes in at all today. Says he's sleeping in and nuts to you. Asks that you kindly 'kiss it.' It's his last day."

"Last day?" Keeney felt about as confused as a color-blind bull. "So who's—"

"You are. You're the new owner. Sunshine State's off to the Sunshine State, and not a day too soon, you ask me—or really anyone on the planet who's met the man. Just as soon as I sign the deeds on Monday, making it legal. You should come to the closing, too—and Reenie—and I'll just sign it over to the two of you there, and then it's all yours, free and clear. I am not a partner, I am not a boss, I am a friend who will occasionally stop by and see what's new on the racks. And if you have our titles prominently displayed."

He told Wink he must be goofy in the head; he couldn't waste his money like that.

But Wink was shaking the noggin in question. "It's money I never really earned, believe me. Ill-gotten booty."

"Listen," Keeney told him, "those girls see you as being just as much a part of that whole thing as them. Or almost as much. I understand you've got some feelings of pride, making money from that, but I've talked to Reenie about this many times, and they do *not* feel, neither one of them, that you've been taking advantage of them or—"

"Not money from that. Not the girlies. This is extra, from the *Tribune*. Trust me. This is free money."

Keeney wasn't clear what he meant by that—*free money*. Wink appeared almost itchy as he said it, and it reminded him of something his new bride had told him regarding her old cuddle-buddy's war injuries, both physical and unseen. Although Wink had never confided any of this to him personally, Reenie claimed the guy was carrying around a lot of screwy feelings of guilt about the way he'd won his Purple Heart—that he'd actually been hungover and not following instructions or something and that from the day she met him till the end of the war, he'd seemed uncomfortable about enjoying civilian life, like he didn't deserve it.

He tried to tell the guy he could just take out a small business loan from the GI Bill, buy it from the old goat himself, direct.

"Save that for the *next* location, when you branch out. Or for a delivery truck or something. This is a wedding present. End of discussion." And as if to make it final, Wink walked over to the cash register and dropped the keys on the little worn wooden counter, and they stood and stared at each other for a time.

This business about a wedding present, on top of his insistence that Reenie needed to sign the papers, too, made it pretty clear, Keeney thought, what this was about. Even more than the issues with his injury and discharge, the guy felt guilty about the way he'd treated Reenie. Or *felt* he'd treated her. As far as Keeney could tell himself, Reenie didn't seem to have any real beef with her old flame. But they both got the idea sometimes that Wink felt he'd treated her a little like a victory girl, never a serious girlfriend or potential wife. *All the better for* me *to come along,* was the way Keeney saw it, but if the guy needed to make some grand gesture like this for it to sit right with him, peachy.

"Thanks then," Keeney said finally. "You're something else."

"As are you," Wink said. "And you're welcome. With only one string attached." He raised a finger in the air. "Not really a condition. A request. I want you to help me with something. Once you're settled in, just let me shoot a photo essay of you running this place, showing how you make it work, the daily stuff and how you've adapted."

Keeney sucked his teeth. He wasn't crazy about having his picture taken, even when the hook was out of sight. Then again, folks stared all the time anyway, especially kids and 4-F types, so what the hey? What he'd seen of Wink's more serious photo work, it probably would turn out pretty nice.

He asked Wink if there'd be half-naked girls in the shots, prancing around the shop, flashing their ta-tas while he sold magazines and newspapers and gum.

Wink grinned. "Not unless that's how you normally run this joint. And if it is, I think maybe I *do* want to keep a piece of this, because you're sitting on a gold mine, my friend!"

"Too late," he told him. "You're out."

"Cheap bastard," Wink muttered. "Fucking ingrate."

"Degenerate," Keeney shot back.

Wink stuck out his hand to shake, and it turned into a little bit of a quick embrace—not much, just a backslapping shoulder grab, the way things sometimes got back in the service, when no one wanted to choke up and get gooey about things, but they sort of were. Keeney didn't want to think about it too much and get all blubbery, but thinking about his hand and the "adapting" Wink was talking about made him think about how far he'd come himself since going through physical therapy. And not just in operating the hook. He remembered how he'd thought, lying in that hospital cot, that the world was pretty much a dark place that took things from you. And maybe it was, if you didn't make an effort to fall in with the right group of people, in which case,

maybe all bets were off on the world making any headway in the
taking things department.

At the door, Keeney told him, "You're the swellest guy ever
once screwed my wife."

"*Once?*" Wink said, grinning like a goddamn movie star. "Stop
kidding yourself, brother!"

Keeney told him he'd have to ask him to leave if he was going
to engage in such risqué banter. "I own and operate an upstanding establishment here, sir."

"Yes," Wink said, tipping his hat to leave. "You do."

84

Mr. Price was still pressuring them to sell out. He'd just appear,
unexpected, to "say hello" and start in again as if they'd never
been through it before.

Wink was starting to wonder if the man considered him a
softer touch than Sal. Lately, he seemed to show up only when
she was upstairs or in the darkroom or, more often, out on an errand. Maybe he'd switched tactics because they'd married and it
was all common property, but Wink suspected, more likely, Sal
was just too frank with the man and wouldn't listen as politely as
Wink tried to do.

Each time, Wink tried to act like he was hearing him out,
then suggest that maybe at another time, in the future, but right
now it just wasn't feasible.

Mostly he managed not to be rude because of what he'd
learned about the man since they designed the card deck for
him. And he was afraid if he lost his temper with Jericho Price,
it might not be the only thing he'd lose.

Lately, Price's tactic seemed to be to make it "absolutely clear" that he had no interest in the camera shop itself—"just the licensing, images, and all other entities held by S&W Publishing."

He said it like he was doing them all a huge favor in not trying to take away her pop's twenty-year business.

There *was* one thing Wink was damn glad to sell. And it was a relief to see the generous whim he was starting to consider slightly foolhardy benefit him in some way beyond just making him feel like less of a heel.

He'd given Keeney a week or so to set up shop, get the place reconfigured the way he wanted it without any input from the old man, and then he approached him again about shooting a photo essay. Keeney could hardly turn him down.

The first day Wink spent following him around the tiny shop, it was obvious the guy was straining to act natural, slipping into wooden poses with each click of the Argus. But by the second day, Keeney got used to him being there or forgot about him, because the shots were incredible. Going over the contacts in the darkroom, with Sal peeking over his shoulder, he thought he'd almost call them powerful and moving.

His pal from back in the Pacific, now a photo editor at *Life,* thought so, too.

85

For the second night in a row, she stirred around one a.m. from dreams of being out in the middle of Lake Michigan, rocked by waves, and sat up, light-headed, queasy, and slipped out from beneath the gangly trap that was her long-limbed new husband and just made it, quietly enough not to disturb him, to the bathroom to throw up. If she hadn't known that morning was only an option, that sickness could come at any time of the day, and if she hadn't been well aware she was significantly late, she might think she was coming down with something.

Yeah, boy! she thought. *I'm coming down with something, all right.*

This second night, after emptying her stomach as quietly as possible, she pulled off her nightie, uncovering the stomach in question, and examined it in the mirror.

This was as flat as it would ever be. Tugging Wink's ratty robe down from the back of the door, she left the nightie on the floor and put the robe on instead and went out into the hallway and down the stairs, turning on lights. In the studio, she began setting up for a shoot, positioning the lights, the camera, arranging some throw pillows on the wooden riser.

She heard Wink on the stairs, tentative, probably still asleep. "Babe?" he said. "Everything okay?"

She almost laughed. He sounded so quiet and unsure, as if maybe she were a prowler. What if she *had* been—calling her babe and being gentle would disarm a prowler?

He stood before her now, squinty-eyed and swaying from sleep. "What's the idea?"

"My swan song," she said and dropped the bathrobe. "You need to get it down for the record. Before it's gone."

"Gone?" he said. He still didn't get it.

"Changed. Everything changes, sweetheart. It's okay." She was laughing at him a little now, mostly because he still seemed so confused, partly to keep from crying and worrying him more. She patted her belly and a look came over him. Maybe he finally got it, the big dope. She knew she was grinning at him like a moron, even if she felt like she might start seriously bawling any second. These would probably be totally unusable—full nudes, bush and all, with a grinning girl with misty eyes, pointing to her slender but seemingly unremarkable midsection—but she wanted them anyway. For posterity.

"Just take my picture, dear. Take *our* picture."

86

He came across a letter one day, among the general camera shop correspondence and bills, that looked like fan mail, addressed to Weekend Sally in care of the store, though they now had a separate PO box down the street for such things. Right off, it was a little troubling, that much alone.

On a single piece of lined legal paper, handwritten, it said only this:

pricktease

It was postmarked from right there in Chicago. He burned it immediately, keeping it from Sal.

But he couldn't hide everything. She claimed that lately she'd begun to notice the occasional "creepy hoodlum teen" looking shifty, looking like he was watching her or following her. Wink didn't imagine it would be very reassuring to her to admit that if it were a threat, he didn't think it was threatening in a particularly sexual way because he was pretty sure they were watching and following him, too.

Another time, soon after, returning one night from taking in a Loretta Young picture with Reenie and Keeney about a pretty farmer's daughter going to the big city and having to change her plans, Wink found a pane of glass smashed on the back door. Likely, it was kids again, hooligans. It seemed like an exact replica of the broken pane he'd repaired about three years before.

"This," he said, trying to get her to laugh about it, "is where I came in."

But he wasn't honestly sure it was something to laugh about.

87

They already had names picked out for the baby. If it was a girl, Manuela, her own mother's name, though they'd probably just call her Manny. If it was a boy, Billy, in honor of Chesty. That one had come from Wink. He insisted.

Wink had a game he played with the baby. He'd pull back her blouse and place his lips to her belly and blow a wet raspberry so loud it made her nervous the baby would be born deaf. It vibrated and buzzed like one of those reducing machines with the belt you strapped around your middle and it shook you to pieces. (Reenie had purchased one with her money from one of her first photo shoots, but Sal refused to even try it, and anyway, Reenie never looked any different no matter what she did.)

Even if she got him to knock it off with the raspberries, he'd feel around to see if he'd provoked any response. If he felt a few kicks or rolling maneuvers, he'd try it again or move on to the next assault—the photo lights. He was convinced the baby could see light and dark at this stage, and so he'd try to wake it up by turning on all the lights in the studio. Usually this did produce a few flutters, but then it would stop. She'd tell him that the damn lights were so hot, he was probably warming up the poor thing and making it drowsy. "It's not a rotisserie chicken," she'd say.

Wink usually seemed to feel remorse at this point and would pat her bulge gently, give it a kiss, and whisper, "Sorry, baby. You go to sleep now. Your daddy got a little carried away." But sometimes he was too wound up, and any suggestion that the baby had dozed off only spurred Wink on to try one more time, and he'd turn on the radio and blast brassy big band music and keep feeling around, trying to make it fidget, until she'd have to tell him to take some pictures, just to get him to stop groping her stomach like a melon and turn down the music.

She didn't mind posing for him like this, though she thought she would. She thought she'd feel huge and bloated and anything but sexy, but the truth was, she sometimes felt very sexy. And since these photos were for no one but them, who cared if she was no longer pinup material?

To loll around nude in her state was so much more languid and lazy and swell. She imagined it was probably how those large Italian gals must have felt, a few centuries back, that they'd seen many times right up Adams at the Art Institute on free-admission-Monday nights. She liked to think, if he had his right hand back in shipshape order, these were the kind of pictures Wink would be making, only with oil paints and with big gaudy frames for wealthy patrons who would applaud him for just entering a room—not the kind of pictures you created under a fake name and delivered in manila envelopes and reproduced on cheap pulp and wrapped in brown paper. It was a little hard to explain the difference, but there seemed to be one.

88

He heard the voices before the pounding—a low murmur of slurred words and half-suppressed laughter: drunks out at the front of the shop, trying the handle.

It was almost eleven on a Saturday night. And the worst possible time: he was shooting Sal in the altogether, baby belly and all. "For no-body but you-oo," she'd cooed, loving it, lolling like a wave against the tumble of half a bolt of dark velvet he'd unrolled across one of the low risers.

It wasn't the first study he'd shot of her like this, but it only got better each time. And she was noticeably bigger in each session, a state he found surprisingly beautiful. He loved experimenting with lighting the curves and roundness she now offered, and as much as he kidded around with her in these private sessions, once even coaxing her onto Chesty's aunt Sarah's ridiculous bear rug, it was still sometimes all he could do not to get choked up.

But now there was this pounding and monkeyshines. "Cover up," he said and stepped out into the hall, moving to the front of the shop and turning on more lights. He supposed they might be legitimately confused about the shop being open this late—had seen light from the little studio area in the back cascading out into the dark hall—but mostly they were certainly drunk and even more certainly foolish.

"*Closed!*" he called, waving his arms to go away. "*Eleven p.m.! . . .*" adding, under his breath, ". . . jackasses . . ."

There were several grinning faces shoved down close in the

glass of the front door, but one in particular stuck out front and center: puffy, like something underwater, a distorted halibut over at the Shedd Aquarium.

But slightly more familiar than any anonymous halibut. He recognized him from the sports page—or at least the brand-new scar, just over the bushy left eyebrow. It was Jo-Jo "Kid" Fortunato, the Cicero Sicilian, local middleweight contender who'd won a big fight the night before. And he looked pie-eyed, out celebrating, no doubt.

Keeney had asked him, just yesterday, if he wanted to get a couple tickets, and he'd declined, telling him boxing wasn't really his cup of tea. The truth was, he could hardly stand to leave Sal alone these days, even though the baby was still months off.

"Bring out the girlies!" they chanted, pounding on the door, laughing hard. "Bring out the girlies!"

With a crash, the glass shattered, and the boxer came toppling through. A half a second of silence followed, everyone stunned, his cohorts behind him staring in at their fallen leader, hunched over, halfway through the frame of the door. Then there was yelping and glass bottles skittering on the sidewalk and a shriek from behind Wink, which had to be Sal, trying to get covered up and probably still in the dark as to what the Jesus H. was going on out front.

The prizefighter was cut up and bleeding when he righted himself, bellowing, "Weekend Sally! Come out, come out!" and his entourage, a gal or two among them, laughed now, maybe relieved he hadn't been guillotined by the falling glass.

"Go!" Wink said and the group fell back, some of them latching onto the boxer by the coat, pulling him back out onto the sidewalk and away.

Wink stood there, listening to the retreating shrieks and more bottles rolling on the sidewalk, trailing off into the distance.

89

It sounded like they'd fled, so she stuck her head out in the hall. "Sweetie?" she said, and then when she saw the damage, the glass glinting across the floor out front, "Oh my God!" She started toward him, but he held out his hand like a traffic cop.

"Don't! You've got bare feet."

He was right. She backed away, telling him he should maybe call someone—the cops?

"We don't need a cop," he said, "we need a new window." Moving to the phone behind the counter, he said he'd try Keeney, see if he could help him with the mess.

Suddenly, he was back, lurching through the front door—a huge, grinning man with cuts on his face, and he was pointing at her. "Knew it!" She turned for the stairs, seeing Wink step out from behind the counter to intercept the intruder, but the man just shoved him back with one hand and kept going, Wink sounding hurt, like he'd fallen hard back there or had the wind knocked out of him. She lurched toward the stairs but lost her footing, stumbling with a heavy weight suddenly on her. "Whoopsy!" He laughed, rolling off her, the two of them fumbling, trying to get to their feet. He'd miscalculated the first step, whether from being drunk or from his injury with the door, and probably meant to grab her rather than fall on her. She heard a woman shrieking that sounded an awful lot like her, and she flailed, all hands and nails, pushing him away, kicking, scratching, and he tottered back a little, weaving slightly on the bottom step with part of the robe in his fist, still grinning like he'd caught a prize, but his eyes were swollen and half open, and his words were slurred. "Mr. Price *said* you was here!"

He tore the robe, pulling it open, hanging on to both pockets. She screamed, squirming, trying to snatch it back and close it.

But he just stood over her, staring and squinting at her naked body, looking confused, looking like he was trying to refocus. Finally, he muttered, "Holy *crap,* lady! You're *huge!*"

Behind him, Wink appeared, swinging the sash weight he used to strengthen his lame hand and bringing it down on the guy's skull.

The big jerk slumped forward, and she didn't have time to scramble out of his way, so he fell on her again. She screamed and kicked, but Wink had him off her in no time, yanking him back by the collar, rolling him off. He was either out cold or at least too groggy to fight, as Wink heaved, dragging him away from her, the guy's huge head thumping down the stairs. She watched him trail away behind her husband, out the back door, into the alley.

Wink was out there for just a moment or two—she couldn't hear anything else—and then he was back inside, moving fast, throwing the bolt on the back door, and rushing to her side.

"Jesus Christ, Jesus Christ . . . ," he kept repeating as he knelt on the bottom step, trying to examine her.

"No, no. I'm okay." It didn't feel like she could stop shaking her head as she gathered the torn robe back around her, feeling the last thing on earth she wanted right now was to have her body scrutinized further, though she did find she was rubbing an elbow and a hip and the small of her back, spots she'd banged up stumbling against the stairs.

"Yeah, but—what about the—"

She knew what he was thinking, but she doubted the baby had gotten squashed. "I banged up my *side,* yeah, but . . . He fell on me a little, but off to the side, not on the baby. More on my pride."

"Jesus Christ," he said again, the veins on his neck throbbing. She'd never seen him look like that—her gentle artist, her sly smart mouth. He looked like he wanted to kill—or as if he possibly already had.

"I think he . . . figured it out there right before you cracked him on the head." It was reassuring, to a degree. Of course, she wasn't sure what would have happened if the big goon *hadn't* realized she was expecting. Maybe he just would have looked at her, leered at her, getting a thrill from checking her out in the flesh, and that would have been the end of it. Maybe he *wouldn't* have done much more than that even if she wasn't expecting. It *was* possible he hadn't had any intention of forcing himself on her or anything like that . . .

Maybe.

90

Keeney rushed right over with some scrap lumber and plywood and helped him board up the front door while Reenie comforted Sal and helped her pack some things.

When the girls were upstairs and out of hearing, Keeney asked what he'd done with the intruder, if he'd called the cops. Wink explained that no, he hadn't, and why he hadn't—who the intruder had been.

"Shit on a shingle!" Keeney said, low and worried. And when he told him he'd dragged the boxer into the alley, the ex-marine insisted that might not have been far enough. "You don't want him coming to and coming back in for a second wave. Shit, pal,

even that silly little Dugout Doug managed to make good on his
'I shall return.' Let's you and me drag this monkey into my truck,
drop him somewhere else to recover, far away. Some other distant alley." Keeney hefted the sash weight he'd used. "You sure
you didn't kill him?"

They went to check on him, Wink bringing along the sash
weight just in case, but Kid Fortunato had taken a powder.

He'd left him right there, half propped up against the down-
spout, in a heap. He'd looked like a sack of old clothes left out
for Goodwill.

Wink wasn't sure if he should feel glad about the fact that he
probably *hadn't* killed him or panic that this meant he might return, as Keeney had said, like General MacArthur. His main impulse was to just get far away and figure this out later, and he
doubted Sal would have any objections to this plan.

"We'll keep an eye on the place," Keeney said. "You just get
out of here." He offered him Reenie's car, the old Buick, and
even in that hurried moment, Wink couldn't help but think the
sly dog was playing pretty generous with a gift she'd been given
by an old boyfriend.

The first safe place he could think of was four or five hours
away. If the idea of sudden travel had come up a few hours ago,
he would have said no way, he was too tired to drive anywhere
tonight. Now he felt as alert as a goddamn German shepherd.

91

Because they'd arrived well after midnight, her first real view of
the place was bright and early the next morning. She woke to
the sounds and smells of a panfried breakfast and the whole

house creaking with quiet activity. There was a radio on, far too low to make out—old-timey hymns, maybe?

The little bedroom window was dusty and warped with imperfections, but it was enough to see the flat farmland and the distant edging of trees and the overcast sky all around. Michigan, all right: midsummer, yet gray as bachelor's laundry.

She remembered now. Wink had slept on the floor. There wasn't room for the two of them to even spoon, in her condition, in his narrow boyhood bed. His uncle had announced that there weren't any double beds in the whole house, but he'd figure out something "more matrimonially suitable" for the future.

She could have used a bathrobe, but she was unclear what Wink had managed to stuff in the suitcase that still lay unpacked under what he had identified as a chick incubator, taking up one end of the small room, and she didn't relish bending over to get it, so she put on what she'd had on during the drive, including her raincoat, and took her chances on the narrow rickety staircase.

She could have used a husband, too—he was not waiting for her in the kitchen. His uncle Len, long and lanky as that actor Raymond Massey, if not Lincoln himself, seemed sheepish to see her, as if he needed his nephew to interpret.

"Didn't want to wake you too early," he said. "So I held off on breakfast for a good while." She glanced at the clock. It was seven-fifteen.

"The boy, he's up to the store. Fetching the Sundays. For the real estate ads. Feels, also, that you're needing *orange juice,* so . . ." He said this last as if Wink had run out for frankincense and myrrh.

She stood there, not sure what to do, trying to cover her belly with the raincoat. It barely closed these days.

As dim and dreary as the morning light was, compared with the endless blackness last night in that long, terrified ride, this seemed bright and startling, washing in on the dingy linoleum and the chipped dinette. They'd rocketed through a lot of desolate night, driving all the way from Chicago to . . . *nothing,* a turn off the highway in about the middle of the state that he swore was St. Johns.

The old man cleared his throat a little. It appeared he felt as awkward and disoriented about all this as she did. "You're going to be fine," he said, pulling out a chair for her at the kitchen table. "Just fine."

Wink had several large newspapers with him and a bottle of orange juice for her and a sack of cinnamon doughnuts for his uncle—or so he said. She actually only sipped the orange juice but wolfed down three of the doughnuts.

She asked him what he was doing; if he was looking for a job or something.

He opened the paper so she could see. "A farmhouse."

"But what will we—?"

"He can partner with me," Uncle Len said. "If he wants. Or if something better comes along, that's fine with me. Whatever you young people—"

"Here?" she said, and then felt bad for how it might sound to his uncle. "But—wait. Can you tell me about the hospitals? And—"

His uncle, it turned out, seemed convinced her condition presented no problem. "I've oversaw many a birth, believe you me."

Wink looked skeptical, himself. "Any you didn't end up milking or eating?"

"A mammal is a mammal," the older man grumbled, swatting his nephew playfully. "You never paid much attention in school, did you, son, other than them art classes? Any rate, there are plenty of knowledgeable ladies living on farms nearby, if you were to get in a pickle. But I'm pretty certain I would know enough myself to keep things moving along, if it came down to it."

She already liked this old guy a lot, and it was clear he was bending over backward to make them both feel welcome and safe, but the idea that it might come down to him rummaging around in her business like she was a cow or a horse or something was frankly horrifying.

"Of course, I'm not saying you couldn't make the county hospital. You might could. First babies sometimes take their sweet time . . . We could drive over there, clock it on the odometer, see what you think."

"So there is a hospital? A modern hospital with regular . . . stuff?"

Len shrugged a little. "Well, you know—it's not like you'd find down in Lansing or Ann Arbor, granted. But . . . ."

She liked the sound of those places. She'd at least heard of those places. She hadn't heard a *lot,* just enough to imagine secure little tree-mobbed college towns with reliable hospitals and public schools. And actual residential neighborhoods. The prospect of a yard with a fence and a lawn struck her as far rural enough—settling *here* in this flat land of tractors and dust seemed like an overreaction to the crisis at hand. She'd never lived outside of the Loop, and if she was going to have to abandon her lovely tall buildings and lights and rattling El and shimmering lake—and Reenie, wonderful Reen—and hide out in the hinterlands, she'd at least like to feel there was an outside chance it could be bearable.

"Wink," she said. "Could we maybe take a little drive and . . ." She wasn't sure how she was going to end this sentence: either *just slow down and think about all this* or *at least go take a look.*

She wasn't sure herself what she wanted—other than not having Wink's bachelor uncle, potentially, as her midwife.

Wink exhaled a little frustrated puff. She knew he was exhausted and unsure. She knew he was doing everything he could imagine to do right by his new little family here, and for a moment she felt like she was asking too much—the poor guy probably once saw himself ending up more like his uncle Len, free from the burden of a pregnant wife and the prospect of a family, not to mention having to protect them from creepy men and criminals. It was a lot to pile on a guy who'd probably pined for his freedom all through his military service, only to come back home and immediately find himself at the service of a needy woman. If he had his choice now, if he could do it all over again, she didn't doubt that three years ago he would have just jotted down her first husband's message, slipped it through the mail slot, and kept on walking, never even setting foot in the camera shop.

But he also seemed distracted by something in the paper, only half listening, and then he pointed to it and turned the paper her way. It was under a column marked BUSINESS OPPORTUNITIES. It was a retail storefront for sale in downtown Ann Arbor.

There were several, actually. Some of the town names she didn't recognize, but he said they were right around there, too.

He was getting up from the kitchen table now. "Let's just go for a little joyride then, see what's what."

92

He thought she might settle for just driving down to Lansing instead, since it was only twenty miles away, but the prospect of the retail space in Ann Arbor had piqued her interest.

It seemed to Wink that now, in the overcast daylight and flat open spaces, it might finally be a little easier to talk about what had happened and maybe, a little, start to talk about what they wanted to do.

Reaching over to pat her belly, he asked how she was feeling.

"Safer," she said. "Ready to talk, I guess."

They hadn't talked much during the drive the night before. She'd seemed too shocked, and he'd been resisting a strong impulse to rant and cuss and carry on—resisting this partly because it wouldn't help matters and would likely upset her more, but mostly because he honestly had no earthly idea what they were going to do. Reenie's so-called Boyfriend Bucket, as Keeney called the Buick, had a radio, thank God, so they'd sat there wordlessly washed over by delirious dance bands, silly and stupid and dreamy, coming around under the lake, all through Gary and the Indiana Dunes and the Michigan resorts, and they never reverted to conversation even as the big stations faded, replaced by static and farm reports and distant-seeming, high-pitched whistles that sounded like lost souls and "haints" or messages from the Arctic Circle.

The floodlights came on in the barnyard just as they pulled alongside the porch, and his uncle met them at the screen door in his robe, his deer rifle resting like a broom, handy to one side, leaning against the glider. They hadn't had a chance to call ahead, but he must have read something on their faces because he didn't ask questions until they got Sal settled upstairs in his old room and they could talk alone back out on the glider where they were less likely to disturb her.

He wasn't sure he'd ever seen his uncle up so late, except possibly the night of Wink's high school prom. It felt strange introducing his only real remaining relative to his wife in such awkward and awful circumstances, but that was the way it happened, and it couldn't be helped. He felt sure his uncle wouldn't grow to adore her any less because it had occurred so imperfectly and so late at night, coming in so bedraggled and bewildered, like gypsies or Okies.

It helped, he knew, that he didn't tell him *exactly* what happened.

He'd had the whole drive from Chicago, listening to the radio, to decide how to phrase it, and so he told him that there was this "known underworld figure" who'd been wanting a piece of their business—letting Uncle Len assume he meant the camera shop itself—and that this person had been intimidating them in various ways and that earlier that night "one of his henchmen, this boxer he promotes, really just a thug" smashed their front door and "accosted" them a little and "really spooked Sal."

It was close, though, Wink thought. No point risking his uncle disapproving of Sal by telling him they were in the girlie-picture business and that his wife had actually been stark naked when the drunk boxer lunged on top of her. He needed his uncle to like her. He didn't have enough family left on this earth to have them at odds with each other.

Or disapproving of me, too, he thought, for engaging in what Uncle Len would surely see as corrupting a woman's virtue.

"I hope you ran him off, this hooligan?"

"I ran him off, sure, but it's not something we can go back to." He said it without checking with Sal. They hadn't conferred about any such assessment or decision, it had just seemed like the thing to say.

And then early that morning, after only a couple hours' sleep, he set out on his own, again without conferring with her.

Bushed though he was, it had been bracing to find himself standing facing downtown St. Johns after so long. Gazing down the short stretch of storefronts, he'd tried to refamiliarize himself, wondering absently if there was any kind of store there where, if it weren't Sunday, they could purchase a larger mattress. It seemed doubtful.

He picked up the papers and orange juice and doughnuts and enough change to call long distance from the corner phone booth, the main purpose of his early errand.

"I've been through the sports pages and the obits and the police beat page for all the locals," Keeney said when he reached him at the news shop. "Reen's brothers are asking around, to boot, and so far, nothing. My belief is, he lives."

"The monster walks among us," Reenie chimed in in the background, trying to crack wise in a half-assed Karloff.

"Or," Keeney went on, "let's say he *didn't* pull through. Let's face it: that was no flyswatter you smacked him with, brother. In which case, what? Price just has him on ice somewhere? *Maybe*. Hoping to distance himself, looking to avoid any exposure on the monkeyshines he's been pulling with you . . . ?"

Wink thought he would hardly call it monkeyshines, watching that drunken lug flounder on top of his naked, knocked-up wife. But such nitpicking mattered little at this point. They were where they were now and had to find their way forward.

"I say he lives," Keeney told him. "And I suggest you two follow suit."

From the phone booth, he had a great view of the grain elevator across the street, and he thought of Chesty and how that stuff was more dangerous than most people knew. When things started heating up, it could all blow, just like it had for him.

. . .

He reported all this to her now, in the car heading down to Ann Arbor, along with an apology for rushing to the farmhouse option, and he asked her what *she* thought they should do.

"We should do what your uncle did," she said. "To your room, I mean."

He'd mentioned before about the reorganizing and purging his uncle had done on his behalf, in his absence, and he thought he'd seen her taking in the room with that in mind last night before they turned off the lights.

"Pare it down?" Wink said.

"Pare it all down. Figure out what's important. To us, I mean. Item by item."

It sounded like a sensible approach. He wouldn't have expected anything else from her. But despite this plan, they didn't really get very far with it before they found themselves caught up in the rhythm of the road and a good old-fashioned Sunday drive.

93

She liked the looks of it, what she saw. Ann Arbor seemed like a lively little college town, with a drippy, dreary sky, and the streets bustling with bobby-soxers in summer school and their daddies' old hand-me-downs—oversize oxfords, shirttails untucked, baggy dungarees. It was no bustling city, true, but at least, just driving around for the first time, she never once saw a prize-fighter or any menacing hoodlums break a plate-glass window or disrobe a pregnant lady. When she pointed this out to Wink as something the town was lacking, he didn't smile but said, "Wait until football season—you maybe spoke too soon."

Nestled on the edges, there were the houses she'd pictured, outdoing themselves with not only lawns and fences but porch swings to boot. Along a shady side street to the west, they passed a young mother pushing a stroller who looked no older than the girls who'd worn men's trousers closer to campus—a former coed recently turned missus?

Sal wondered how the two parts of this town overlapped. It appeared sleepy enough, yet the place had to be brimming with progressive thinkers—bearded eggheads and artists, even. Conceivably, secrets of a bohemian past might be more common here than one might think, porch swings or no. University art classes required life models—*some* gal around here must have taken the job at least once, maybe on a dare, maybe in a bind. Even the unconventional had to live somewhere.

The retail space they were considering was on a street called Liberty, back downtown. While looping around to make another pass by it from the other direction, but still smack in the residential section, the bright masonry of the Argus Camera Company headquarters suddenly appeared before them as if plunked down amid the elms and maples. "Hey!" Wink said. "Home of the Brick! How's about that for a sign, boy!" He sounded so peppy about the whole adventure, she wondered if he was putting it on a little thick; if he was actually, in fact, as nervous and scared as she.

They drove by the university hospital complex, a gleaming cluster of towering buildings on a steep rise with a view of the river, looking as big-city as any she could hope for. Easing up on the gas, he slowed through the hospital zone. Here the sidewalks seemed almost crowded with young, bright-looking people in white lab coats and nurse's uniforms. Wink jerked his head in their direction, swerving slightly, as if he intended to pull alongside. "So should I ask if they know where babies come from or . . . are we all set on that front?"

She swatted him for this, but couldn't help laughing a little, and they continued on past apartments and dorms and signs that said OBSERVATORY and CLARK'S TEA SHOP. This last struck her as a cozy spot where she might sit and chat with a friend. Not the Zim Zam, but cozy.

Something felt settled, and though they were far from "all set," as he'd just said, it was clear they'd ruled out a few options already, like the possibility, regardless of what else they decided to do, that she would be giving birth on his uncle's kitchen floor, following instructions from the animal husbandry section of the *Farmer's Almanac*.

94

The retail space was right downtown, in the midst of the U of M campus. He liked the shop a lot, though there wasn't quite as much square footage as they had in Chicago. The upstairs *could* be used as a living quarters here, too, but he thought it would be pretty cramped, especially once the kid arrived. And, as he pointed out to Sal as they toured the shop, if they wanted a studio space here, they'd have to give up half the upstairs.

She frowned at this, grabbing him by the arm. "Wait. I'm not sure we're going to still . . ."

"*Portraits,* I'm talking about, Sal. Remember? People get married, have babies . . . *customers'* portraits." He tried to be soothing about it, knowing how jumpy she was feeling. *Right,* he thought to himself, *we're going to start cranking out the girlies* real *soon. Maybe Thursday* . . .

As he looked around again at the rear of the store, checking the alley door and heading back upstairs to get another look at the size, he left her talking to the real estate agent by the counter in front.

"My husband," he heard Sal saying, as if by way of explanation, "is a professional photographer." She sounded proud of him, though God knew what for.

He stayed up there, trying to think it through.

So they would need a separate place to live, as well. If not right away, then soon.

Plus, there was no El here. They'd need to buy a car once Reenie reclaimed the Buick.

Also, they'd need to invest in a lot of advertising. There wouldn't be any regular customer base to count on, not for a while. . . .

Their whole life would be different here, and it wouldn't come cheap.

He thought of the beautiful houses they'd seen coming into town today: wide porches and elm-lined avenues on the west side of town. It looked like the place where lemonade and sheep-dogs had been invented. Sal had actually smiled.

Standing on the back fire escape, he peered down into the alley. On the brick wall near the rear of the store someone had written, in gory red paint, KILROY WAS HERE.

People here seemed to jaywalk as a matter of course, cutting across the street at will. He felt silly waiting at the light with so few cars on the street and everyone else crossing, so he took her arm and did the same.

They'd grabbed a hamburg sandwich at a diner handy to the store called Red's Rite Spot, a friendly little place with a limited menu, and the "paring down" discussion had really taken off there with *Do we need to live in Chicago?*

After a dessert of pecan rolls, they strolled toward campus, and it became *Do we need to live in a city* like *Chicago?*

He didn't think so, and he said as much as they crossed against the light.

Next, they stopped in Drake's Sandwich Shop. He remembered this place as a kid. They had candy, rows of it along the wall, in scientific-looking jars. Despite the pecan roll, Sal insisted the salesgirl take down five separate jars, filling little paper bags. He'd never seen her so excited about candy.

"Quite a place," she said, chomping on a root-beer barrel.

"Do we need to run a camera store?"

She shrugged. "If it's profitable. You mean is it some kind of family heritage? No. We could run a different kind of store."

"I could work in an office."

She laughed. "You could not."

"I might. If it was something interesting."

"Well, that answers itself then," she said.

He was thinking of Argus Camera, though he didn't tell her this. A decision like that seemed several dozen steps down the line.

She said, "We'll need to at least secure our stuff back there, hopefully get it moved to wherever we're going to be, even if it's just for a while . . ."

"Absolutely," he said, glad she was thinking it through and wanting to keep the questions coming. "What about our friends back home?"

"Like Reenie?"

"For example. How do you feel about that part of it?"

"A little sad," she said. "But they'll visit, I'm sure. And Reenie's probably easier to take in shorter installments, I imagine. Would we need to sell the shop?"

"Maybe we could rent it out for a while? I guess I'm not sure." He countered by asking if she thought they needed to plan on *never* moving back.

Through a mouthful of licorice wheels, she said, "Maybe not. I'm really not sure about that yet. But I could live with that, if we had to give it up."

Across from Drake's was the shady green center of campus they called the Diag, and they crossed over and walked up its angular path. There was an art museum there that was certainly no Art Institute, but looked promising.

She had another one for him: "Do you need to keep making girlies?"

"No." He stopped her now, wanting her full attention. They were standing near a giant *M* embedded in the sidewalk, facing each other. This felt important to say. "I do need to keep making pictures, though. And I need to be with you. And *you*," he added, touching her belly, hoping he'd feel the baby kick. "That's pretty much the extent of it on my end."

He was aware that he continued to think of it as *making* pictures, rather than *taking*—his drawing and painting background would probably never leave him, and he imagined that even if he continued farther down the path of more journalistic photography, he would continue to think of it as *making* pictures. Not that they would necessarily be posed or concocted, but there was a difference, he felt—something inside himself, maybe, that made him feel he belonged more in that Hopper room at the Art Institute than in a smoky saloon with the newsies, chasing the latest scoop.

"So you don't need to watch skimpily clad ladies undress every day?"

He pretended to ruminate, rubbing his chin. *"Every* day? *No* . . ." and she socked him in the breadbasket.

Diving back up to St. Johns, the North Star twinkled dead ahead, and the whole night sky surrounded them. They had their windows down, chilly air and lightning bugs whizzing by, and Sal had her legs stretched out, propped up on the dash. He couldn't imagine how she was comfortable like that, but she seemed lively enough, already working the figures, scheming how they might finance all this.

"Keeney's hoping to expand one day," she pointed out. "He aims to own a chain of news shops. And since you just *gave* him that one, maybe he's already in a position to buy a second location. You know, with the GI loan and all."

He'd expected it would be more of an ordeal introducing the topic of selling off the shop back in Chicago—the place that had been her home since she was a girl and the only thing she had left that connected her to her folks. And to Chesty. But she said, no, she had plenty of things to remember them by. They would need to retrieve all the contents of the apartment anyway, and a lot of the shop. The darkroom equipment, especially, plus a lot of the more expensive inventory that would require taking a bath if they had to sell it off at fire-sale prices. She would have all her old furniture and pictures and her "sentimentals," as she called them. "The rest of it, that's just a building," she said. "And you know—a neighborhood."

He thought she didn't sound quite as sure as she made out, but she wouldn't let him pursue it. Any attempt to further deliberate over selling out was met with firm resolve from Sal: they were moving forward. Damn the torpedoes.

95

Safe in the shade of the porch, she was making another list on a notepad on her lap, glancing up every now and again to watch him out there helping his uncle with something Len called "the Chicago" and Wink called "the red," but as near as she could gather was winter wheat. It was strange seeing him roll up his sleeves and pitch himself into such a farm-boy chore. She couldn't decide if he was just very adaptable—much in the way he picked up photography and darkroom techniques so fluidly— or if she was witnessing his true and natural calling: agriculture. Picturing herself just as sun beaten and prematurely Okie-fied as Chesty's mother back at the funeral in Breakey, Nebraska, Sal found the prospect of a similar life alarming, yes, but she did have to admit there was something pretty sexy about the way he hitched up the old pair of dungarees Len lent him, the way he seemed to know not only nicknames for crops but also his way around farm machinery.

"You're in luck," Len had teased him, clapping his arm around him and leading him to the barn. "I got a special left-handed combine outfitted just for you," and he was operating it now, the big machine jouncing along into the hazy orange ball that was the lingering sun, throwing back a cloud of airborne chaff. She thought of getting the Argus and taking some pictures, and she was also wondering if this was the type of wheat used to make cake flour.

Wink hadn't picked up the camera for days now, and it worried her some.

She'd tried to get him to give her a ride on the big machine, but he wouldn't allow it. "On account of the baby," his uncle explained, though she was pretty certain the combine didn't shake much more than Reenie's Buick.

As much as she appreciated the way Len joshed him about his hand and made him feel as if life was moving right along, she couldn't let her husband grow too comfortable here. Not that Len's solution regarding the beds was aiding much in that regard. He'd ultimately assembled a collection of rusty piping pulled from the barn that turned out to be a squeaky army barracks cot, and he lashed this snug up against the existing single bed in Wink's old room so neither of them would slip through the crack and hit the floor. Each night in the strapped-together beds reminded her that this was *not* going to be their fallback position if Ann Arbor didn't work out. Not on her life . . . Which was why she was working on her lists.

Len had brought her a tall glass of cold buttermilk, insisting it would be good for the baby, though personally, she'd rather have a bottle of Vernors like Wink was drinking out there. Len didn't seem to have any beer or hard liquor in the house, and she was surprised to discover this, knowing the man was related by blood to Wink, but Wink didn't seem to be kicking up a fuss about it.

She tried to get down the buttermilk as she worked on the list on her lap.

The list was her own attempt to remain organized. This was all happening in such a rush; she wanted to be sure to stay on top of it. Or as on top of it as she could.

She had a couple lists going at once on this notepad, hopping from one to the other. One list was the personal belongings and store inventory they'd left back in Chicago and how best to deal with different categories of items. The biggest list was the one inspired by Len's paring down of Wink's childhood room—her "life's essentials" list. She'd made a lot of headway on that one already, thanks to her husband's willingness to really talk it through. She loved that Wink had pared it all down to just she and the baby but also included making pictures as a necessity. She wasn't sure she'd love him quite so much if he hadn't included that, too. The guy was an artist down in his bones, end of discussion. Even out there right now, working those monotonous rows of wheat, she imagined his eye was framing composition through the dusty window of the combine, grasping fleeting mental snapshots when it all lined up just right, following the rule of thirds.

The list on top right now had to do with who, potentially, meant them harm.

She'd resisted titling this list, unable to bring herself to write something as alarming as ENEMIES at the top. Certainly, she hadn't reached the point of cataloging her enemies, had she? But she did want to better understand where they stood.

It was really more of a chart than a list. She'd drawn three columns. The far left column contained the men who'd first come by after Chesty's death. Federal agents, they'd decided—more military-intelligence types than the ones that followed. Their own probing questions at the naval hospital out in California had prompted that visit, fanned by her taking the Swans Down story to the *Tribune*—a paper run by a known isolationist who was, as Sunshine State had pointed out, no fan of the administration or America's involvement in Europe. But that sort of bled into the next group of visitors, which also seemed to be federal men of some sort, though they'd been there after Wink's allegedly "un-American" photo of Keeney standing on a corner, minding his own business, ran in the *Trib* and there'd been those responses to the editor claiming Wink's intention was to condemn the government's treatment of returning vets. She'd discussed that one pretty thoroughly with Mort Doerbom, back when they were dating and they all got arrested at the beach, and it was Mort's opinion that those two visits, though separate inquiries from different departments, were both part of a much larger investigation being orchestrated between the FBI and some congressional committee that was apparently really heating up.

So. How best to organize this list . . . ?

She was still a little confused, and it was fouling up her system. She wasn't sure if she should put the two incidents in separate columns or lump them together. . . .

In the third column, the two men that didn't show their badges—these were *not* local plainclothes detectives trying to "clean up" their neighborhood after the North Shore arrest exposed the secondary purpose of the camera shop. She had to assume now that they were more of Mr. Price's bunch. Or if they *were* police officers, they were working for Price as well, in their off-hours.

She scratched these two out of the middle column and moved them to the third column, joining Jericho Price and his drunken contender and, now, she had to assume, every leering teenager and loiterer she'd seen on the sidewalk in recent months; every scribbler of obscenities; every threatening, little no-account vandal. Some of these, of course, could just be mindless nitwit kids, looking for trouble with no instruction from anyone else. Dirty words on the alley wall, broken windowpanes—that could simply be the work of irate neighbors or random burglars, nothing more. Sure. But at this point, just to be safe, she thought she ought to count it all under Jericho Price.

The far-right column, it appeared, was winning by a landslide.

The baby kicked, and Sal said, out loud, "I get it, I get it. Kicking Mommy's not necessary."

The guy had been very persistent about the trademarks. And were they really worth it? After all, she told herself, the trademarks weren't all that lucrative a thing; they'd just provided her with a feeling that she had a say in all this, that she was at the wheel. It had helped her feel less like she should feel exploited.

Despite all this talk of paring it down, she had to admit to herself she maybe wasn't as carefree about walking away as she'd been putting on with Wink.

It was difficult to stomach the notion of getting chased off a place she'd worked so hard to hang on to—originally hanging on to the shop for the sake of her parents and Chesty, then for this new growing family she'd found herself in. Heck, she'd taken off her clothes in order to hang on to that place!

Well, not entirely. That wasn't completely fair. Honestly, there'd been other factors in doing the girlies, she knew. She couldn't have enjoyed doing it quite so much if it had merely been a matter of paying the bills and taxes.

She thought of what Reenie liked to say about life being what actually happened—she'd been saying that a lot since she eloped with Keeney.

And this was not exactly the same as being *chased off*—not if it meant taking hold of their life and planning a new path for themselves. It felt okay when she thought of it that way.

The baby kicked again.

"All right, already!" she said, patting her belly, then pushing up out of the glider. "I'm doing it, baby. Keep your pants on—or dress, as the case may be."

Out on the porch steps, she raised her hand high, hoping to wave him in. Hopefully he was at a good stopping point to take a break and drive her into St. Johns to the pay phone. She didn't want to use the one in the house and risk having Len overhear her conversation with Mort Doerbom.

It was as awkward asking for his help as she thought it would be, though he acted very civil, as genteel as ever, even asking after her health. She admitted she was expecting, and he said, "Yes, that's wonderful. That's why I asked, actually. I uh, happened past the shop a little while ago and happened to glance in and I *thought* so . . . Well, congratulations. To both of you. That's very exciting."

He didn't sound excited, but it wasn't really the purpose of the call, so she moved on, telling him briefly what had happened and asking him if he could draw up a document with which they could sign over S&W Publishing and its licenses and trademarks to Mr. Jericho Price, free and clear—something they could sign and pop in the mail back to Mort and have him deliver so they wouldn't have to deal with the man directly.

She watched Wink as she spoke, waiting just outside the phone booth, still in his borrowed work clothes, hands in his pockets. She wasn't sure she'd ever seen his arms sunburned like that. She'd always thought of him as the indoor, night-owl type. *Not a lot of tanning going on in the darkroom . . .*

When she told Mort to send the bill to the same address, in care of Wink's uncle, Mort told her, "Don't be absurd. This is a wedding present. Or a moving present—whatever." And then he asked to speak to Wink.

When she cupped the receiver and opened the folding door to tell him, he squinted back at her as if talking to Mort was the last thing he wanted to do. Besides, Wink didn't need to give his permission. She'd already cleared it with him on the drive to town. He'd shrugged and said, "It's yours to give away or not, Sal. It's always been." But he took the phone now, plastered on a wincing little smile, and said, "Hey, Mort. How're tricks?"

She'd never heard him say anything so trite, and she chalked it up to his discomfort. She stayed in the booth, curious to know what this was about. It was a tight fit with her belly, but Wink tipped the receiver away from his ear, and she squeezed up against him to listen.

"Dutton. Listen. I understand your immediate concern is primarily potential retaliation—the intruder and altercation the other night, making sure you're all safe. Only natural. But in terms of these federal agents who were coming around earlier, I feel I should advise you, unofficially, that they have since been round to ask *me* questions about your activities—"

"Christ on a duck." Wink inhaled deeply, like he was bracing himself. "What'd you tell them?" Sal found she'd started stroking his chest, as if this might calm things down.

"I told them nothing, really, partly because I know my rights and partly because I don't know the answer to such personal questions as what your political leanings are, if you *are* a subversive, whatever in the wide world that means. But I have to say, these investigators appear to be people with a real agenda. Have you heard of HUAC?"

"I *think*," Wink said. "Something to do with industrial cooling systems, or . . . ?"

There was a pause on Mort's end. "Well, no matter. Suffice it to say I took it upon myself to contact some *actual* free speech advocates I know out east—not like your Mr. Price—and it sounds as if certain elements on the federal level are currently beating the bushes for pawns to help them stir things up in the coming months. Really bring their agenda to the fore. They appear to be intent on finding any accomplice to help execute their investigations, no matter how coerced. The way these people think, it makes your Mr. Price look like small potatoes, and so I'd be cautious in returning to Chicago, were I you. If you do return, I've been thinking they might actually try something as manipulative as charging you under the Mann Act—that is, transporting a female across state lines for immoral purposes."

"What?"

"I know, I know. Never mind that she's your legal spouse and you'd merely be returning to your home or that immoral purposes, at this stage, I'm sure, would only be to assist you in producing cheesecake . . . I could thoroughly imagine these people employing just such a spurious distortion of the statute. But this is only one tack they might take I thought you should be wary of. These people seem capable of all manner of trumped-up charges simply to get witnesses before them and making the sorts of allegations they clearly want them to make. I . . . I'm just saying be careful."

There was a long pause while they waited for more. There wasn't more. Finally, Wink said, "Thank you, Mort. I appreciate the straight dope on this. I mean it."

After he hung up, she asked Wink if he understood any of that.

He shrugged. "I guess just . . . *Don't go back to Chicago?*"

What *she'd* taken away was *Stay away from J. Edgar Hoover and overzealous congressmen,* but her husband's interpretation seemed like a more practical approach.

"Let's go," he said. "We should get home before it gets dark."

She followed him to the Buick, not saying what she was thinking: that she hoped the farm wasn't really going to end up being *home* home and that they would soon be in a place where they didn't think in terms of the dark.

96

The day they drove down to talk to the Ann Arbor bank about buying the store, they got there an hour before their appointment, so he drove out past the stadium and showed her where Uncle Len once took him to see his first real football game. Then they crossed back down to the river. He couldn't figure out where the beach was, but he remembered, very young, visiting some cousins or someone and swimming in the river.

She frowned a little when she saw the murky water and said, "Count me out on that one, pal." He wondered if she was thinking of the trouble they'd had at the last beach they visited.

At the bank, while the loan officer was going over their application for a GI loan, he and Sal got to talking about just how long they might be able to make do living over the new shop and the pressing need to find a better place to live.

The loan officer stopped reviewing their application and watched them discussing this, smiling as he waited. When he had their attention, he had Wink sign at a few designated spots and then acknowledged he'd been eavesdropping, saying, "Sounds like you're looking for a place to live, too, maybe?"

Wink suspected he had the job on account of he was probably a vet himself. He seemed about his own age, mid- to late twenties. Short stocky guy, but handsome. Rode a tank, was Wink's best guess.

The guy nodded his head a little, looking like a doctor dishing out a troubling prognosis. "Well, housing's tight here, just like anywhere. Maybe more so in a town like this, all these fel-

las coming back to school. They're building, though. Like gangbusters. If you can wait for construction—"

Wink patted his wife's belly. The loan officer's eyebrows
jumped a little, like Wink had passed gas or done something really off-color. "Sort of on a schedule," Wink reminded him. "Already built's *far* preferable."

"Say!" The loan officer snapped his fingers. Wink had never
known a guy to actually snap his fingers when getting an idea,
outside of in the movie pictures, but this character did it. "I know
of *one* house actually—beautiful place, right next door . . ."

For a second, Wink thought he meant right there, adjacent to
the bank, but the guy cleared this up.

"Next to *my* house, I mean. In the Burns Park neighborhood.
For sale by owner."

They'd passed that neighborhood, he was pretty sure, going
out to the stadium earlier. It looked a great deal like the one she'd
liked coming into town, the one the real estate agent had called
the Old West Side.

The loan officer was smiling wide. "We'd be neighbors!"

Wink told him to set it up, and he said he would; that he'd
even bring them over there personally, put in a good word for
him with the seller.

They shook hands. It was all falling into place.

The muggy weather and the dwindling supply of clothes they'd
packed continued to remind him of the need to get all their stuff
in one state. He was working on it. This time of year, Uncle Len
couldn't really afford to leave the crops for even one day, but he
did, hauling one load of furniture and darkroom equipment from
Chicago to Ann Arbor in his ancient REO stake truck. Meanwhile, Keeney and Reenie were working on packing the apart-

ment and the shop and would drive a load of mostly housewares in Keeney's panel truck while the Rooney brothers minded the news shop. Wink estimated that would probably leave him with one return trip, probably with Uncle Len's truck, to get the last of it, but he would wait to do that till they had everything in order in Ann Arbor.

The current owner of the retail space had agreed to let them store their property on the premises before the closing, a thing which Wink found damn neighborly. "This," he told Sal, "is why we're in Michigan now. You picture this kind of cooperation going on back in the city?"

Sal didn't say one way or the other whether she could picture that, just made a little face. Lately, the baby was making her very tired. He could tell she needed a place of her own and soon.

97

She'd been holding it in as long as she could, but Sal finally had to admit after a few days of this that she was just too exhausted to continue carting herself back and forth to his uncle's farm. So they were staying at a motor court out toward someplace that was honestly called Ypsilanti until tomorrow, when they'd have the closing on the new shop and they could move in there, at least for the time being. The cold snap they'd driven into had passed, and it was just plain sticky now—not a fun time for a pregnant lady, summertime in southeastern Michigan.

She tried to think positive thoughts about the Burns Park house they'd be looking at tomorrow, after the closing for the shop. If it was as great as it sounded, maybe they wouldn't even have to temporarily move the rest of their household stuff into the new camera shop. Maybe, very soon, they'd finally be home, not waiting up on the farm or in this Ypsilanti place.

Wink had tried to cheer her up earlier with some claim that the original Rosie the Riveter—the tough gal behind the famous picture—lived right around here. She wasn't sure where he got *that,* and besides, it wasn't going to make her feel any better about living out of a suitcase.

She watched him through the open window, crossing the dark parking lot from the manager's office. He'd been using the pay phone to check on several elements of the whole exhausting upheaval, and from the way he was walking, she knew something was wrong.

He said it right away, as soon as he was through the door. "The shop is gone."

She didn't understand how this could be. "You mean they got a better offer, or . . . ?"

He was shaking his head, jerking his thumb in the direction of—what? The pay phone? Downtown Ann Arbor? "The *old* shop," he said. "*Your* shop. There was a fire."

Apparently, Reenie and Keeney were fine. The second load, mostly of housewares they'd packed for their trip out to Ann Arbor the next day, was also safe. Keeney hadn't felt his panel truck would be secure enough out on the street, so he'd parked it in a garage for the night, ready to go the next morning. They were at the Berghoff, having a late dinner, when they heard the sirens coming up Adams.

Keeney told him the fire inspector told him, "Well, it looks like they at least waited till you were safely out," and that Reenie had said this:

"Bilge. They were just waiting for dusk."

What had burned was mostly overstock in the basement—supply inventory, the photo paper and darkroom chemicals, boxes of Kodak film, and a wall of the specials they'd published themselves. And, of course, the building itself. There would be no third load of belongings coming from Chicago.

She reminded Wink that they had insurance on the property, that even if they could no longer sell it or use it as collateral, between his savings and the insurance money she'd collect and the lenient nature of GI loans, they'd be okay. She wasn't going to cry about it.

Still, it didn't stop her from trembling. She'd lived there since she was a little girl.

"I know," Wink said, putting his arm around her and rubbing her belly. "We'll be fine. We'll be just jake, just dandy . . . Those fucking ass-fuckers."

98

He supposed it was possible Price had nothing to do with the fire. Maybe it was Kid Fortunato, acting alone, paying them back for the KO in the alley. But either way, it didn't matter. Those people were involved, either way, no matter how much of an arm's distance the fake Little Lord Fauntleroy liked to keep from the rough stuff.

And so Wink got out the papers Doerbom had just sent him and they got the manager of the motor court, who had a little cardboard sign in his bug-screened window announcing he was also a notary public, to notarize their signatures. And then he escorted his wife back to their unit, where he took a match and burned the bottom of the document, fanning the flame just until it had eaten away their signatures, then snuffing the edge with a hiss in the toilet. Part of the embossing seal remained, a raised arc of blisters that indicated it had, moments before, been official and legally binding, and then he borrowed Sal's lipstick and wrote in red across it:

ALL DONE!
CALL IT
A DRAW.

He folded it back up, sealed it in a business envelope addressed to Price (no return address), put the whole deal in the manila envelope addressed to the lawyer, and walked it back to the big mailbox by the manager's office.

He knew in his gut that would be the end of it. Because guys like Jericho Price sometimes went after things just to go after them; just to squeeze some of the juice out of the lemon. Since they had no creative talents, once the lemon was wrung dry, guys like that were shit out of luck. Whereas, Wink knew, he and Sal would go on to do other things in their lives. He would create other images. Sal would have other projects. They wouldn't live and die by Weekend Sally or Winkin' Sally, whichever the hell was which.

The licensing had never honestly felt like all that much of a priceless commodity to Wink. They'd made a nice profit on the specials, but only because Sal had calculated ways to keep the overhead costs down, to put them out for cheap. And the fan mail that had come in, in care of all the preexisting magazines, that had been satisfying and rewarding in a way, and it helped sell each subsequent photo story they pitched, sure. But it wasn't as if Betty Grable and Rita Hayworth were looking to buy the movie rights to make some watered-down Hollywood version for MGM—*The Two Sallys* or something. There was only so much actual value in the trademarks. No, Jericho Price had wanted to horn in, mainly, just to horn in, because he couldn't bear to see these upstarts make something of their own.

Price must have known, too, especially once Sal was about to be a mother, that the girls probably wouldn't be modeling much longer. They would have to find another pretty girl. Or two. And as long as they were changing girls, why not cook up new catchy names for them? Different pretty girls, different catchy names . . . Wink adored Reenie and, obviously, Sal, but what was the difference, really?

No, it really wasn't that much of a unique commodity Price had been trying to get his hands on. He'd just wanted to wring the lemon dry. He just wanted to *push*.

Which, of course, made him a fucking ass-fucker, as he'd already stated, but it didn't mean he'd actually stand to gain anything in all this.

Wink stood at the edge of the gravel turnaround, looking out past the dark road for a moment, wondering which light out there might be the home of the real-life Rosie the Riveter, that biceped, grin-and-bear-it girl with grit, and if, in fact, she was still out there. He felt pretty sure she was. They hadn't all turned back to housewives.

He wondered, too, if his own mother might have done something like Rosie—rolled up her sleeves and did what had to be done. He knew he'd likely never know anything about her life after he got sick and she hightailed it, but he liked to think that at some point, she'd landed somewhere downstate like the Willow Run Bomber Plant, that she'd ended up doing something on behalf of the war effort, doing her part, getting by. The thought made him like her more, picturing her with her hair in a bandanna, toughing it out.

Turning to head back to his own amazing woman—this wife of his who had just been told the only home she'd ever known had been torched and yet was facing it not with unstoppable sobs and shrieks but unflinching plans and agendas of what they must do next, what was on the docket for tomorrow and the next day, he had the thought that *Maybe if the baby's a girl, rather than Manuela, maybe we should name her Moxie . . .*

99

She'd never heard them before coming out here, but the heat bugs, as Wink had explained they were, were buzzing and screaming at a high zingy pitch when Reenie and Keeney pulled in with their stuff the next day, the last load of belongings they'd gotten away with before the fire, and Reenie hopped off the running board, skirt flying, before Keeney even got it into park.

"Easy, tiger!" he called to his wife. "Settle down now."

They hugged and cried and she'd never seen her friend quite like this, not trying to put up a front. Even Keeney threw his good arm around Wink and pulled him in close.

The good thing was, they didn't have a lot of time to sit and stew over what had happened. They had to meet the loan officer at his home in the Burns Park neighborhood and take a look at this house the neighbor had to sell.

It was late afternoon, and the light through the trees was summer gold on the homey little lawns as they followed the loan officer's car through the residential blocks just south of the university campus. Before they even pulled in the drive, she wanted to live there.

Reenie whistled, low, sitting on Keeney's lap.

"You said it," Sal said.

The loan officer got out of his car, and his wife came out of their house with a toddler in her arms and met them in the driveway. "Welcome, welcome," she said all around, and when she got to Sal, she touched her belly and said, "You hurry up and have that baby, won't you, hon, so our Jack'll have someone to play with?"

It was almost enough, she thought, to make a person forget they'd been the victim of arson in the past twenty-four hours.

Then the homeowner came out on his porch. He was all smiles and hearty handshakes with the men, declaring, "Good neighbors let their current neighbors help pick their future neighbors!" He said it twice, as though he thought it was clever, something to be needlepointed on a sampler.

He was a professor of some sort and would be teaching somewhere else in the fall, so they needed to sell. His wife and two kids were up north at a camp called Michiana or something, so the kitchen and laundry room part of the tour, he explained, would have to be left in his own "incapable hands." She found it a little annoying, the way he seemed to be both apologizing for his lack of domestic knowledge and also bragging about it, but the house was adorable, especially the kitchen, and the dining room with French doors and built-in glass-fronted bookcases. It *seemed* like a professor's house, she thought. And there certainly was enough room.

Wink and Keeney roamed the far regions of the house, mostly with the loan officer—and, now, potential next-door neighbor—as their guide, stomping around and discovering all manner of manly fun, like a workshop in the basement and a den in the attic.

When they asked to see the garage, the loan officer said he'd walk them through it, since he needed to check back in with his wife anyway, and the two of them trooped out after him, talking excitedly, leaving her and Reenie alone again with the home-owner.

He seemed suddenly nervous, or maybe he'd just reached the far edges of his reserve of small talk. Finally, he said, "Now who's with whom here?"

It was so silent, she could hear the heat bugs again, even inside.

"Kidding!" he said, nodding toward her belly. "I see at least one of you is married."

Sal snuck a glance at Reenie, who curled her lip in disgust. She seemed to be saying, *What's this clown's deal?*

She was standing alongside Reenie when she realized he was looking at them sideways, in profile. She recognized, too, that she'd undone an extra button on her own blouse. But why the hell not—it was in the upper eighties, she was getting ready to give birth to what was starting to feel like twins. She was enti-tled. The other thing was, it was so humid, she'd been afraid her hair would frizz up on her, so she had it covered with a light-weight scarf, a sort of dark lavender, and she decided, later, that this is what made him notice her: if you were to squint, she might look like a brunette. And, of course, Reenie looked like Reenie.

"Will this be your main residence or—you know—just a hide-away for the *weekend?*" The man actually winked. A shimmer of nausea swept over her.

As soon as he said it, he had one hand up, waving it as if wip-ing clean what he'd just said. "Don't mind me, ladies. See, I was in the service and, well . . ."

She could have taken this last to mean he wasn't right in his head, that he had a plate in his skull or was nervous-in-the-service, as they used to call it, but she knew better than that. She knew what he meant.

And she was certain of it when she looked up a moment later at the creak of the screen door and moved to the window over the kitchen sink to see him striding across the yard to talk to his neighbor, their loan officer.

Reenie joined her, peeking through the lace curtains, watching them back there by the property line, the two men peering back at the house, not taking their eyes off it as they leaned close to each other, talking low, conspiring, two citizens on high alert as if there were dangerous intruders in their midst.

100

He loved the whole house, but especially this attic den the owner had built in a walk-up garret above the second-floor master bedroom. The oval windows at both ends gave a view down to the sloping backyard and the park just beyond where kids were playing baseball and out the front window, a canopy of tree-tops running north to ring the Diag and the campus.

He imagined walking to work at the new shop up on Liberty. From here, it would be a snap. Reasonably close enough, too, if he ever got a job at the Argus headquarters—a possibility he'd been mulling over all week.

This would be a great space for a little studio, he thought, a place to work on his own private stuff.

It smelled of cherry pipe tobacco, but he imagined that could be remedied with a solid airing out. There was a bar, of sorts, at one end, with cabinets built into the eaves. In one, he found a stack of unused ration stamps, no longer any good, a Japanese flag and some other war souvenirs, and a stack of girlie magazines.

He didn't have to dig very far to find one with his wife on the cover. There were even more with Reenie. He thought he even recognized the spine of one farther down that they'd done themselves, one of their S&W Publishing specials.

He thought Sal would get a charge out of that, and he wished she could come up, but she'd said climbing that many stairs was beyond her today, that he'd have to describe the attic to her.

As he was returning them to the cabinet, he heard some sort of commotion out back and went to the rear window to look.

Down below, in the backyard, he saw Reenie glaring at the loan officer. It was hard to see her whole face, this high up, but from the set of her bony jaw and the cock of her hips, he was pretty sure she was letting him have her worst black Irish evil eye. Keeney began pulling her back toward the driveway, corralling her into the car. Wink couldn't hear what she was saying, but it didn't seem likely it would be appropriate to the neighborhood. She stuck out her tongue. He watched the loan officer cross back into the house, shaking his head, and heard the sound of him downstairs, coming up. Sal appeared in view now, hugging herself, arms crossed over her belly, moving toward the driveway, looking small for a lady expecting and more weary than mad.

He started down the stairs. Halfway down, on the second-floor landing, he ran into the loan officer. He was smiling to beat the band, wiping sweat from his forehead with what appeared to be a complimentary ink blotter from the bank, a fact which Wink took to mean the guy didn't have the sense to carry a handkerchief. "You know," he said, leaning against the railing as if they were just shooting the shit, as if Wink didn't have loved ones downstairs clearly upset and pulling up stakes, "funny thing . . . My neighbor, he's just not so sure about selling right now."

Wink was listening, but he was moving, too, heading down the stairs. The loan officer followed, still talking. "Probably why he didn't go through a real estate agent to begin with. Maybe his heart's just not in it yet . . . Folks live here, it ends up meaning a lot to them . . . *you* know. Anyway, I feel bad about it, but I can sure help put you in touch with some of the developers on the edge of town—some of those new ranch-style houses are quite affordable and stylish, I think . . ."

Wink was hardly listening now, the guy rattling off all kinds of rationales. He didn't bother pointing out that the professor had said he was moving, that he had to sell.

"Maybe this wasn't exactly your kind of neighborhood, anyway. You're probably used to a little wilder life in the big city, I imagine."

Wink stopped and faced him. He would not punch him. They'd made some decisions about their life, he and Sal, and he was going to have to make this new chapter work, come what may. They still had to deal with the bank, and he had to be civil. But he did say, "You imagine, huh? That's what you imagine?"

101

It wasn't the beautiful elm-lined neighborhood she'd had her heart set on. It wasn't the avenues of the Old West Side, and it wasn't anywhere near that Burns Park area, in the heart of the town. It didn't feel like it was even part of the town, especially a town that made reference to trees right in its name. This was out in the open—nothing more than a cow pasture, it seemed like. A dilapidated barn was the nearest man-made structure she could see, and that was far off to the west. The only thing keeping her from feeling they might as well be back at Wink's uncle's, setting up a tent in the back forty, was the graded, winding road, running all through it, and the foundations that had been poured. It looked, she thought, like a memorial cemetery for giants. It wouldn't feel as barren, once there were walls on these houses. In fact, the neighbors would be packed in on either side far closer than anything they'd looked at so far.

Most of the houses were going to be that bare-bones ranch style, but she spoke to the developer personally and insisted they get one of the few with a second floor, maybe even an attic. "It's always better when there's an upstairs," she explained to Wink. "You and I never would have *been* if I hadn't had extra room upstairs." She grinned and tugged at his coat, pulling him close, and he grinned, too, thinking what she was thinking—of the apartments above the shop back in Chicago, of course. But she could see the real estate man, standing just beyond him, hands in pockets, and looking a tad flummoxed, frowning a little, eyebrows disapproving, and she almost spoke up and explained what she meant to this eavesdropper, thinking he might have taken her "upstairs" to mean her bosom, her bustiness, not the apartment.

But she decided to just let him think whatever he wanted to think. She knew what having an upstairs meant, and the man she loved knew what it meant, and all the rest could go to hell— or, at least, to the privacy of their own home to think their own dirty thoughts in peace.

And soon, now, they would be able to do the same.

Epilogue

She knew what was in the trunk without having to examine every last thing the boy was uncovering, digging around in it now that he'd dragged it down to the front hall, and she sat in the empty dining room just through the archway and did her best to respond as he called out questions, occasionally crossing over to show her a curled photo or piece of equipment. "That's a flashbulb . . . ," she said, thinking even he should know that one. She identified the safelight, the film pack tank, the remote release bulb. "Some sort of wartime pinups . . . ," she said.

He seemed to know what the enlarger was and not to open the packs of unexposed Kodak photo paper, though she doubted it was still any good. She knew he couldn't have been expected to identify the leg makeup or two-sided tape they used to hold the wigs and costumes in place.

"That all stays with me," she said. "All of it."

She didn't know the name of the facility or even what state it was in, but she knew she could take a few belongings with her, even those too big for the room they would give her. Each resident would have a storage space, Billy had told her over the boy's tiny Dick Tracy phone.

She knew this last was a cell phone, but she also knew how much it deviled her son, and the grandson, to think she was still living in an ancient time. She even knew that the cell phone could miraculously take pictures with less effort than picking your nose, though they weren't true photos in any sense, and that the boy had

been using this system to send Billy updates on the house and supposed repair problems he'd discovered while emptying it, all sent
through the air to California with the help of computers.

She knew that people did it this way now—they could empty
and sell off a house that they hadn't set foot in for years.

There were certain things that were crisp as an amber filter with
panchromatic film and still others that remained out of focus—like
what this young man's name was, the one packing up her house,
though she was pretty sure he was her grandson. Her son Billy's son
from his second marriage. And what the boy's wife's name was. Or
if they even were married and not just living in sin.

She knew the Argus C3 the boy held in his hand had been
owned by two husbands. She knew it was manufactured by the
Argus Camera Company, originally of this very town, that her
husband Wink had used this very camera, this Brick, as it was
called, to finally do better than finalist and win the Pulitzer. She
knew that was in 1954, for a photo essay of Jonas Salk—an average day with his family and codiscoverers, shot all around Ann
Arbor.

She couldn't remember the address of this house they were in,
but she knew it was in Ann Arbor, too, and it was the only place
she'd known as home since late 1947, back before the town bound-
aries had moved far beyond them and there were trees outside, providing cover, providing the landscaping company an excuse to
overcharge her son for raking leaves because, as she also knew, you
still couldn't rake leaves over the computers.

She knew that Wink had worked for Argus for a time as a
consultant and executive director while still doing freelance
photographic essay assignments for Life, Time, Playboy magazine . . .

She couldn't remember what the machine was she was hooked

up to now—what it did or who had hooked it up to her. But she did know she was supposed to leave it alone and not fool with it.

She did remember the name of Wink's doctor—Zaret, it was. Or maybe Zater—the hopeful, energetic fellow up at the university hospital who'd tried, twice, to restore full use of his right hand through experimental surgery. Neither attempt worked, but neither did it make his hand any worse. And, as Wink had put it, the fellow meant well.

She knew Wink had never managed to properly retrain his own hand enough to paint or illustrate but did go on to teach photography and journalism at the U of M after selling the camera shop downtown on Liberty. Going out on the occasional photojournalism assignment, and into town for classes, he felt, took him away from their home plenty enough.

The boy had seen the girlies in the trunk, but he didn't seem as worked up as she'd thought he might be. Maybe he'd seen enough these days on the computers. He was a grown man, after all—but he did seem captivated by one shot in particular and, after standing in the archway squinting at it in the late-afternoon sun, he brought it to her.

"Gram," he said. "This looks like the old cottage up north, but who's the lady?"

It shook in her hand, but she knew what it was. Judging by the hairdo, 1950 or '51; judging by the location—the sparkly ripple at the water's edge, the curve of pine trees along the beach, and the white puffs of clouds—summer. She must have just been starting to get her figure back after baby number two—Baby Manny, they'd called her at that point—and she was clowning by the lake with one side of her suit unhooked, her bazoom poking out like one large, winking eye.

She wondered where the kids were—maybe napping back in

the cottage. It looked bright, like midafternoon. Maybe Billy and Manuela were off on a day trip to Petoskey or Traverse with their aunt Reenie and uncle Keeney, if they were there visiting, which they often were. They certainly weren't right there on the beach with them. She didn't think she would have carried on like that so that anyone could see.

ACKNOWLEDGMENTS

Special thanks to Bob and Connie Amick, Huck Lightning, Bruce Amick, Walter Amick, the Ann Arbor District Library, the Argus Museum, Vicky Baker, the Bentley Historical Library, Guy Berard, Nan and Stan Bidlack, Bill Brown, Jere Burau, Cheryl Chidester, Bill Cusumano, Dominique Daniel, Bonnie Delaney, Meg and Brian Delaney, Tim Delaney, Cecile Dunham, Rachel Eckenrod, Elk Rapids Village Market, Elmers Glue, Ithamar Enriquez, Erik Esckilsen, Gina Fortunato, Dr. David Freiband, Al Gallup, Deb Garrison, Matt Garrison, Janice Goldklang, Jennifer Green, Alison Griffith, Rich Griffith, Manuela Guidi, Naomi and Ted Harrison, Carol Holsinger, Dave Keeney, Leonard H. Lillard, Fran Lyman, Mike Madill, Maria Massey, Matt Miller, Pamela Narins, Sunny Neater, Chuck Pfarrer, David Platzker, Steve Rogers, Eric Revels, Jonathan Sainsbury, Vanessa Hope Schneider, Grace Shackman, Jack Spack Jr., Elaine Spiliopoulos, Joe Veltre, Dietmar Wagner, Deb Waldman, Suzanne Wanderlingh, Caroline Zancan, and Dave Zaret.

A NOTE ABOUT THE AUTHOR

Steve Amick is the author of *The Lake, the River & the Other Lake*. Born in Ann Arbor, Michigan, he received a BA from St. Lawrence University and an MFA in creative writing from George Mason University. His short stories have appeared in *Playboy, The Southern Review, New England Review, Story, McSweeney's,* in the anthology *The Sound of Writing,* and on National Public Radio. On walks with his wife and young son, he often passes the original Argus Camera building.

steve-amick.com

A NOTE ON THE TYPE

This book was set in Fairfield, the first typeface from the hand of the distinguished American artist and engraver Rudolph Ruzicka (1883–1978). In its structure Fairfield displays the sober qualities of the master craftsman whose talent has long been dedicated to clarity. It is this trait that accounts for the trim grace and vigor, the spirited design and sensitive balance, of this original typeface.

Composed by Creative Graphics, Allentown, Pennsylvania
Printed and bound by Berryville Graphics, Berryville, Virginia
Book design by Robert C. Olsson